BREAK THROUGH

COLIN GEE

1

'Breakthrough'.

The second book in the 'Red Gambit Series'.

WRITTEN BY COLIN GEE

Dedication for the Red Gambit Series.

This series of books is dedicated to my grandfather, the boss-fellah, Jack 'Chalky' White, Chief Petty Officer [Engine Room] RN, my de facto father until his untimely death from cancer in 1983 and who, along with many millions of others, participated in the epic of history that we know as World War Two, and by their efforts and sacrifices made it possible for us to read of it, in freedom, today.

Thank you, for everything.

The 'Red Gambit Series' novels are works of fiction, and deal with fictional events. Most of the characters therein are a figment of the author's imagination. Without exception, those characters that are historical figures of fact or based upon historical figures of fact are used fictitiously, and their actions, demeanour, conversations, and characters are similarly all figments of the author's imagination.

Foreword by Author Colin Gee

The series deals with the violent events that commenced in 1945, through to the end of hostilities in the autumn of 1947; from birth in the mind of man through to the terrible conclusion.

All I have set out to do is relate the events as faithfully as is possible, and to leave the reader to decide the worth of those who wore different uniforms, and fought for different causes and reasons.

The reader will note that, in some areas, I refer to the 92nd Colored Infantry Division. This is an actual formation and I reflect its WW2 title faithfully. It is not for me to comment further on the reasoning and prejudices of those times.

Some readers of 'Opening Moves' have asked me whether or not I have an unhealthy respect for members of the Waffen-SS.

My answer is an unequivocal no.

In any field, excellence is to be admired, and any historian examining all the facts behind the service of World War Two's fighting formations would, in my humble opinion, find it very difficult to justify not placing the members of the prime Waffen-SS formations in the top drawer of fighting elite.

Some, probably those who do not possess balanced knowledge, will always align themselves with popular myths and misconceptions, and will tend to lump the field soldiers in with those who defiled the uniform, their nation, and mankind, by serving within other agencies, such as the camps. Those who served in such places should be universally reviled.

I do not seek to excuse the excesses that were undoubtedly performed by some of the Waffen-SS, neither those well documented, nor those unheard of. Neither am I so stupid as to believe that we, the Allies, fought the war according to Queensberry rules. I know for a fact that we didn't.

Within the ranks of the Waffen-SS there were psychopaths and sadists, and many are household names, or at least were, until the generation that fought them started to die out.

Such individuals also existed in the Royal Navy, the United States Army Air Force and the Canadian Army to name

4

but three. However, I cannot name one such individual, as the Allied excesses received no coverage of note.

We won, and so no one was going to haul us up before a judge and hang us, were they?

Had the Axis triumphed, then maybe the Allied author of the 'No prisoners' order in Normandy would have had his day in court?

The political system that the German soldiers fought for was fundamentally flawed, and so lacking in moral restraint as to beggar belief, and nothing about it should ever be excused, dismissed or denied.

There are no bad peoples, just bad people. That is a view I have held since I grew up and developed an understanding of human nature. Many of the soldiers wearing field grey were good men, brave men, and soldiers par excellence.

War, by its very nature, brings up peaks in human behaviour, be it in the field of endeavour, science or horror.

For me, there are a number of unbelievable acts of courage that can be attributed to soldiers in WW2.

Of course, most of them went unrecognised and unrewarded.

Some continue to stir the heart to this day.

Pointe-du-Hoc and the US Ranger assault, the 116th/29th Infantry's assault on Omaha, and Otway's 9th Para Battalion and their assault on the Merville Battery, all on D-Day.

The 82nd US Airborne's crossing of the Waal River during Market-Garden; 13th Guards Rifle Division and numerous others in the hell that was Stalingrad.

That is by no means an exhaustive list, but it serves my point, I hope, because I believe it is difficult for anyone but an historian to add the likes of the 352nd Infanterie Division of Omaha fame, 'SS-Der Fuhrer' Regiment during the Battle of Moscow, or the 1st Fallschirmjager Division at Monte Cassino.

Post World War Two, the Soviets became our de facto enemies, and so our view of them became jaundiced too.

In regard to Stalin and Beria, it is difficult to find any redeeming matters, I grant you.

But we must never forget that the Soviet people displayed an incredible national determination and an ability to sustain suffering on an unparalleled scale, and we applauded them for it, all the way to the centre of Berlin.

It was subsequent events that made them pariahs in our national psyche.

I have said enough for you to understand where I am on this matter. This is not a crusade, just my weak attempt to do justice to men and women in all uniforms who fought courageously, and with honour, for whatever cause.

I hope that you enjoy it.

Again, I have deliberately written nothing that can be attributed to that greatest of Englishmen, Sir Winston Churchill. I considered myself neither capable nor worthy to attempt to convey what he might have thought or said in my own words.

Those with an eye for detail will notice that the name of this book has changed. I produced 'Stalemate' as the second in the series, but it achieved in excess of 300,000 words and was too cumbersome. Therefore, it seemed sensible to split it into two parts. This is the first of those parts.

My profound thanks to all those who have contributed in whatever way to this project, as every little piece of help brought me closer to my goal.

In no particular order, I would like to record my thanks to all of the following for their contributions. Gary Wild, Jan Wild, Mario Wildenauer, Loren Weaver, Pat Walsh, Elena Schuster, Stilla Fendt, Luitpold Krieger, Mark Lambert, Greg Winton, Greg Percival, Brian Proctor, Steve Bailey, Bruce Towers, Victoria Coling, Alexandra Coling, Heather Coling, Isabel Pierce Ward, Ahmed Al-Obeidi, Hany Hamouda, and finally, the members of the 'Red Gambit' facebook group.

Again, one name is missing on the request of the party involved, whose desire to remain in the background on all things means I have to observe his wish not to name him.

Again, to you, my oldest friend, thank you.

The cover image work has been done by my brother, Jason Litchfield, and his efforts have given the finished article a professional polish beyond my dreams. Thanks bro.

Wikipedia is a wonderful thing and I have used it as my first port of call for much of the research for the series. Use it and support it.

My thanks to the US Army Center of Military History website for providing some of the out of copyright images. Many of the images are my own handiwork.

All map work is original, save for the Château outline, which derives from a public domain handout.

Particular thanks go to Steen Ammentorp, who is responsible for the wonderful www.generals.dk site, which is a superb place to visit in search of details on generals of all nations. The site had proven invaluable in compiling many of the biographies dealing with the Senior officers found in these books.

If I have missed anyone, or any agency, I apologise and promise to rectify the omission at the earliest opportunity.

This then is the second offering to satisfy the 'what if's' of those times.

Author's note.

The correlation between the Allied and Soviet forces is difficult to assess for a number of reasons.

Neither side could claim that their units were all at full strength, and information on the relevant strengths over the period this book is set in, is limited as far as the Allies are concerned, and relatively non-existent for the Soviet forces.

I have had to use some licence regarding force strengths and I hope that the critics will not be too harsh with me if I get things wrong in that regard. A Soviet Rifle Division could vary in strength from the size of two thousand men to be as high as nine thousand men, and in some special cases, could be even more.

Indeed, the very names used do not help the reader to understand, unless they are already knowledgeable.

A prime example is the Corps. For the British and US forces, a Corps was a collection of Divisions and Brigades directly subservient to an Army. A Soviet Corps, such as the 2nd Guards Tank Corps, bore no relation to a unit such as British XXX Corps. The 2nd G.T.C. was a Tank Division by another name, and this difference in 'naming' continues to the Soviet Army, which was more akin to the Allied Corps.

The Army Group was mirrored by the Soviet Front.

Going down from the Corps, the differences continue, where a Russian rifle division should probably be more looked at as the equivalent of a US Infantry regiment or British Infantry Brigade, although this was not always the case. The decision to leave the correct nomenclature in place was made early on. In that, I felt that those who already possess knowledge would not become disillusioned, and that those who were new to the concept could acquire knowledge that would stand them in good stead when reading factual accounts of WW2.

There are also some difficulties encountered with ranks. Some readers may feel that a certain battle would have been left in the command of a more senior rank, and the reverse case, where seniors seem to have few forces under their authority. Casualties will have played their part but, particularly in the Soviet Army, seniority and rank was a complicated affair, sometimes with Colonels in charge of Divisions larger than those commanded by a General.

It is easier for me to attach a chart to give the reader a rough guide of how the ranks equate.

T UNION	WAFFEN-SS	WEHRMACHT	UNITED STATES	UK/COMMONWEALTH	FRANCE
SOLDIER	SCHUTZE	SCHUTZE	PRIVATE	PRIVATE	SOLDAT DEUXIEME CLASSE
EYTOR	STURMANN	GEFREITER	PRIVATE 1ST CLASS	LANCE-CORPORAL	CAPORAL
Y SERZHANT	ROTTENFUHRER	OBERGEFREITER	CORPORAL	CORPORAL	CAPORAL-CHEF
ZHANT	UNTERSCHARFUHRER	UNTEROFFIZIER	SERGEANT	SERGEANT	SERGENT-CHEF
Y SERZHANT	OBERSCHARFUHRER	FELDWEBEL	SERGEANT 1ST CLASS	C.S.M.	ADJUDANT-CHEF
RSHINA	STURMSCHARFUHRER	STABSFELDWEBEL	SERGEANT-MAJOR [WO/CWO]	R.S.M.	MAJOR
LEYTENANT	UNTERSTURMFUHRER	LEUTNANT	2ND LIEUTENANT	2ND LIEUTENANT	SOUS-LIEUTENANT
ENANT	OBERSTURMFUHRER	OBERLEUTNANT	1ST LIEUTENANT	LIEUTENANT	LIEUTENANT
LEYTENANT					
PITAN	HAUPTSTURMFUHRER	HAUPTMANN	CAPTAIN	CAPTAIN	CAPITAINE
YOR	STURMBANNFUHRER	MAJOR	MAJOR	MAJOR	COMMANDANT 1
LKOVNIK	OBERSTURMBANNFUHRER	OBERSTLEUTNANT	LIEUTENANT-COLONEL	LIEUTENANT-COLONEL	LIEUTENANT-COLONEL 2
KOVNIK	STANDARTENFUHRER	OBERST	COLONEL	COLONEL	COLONEL 3
L-MAYOR	BRIGADEFUHRER	GENERALMAJOR	BRIGADIER GENERAL	BRIGADIER	GENERAL DE BRIGADE
LEYTENANT	GRUPPENFUHRER	GENERALLEUTNANT	MAJOR GENERAL	MAJOR GENERAL	GENERAL DE DIVISION
POLKOVNIK	OBERGRUPPENFUHRER	GENERAL DER INFANTERIE*	LIEUTENANT GENERAL	LIEUTENANT GENERAL	GENERAL DE CORPS D'ARMEE
AL-ARMII	OBERSTGRUPPENFUHRER	GENERALOBERST	GENERAL	GENERAL	GENERAL DE ARMEE
SHALL		GENERALFELDMARSCHALL	GENERAL OF THE ARMY	FIELD-MARSHALL	MARECHAL DE FRANCE
		* OR ARTILLERY, PANZERTRUPPEN ETC	1 CAPITAINE de CORVETTE	2 CAPITAINE de FREGATE	3 CAPITAINE de VAISSEAU

ROUGH GUIDE TO THE RANKS OF COMBATANT NATIONS.

Breakthrough

The Second book in the 'Red Gambit' series.

13th AUGUST TO 6TH SEPTEMBER
1945

Book Dedication

This book is dedicated to two men with whom I was fortunate to serve in my former uniformed years within Royal Berkshire Fire Brigade, as it was once known.

Firstly, Divisional Officer Ken Reed, footballing expert and man's man, who was the finest leader of men I encountered in thirty-two years in the service; a courageous and humble man whom I greatly admire. Without him I might have been left floundering in the early days.

Secondly, Harry 'Hit it where it shines' Woolhouse, gnarled ex-London fireman and snooker player, who courageously stood up and was counted. You acted to my great benefit when the liars' voices were raised and my back was to the wall. Harry, you conducted yourself with great honesty and integrity, and I never got to say thank you. So I say 'thank you' now.

Although I never served in the Armed forces, I wore a uniform with pride, and still carry my own long term injuries from the demands of my service. My admiration for our young servicemen and women, serving in all our names in dangerous areas throughout the world, is limitless.

As a result, **'Combat Stress'** is a charity that is extremely close to my heart. My fictitious characters carry no real-life heartache with them, whereas every news bulletin from the military stations abroad brings a terrible reality with its own impact, angst and personal challenges for those who wear our country's uniform.

Therefore, I make regular donations to **'Combat Stress'** and would encourage you to do so too.

Index

Contents

18

19

My thanks to...

The purpose of this series is to inform the reader about the soldiers who fought in those desperate times that followed the Soviet invasion of the western half of Germany.

In order to ensure that I have balance, I spoke to many veterans of that conflict, men and women, who paraded under different flags, and faced each other across the no man's land divide.

This is a work about human beings, and their capacity to endure. In that regard, the books can sometimes depict matters graphically, the better to illustrate what our forefathers dealt with.

It is my hope that I have not judged, only reflected faithfully their actions, and more importantly, their spirit and courage, regardless of the colour of their uniform.

I confess that I have occasionally had to use some license to fill in small gaps in events, or, where conflicting accounts exist, I have examined the facts and make a judgement on how best to present disputed events to the reader.

It is a fact that bravery knows no national boundaries, and that the other side always have their honourable and courageous men too. I hope that I have reflected that, and done due honour to all those about whom I have written here.

The events which brought me to write the 'Red Gambit' series have been outlined previously, as have the major contributions of some of the more important characters.

My grateful thanks have already been offered up to the families of John Ramsey, Rolf Uhlmann, Ernst-August Knocke and Marion J. Crisp. The contribution made by Vladimir Stelmakh cannot be overestimated, and the value of the personal documents of Arkady Yarishlov was immense.

I am indebted to those members of the French Deuxieme Bureau who risked much to ensure that their colleagues received the laurels they deserved, as I am to the Foreign Legion librarians and personnel of all origins, who gave me all the information I asked for, and helped me understand the espirit de corps of one of the world's prime combat formations.

I deliberately did not include some others in my first book. I omitted them to try and maintain some suspense for the reader who does not know everything of those times. I make amends now.

Tsali Sagonegi Yona gave me much assistance, but modestly played down his role in certain momentous actions. It fell to his proud family and the keepers of his Aniyunwiya tribal heritage to enlighten me on his full contribution to the events of which I write.

Lieutenant-General Sam Rossiter USMC [Retd] proved a mine of information, not only on the clandestine world of special operations, but also on the machinations of SHAEF that escaped description by the formal historians and, on occasion, by Eisenhower himself. Semper Fi!

Pompeia Collins was a very formidable lady, and she gave me everything I could ask for, and more, regarding her adopted son's war. Unfortunately, she passed away before she could see stories of her Julius in print.

Access to the personal papers of Roberto Di Castillio de Sangre proved of great assistance, and introductions to a number of veteran's helped fill in many blanks regarding the Spanish involvement.

My greatest omission was to fail to mention the assistance I received from the Nazarbayev family. Piecing together all the events from the word of mouth stories of the Nazarbayev's themselves, anecdotes from comrades through to personal diary entries of those who fell before the firing ceased. Thanks to all of you, and my respects and sympathies for the sacrifices your family made for all of our futures.

With the help of all these documents, the personal memories of the above, and others, I have been able to put together a story of the last two years of World War Two, or as they became known, World War Three, years which cost many lives, and which left such an indelible mark on those who fought on both sides.

The events that led up to the Soviet assault are well known. I have tried to combine the human stories with the historical facts, and to do so in an even and unbiased manner. In my humble opinion, the heroes wear different uniforms and only in one specific area are they on common ground.

They are all ordinary human beings.

The story so far.....

As this book forms part of a series, I would recommend that you read all books in sequence. 'Opening Moves' deals with the political decision making behind the Soviet attack, and the first assaults into Allied occupied Europe.

In any case, as a reminder, this is the story so far.

The Soviets have been presented with reasons, seemingly substantial, to suspect treachery from the Allies.

Stalin and his cronies harness the indignation of the Soviet Officer Corps for their own Imperial intentions, and plan a lightning attack on the Western Allies in Germany.

Elsewhere, the US Atomic Bomb test was a failure, and Soviet intelligence secures American information that permits their own Atomic project to advance.

Rumours of a Soviet attack do not arrive in time, despite the best efforts of some German POW's, who work out what is happening, and make a daring bid to get to the Allied forces in Austria.

The war starts, commando attacks and assassination squads preceding the ground forces, Soviet air force missions reaping huge benefits and reducing the Allied air superiority to parity at best. Initial Soviet advances are made, but the resilience of the Allies is unexpected, and the Soviet leadership develops a sudden respect for the 'soft' capitalist troops. The war descends into a gutter fight, not the free flowing fight that the Soviet High Command had envisaged would take place once they broke through the front lines.

The USSR's new ally, Imperial Japan, rearmed with captured German weapons, starts making inroads in China, as well as taking advantage of subterfuge to deal heavy blows to the US Pacific Fleet and Pacific ground forces.

The world is plunged again into combat.

Casualties are horrendous on both sides, and Allied commanders find themselves unable to regain the initiative, constantly responding to the Soviet assaults.

The German Army, displaying incredible resilience, commences reforming, promising to commit substantial numbers to the Allied forces.

The Soviet Navy plays its part, its submarines, many of which are former U-Boats, wreaking havoc on the Atlantic reinforcement programme.

However, the American war machine begins to whirr again, once more underestimated by an enemy.

Men and weapons, slowly at first, begin to flow from the camps and factories.

Also, the Allied Air forces recover, showing great resilience and taking the Air War back to the Soviets.

In particular, the Soviets have failed to appreciate the heavy bomber force, a mistake of immense proportions, but perhaps understandable, given their own bomber force's capabilities and the rushed nature of their strategic planning.

None the less, the Red Army continues to make inroads into the Allied defences, and the rate of attrition is awful.

Whole divisions can be swallowed up in the smallest of battles for the most insignificant of locations.

The Soviet plan has allowed for a number of phases of attack, with substantial reinforcements under central command, ready to be fed in when needed.

Despite some serious setbacks, the Red Army launches its second phase on 13th August 1945.

Fig #32
European map with relevant locations.

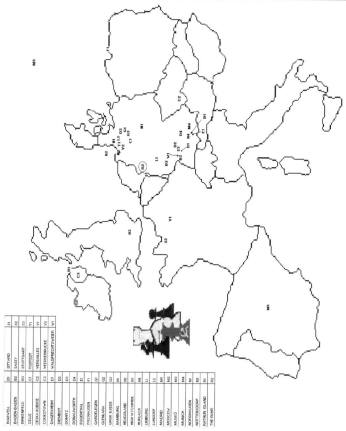

Artillery is the god of war.

Iosef Stalin

Chapter 55 – THE WAVE.

<u>0255 hrs Monday, 13th August 1945, Europe.</u>

Whilst not as big a bird as the Lancaster, or as potent a weapon in general, the Handley Page Halifax Bomber had seen its fair share of action and success up to May 1945.

NA-R was one of the newest Mark VII's, in service with the Royal Canadian Air Force's 426 Squadron, presently flying out of a base at Linton on Ouse, England.

Tonight, its mission was to accompany two hundred and forty-one aircraft and their crews to area bomb woods to the south-east of Gardelegen.

The Halifax crew were relatively inexperienced, having completed only two operations before the German War ended, added to four more in the new one.

The night sky was dark, very dark, the only illumination provided by the glowing instrument panel or the navigators small lamp.

Until 0300 hrs arrived, at which time night became day, as beneath the bomber stream thousands of crews operated their weapons at the set time. Across a five hundred mile front, Soviet artillery officers screamed their orders and instantly the air was filled with metal.

From their lofty perches, the Canadian flyers witnessed the delivery and arrival of tons of high explosive, all in total silence, save for the drone of their own Bristol Hercules engines.

They watched, eyes drawn to the spectacle, as the Russian guns fired salvo after salvo.

Their inexperience was the death of them, as it was for the crew of K-Kilo, a Lancaster from 626 Squadron RAF.

Both aircraft, their crews so intent on the Soviet display, drifted closer, until the mid-upper gunner in UM-K screamed in shock and fear as a riveted fuselage dropped inexorably towards him.

29

Aboard the Halifax, the crew was oblivious to their peril, the Lancaster crew resigned to it, as contact was made with the tail plane and rudders, the belly of the Halifax bending and splitting the control surfaces.

The Lancaster bucked slightly, pushing the port fin further up into the Halifax where the ruined end caught fast, partly held by a bent stay and partially by control wires caught on debris.

The Halifax captain, a petrified twenty-one year old Pilot Officer, eased up on his stick, dragging the Lancaster into a nose down attitude and ruining its aerodynamic efficiency. The young pilot then decided to try and move left, and at the same time, the Lancaster pilot lost control of his aircraft, the nose suddenly rising and causing the port inner propeller to smash into the nose of the Handley Page aircraft.

Fragments of perspex and sharp metal deluged the Halifax's pilot, blinding him. His inability to see caused more coming together and the tail plane of the Avro broke away, remaining embedded in the belly of the Halifax.

Both aircraft stalled and started to tumble from the sky. Inside the wrecked craft, aircrew struggled to escape, G forces building and condemning most to ride their charges into the ground.

NA-R hit the earth first, with all but two of its crew aboard. The resultant explosion illuminated the area enough for many Russian soldiers to watch fascinated as the ruined Lancaster smashed into the ground some five hundred yards north, four parachutes easily discernable in the bright orange glow which bathed the area.

Fire licked greedily at one of the NA-R crew's white canopy, taking hold and leaving only one man to witness his comrade's fate, plunging earthwards, riding a silken candle into the German soil.

The Bomber stream tore the Gardelegen Woods to pieces, destroying acres of trees and occasionally being rewarded with a secondary explosion. Seventeen more bombers were lost but they reported success and the obliteration of the target.

Unfortunately for them and, more importantly, the British and Canadian units in the line at Hannover, the units of

6th Guards Tank Army that had occupied hidden positions in the target area had moved as soon as night descended on the countryside. Apart from a handful of supply trucks and lame duck vehicles, nothing of consequence had been destroyed.

At Ceska Kubice, the results were far better, with the Soviet 4th Guards Tank Corps and 7th Guards Cavalry Corps still laagering, hidden and believing themselves safe. Medium and heavy bombers bathed the area in high explosives, destroying tanks, horses and men in equal measure. It was an awful blood-letting and the survivors were in no mood to take prisoners when the New Zealand crew of a stricken Lancaster parachuted down nearby. Cavalry sabres flashed in the firelight, continuing on when life was long since extinct and the victims no longer resembled men.

On the ground, the results of Soviet attacks on the Allied units were quite devastating, as the Soviet Armies resorted to their normal tactic of concentrating their attacks, focussing on specific points.

Whole battalions were swept away in an avalanche of shells and rockets.

On each of the five chosen focal points breakthrough was achieved swiftly, the leading Soviet units passing through a desolate landscape, tainted by the detritus of what a few minutes beforehand had been human beings and the weapons they served.

Occasionally, a group of shell-shocked troops rallied and fought back, but in the main, only the odd desultory shot greeted the advancing Red Army.

The reports of advances were immediately sent back and within twenty minutes Zhukov knew he had all five breakthroughs ready to exploit, and ordered the operations to go ahead as planned.

Ten minutes after Zhukov's orders went out, a bleary eyed Eisenhower, woken from his much needed sleep to swiftly throw on his previous day's shirt and trousers, learned that he no longer had an intact front line and that a disaster was in the making.

31

Swift telephone conversations with his Army Commanders took place, each man in turn receiving a simple order.

"Reform your line, General, reform your line."

Each was different, for McCreery had problems contrasting those of Bradley, who had worse problems than Devers et al.

Eisenhower felt like Old Mother Hubbard. He already knew that he had probably just lost the best part of three divisions of good fighting troops and he sought replacements. The cupboard was all but bare.

Some units were coming ashore in France, some in England. A few were already moving forward to their staging areas near the Rhine, ready for operational deployment.

Setting his staff to the problems of logistics, he let them take the strain whilst he sucked greedily on a cigarette and watched the situation map as the disaster unfolded.

Report followed report, problem heaped on problem, as the Red Army moved relentlessly and surprisingly quickly forward.

Ike stubbed out number one having lit number two from its dying butt, spotting the normally dapper but now quite dishevelled Tedder approach, half an eye on his Commander in Chief and half a horrified eye on the situation map.

So shocked was the Air Chief Marshall that he stopped, mouth open wide, watching as blue lines were removed to be replaced by red arrows.

Eisenhower moved to the RAF officer, who seemed rooted to the spot.

"Arthur, they've hit us bad and we're in pieces as you see."

The Englishman managed a nod accompanied by a grimace as arrows, red in colour, appeared moving north of München.

"I want maximum effort from you, maximum effort. Get everyone in the air that can carry a bomb or a machine-gun. I will get you my list of target priorities within the next hour. Send everyone, Arthur, even those who have been out tonight."

That drew a dismayed look from Tedder, this time aimed at Ike.

The complaint grew on his lips but withered under Eisenhower's unusually hard gaze.

"Arthur, I know your boys will be tired, and I know the casualties will reflect that. Send them in later if you must, but send them in, come what may. Are we clear?"

Tedder stiffened.

"Yes, General, we are clear. There will be a turnaround time in any case, so I can rest them, but it is a long time since they have done day ops."

Eisenhower, both hands extended palms towards his man, spoke softly.

"I know, Arthur. I am asking a lot of them but I think much will be asked of many this day, don't you?"

The Air Chief Marshall couldn't buck that at all; especially as he caught the stream of arrows around München grow further out the corner of his eye.

"Very well Sir. I will get them ready for a maximum effort. Target list will be with me by five?"

"I will do my very best, Arthur."

The man sped away, his mind already full of orders and thoughts of incredulous RAF officers reading them as tired crews touched down at bases all over Europe.

No one was going to be spared on this day.

Four Mosquitoes of 605 Squadron RAF had been tasked with destroying a Soviet engineer bridge laid over the Fuhse River at Groß Ilsede, the main road bridge having been dropped into the water by British demolition engineers some days previously.

The plan was for the lead aircraft to mark with flares to permit the rest of the flight to drop accurately.

Squadron Leader Pinnock and his navigator, Flying Officer Rogers, both knew their stuff inside out and the Mk XXV Mosquito arrived on time and on target, releasing its illumination.

Flight Lieutenant Johar, a Sikh and the squadron's top bomber, was confused. The landmarks were quite clearly right;

the parallel railway, the watery curve, both present and yet it wasn't there.

Johar streaked over the target area, his bombs firmly on board, closely followed by three and four, equally confused. Navigators did checks and came up with the same result.

"This is the right place, dead on, Skipper, no question" Rogers holding out his handwork for his boss to examine.

"Roger Bill," Pinnock decided not to bother with the normal banter involving Rogers' name and radio procedure that whiled away hours of lonely flying for the pair.

Thumbing his mike he spoke to the others.

"This is Baker lead, this is Baker lead. Mission abort, say again mission abort. Take out the rail track rather than dump ordnance."

The bombs rained down, savaging the track running to the east of the Fuhse, rendering it useless for days to come.

605's professionalism was such that no more was said over the radio until they touched down at Wyton some hours later.

The base adjutant, debriefing the crews, insisted that there must have been a navigational mistake until all four navigators produced their documentation, setting aside his first query.

This raised a rather interesting second one.

"My rule is, if you meet the weakest vessel, attack; if it is a vessel equal to yours, attack; and if it is stronger than yours, also attack."

Admiral Stepan O. Makarov [1849-1904]

Chapter 56 – THE SINKINGS

<u>0603 hrs, Monday 13th August 1945, aboard Submarine B-29, Irish Sea, Two miles north of Rathlin Island.</u>

Somewhere to the north of B-29 lay another Soviet submarine, probably drifting slowly up into a firing position on the unsuspecting enemy vessels. The ex-German type XXI U-Boat, now crewed by Soviet naval personnel, had been pulled from its patrol off the French coast and sent to operate out of Glenlara.

The two boats intended for the Irish Station had only just been tested as seaworthy and the Soviet Naval Command needed a capability in British home waters, and B-29 was it.

The Type XXI's represented the peak of submarine development, and had the Germans produced them in large enough numbers things may have turned out differently for the western allies. Soviet submariners were now demonstrating the vessels capabilities off France, America and Ireland, sinking a large number of enemy vessels without loss. Capable of schnorkelling virtually indefinitely, the XXI's were designed to operate constantly submerged, confounding the enemy AS tactics.

B-29 had been very successful over the last few days, sinking a number of merchant vessels. Even though it had been stressed that naval targets were a secondary priority, Captain 3rd Rank Yuri Olegevich Rybin had been unable to resist the big battleship he thought was the Duke of York, sending her to the bottom of the Atlantic with four deadly torpedoes. The riposte from the escorts was misdirected and B-29 slipped quietly away, popping up twelve hours later to rip open an escort carrier and a large tanker with a six shot spread.

With only five fish left, Rybin chose to drop back closer to shore and the rearming base secretly established at Glenlara in Eire.

His plan did not survive the mouth-watering encounter with the large shapes in the fog. Initially drawn forward to make visual contact by his sonar reports, a snatched look through the periscope promised more gross tonnage than he could have ever dreamed of.

A contact report was sent to headquarters and a swift reply was received, the commander there trying to put B-29 and the arriving ShCh-307 into an ambush position north of Rathlin Island.

This he did with ease, and both submarines now lay in position for the kill.

0629 hrs, Monday 13th August 1945, aboard Submarine Shch-307, Irish Sea, four miles north-north-east of Rathlin Island.

Kalinin had managed to get his submarine a long way, despite being harassed and attacked on a daily basis in the North Sea. He had made a feint towards the northeast coast of England, killed a fishing trawler to draw attention, and then reversed course, slipping around the tip of Scotland and taking the risky route between Skye and Lewis to make up time.

307's sonar was picking up engine sounds, exciting the operator, who recognised them as belonging to larger, more valuable beasts.

His periscope shot up and down in an instant, but long enough for Kalinin to see little but the fog and a number of dark shapes.

Starting his attack, he repeated the process every two minutes, pleasantly surprised that the shapes were becoming more distinct with each cycle. Information was constantly updated, and his torpedoes prepared for their short but deadly journey.

36

His scope broke water for the sixth time, and he on this occasion he dwelt long enough to fix two images in his mind.

Bearings revised and computed, he ordered the target book to be made ready at the navigation station. This was once the property of the Kriegsmarine, written in German but with neat, handwritten Russian notations.

'First, the warship.'

In control of himself, he calmly opened the book at the intended page and was immediately satisfied that he had his quarry.

His officers waited eagerly, the routines observed as normal. Turning the book around so they could see more clearly, he placed a finger on the silhouette of the vessel they were about to kill.

Eyes sought the shape and married it with the bold handwritten Cyrillic text indicating the USS Ranger, aircraft carrier of fourteen thousand, five hundred tons displacement. Aircraft carriers were an exception to the warship rule, mainly because they were being used to transport aircraft reinforcements to mainland Europe, and that had to be prevented at all costs.

Word on the identity of their intended victim spread swiftly through the crew, and it was necessary for some of the older senior ranks to calm their younger crewmates.

For the second target, Kalinin had to go searching, and, as he turned the pages, his officers found other distractions. After all, what could be as good as a juicy Amerikanski carrier?

Kalinin slid a piece of paper in between the pages and moved back to the periscope stand. Opening the book at the mark, he took in the image once more and ordered his scope raised.

Now the vessel was revealed more clearly as the early morning fog had disappeared; what he saw was definitely the shape he had identified in the target book.

"Down scope."

He opened the book and alternated between examining his prize and looks at his officers, drawing them in as they realised that there was more to be had than an Amerikanski flat top.

"Fortune smiles on us today, Comrades. We have an illustrious guest."

There was expectant, almost childish schoolboy silence throughout the control room as Kalinin placed the open book down and tapped the image.

"An illustrious guest indeed."

Gasps of surprise and softly spoken oaths filled the heavy air, as each man identified the RMS Aquitania, a four-funnel liner. A beast of over forty-five thousand tons, she would undoubtedly be carrying many troops, and sinking her would be a huge victory for the Soviet Navy.

"Comrades, we attack."

A similar scene had been played out three thousand yards to the south-west, where Rybin and his crew had experienced a similar wave of euphoria after identifying the two prime targets lining themselves up in front of his tubes.

Sonar identified a number of smaller craft, escorts flitting around their charges like nervous sheepdogs, hounds that sensed a wolf in the hills.

B-29's periscope broke the surface again, and more information was relayed for the firing solution.

'Perfect.'

Rybin manouevred his boat gently on steerage power only, turning her gently into the correct angle.

The excitement in the boat was tangible, the atmosphere heavy with expectation and fear, the ever-present companions of the submariner.

The German contractors, hijacked when they had left Danzig, still remained onboard, but were not now permitted to be at the controls during attacks.

Starshina 2nd Class Mutin, overseeing the planes crew, was as excited as everyone else, but became distracted by it all, watching his captain formulate the attack rather than his own station. One of his planesmen, a young Matrose, sneezed, his eyes watering and his body gathering itself for a repeat. In the act of sneezing, the plane angle altered imperceptibly.

Rybin ordered the scope up for one last check.

A swift look told him that something was wrong and he screamed at the Starshina, the man's horrified silence quickly giving way to rapped out orders, bringing the vessel back down to its attack depth again.

Incandescent with rage, but sufficiently in control to proceed, Rybin checked bearings and shot, six torpedoes fired and running in short order.

The Starshina was relieved and placed in the custody of the Senior Rating for a later court-martial.

Twenty seconds after B-29 attacked, Kalinin had his own fish in the water, two torpedoes targeted on each of the prime vessels.

Immediately after their release, he had gone deeper and turned west, intending to slip through to Glenlara and the supplies he desperately needed. Maybe another captain might have reloaded his last two torpedoes and gone after the group again, but Kalinin had survived thus far on his judgement, and he judged that he might need them before the coast of Eire offered up its comforts and promise of safe haven.

In the control room, he went into his routine as the stopwatch counted down. His rendition of Tchaikovsky grew in volume, heading unerringly to its intended climax.

The crew of Shch-307 were not disappointed and it seemed all four torpedoes found their mark.

Onboard B-29, things were more subdued. The young Starshina was popular, but no one could deny his guilt and that he had placed the whole crew at risk.

The senior midshipman had the stopwatch and looked confused when explosions started to hammer through the water.

"The other boat, young Alexandrov, the other boat."

39

Nodding his understanding, the midshipman returned to his task, using his fingers to bring the count down from five to impact.

His countdown came to naught.

Repeating the process, he was again unrewarded.

Rybin remained poker-faced but inwardly seething.

Third time lucky, and the midshipman's effort was rewarded with a deep rumble, which sound filled the boat and eased the tense situation.

Two more followed in quick succession, but the final fish failed to hit home.

None the less, three hard hits had been achieved and reloading was already underway. B-29 could be back in the attack very soon.

Rybin went to the chart table and looked again at the scenario, trying to find out what went wrong with the attack and the waste of three valuable fish.

The scared sonar operator's shouted warning rose above the hubbub in the control room, and immediately the submarine was thrown about by a pair of explosions close by.

'Aircraft dropped depth charges,' stated the clinical part of Rybin's mind, which also knew the answer as to how they had spotted B-29.

'That idiot Mutin.'

After the attack, the XXI had gone deeper and manoeuvred back around to head east, trying to stay in an attack position.

Quickly mapping out the scenario, Rybin ordered a further dive and turn to port, heading in towards the escorts and his previous targets.

More explosions followed as the attacking Sunderland put the rest of its depth bombs on the money. It could not really miss, seeing as the enemy sub was dragging a large white fender with it wherever it went.

Actually, it wasn't Mutin's fault at all. Fate had dealt badly with B-29, conspiring to catch a floating fender's line with the periscope and causing the submarine to pull it along, leaving a very obvious mark on the sea for the Sunderland crew to follow.

40

Bulbs shattered and joints burst as the vessel was engulfed in the pressure waves. Shaken from stem to stern, the vessel screamed in indignation as German engineering was tested to its fullest degree. Limbs were broken and flesh was torn, as men were dashed against unforgiving surfaces.

However, the XXI refused to die, and its crew rushed to their damage control duties, intent of keeping the sea at bay.

The young Starshina Mutin was saved from his courts martial, his neck broken when he was dashed against a watertight door.

Elsewhere in the boat, two others had been crushed to death when a torpedo was shaken loose during the reloading; others were injured in the desperate fight to stabilise the weapon.

A fire in the engine room had been quickly extinguished, partially by the prompt action of the 2nd Engineering officer, and partially by the inrush of seawater, which leak was serious and already being attacked by the engine room staff. Willing hands removed the badly burnt and screaming Starshina to the sick bay where he died, even as his engine room crew triumphed over the leaks.

The sole serious casualty in the Control room was Rybin. The unconscious commander was on the deck, flopping about with the movement of his craft, a very visible crescent of blood on his forehead where he had impacted a control valve at speed, the shape precisely mirrored in the wound, down to the serrated finger grips on the outer edge.

Grimacing from the pain of a broken finger, Senior Lieutenant Chriakin took command and dived, also turning back 180°. Unknown to him, the manoeuvre also dragged the fender below sea level, removing the marker that the now toothless Sunderland was using to call down the vengeful destroyers.

B-29 would live to fight another day.

Kalinin, as per his usual practice, manoeuvred away rather than inspected, and only raised the periscope when he felt secure.

A swift rotation of the scope yielded the unforgettable image of dying leviathans, the Aquitania ablaze and attended by smaller vessels, seemingly intent on saving life. The USS Ranger was low in the water, so low that her flight deck seemed almost a continuation of the water that was about to claim her.

Intent on leaving the area as safely as possible, Kalinin ordered a course to northwest, removing ShCh 307 from the scene at best speed.

Who hit what would actually not become clear until the end of hostilities, but Kalinin felt sure he had a piece of both vessels, in which he was absolutely correct, none of his torpedoes having been fired in vain.

His first two had struck the Aquitania on her port side, one amidships, the second fifty feet before her stern. Either might have been fatal to the venerable liner, but in tandem, they ensured her end, the resultant fires inhibiting the evacuation of her crew and passengers.

His last two torpedoes had struck the USS Ranger forty feet short of her bow and amidships, the former being right on a bulkhead division, causing the loss of the bow section to flooding. Damage to the next bulkhead meant that the vessel then hastened her own end as momentum drove her forward, causing weight of water to rupture the damaged bulkhead, flooding a further compartment and giving the aircraft carrier a pronounced nose-down aspect.

The latter strike failed to explode, but still penetrated the skin of the warship, permitting the sea to make more steady inroads.

B-29's torpedoes had condemned the carrier to the depths, flooding her engine spaces and denying the power to drive the fire fighting mains. When Kalinin had looked, he saw little smoke coming from her, but had not realised that below decks the blazes were running out of control.

B-29's third torpedo, the first one to detonate, had struck a RCN Corvette fussing round its charges, which

42

corvette had vanished beneath the waves in less than a minute, taking every soul on board with her.

As both submarines now moved away, the sonar operators became the only point of contact with the battle they left behind them.

Sounds of a large vessel sinking beneath the surface were interpreted as the carrier, and both crews claimed her as their own.

It was USS Ranger that succumbed first, the Captain abandoning ship reluctantly, the delay in abandoning ship costing more men their lives as she rolled over and nosedived to the bottom, three hundred and fifty-six of her crew still entombed in the hull. The sinking vessel took an important cargo down with her; one hundred and twenty-one replacement aircraft for the European War.

Around Aquitania, the efforts of fire fighting and rescue went on for many hours. The big liner resisted, and all the time more lives were being saved as she remained stubbornly afloat. Her passengers consisted mainly of US and Canadian air force personnel returning to the ETO from their mother countries, and many had been lost in the explosions and fires. But thanks to the Herculean efforts of the escorts, and the reluctance of the old ship to die, many were saved to fight another day.

Her killer was too far away to hear when the SS Aquitania slipped grudgingly beneath the water at 0914 hrs.

At least five hundred and thirty air force personnel perished in the tragedy, along with one hundred and ninety-seven crewmembers. Over the next few hours, the escort vessels put the survivors ashore in Northern Ireland, one thousand five hundred and fifty-one trained personnel having been saved from death by their excellent efforts; one thousand five hundred and fifty-one aircrew and ground staff who now possessed a very clear hatred of submarines, and all things Russian.

The following day both B-29 and ShCh 307 made their landfall at Glenlara, B-29 beating Kalinin's boat in by two hours precisely. Standard procedure required the submarines to stay on the bottom during daylight hours, and surface at night when prying eyes could not see them. Kalinin dropped '307' to the bottom and ordered 'minimum crews' on watch so his men could rest as best they could. '39' ignored instructions and surfaced close to shore, the Senior Lieutenant deciding that the risk was worth getting proper medical attention for his wounded comrades, amongst whom was a gravely ill Rybin, whose depressed skull fracture needed urgent care.

Carried out under the watchful eye of the Soviet Marine commander, Senior Lieutenant Masharin, the medical transfer was swift and well drilled, and the three submariners were quickly in the small hospital facility onshore.

B-29 then sank to the bottom, where her crew also rested under the protective gaze of their IRA allies.

1059 hrs, Tuesday 14th August 1945, Hotel Regina, Madrid, Spain.

The Commander had been to Madrid once before, so he expected the heat. None the less, he still recoiled on leaving the protective coolness of the lobby, discretely shadowed by Vassily Horn, one of the two members of the team who had joined the group in Madrid.

Both new men were German-born communists, official residents of the Spanish capital, and long time NKVD agents.

Strolling out of the Hotel Regina, the expected contact was immediately apparent, struggling as she was with her two large suitcases. Taking a second to study the shapely form, he approved of the simple but classy red dress with crocodile leather shoes and a patent white leather bag. Her ensemble was completed by a classically Spanish white silk bow at the back of her head, bringing her long jet black hair into a solid line down her back.

44

She turned round and the Russian was slightly disappointed.

However, although not beautiful by any estimation, her make-up was well applied and achieved much, and the middle-aged woman still presented some charm to the eye.

Horn was settled into a raffia chair adjacent to the main entrance, and seemed engrossed in the latest edition of 'ABC'. Appearing the gentleman, Mayakov offered his assistance, exchanging code words satisfactorily, and took charge of both cases, following the woman through the hotel foyer and into the lift. Nothing further was said until both were safely behind the door of his attic suite.

Pleasantries complete, he confirmed that his contact was one Maria Paloma. He already knew that and more besides. The woman was an NKVD sleeper agent, born of good communist stock, and activated solely for this mission. She knew better than to ask whom he was.

Professional in her approach, she confirmed that all requirements had been met, even down to hand drawn extras that should be of great assistance.

"If only you could give me some idea of your mission, Comrade, I am sure I could do more."

Nodding in acceptance of her efforts, he examined her map work as he listened and, seemingly at random, Mayakov selected the relevant one and relaxed back in his chair as she continued.

"My job gives me access to most of what you required. The hardest items to obtain were the boots, Comrade, but they are all there, and all the correct sizes. Do you want to check?"

He smiled and shook his head gently.

"I am sure you have performed your duties, Comrade Paloma." Indicating the plan in his hand, he praised her extra work.

"Just quickly, Comrade, this market area here," he indicated a patch of land immediately adjacent to the road junction.

She looked briefly just to confirm where he meant.

45

"Yes, that's the El Pardo market, held every Tuesday and Friday. Very well attended. I go regularly myself, which is how I know this area."

"Thank you, Comrade, I need keep you no longer."

Holding out an arm to steer her away from the table, he rapped the knuckles of his other hand on the wall three times.

"Comrade, if that place is of interest to you, perhaps you should know that it is not far from the Presidential Palace, and that the Caudillo travels that very road to Madrid nearly every day."

The NKVD Major looked at the woman with feigned surprise.

"General Franco? Really? Then we must be extra careful with our planning."

The room door rattled to four firm knocks and another man was admitted.

"This is Vassily. He will take you where you need to go, and thank you once again for your service to the Motherland, Comrade Paloma."

Switching his attention to the raffishly handsome young officer, who normally went by the name of Oleg, he cautioned him as a father to a son.

"Don't do anything to attract attention, and make sure you are back here by three o'clock at the latest, Leytenant."

"Yes, Comrade Major. Shall we go, Comrade?"

More pleasantries were exchanged.

Opening the door, he stepped back to allow the woman through first, his eyes catching those of his commander, confirming understanding of his instructions.

2312 hrs, Tuesday 14th August 1945, Parque del Buen Retiro, Madrid, Spain.

Just after eleven o'clock in the evening, two Guardia Civil troopers were walking down the narrow path leading away from the Estanque Del Retiro, a circular pond within Madrid's most popular park. The elder of the two checked

46

around quickly and made his excuses to his younger comrade, as he disappeared into the bushes to answer his call of nature.

The younger but senior man taunted his comrade for his weak bladder, but took advantage of the situation and slipped a cigarette between his lips.

He drew in the smoke, welcoming its rich flavour and, content with his lot, casually examined his surroundings.

His eyes looked but did not see, and it was not until the third time of looking that his brain registered what was drawing his attention.

Hanging from a bush on the other side of the path was a white bow. Or at least most of it was white, as the moonlight betrayed the random presence of a darker, more sinister colour.

He drew a torch from his belt, flicking the switch and illuminating the ground, immediately revealing signs of disturbance.

His comrade returned, silent and alert, focussed on the revelations in the torchlight.

Both guardsmen gasped as one when the beam swept over a dainty foot. They moved forward in an instant, but the woman was well past help.

Face down in the dirt and devoid of any clothing, she was long dead, although the signs of rape and sodomy were still clear for anyone to see, as were the scratches and cuts from her vain resistance. Less apparent was the bruising to her neck where she had been strangled prior to the other indignities that had been heaped upon her, in the name of providing 'motive' and providing the young Leytenant perverse satisfaction.

Had NKVD Major Mayakov used his real name and stated any other time but three o'clock, then Maria Victoria Paloma would still be alive, and Oleg Nazarbayev's sadistic sexual urges would have remained unsatisfied.

Never give in.....never, never, never, never, in nothing great or
small, large or petty, never give in except to convictions of
honour and good sense. Never yield to force; never yield to the
apparently overwhelming might of the enemy.

Winston Churchill

Chapter 57 – THE FRONT

<u>1140 hrs, Monday 13th August 1945. YQ-B, Airborne over
Northern Germany.</u>

The RAF's 616 Squadron had spent its last few
months like nomads, moving from base to base with the
German withdrawal and now, falling back with the Soviet
advance. Having received attention from ground attack
aircraft on the 6th August, they had left their field at Lubeck
and fallen back to Quackenbrück, southwest of Bremen, a
former base that they knew was adequate for their needs.

Reorganising the ravaged squadron took time,
especially as they could not call upon other fighter units to
scrounge spares and compatible equipment, for 616 flew the
Gloster Meteor, Britain's first operational jet fighter aircraft.

This morning, 616 Squadron was tasked with flying
top cover to a large air raid tasked with striking the rail yards
in Winsen, and also knocking down a number of bridges
spanning the Luhe River, from Winsen south through
Roydorf and Luhdorf down to Bahlberg.

The mission had been thrown together quickly in
response to the huge Soviet attack, and it had all the
hallmarks of Fred Karno's circus, as different squadrons
jostled to secure their places in the grand scheme.

RAF Bomber squadrons, who normally flew at night,
were accompanied by NF30 Mosquitoes whose normal
working day also started when the sun went down.

The ground attack squadrons flew ahead, savaging static and mobile anti-aircraft positions, beating up anything that might stop the bombers.

An attempt to keep some sort of formation had been given up as a bad job and so the six heavy bomber squadrons flew more as gaggles than an organised stream, each aircraft seeking out its objective individually, although pathfinder Mosquitoes were tasked to mark the main targets.

616 Squadron had nine airworthy Gloster Meteors that morning, and every one of them was committed to this maximum effort call.

Ahead of the bomber force, the ground attack boys were having a field day, and at higher levels, the RAF Spitfires and Mustangs were having good success against the Soviet aircraft trying to respond to the incursions.

Flight-Lieutenant Pieter De Villiers was a South-African who had shipped to England when the mother country called. He had served with distinction throughout the conflict, accruing four kills and thousands of flying hours in his five years of war, all but the last ten months flown in various marks of Spitfire. Now he rode the sky in a Meteor F3 jet fighter, the best that Britain could provide, flying shotgun on a squadron of Lancaster's due to visit hell upon Bahlberg.

Scanning the sky left and right, high and low, he spotted the dots to the southeast. Focussing in, he counted at least twenty and confirmed they were inbound, all in a matter of two seconds.

"Gamekeeper, Gamekeeper, twenty-plus bandits inbound, two o'clock, level. Type unknown."

The Squadron commander rattled off his instructions, and the nine Meteors accelerated and manoeuvred to attack. Immediately one aircraft fell out of formation spewing smoke as its portside Rolls-Royce Derwent engine objected to the stresses of full-power and broke down.

The other eight prescribed a steady upward curve, gaining height before charging down upon their enemy, 'matter of factly' identified as La-5's by the Squadron 'know-it-all', Baines.

49

The Soviet pilots turned and rose to meet the aggressor's, climbing at an impressive rate as their big radial engines poured out the power, some firing their 20mm cannon in short bursts to distract their enemy.

In turn, the Squadron Commander employed his own Hispano cannon and was rewarded with an immediate kill, as shells tore through a La5's wing and sent the aircraft spinning away.

Having disrupted the initial attempt to get at the bombers, 616 Squadron concentrated on ensuring none broke through.

By comparison to the Lavochkin, the Meteor enjoyed advantages in nearly every department. True to their teachings, and on this occasion, the attack plan, the Russian pilots tried to draw their enemy downwards where low altitude was normally an equaliser for them. Not so against the Meteor, and four Soviet pilots were already under silk as their abandoned aircraft crashed beneath them. A fifth La-5 carried its pilot into the ground.

The Soviet pilots did not lack courage, but the La-5 was a short-legged aircraft at the best of times, and combat manoeuvres were always heavy on fuel. They broke off the attack and dived for the ground as they fled eastwards. Ordering Blue flight to pursue, the Squadron Commander took the remaining five aircraft back to their position above the bomber force, just in time to spot the approach of a large force of fighters from the northeast, which Baines believed to be the latest Yakolev's.

By design, the Soviet air commander had used the La-5's to draw off the escorts and delayed sending in his high-altitude Yak-9U's to give them a clear run at the bombers.

It nearly worked, but for the Meteor's excellent climb rate and higher speed.

Despite that, one Lancaster fell victim to a speculative burst at range, the Yak's 20mm ShVAK cannon striking home and reducing the nose and cockpit to a charnel house. The huge bomber fell away as the living attempted to escape, leaving dead men holding shattered controls. Only four white mushrooms marked successful bail outs.

Summoning back Blue Flight, the Squadron Commander led his men into a side attack, disrupting the Yak's and chopping three from the sky before they could properly react.

Below, De Villiers drove his own flight upwards, throttles to the max to get back to his charges.

His eyes focussed on the battle above and he saw the orange blossom of a large explosion, not realising that his commander and a junior Soviet pilot had come together in the melee, both aircraft disintegrating in a fireball, both pilots instantly dead.

Another Meteor was falling from the sky, one wing removed at the fuselage, rotating madly like a sycamore seed pod, a victim of cannon fire. The G forces held the wounded pilot in place all the way to its end.

Two more Yak's were going down, one falling in a huge fireball to explode two thousand feet above the ground.

De Villiers throttled back and swept in behind a pair of Yaks intent on breaking through to the Lancaster's of 460 Squadron.

His four Hispano cannons dispatched the first with ease, the heavy shells knocking the tail assembly into pieces, the Yak simply dropping away and rotating uncontrollably all the way to its end.

The second aircraft suddenly slowed, and De Villiers overshot his prey, registering the lowered undercarriage as he went and mentally congratulating his opponent. A steady rattle told the South African that his aircraft had been hit. His controls seemed fine, and he recovered his position in time to watch his wingman dispatch the second aircraft.

Probably a dozen Yaks had now been downed for the loss of two Meteors, plus one further jet staggering away streaming smoke from a damaged engine.

None the less, the Russian pilots drove in hard once more and succeeded in chopping another bomber from the sky before the remaining Meteors reorganised and forced them off again.

51

A pair of Yaks limped away, smoking badly, damaged and out of the fight, only to be chopped from the sky by a flight of Typhoons returning from savaging the Flak positions around Bahlberg.

Anxious to join in further, the four Typhoons applied power and rose higher, clawing another Yak from the sky before they were spotted.

Their arrival was enough for the Soviet Regimental Commander and he called off the attack, satisfied that his last burst had damaged another of the huge British bombers. The Yaks hauled off and dived away for the relative safety of their own lines.

Flying Officer Baines slid in behind the fighter that had just knocked lumps off a Lancaster and sent a stream of cannon shells into it, transforming the aircraft into a flying junk yard in the briefest moment and killing the pilot instantly.

The now leaderless Soviet Regiment withdrew to lick its wounds.

Realising that he was now the senior man, De Villiers organised his surviving aircraft, positioning the group correctly once more, just in time to watch 460 Squadron drop their bombs and turn for home.

The damaged Lancaster struggled to keep up but fell out of the bomber stream, as more smoke and then flame leapt from its starboard inner engine and wing. AR-L lost height, and De Villiers watched as parachute canopies started to appear.

Fascinated though he was, he dragged his eyes away to survey the sky. With no threat apparent, he returned to the stricken bomber. With detached professional interest, he watched the fire grow and engulf the inner starboard wing. He also counted six canopies floating in the breeze.

The Lancaster bled height as the pilot struggled to land his charge, and all the time the fire developed.

Reaching a critical point, the wing failed and folded at the junction with the fuselage. In the Lancasters, Typhoons and Meteors above, numerous watchers spoke many a word of prayer in recognition of the brave man, who died as the inferno struck the ground and exploded.

Tearing his eyes away from the crash site, De Villiers assessed the mission. Of nine meteors, two had been shot down, including the Squadron Commander. Another two had limped away, leaving a grand total of five, including his own craft. The Typhoons, whoever they were, had not lost an aircraft, which was a positive, but that was balanced by the loss of at least three Lancasters that he knew of.

The enemy had paid a heavy price, with five of the Lavochkins felled and over a dozen of the Yaks destroyed. The numbers were in his favour but he knew the overall balance of forces was not, and Pyrrhic victories were of no use to a hard-pressed allied air force.

The raid's objectives were to destroy the railway junction at Winsen and to take out the crossing points over the Luhe River. In the former case, the results were disappointing, with only a moderate amount of damage done. However, in the latter cases, save Luhdorf, the results were excellent. Both the recently repaired road and rail bridges at Winsen were obliterated; similarly the two bridges at Bahlburg.

The crossing points at Roydorf were damaged, but not badly so, and with swift efforts by Soviet engineers the bridges were taking traffic within two hours. At Luhdorf, the Halifax Mk VI's of 347 (French) Squadron FFAF missed the target and dropped their bombs into the centre of the town, killing Russian soldiers and German civilians in equal measure.

<u>1312 hrs Monday 13th August 1945, Luhdorf, Germany</u>

Slowly, Vladimir Stelmakh became aware of his surroundings. The external noises had stopped now but the hammering inside his head continued. By the modest interior light he could see the gunner and loader collapsed over each other, still out for the count.

Stretching out, he kicked the gunners hand and received a reaction, repeating the blow on the loaders dangling leg. Both were alive.

'*Good.*'

Extending his arm, he undid the hatch and pushed upwards, not hearing the bricks slide off it but aware of the extra weight.

He cautiously stuck his head out of the hatch and examined his tank.

The IS-III was half buried in rubble and wood from the building it had parked beside, a gay and pleasant Gasthaus on Luhdorf's Radbrucher Straße.

'*Was*', he corrected himself, assessing the ruins.

He could see fire and smoke. He could see soldiers and civilians rushing round. He watched as an old house slowly collapsed. He realised he could hear nothing, the bombing having robbed him of that sense. He waggled his finger in his ear and withdrew it, the blood from a burst eardrum apparent on the tip.

He examined the scene further, noting the huge crater to his front, and the ruined carcass of the Regimental Commander's tank decorating the rim.

Stelmakh stiffened and saluted whatever was left of a man he had admired.

He slowly took in the rest of the surroundings, noting with relief at the obvious closeness of his own demise, the bomb crater to the rear of his tank, this bomb having flipped another of his unit's tanks on its roof. Again, no-one would have survived, although this tank at least could be recognised for what it once was.

Slowly, Stelmakh climbed out of the turret, becoming aware that his bladder had let go at sometime during the ordeal.

Sat at the front of the IS-III was Stepanov, Corporal, and driver of 'Krasny Suka'. Vladimir didn't like the name but it had been the choice of the crew's previous commander. He had been a popular officer and had died of some medical condition. To change it could undermine crew efficiency, so he was stuck with 'Red Bitch' and had to like it.

Stepanov's mouth moved and he offered up a pack of cigarettes. Stelmakh tapped his ears, and spoke words he could not hear above an internal resonant buzz. Stepanov laughed and indicated his own lack of hearing. Joined by both the gun crew, and sitting on the front of 'Suka', Stelmakh drew in the rich smoke and simply enjoyed living the life he thought he had lost an hour beforehand.

Medics found the four there twenty minutes later. A Doctor swiftly examined them and gave each a clean bill of health. The tankers grinned and thanked the doctor, despite the fact that none of the men could hear a word she said.

The medical team moved on and left the crew to themselves.

Stelmakh, gradually recovering his wits, if not his hearing, organised the crew to start removing the rubble from on and around their tank.

By the time they had finished no hand was free from laceration or bruise, each man having sworn as fingers were crushed, his comrades all buoyed by the fact that the cursing was now apparent, as sound gradually began to filter back into their lives.

It took over two hours to free 'Suka' and drive her to the rally point, as designated by the temporary commander of the regiment, who had done the rounds of his surviving troopers.

The IS-III's were not renowned for their mechanical reliability but Stepanov was a wizard, and the Red Bitch showed her class by starting first time and moving off without problems.

6th [Independent] Guards Breakthrough Tank Regiment had been detached from 12th Guards Tank Corps but had not been incorporated into the new attack, being held back in reserve yet again.

Having not fired a shot in anger in this war, the Regiment now found itself in pieces, leaderless and savaged, casualties particularly heavy amongst the motor riflemen and support troops. Five of twenty-one IS-III's were total write-offs; another two would need a lot of attention before being declared fit for service.

As 'Suka' made her way through rubble strewn streets and past shattered houses, Vladimir Stelmakh examined his thoughts. Without firing a shot, he was now an acting Senior Lieutenant, and commander of the 3rd Company.

The red-faced Colonel was apoplectic with rage.

"No, no, no, no, that's wrong, Comrade Mayor."

"I have my orders, Polkovnik."

"Your orders are incorrect, Comrade. This is all incorrect!"

The hard-faced Major remained outwardly impassive but eased the PPS submachine gun at his side to demonstrate his annoyance.

"Don't make this worse than it already is, Polkovnik. You will accompany me now."

"How the fucking hell could I have known they had jet fighters, Comrade Mayor, tell me that?"

As no answer came from the poker-faced NKVD officer, the Colonel kept going.

"The plan was perfect, executed well, and the regiments pushed hard."

The deadpan face revealed nothing.

"Even then, with the enemy advantage, we have downed three heavy bombers and savaged their jet force for fuck's sake!"

Silence carries its own menace, especially when accompanied by grim purpose.

"You cannot be serious Comrade. General Sakovnin simply cannot be serious!"

Turning around to the large window looking out over the former Luftwaffe airfield of Wittenberg, he watched as the remnants of his three savaged regiments were put back together by harassed ground staff. The La-5's had lost five of their number, the two regiments of Yak's had returned with only fifteen of thirty-one that took off, and four of them were probably write-offs according to first reports.

Turning to his accuser, he went on the offensive.

"The Division needs my attention as you may notice. Tell Comrade General Sakovnin that I will send my report as quickly as I can, but I must get my regiments reorganised."

The NKVD officer remained unmoved.

"You are dismissed, Comrade Mayor, and I want no more of your nonsense."

He sat down, making great play of reading a sketchy report on the engagement, all the time concentrating on every sound from the man on the other side of the desk.

He never heard the shots that killed him, dying instantly, executed on the orders of the Chief of Staff of the 15th Air Army. His plan had been good, anticipating an enemy bomber attack and utilising the strengths of his aircraft, but intelligence had failed to notify him of the possibility of enemy jet fighters. A simple, but costly, error. None the less, a scapegoat was needed and Colonel Garinov, Commander of the decimated 315th Fighter Division, was an appropriate choice to save General Sakovnin's neck.

By the Way of the warrior is meant death. The Way of the warrior is death. This means choosing death whenever there is a choice between life and death. It means nothing more than this. It means to see things through, being resolved."

Yamamoto Tsunetomo.

Chapter 58 – THE SAMURAI.

<u>0904 hrs Monday, 13th August 1945, Headquarters of the Manchurian Red Banner Forces, Pedagogical Institute, Chita, Siberia.</u>

Marshall Vassilevsky was in high spirits. The plan was proceeding pretty much as planned, with the newly strengthened Japanese Army making big inroads into the Chinese defences centrally and to the south.

His own ground forces were driving deep into Northern China, courtesy of an agreement with the Chinese Communist forces, who stepped adroitly aside, exposing the Nationalist forces to a series of lightning flank attacks.

However, the planned paratrooper deployments had been cancelled. The heavy losses in valuable aircraft were only partially to blame, the success of the ground offensives actually meaning that the majority of the airborne operations were made redundant.

The Chinese and American air forces, possibly lulled into a sense of false security by the decline in Japanese air power, had been dealt significant blows. Main amongst these being the wholesale destruction of the base at Chengtu, along with heavy losses inflicted on the 58th Bomb Wing, recently returned from the Marianas, the 312th Fighter Wing and the 426th Night Fighter Squadron, all of which had called Chengdu home.

Vassilevsky, warmed by the fresh coffee he was consuming, observed his CoS and frowned. Colonel-General Lomov, his briefings normally easy and pain free, was preparing the daily delivery but seemed unduly concerned for the first time.

58

The normally calm officer was in animated discussion with the senior Japanese Liaison officer, Major General Yamaoka.

The Marshall cleared his throat to attract their attention, and both men advanced, one holding a map, the other a newly arrived report from General Yasuji Okamura, commander of the China Expeditionary Army.

"Well, Nikolai Andreevich, what's causing you such concern?"

"Comrade Marshall, General Yamaoka has received information regarding the US tank force that went missing."

The map was spread on the large table, the corners held down with pencils, and, in the absence of anything more suitable, Vassilevsky's pipe and cap.

The area of concern lay in one of the most important areas entrusted to the Japanese Army; the southern assault towards Nanning and Qinzhou, subsequently angled towards the Indo-Chinese border.

Up to now, progress had been spectacularly good, but that had changed.

Lomov's morning report would have indicated that the enemy resistance had stiffened, and that the advance had come to an abrupt halt.

With the arrival of the new information, it seemed clear that there was a definite possibility of an enemy counter-attack, supported by the US Tank brigade that had so mysteriously dropped out of sight a few days beforehand.

"So, what does Okamura propose to do about it?"

Whilst he mused openly, the question was really a challenge to him, a spur to read the situation and the response.

Yamaoka grabbed a pencil.

"Sir, the 63rd Special Army is now further forward than indicated on the main map," he gesticulated at the wall behind him, both Soviet officers checking out the last recorded position of the newly-formed and extremely powerful 63rd.

The sound of a pencil on paper drew them back, Yamaoka circling the general area of concern before notating the map with 'Suwabe' and 'Minamori', the two sub-commands of the 63rd.

"Oh that's good. That's very, very good."

59

Vassilevsky could see that the enemy would, most likely, run straight into 'Suwabe'.

'Unless?'

Standing up straight and loading his pipe, the Marshall descended into silent thought, a process his senior men knew well not to interrupt.

Striking a match, Vassilevsky pulled on the pipe, puffing out the rich smoke that still bothered Yamaoka's eyes to the point of tears.

"They will come there I think, to the north of the assault forces and the 63rd."

The tapping finger drew both Generals down again, taking in the details that had stimulated their commander, finding the same reasons that had made him convinced.

'Wuzhou?'

Yamaoka turned and clicked his fingers to an aide, the folder he required made immediately available.

"Sir, at Wuzhou are..."

He tailed off as the shaking head indicated he had missed something vital, the tapping finger returning, this time to a more specific point where the finger waited, ready to describe a route east and then south, bringing the enemy into the flank of the attacking bottleneck.

"I would concern myself more about who is at Gulping than Wuzhou, General Yamaoka, for I think it is they who will have to fight like the devil."

Both officers could see it clearly now.

The blocking force, causing the attackers to build-up in one area, the mobile tank force smashing hard into the flank of the stacked-up formations.

Add probable enemy aircraft attacks into the mix, and there was a serious problem for the 6th Area Army.

"Do you have anything that can stop them apart from," Vassilevsky looked at the notations, "The 85th Infantry brigade?"

'Not that one of your infantry brigades would stop a determined armoured force at any time!'

"Sir, the 85th Brigade has not progressed beyond Tianpingzhen, there being a high sickness rate, some sort of stomach problem, hospitalising many of the men."

Keen to show that the Japanese Army had its own house in order, Yamaoka quickly spoke again.

"Kempai-tai units are already with the 85th resolving the problem."

No-one needed any illumination on how the problem was being solved.

"However, Major-General Suwabe sent part of his detachment ahead to the area as a cover, which will now prove very useful to us."

'I suppose Gulping is too much to hope for?'

Both Russians shared identical thoughts.

"Here, from Gulping to Mulezhen. Suwabe has positioned his 3rd Brigade."

Neither Soviet officer was any the wiser.

"3rd Special Obligation Brigade is partially armoured Sir."

Something broke through the haze in Lomov's mind.

"They are a new formation, aren't they, General?"

The nod was full and unequivocal, as was the broad smile that accompanied it.

*'Ah, one of **those** new formations.'*

Vassilevsky relit his pipe.

"Then it seems we have no problem of note there. Proceed, Comrade Lomov."

<u>1255 hrs Monday, 13th August 1945, 3rd Imperial Special Obligation Brigade 'Rainbow', Nanjincun, near Guiping, China.</u>

Captain Nomori Hamuda stood silently in front of his tank, his crew lined respectfully behind him. The five of them stood in silence as the Shinto priest performed the Harai ritual of purification, a small array of fruits and vegetables placed on the vehicles hot armour plate.

Despite the fact that the metal beast had been their virtual home for the last month, it was only now, on the verge of action, that Hamuda had permitted them time to conduct the important ceremony.

61

Like most of the men of the 'Rainbow' Brigade, Hamuda had been a member of 3rd Japanese Tank Division, fighting a long and bitter war against the two distinct armies of China. Communist and Republican forces had cooperated and come together to oppose the Japanese occupation in a little known war that claimed millions of lives since its start in 1937.

When volunteers were called for to train with a secret unit, Hamuda immediately put himself and his crew forward for the mission, plucking them from the 17th Tank Regiment and into the unexpected delights of getting to grips with the new presents their covert allies had bestowed upon them.

The five men dutifully bowed on cue, honouring their own particular vehicle as the Harai drew towards its close.

Hamuda appreciate its beauty, but knew nothing of its history.

First, it had been known simply as the VK3002, the product of design work within MAN, or Maschinenfabrik Augsberg-Nürnburg AG as it was more properly known. This particular vehicle had been salvaged from the ruins of the 6th August 1944 Allied Bombing raid on the MAN production line and had been sent off for operational duties on the Russian Front. It was assigned to the commander of 2nd Platoon, 1st Company of Panzer Regiment 'GD' of the elite Großdeutschland Panzer-Grenadiere Division. It was lost in its first action during the counter-attack on Wilkowischken in the autumn of 1944. The new Soviet owners used it against the former owners, claiming five kills before the vehicle found its way into the hands of new masters once more. Bulgarian tankers employed her in limited action before she was again sent east on a railway flatbed, but this time, further than even those German engineers who had designed and built her could have envisaged.

To Hamuda and his men, she was affectionately called 'Masami', the 'Elegant Beauty', and in the Rainbow Brigades' 1st Tank Company she had thirteen sisters, all equally loved and equally deadly.

To the Germans, she was officially known as the Sonderkraftfahrzug 171, Panzerkampfwagen V Ausf. G.

To any allied serviceman who had encountered her or her sisters before, she was simply known as the Panther Tank, and she was very much to be feared.

The 3rd S.O. Brigade 'Rainbow' was the right flank of a Japanese attack intended to cause consternation in Allied circles, aiming as it was for Nanning and points westwards. It was intended to reinforce the excursion that had previously secured a route to the Indo-Chinese border, and to threaten US-Chinese supply routes from India into the vast hinterland of China itself.

The main strike unit had been the Japanese 3rd Tank Division, but concern over the disappearance of an American armoured unit had resulted in the Rainbow Soldier's temporary reassignment from the Suwabe Detachment to provide strength if a stand-up fight took place.

Leading the 3rd Division's drive on Nanning was the 6th Japanese Tank Brigade, and it had successfully overwhelmed every impediment posed by the Chinese Nationalist forces, inflicting huge casualties.

This brought cries for help, which prompted the swift redeployment of the 1st Provisional Tank Group, a mixed Chinese and American armoured force.

The Japanese armour was not capable of holding its own in a stand-up fight with modern enemy tanks, and 1st Provisional sported many Shermans and a handful of Hellcat Tank-destroyers, which were all capable of dealing with the standard Type 97 with ease.

Nationalist officers assured the US officer commanding 1st PTG that the Chinese 22nd Division would hold north and south of Xingye, where more favourable terrain meant that the Japanese armour advantage was greatly reduced. A further division of Chinese troops was promised to reinforce the position, especially as the Japanese tank force had been successfully halted and it was likely that a different approach would shortly be made.

Indeed, intelligence suggested that the attacking Japanese forces had moved up two infantry divisions to carry forward the assault, which bottleneck of forces looked

63

particularly inviting for the US officer commanding 1st PTG and for which he planned a stellar coup.

1st Provisional would strike over the Yujiang River at Guiping, driving straight down Route 304, seemingly aiming at Wuzhou.

In reality, leaving the 6th Chinese Tank Battalion to secure their rear, the bulk of the Group would turn right near Baishahe, and follow Route 211 all the way to Rongxian, cutting the Japanese supply lines and placing a powerful force behind the attacking formations.

Some of the armoured infantry, supported by the 4th and 5th Chinese Tank Battalions, would then be detailed to hold the area around Rongxian, securing the area against any Japanese counter-attack.

Lieutenant Colonel Albrighton would then lead his remaining three tank battalions and infantry into the rear of the Japanese assault forces and cause havoc.

The plan was bold and relied on speed and surprise, but the roads were familiar to Albrighton's Chinese second in command, and Japanese reconnaissance capability was almost nil.

1325 hrs, Monday 13th August 1945, YongYang near Guiping, China.

American-Chinese forces:-
1st Provisional Tank Battalion of 1st Provisional Tank Group, 2nd Battalion, 66th Infantry Regiment and 22nd Artillery Battalion of 22nd Chinese New Infantry Division, all of 56th Chinese Corps.

Japanese forces:-
1st Tank Battalion, 3rd Special Obligation Brigade 'Rainbow', temporarily assigned from Suwabe Detachment, attached directly to 63rd Special Army.

The ceremony completed, Hamuda detailed his men to the routine maintenance tasks needed to keep his new thoroughbred operational. With the work in full swing, he moved towards the tank of his second in command, Lieutenant the Marquis Hirohata, who was in conference with the company's senior NCO, Sergeant-Major Kagamutsu.

As ingrained in them since birth, the two junior men acknowledged their leader with respectful bows as he approached, which were returned in kind.

Kagamutsu and Hirohata had been arguing about the best way to stow their Katana swords when on the road, an argument which had been going on ever since the Company had first received its new vehicles.

Kagamutsu argued that there was no place for a sword inside the fighting compartment, preferring it outside in the tube container holding the barrel cleaning equipment.

Hirohata, carrying his family's heirloom, a priceless blade crafted by legendary sword smith Hikoshiro Sadamune, preferred to keep his closer to hand, and secured it against the cage stanchions within the tank's turret.

Thus far, Hamuda had avoided being dragged into the argument, and had every intention of continuing to avoid the on-going squabble by dealing with more mundane military matters.

Despite the differences in station, Hirohata and Kagamutsu were committed friends. The former was a member of the peerage, his father having been granted the title under the Kazoku system for military services to the Emperor, the latter was the son of a fisherman, and even though they had both been brought up within ten miles of each other, they had lived very different lives.

Their relationship was built on soldierly comradeship and shared dangers. That Hirohata still drew breath was solely down to the bravery of his Sergeant-Major, whose face bore the burns caused by the fire that should have killed the young Marquis. The blaze claimed the lives of the five other officers of 3rd Tank Division who had bunked in the wooden hut, but Kagamutsu had plucked the young Lieutenant from the building, even as it started collapse on top of them. The young Chinese culprit had been apprehended swiftly and was brought before the unit commander. Major Kaneda had beheaded the youth on the spot.

Unfolding his map, Hamuda cleared his throat noisily to draw a line under the pair's ritual squabbling.

As the business of the march was being discussed, a shouted warning stopped them abruptly, eyes swivelling upwards to confirm the friendly nature of the approaching aircraft.

Around the positions, AA gunners tensed, ready to hurl death into the air.

Private Asego had been the man to shout and his eyes were the finest in the unit. It was a full ten seconds before any of the three could verify that the aircraft were indeed friendly.

A Mitsubishi Ki-46 reconnaissance plane was being shepherded back towards friendly lines by a group of four Ki-84 fighters, having conducted a mission to gather information about Chinese forces around Xingye.

Two of the fighters broke off from the formation, circling back to port over the Heights of Jianzhuding and lazily lost height, heading away from the Rainbow tankers to the south.

Sounds of firing followed and the keener eyes of Asego confirmed that the aircraft were strafing something on the ground.

Lacking any means of swiftly communicating with the troops on the ground, the flight leader had ordered two of his pilots to attack the enemy force on the road, in order to try and warn the tank force that they were not alone.

Hamuda swiftly grasped the situation and ordered his unit to readiness. Correctly assessing that the attack had been carried out the other side of the river, he ordered his tanks to prepare to move out.

On arrival at his command tent, a sergeant passed him the radio handset, unit commander Major Yamashio already informed and planning his own response to the obvious Chinese advance.

Fig #33 - Yujiang River dispositions.

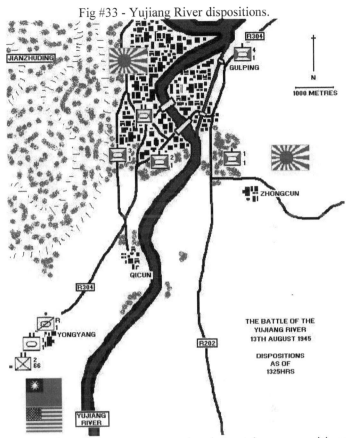

1st Company was ordered to take up positions bordering the river, oriented to the west, remaining silent for a flank ambush when Yamashio ordered it.

2nd and 3rd Companies had crossed the river previously and would remain in position, guarding the approaches to Guiping. 4th Company would remain in situ as a reserve.

With the improved communications offered by all the newly-arrived German equipment, Yamashio expected to be able to better control his battalion's responses, and so was light on specific orders, enjoying a freedom of operation and command almost unheard of for a Japanese tank unit commander.

Hardy hated the Chinese with a passion. They were useless soldiers, so he told himself, unable to digest the simple soldierly arts let alone the complexities required of the tank man.

And yet here he was, commanding an M5 light tank with Chinese crew, and leading his whole unit into battle.

The unexpected strafing attack by the nip fighters had been ineffective, killing solely one useless chink tank commander who couldn't keep his head down.

Apart from that, the advance had been uneventful as the column pushed up Route 304 towards their first objective, the Yujiang River bridges at Guiping.

Raising himself out of the cupola, he brought his binoculars to his eyes, taking in the relatively open landscape into which he was driving. Hardy shuddered at the memory and quietly thanked his god that he wasn't back in France, where such terrain meant Paks and Panzers, which always brought death and destruction in equal measure.

As they passed the left hand junction with the county road Teo Li, his gunner, began chattering excitedly and the tank halted abruptly and without orders. Whilst Hardy could normally manage to issue orders and could understand much of what his crew said, at this moment, his ability to comprehend the increasing pitch and rapidity of his crew's agitated conversation was non-existent.

The gunner alternated between looking down his sights and sending an imploring look directly at his American commander, accompanying both with increasingly panicky words. Hardy shook the man's shoulder and calmly used his best Chinese to find out exactly what the problem was.

He was in the process of isolating key words like 'Japanese', 'Tank' and 'big' when something sounding like an express train rocked his tank as it passed close by.

68

Fig #34 - Yujiang River ambush positions.

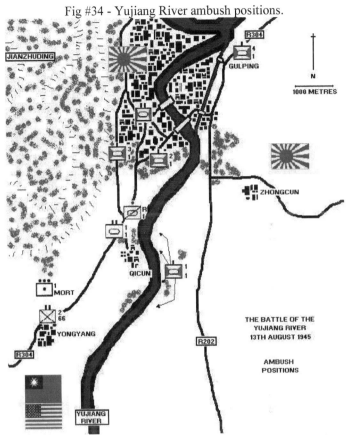

Ordering his tank to head for some isolated buildings just off to the right, he stuck his head back out, the binoculars again probing for enemies.

A second shot betrayed the enemy position.

The radio was in his hand in an instant, sending back a contact report as his tank dropped in behind the farm building, screening him from the Shinhoto Chi-Ha that had engaged the Stuart tank.

He dismounted and moved to the corner of the building, from where he immediately spotted a second Shinhoto. The 47mm gun was engaging the next US vehicle

69

in line, with more success it seemed, as a burst of smoke followed the sound of metal on metal.

Climbing back into his tank again, he informed the unit commander of the latest development and was told to reconnoitre further forward around the flanks, if safe to do so. Which order he immediately interpreted to his own ends, determining the move totally unsafe and electing to remain in place until the medium tanks took care of business.

Li's mouth was still working overtime, but the man was clearly calming down, as his pitch started to descend to more normal levels.

Cigarettes appeared and Hardy tried to calm his men further, all made jittery by the panic of their gunner. He spoke softly to the man.

"Ok then, Teo Li, you've been in action before. What on earth got into you? You've seen a Shinhoto before, haven't you?"

The look from the frightened Chinese was a mix of disbelief and contempt. "That no Shinhoto, Hardy Sergeant. That bigger tank."

This started the rest of the crew off again and the chatter again climbed in pitch and intensity. Hardy, his dislike of serving with the Chinks reinforced, dismounted once more and moved to watch the armoured exchange.

An M4A4 had stopped to engage the Japanese tanks and was rewarded with a first shot hit, splitting the track of the stationary tank adjacent to the road. A well aimed reply struck the Sherman on the glacis and ricocheted skywards with next to no damage done, a gleaming scar the sole testament to the strike.

The American gunner nonchalantly adjusted his aim and dispatched the Shinhoto through the hull, watching as three panicked crew members abandoned their tank before putting a second shot into the smoking vehicle.

Hardy thought the shooting was impressive and nodded approvingly when the second Sherman killed the other Shinhoto with its first shot.

Inside the two lead Shermans, the relaxed atmosphere generated by easy kills evaporated in an instant as first one then the other gunner brought their sights to bear on a third enemy tank.

The first gunner remained speechless, transfixed by the sight.

The second gunner had the presence of mind to report the new target.

"Enemy tank, two o'clock, range 900 yards."

The Commander looked for the new target and found it, euphoria turning quickly to fear.

Never having seen one in the flesh before didn't mean that the vehicle wasn't instantly recognisable, and every man that saw it knew that death was a moment away.

Hardy had turned back to his own vehicle when the sound of a heavy gun reached his ears, accompanied by the thundering whoosh as it slid closely by its intended target.

"What the fuck?", although somewhere in the recesses of his memory he recognised the sound and his stomach flipped.

The two M4's were reversing, smoke pouring from their labouring engines and from smoke grenades lobbed by the crew to cover the withdrawal.

Hardy knew the answer before he looked, just in time to hear the big gun roar again and the first Sherman explode into a fireball from which no-one escaped.

It was the sound of a Tiger I's 88mm gun that he had recognised, and sat on the road eight hundred yards away, was a fully operational example of the deadly German tank.

By the time Hardy had composed himself, the tank had eaten fifty yards off that distance, firing on the move without success.

The American battalion commander contemplated relieving the idiotic Lieutenant who was screaming about Tiger tanks. Before he made the decision, the man's radio transmission ended abruptly.

The second Tiger's arrival gave Hardy the impetus he needed, and he was in his tank in seconds, issuing orders, anxious to get his tin can out of the way of the leviathans.

Swiftly conversing with the unit Commander, he pushed out to the right, heading towards the river, looking for

71

a way round on the right flank, as other's were looking on the left.

Hamuda calmed his men, listening intently to the reports of combat coming from the tanks of 2nd Company, marrying them with the evidence of his eyes.

The American Sherman and Stuart tanks were expanding their line and firing rapidly, presenting excellent flank targets to his company's Panther tanks. A fact he reported, keen to get into action before 2nd Company claimed too many. Through his episcopes he could already see six American tanks burning, but there were plenty more.

An American M5 Stuart tank emerged from the buildings five hundred yards to his front. Fearing discovery, Hamuda asked for permission to open fire, and his headset crackled with a new voice, that of Major Yamashio, giving 1st Company permission to engage from their flank position.

Selecting the enemy Stuart tank as his first target, he warned his company to prepare.

The Panther's gunner took careful aim and waited for the order.

Two seconds later it came and the firing button was pressed, sending a 75mm armour-piercing shell on its way.

The Panther's 75mm gun could penetrate the M5 Stuart many times over and its high-velocity shell passed through the vehicle and buried itself in a small mound behind the American tank. Its journey through the US light tank had been catastrophic. On its arrival at the glacis plate of the Stuart, the AP shell had easily penetrated the metal plate before messily destroying the co-driver, proceeding on to amputate Teo Li's left leg at the knee and finally smashing the rear-mounted engine virtually in half, before exiting the back of the tank.

The crew bailed out at speed, all save Li, whose screams of pain and fear harried the fleeing tankers until a second shell from the Panther smashed the tank into silence.

The Stuart driver was struck down by a burst from Hamuda's hull machine-gun, the gunner walking the tracers across the ground and into the running figure. Using the distraction, a breathless Hardy found refuge in an animal pen, diving over the wall into the deposits of the previous occupiers.

He lay there, trying to make himself as small as possible, not knowing what it was that had killed his tank and men.

Other Panthers were also engaging and five more Shermans had been destroyed. The Japanese gunners were doing their best and, whilst they were not up to the standard of German panzer crews, being sat in an invulnerable tank, killing enemy armour with side shots, wasn't too difficult.

Caught between the 2nd Company's Tigers and Shinhotos to his front, and the Panthers of 1st Company to his right, the American commander rightly called a withdrawal of all three companies committed to the advance.

The accompanying Chinese infantry had already made their own decision, withdrawing to safety immediately the Shinhoto's had opened fire.

To the rear of the column, a battery of 105mm Howitzers was brought online and targeted on the enemy tanks to the Battalion Commanders front. The 81mm mortars of the Provisional battalion's mortar platoon commenced dropping smoke to the right flank of the unit, trying to mask the Panthers from their quarry.

Hamuda ordered his company to switch positions to counter any enemy artillery fire, and to try and seek better firing positions. The euphoric commander of 2nd Company committed an error, and did not shift his company until the first heavy calibre shells started to arrive. The battery's third salvo caught another Japanese tank, a basic Type 97 Chi-Ha, throwing the wreck on its side and killing the crew with the concussion.

By now, 2nd Company was scattering, permitting the savaged allied tankers to withdraw in good order, leaving nearly half of their number on the field, twenty-three wrecks testament to the capabilities of the gunners and their German weapons.

1st Company found themselves without targets as the American tankers used the terrain to mask their retreat. Some commanders contented themselves with the occasional shot at moving trees and bushes without further success, something which Hamuda called a halt to as it wasted ammunition.

One of 2nd Company's Tigers halted and its deadly 88m spat a shell out. Hamuda noted the sudden pall of smoke from beyond a group of huts, which quickly turned into the traditional fireball that tended to mark the demise of a Sherman tank.

His professional eye swept the field, counting out the pyres and concluding that the two companies engaged had destroyed twenty-five enemy vehicles in total. Only two of the four tigers of 2nd Company had engaged, whereas all of 1st Company's Panthers had taken the American unit under fire. Hamuda's own tally amounted to two tanks destroyed and another hit. He had already decided to employ the German system for recording tank kills, and was looking forward to displaying two kill rings on his gun barrel. Some of his unit's tanks had possessed rings earned by their previous owners, but his own late production Ausf G had apparently been a virgin until this day.

Across the river, the Allied artillery made a spectacular kill.

During 1944, the top armour of the Tiger I was increased to 40mm. The tank struck by the shell was a pre-44 model, whose armour was still the 25mm production standard thickness, which yielded easily to the force of the strike.

The whole crew were killed instantly and Hamuda knew he had just watched the 2nd Company commander die.

In almost slow motion, he watched as the Tiger's turret was propelled up and left by the internal explosion, gently rotating, barrel over turret. Through his binoculars he watched as it crashed to the earth, coming to rest upside down on an animal pen. He swore he saw a face appear at the moment of impact.

American artillery continued to mask the withdrawal for some time, but failed to secure any more kills and the battle was over within twenty-four hectic and bloody minutes.

Hamuda called for his supply vehicles and withdrew to a safer place to replenish, using the opportunity to discover the facts of the battle.

To his chagrin, he learned that many of his gunners had failed to score hits, let alone kills, and that most of the damage had been done by five of his tanks.

Kagamutsu had enjoyed success four times whereas Hirohata had five kills to his name, four of which were American Shermans. Two others of Hamuda's Panther unit had a brace each, leaving the other successes to their comrades in 2nd Company.

None the less, Rainbow's war had got off to an excellent start.

"One minute can decide the outcome of the battle,
one hour - the outcome of the campaign,
and one day - the fate of the country."

- Russian Field Marshal Prince Aleksandr Vasilyevich Suvorov

Chapter 59 – THE WITHDRAWAL

<u>1455 hrs Monday, 13th August 1945, SHAEF Headquarters,
Versailles, France.</u>

All morning the reports had flooded in, a village lost, a unit overrun, and a myriad of information from hard-pressed commanders desperately trying to salvage their units from the maelstrom.

Some units stood and fought, others simply withdrew under pressure. Some ceased to exist in defiant defence, whilst yet others ran away.

The staff of SHAEF were desperately trying to bring together the big picture so that their General could make informed choices, rather than trying to fire fight each individual report that arrived from his senior commanders.

Rather surprisingly for Eisenhower, it was Bradley that was least forthcoming with information, the normally genial and calm general clearly rattled by what was happening to his units.

It had taken all morning to establish that 12th Army Group's frontline had been badly broken, Soviet units seemingly pouring through and driving hard into the heart of the Allied Occupation Zone.

Having just got off the phone with General McCreery, Eisenhower savoured the positives of the call. Soviet attacks had taken place, but not at the heavy level of Central Germany, and not with the same effectiveness. Leastways, not in and around Hamburg. Hannover was under heavy pressure and the British General did not expect to hold beyond that evening. But still McCreery's report was better

76

than any of the others Eisenhower had endured so far that day.

Opening his third pack of cigarettes, the commanding General examined the situation map, seeing the front sundered at Kassel, Frankfurt, Geissen, Heilbronn and Ingolstadt, the red markers seemingly breeding on the map before his eyes, as tired staff placed up the markers of processed reports.

A red-eyed staff Major attracted Ike's attention and gestured towards the telephone, mouthing the word 'Bradley'

"Eisenhower."

"Ike, this is Omar. We can't stop them."

'Well that is pretty unequivocal', thought Ike.

"Go on, Brad."

"If my brief is still to preserve my force, I have no choice but to conduct a controlled and rapid withdrawal, and to be frank, for some of my units it may be too late already Ike."

"You must preserve your force, that order still stands Omar. You've been updated about Ingolstadt I hope?"

"Yes Sir. Depending on where they go, I don't believe they will be a problem for me just now."

Drawing quickly on his cigarette, Eisenhower focussed on the map to his front.

"So, what do you propose, Brad?"

"The Rhine."

"The Rhine?"

"Has to be, Ike."

Eisenhower's eyes took in the situation, assessing distances from enemy forces to the Rhine, new units arriving at French ports, others available in France, bringing everything together in his mind.

"No good for the British, Brad, no good for the Germans," Eisenhower shook his head at the inanimate object in his hand, "No good at all."

"I understand, Ike. We have to hold the Ruhr in any case, that is a must, so we can establish a defensible line from there up to Bremen, I hope."

77

"There's not as much going on with McCreery at the moment. He should hold for now."

"Regardless, I need to start pulling back now, and to cut the orders, now," Eisenhower didn't care for the school teacher emphasis his General used but let it go, "It means abandoning large areas of Germany to the Russians and the Council ain't gonna like it, Ike, but if I'm gonna have enough Army to kick them back again then it has to be done..."

"...And done now?" Eisenhower completed the sentence.

"Yes, Sir, it surely does."

A few staff officers had stopped what they were doing and were looking at Eisenhower, aware from his posture and expression that the day was about to take a different turn.

"No."

Bradley was actually physically shocked.

"Sorry Brad, but I cannot give up that much ground without a fight. There are other natural lines of defence we can dig our heels into."

"Yes Sir, but none with the worth of the Rhine."

"But none the less of worth, General."

Eisenhower consulted a small map on the table in front of him.

"Too much ground. We can hold them for some time on other lines, Brad. Dropping back to the Rhine in one hit removes other options. I can't sanction that."

"I'm not proposing a mass bug out, Ike. A controlled and fighting withdrawal back to the Rhine, to give myself time to beef up the defences."

"I can buy into that, General, but ceding the ground only when absolutely necessary. There will be other lines to hold, before the Rhine, and I will tell the Council that we will hold them as best we can whilst we prepare the Rhine. Combat engineers have been working hard, but we are light on mines from the reports I see."

Bradley clearly wanted to make certain of his remit, ignoring the point to ensure he understood fully.

"So can I look to drop back on the Rhine?"

78

Eisenhower wanted to make sure his man understood his orders.

"A fighting withdrawal, establishing more defensive lines and holding on to them for as long as is possible, pulling out only to preserve your force. Not a general bug-out to the Rhine. Am I clear, Brad?"

"Yes Sir."

"How long can you keep the Reds away from the Rhine river line for?"

"Mainz worries me. It's the shortest route, and we seem to have half the Red Army committed around Frankfurt and Giessen. I think a minimum of three days for them to get there, but I can hold Mainz for now, Sir."

"Right. Make sure you tie in on your flanks, liaise with McCreery and Devers, particularly work out the plans with Devers, as the join between you is crucial, Brad."

A swift look at the sheet of paper on his coffee table and Ike continued.

"I will cut three of the newly arrived infantry divisions to your command immediately. Details to follow."

"Thank you for that, General, but twenty-three would be needed right now."

"Would that I had them to send you, Brad."

"The Germans?"

Eisenhower overcame an automatic reluctance.

"I am speaking with the Council this afternoon."

"Good, cos I'm sorry to say we need those sonsofbitches right now. Put some of them in the field soon and we can free up some assets and start thinking about hitting back."

Something stirred in Eisenhower's memory as he sought more tobacco. Lighting up, his mind suddenly clicked.

"Did you see that report on those unusual attacks in the Pacific, Brad?"

Momentarily confused by the curve ball his commander had thrown, Bradley switched his train of thought.

"Yes, Sir, I did. Anthrax bombs and infected fleas that carry Bubonic Plague; nasty business, Ike."

79

"Just thinking out loud here but, as the Japs and Russians are allies; do you think that there could be a possibility that they might have given the Reds something in return for the tanks and guns?"

A pause suggested that the ramifications were being swiftly processed.

"Possibly so, but I can't see it. The Soviets are advancing into our areas, whereas the Japs used the nasties to mess up areas under our control. But it will pay to consider the possibility, Ike."

It was a fair point.

"Ok then, Brad. You sort your forces out, dropping back towards the Rhine only if you must, and only as a last resort. Tie in with Devers and McCreery. I will speak to both now, Devers first. I will also speak to Alexander and see if he will cut some more forces out to send around Switzerland to secure the bottom end of the Rhine."

A staff Captain placed a sheet of paper in front of Ike and retreated. Scanning as he spoke, Ike was able to pass on some good news.

"It seems we have some more Air coming on line too. We are steadily making good our losses. According to what is in front of me now, we are at 70% of pre-action numbers and climbing."

"Well that's just fine and dandy, but we are going to need those boys to do miracles, Ike."

"Yes indeed, Brad, as they've been doing since day one."

Placing the paper back on the table, Eisenhower concluded his call.

"Get it done, Brad, and blow everything as you fall back. Every rail junction, every bridge, every airfield, every supply dump. Leave them nothing, and hinder their advance to the maximum."

"Will do, Ike. Good day to you Sir."

"Good day to you, and good luck, General."

Pausing to sign off the aircraft replenishment report, Eisenhower communicated the decision to his staff and commenced his calls to the senior commanders.

80

The four Germans sat opposite Eisenhower, their coffees untouched, impassively listening as he described the military decisions taken that afternoon, decisions that would temporarily condemn the greater part of Germany to Soviet occupation.

The Tech-4 sat in the corner, making her normal record of the meeting.

For the benefit of Dönitz and Von Vietinghoff, a military map had been prepared and Eisenhower rose from the table to approach it. The two German officers took their cue and joined him, whereas Speer and Von Krosigk watched on.

Ike quickly went through the situation that had been updated at 5 o'clock to include the threat to Augsburg and fall of Frankfurt, as well as the withdrawal from Nürnberg. There was no way to dress up the disaster that was unfolding in these men's homeland.

He mapped out the ongoing withdrawal, ending on the most upbeat note, namely his decision not to fall back to the Rhine immediately but to set up other lines to the east, buying time to make sure the great water barrier was as impregnable as it could possibly be.

Eisenhower finished and stepped back as Goldstein finished his translation, permitting the two to do their own closer examination.

Dönitz swept a hand over south-west Germany and fired a question at Von Vietinghoff.

Goldstein spoke.

"Herr Dönitz asks if it is truly necessary to concede so much ground, Sir."

Eisenhower went to move forward, but was beaten to it by Von Vietinghoff.

The ex-General jabbed a finger at a few places on the map and spoke swiftly, so much so that Goldstein had not even started to translate before he was finished.

"Herr Von Vietinghoff says that no defence can be sustained for long at any of the points he indicates, despite

81

the assurances you have just given, and that the Rhine is the first and last line that can be manned and held in time. A slow gradual withdrawal is the best solution."

Eisenhower nodded and inclined his head to acknowledge Von Vietinghoff's understanding of the military position. He also realised that something had just been said that he simply had not properly understood himself until that moment.

"First and last line indeed, gentlemen. We will stop them on the Rhine, and then we will roll them back."

Goldstein ended his translation and waited for the response.

It came from Von Vietinghoff, and was in perfect English.

"To the Polish Border and beyond, Herr General."

Eisenhower's words were repeated back at him, at a time when such an advance seemed impossible to contemplate.

The two Germans returned to their seats, offering up a small explanation of the situation as they saw it for the benefit of the two politicians.

When they had finished, Eisenhower drew hard on his cigarette and stubbed it out before he posed the big question.

"I have been hearing good reports about your soldiers and their willingness to serve. I wonder when we might see some forces free to send forward into action?"

Eisenhower had heard a number of reports, not all of which were good. 'Agents provocateurs' within the ranks causing trouble, and there had been desertions by a number of men from the forming up camps. Even a report of a bloody fight near Emmerich, which ended with over forty men dead and hundreds hospitalised.

'Maybe that is why I feel like I do?'

It was Speer that spoke up, and he candidly confirmed every rumour Eisenhower had heard to be true, detailing additional problems, as yet unsuspected by the Allied Commander. Polish troops, the least forgiving of the Allies, had ransacked a German holding barracks in San

82

Bonifacio near Verona. The Polish troops were outnumbered and quickly resorted to firearms, the resulting fire fight leaving eighteen Poles and forty-nine Germans dead, with dozens more injured on both sides.

Throughout the German forces, a common problem had emerged. German officers had fought long and hard, bound by their oath to the person of the Führer, Adolf Hitler. The Council had immediately instigated a new oath to the state of Greater Germany. Soviet agents amongst the officers had caused great unrest on the matter, citing the unconstitutional nature of the Council that was enforcing the new oath.

In Jülich, the unrest had developed into violence, resulting in the deaths of seven officers. More violence had flared in Freiburg, where another five men were lost. Speer confirmed that GeneralOberst Guderian was engaged in a tour of the forming-up camps, and at each he openly retook the oath as an example, dealing with the concerns of officers head-on, and with great success.

Whilst it was good for Eisenhower to hear that the Council was doing its bit, the important question had not been answered. Not wishing to interrupt, he eased himself in his chair and went for another cigarette.

It was Dönitz who did the job for him. Leaning across to Speer, he tapped the folder in front of the former Minister of Munitions and spoke softly.

Speer conceded with a nod of the head and opened the folder, extracting a set of papers, which he offered up to Goldstein.

When the report was in Eisenhower's hands, Speer read aloud in German, which Goldstein at first translated but a raised hand from Eisenhower stopped him, the General's own copy of the document being typed in English.

Eisenhower scanned the list, conscious of Speer's voice in the background, but distracted by the content before him.

Organised on 1944 lines, the forces presently assembled should have represented a lifeline to a hard pressed Eisenhower.

But.

'Get a grip General! Snap out of it, and don't look a gift horse in the mouth.'

Eisenhower cleared his mind and felt the better for it.

The full tank division was most welcome, as was the motorised infantry one. However, a further nine complete infantry formations was the eye-catching figure that leapt up at Ike, albeit that the units were spread from Holland down to Italy.

One of the formations was a complete 1945 formation, the 319th Infanterie Division, which had served for four years as the garrison for the Channel Islands.

Another of the divisions was heavily motorised with a tank element and represented a former Panzer-Grenadiere style division, now named the Europa Division. With the sole exception of that unit, the other German divisions carried the nomenclature of their former deployment.

Scanning down the list, it was obvious that some support elements were missing from one or two of the formations but, all in all, he was being given an Army of eleven divisions, plus change, all fit to go in harm's way.

He reminded himself that these units were also comprised of good fighting troops, men already tested in battles such as those to come.

Turning the sheet over, projections of a second and third tranche of units over the coming months drew his attention, the figures seeming to offer up so much hope at a time of near despair.

With the return of prisoners of war from Canada and the States, numbers would be further boosted. Certainly, Ike mused, unit strengths could be maintained with reinforcements.

Another piece of the report suggested training with allied weapons and equipment in case of shortages as captured German stocks became denuded, although there was a reference to a report from Minister Speer to come.

Goldstein interrupted his flow of thought.

"And here is a list of the contribution that the German Air Force can make, once logistics are put in place."

84

The second list was no less impressive than the first, containing some twenty separate units, ranging from fighters to reconnaissance.

Speer had deferred to Dönitz, who was speaking very methodically to ensure Goldstein got every word.

"Herr Dönitz stresses that these German Air force units are not ready to contribute as yet, as even spares and facilities have yet to be organised, let alone IFF and signals protocols. In the light of the clear and urgent need for a qualified and competent man to direct Luftwaffe matters, the Council requests that you arrange for General der Flieger Koller to be released from British custody to facilitate the organisation and integration of these units."

Eisenhower couldn't speak for the British but doubted there would be a problem, given the likely benefits to the Allied cause, plus he seemed to recall that Koller was not on the list of those who were unacceptable.

"I will make urgent enquiries as soon as we have concluded our business here, gentlemen."

Acknowledging the translation from Goldstein, Dönitz plunged on.

"There are a number of U-Boats that can be made available, but we are unsure how they would be employed or if they would be necessary. Clearly, there is a large manpower pool of naval personnel who wish to contribute. The Council wishes to liaise with a senior officer of the Royal Navy to discuss what is to be done."

Eisenhower ignored the unintended snub to the USN.

"I assume that will be your responsibility, Herr Dönitz?"

A positive response allowed him to rapidly continue.

"Tomorrow, Admiral Somerville will be attending this headquarters. I will ask that he liaises with you and arrange it for the two of you to have an office to discuss the matter if that is satisfactory?"

Ike understood the simple 'thank you' without need for Goldstein skills.

Anxious to resolve the burning issue, Eisenhower picked up the first report and scanned it again, failing to see the answer he needed.

"Gentlemen, this report doesn't tell me when I can expect these units to be available for combat use."

The Germans received the translation with barely concealed amusement, exchanging glances before Von Vietinghoff picked up the report and pointed at the top of the document, speaking directly at Goldstein and fingering each word he recited.

Dropping the document back onto the table, he added a few more words for the benefit of his council colleagues and sat back in his seat, looking directly at an expectant but confused Eisenhower.

The Major leant across and pointed the same words out to his General, words whose true meaning were simply lost in the translation of the document.

"Sir, it states here that 'the forces available are'. What Herr Vietinghoff states is that these formations are available.......now."

Ike could not help but feel a surge of electricity through his frame at that news, a charge of both positive and negative thought.

Before he could summon up the right response, Goldstein continued.

"Herr Vietinghoff offers himself as a staff officer here in order to plan the integration and use of the German divisions and to act as liaison between SHAEF and the German Army Commander."

Eisenhower knew he had been railroaded, as the Army command was supposed to, by mutual agreement, belong to a SHAEF appointee, with a senior German Officer as Chief of Staff, but somehow it didn't seem to matter at that moment.

"Guderian, I assume?"

Goldstein was cut off as he drew breath.

"Jawohl. GeneralOberst Guderian."

86

Pursing his lips, Eisenhower placed his hands palms down on the table, weighing up the pros and cons, quickly understanding that acceptance was the only real possibility.

"Very well."

Eisenhower stood and walked briskly around the table, extending his hand to each man in turn.

"Thank you, Gentlemen."

Eisenhower was alone in the room; the council, Goldstein, and the Tech NCO, all departed.

Speer had passed over his report, translated into English, with the original German version attached.

His forecast on German weapons production was extremely interesting, anticipating an Allied stand to preserve the Ruhr, and an Allied withdrawal in areas of Germany, necessitating the removal of some manufacturing plants to safer areas, such as were suggested in France.

Ike found this puzzling, and consumed two cigarettes as he pondered the facts. Speer had seemed surprised that so much ground was to be conceded, and yet had already prepared a proposal to evacuate much of the industry in south-west Germany.

The council had suggested that some of their forces commenced training on Allied weapons, and yet seemed to be suggesting that German industry could quickly start to manufacture replacements for losses incurred in the coming battles.

'What am I missing here?'

After a number of calls to his senior commanders, Eisenhower was clear as to where he would commit the Northern European German units when they came on line. In truth, the commitment was blatantly obvious.

Inserting the Germans between McCreery's 21st Army Group and Bradley's 12th Army Group made sense, the more so as the Ruhr would offer a suitable area for the

Germans to defend, and one that they would be well motivated to preserve.

That all pre-supposed that Bradley and McCreery could stifle the Soviet advances for long enough to get the Germans in position. Both had given an assurance that they would give ground slowly to buy time for the deployment, but that didn't stop Ike being anxious and upping his cigarette consumption rate alarmingly.

He tried to convince himself that the imminent arrival of German divisions would have a positive effect on Bradley's 12th, and make their defence in front of the Rhine more difficult for the Soviets to overcome.

The Italian based formations would free up some of Alexander's divisions which would be sent north as soon as possible.

A visit that evening from Austrian leader Karl Renner, promising two and a half Bundesheer divisions was welcome, but did not ease the worry.

The darkness brought too little sleep, as Eisenhower debated and argued with himself into the night.

'I am committed to using them.'

'And why would you not? They are great soldiers.'

'Because they are German, of course!'

'And they fought the commies for four years.'

'Look at the trouble there's been already.'

'Small stuff by provocateurs. Anyway, you need 'em! The Allies need them, and will probably not prevail without them.'

Eisenhower woke, his breathing rapid, his body filled with the unease of a broken night.

He reached across for his cigarettes and drew in the pungent smoke, coughing lightly as his body overcame the nocturnal surprise.

"Goddamn it!"

When the enemy advances, withdraw; when he stops, harass;
when he tires, strike; when he retreats, pursue.

Mao Zedong

Chapter 60 – THE SNIPERS

Monday, 13th August 1945, 1800 hrs, Tostedt, Germany.

Calmly, carefully, and quietly, as is the way of the sniper, the two soldiers crept into the chosen firing position.

Opposite it was the building that had caused all the problems to the battalion assault that earlier that morning.

Soviet dead lay strewn over the open ground in between. The rubble and craters that surrounded and filled the destroyed German town of Tostedt, all heavy with those freshly killed that day.

Allied soldiers from the 1st Canadian Infantry Division's Carleton & York Regiment, stubborn soldiers in defence, filled the positions opposite, from where they had poured deadly fire into the attacking forces, beating them off with heavy casualties.

And then the rain had come, a downpour that masked the sniper teams now moving into their chosen positions, as well as washing away the puddles of bodily fluids freshly formed from the products of the day's butchery.

Adjusting her sights to suit a range of four hundred metres, she risked a swift look through the hole in the side of the American truck, the position from where she intended to wreak her own sort of havoc.

Mortars shells, a mix of HE and smoke, were dropping on the Canadian positions, a small token from the commanding officer to help the sniper teams deploy.

Along with Yefreytor Lena Yurieva Panfilova's team, 360th Rifle Division had been allocated five other special sniper groups, all of which were taking their positions, each with their own allocated fire sector to work once the new attack commenced.

89

Each team consisted of two snipers and two spotters, all of whom could change roles in an instant, as all were deadly marksmen and women in their own right.

Panfilova's number two today was Yarit, a wizened old Siberian Eskimo, whose eyes seemed hardly to open no matter what the circumstances, but whose aim was as deadly as anyone in the unit.

Using whispers and sign language, Yarit sorted out the targets.

The other two in Panfilova's team, Olga Maleeva and Sergey Erinov, had dropped off into a group of fallen trees on the other side of the road and were invisible to the team leader, despite the fact that she knew they were both there.

The specialist sniper sections of 11th Guards Army had little time to do their work before the next battalions were thrown forward. Priorities were the machine gunners, the deadly Vickers and Bren gunners, who were the main culprits responsible for the human detritus filling the space between the snipers and the Canadian infantry positions. The others, the highly effective Canadian artillery of 3rd Field Regiment, were beyond the reach of the sniper teams, but not the ground attack bomber regiment specially tasked with their destruction.

The seconds ticked away, each spotter concentrating on their watch, each sniper keeping their weapon on target, waiting, quietly, as the second hands brought closer the agreed moment of firing and the inevitable death of young Canadians that would accompany the volley.

Panfilova controlled her breathing, relaxed into her rifle, steadied by the crate against which she leant.

Starshy Serzhant Babr Yarit quietly counted away the last seconds.

The Mosin-Nagant rifle kicked, and Lena was rewarded by a red mist that appeared where once her target had crouched behind his Vickers machine-gun.

Switching to the second target, she was greeted with the surprised face of a young soldier, clearly inexperienced, head extended above cover whilst his older comrades had already disappeared from view.

90

The bullet took him just under the nose and carried through the eighteen year old's brain before exiting at the base of his skull, expending its remaining energy burrowing into the wall beyond.

The other teams similarly brought down their targets, leaving the Canadian positions temporarily exposed.

Overhead, the return of the air force bomber regiment encouraged the ground troops, although the older soldiers noted many less aircraft than had flown to the attack some minutes beforehand.

A collective shout, the famous 'Urrah', went up from the lead assault battalion, and the Soviet infantry again rushed forward, this time accompanied by three SU-76 self-propelled guns, sent forward for close support.

Defending Canadian troops commenced firing but the rate of fire was low. Brave men tried to man Vickers and Bren guns, but were mainly struck down as the sniper sections continued their work.

The self-propelled guns also wrought destruction, accurately blotting out nests of resistance.

A movement at an unoccupied window drew Panfilova's attention. She fired a shot at a vague shape and the shape fell forward into view. Rechambering her rifle, she noted with satisfaction the obvious rank markings of her latest success. This bullet had killed the Artillery Observation officer for the Canadian batteries supporting this sector, removing the effectiveness of their support, support that had already been eroded by a swift and savage working-over by the Shturmoviks.

The Soviet infantry were already beyond the line of bodies that marked their furthest progress in the last attack, and few men had been struck down by comparison.

A handful of mortar shells burst amongst the attacking wave, enough to kill and maim a handful of men, but insufficient to halt the momentum of the charge.

With the absence of the Artillery Officer, slain by a sniper's bullet, and the OP team, destroyed by an SU-76 shell, the Canadian infantry Captain had called upon anything he could get to listen on his own radio before yet another HE shell had ended his life.

A second wave of infantry threw themselves forward as two Mosquito Mk VI's arrived, responding to direction from an RAF controller who had heard the desperate plea for help. One was already smoking, courtesy of a brush with Soviet interceptors.

The concentration of advancing Russian infantry drew their attention, and they attacked immediately. Each aircraft mounted four 20mm Hispano cannon in the nose, and these spewed shells into the second wave, ravaging the ranks and destroying men by the score.

Spotting two of the Soviet assault guns, the leader turned and bore down again, this time thumbing off his main strike weapons. All eight 60lb rockets leapt from their racks and bore down upon the Soviet armour.

He did not see his salvo obliterate both SU's as his aircraft was knocked out of the sky by a ZSU-37 covering the attack. It's 37mm automatic weapon severed the tail plane, and the Mosquito drove straight into the ground, killing its crew and more hapless Soviet infantry.

Panfilova grinned at her spotter, both for the destruction of the enemy aircraft and the obvious success of the Soviet attack.

Her good-humour turned to concern as she noticed Yarit was wide-eyed, looking down and up, alternating between the two views swiftly, a look of horror spreading over his face.

The remaining SU76 was moving as fast as it could, desperate to avoid the attentions of the surviving Mosquito.

It was heading straight at their place of concealment, its madly rotating tracks sending mud spraying in all directions as the driver hammered his vehicle.

The Mosquito flipped into a shallow dive and eight rockets sped away, smoky trails indicating the likely landing point.

Panfilova and Yarit tried to run but explosive force moves quicker than a human can react.

92

The first rocket entered the rear compartment of the SU, instantly sending it in all directions as nothing more than scrap metal, its crew evaporated.

The seventh rocket to land dropped at the rear of the ruined truck in which the two snipers were hiding.

After the battle was over, and Tostedt was in Soviet hands, comrades searched long and hard for the pair. Of Yarit, there was simply no trace. The sniper unit's senior Non-com was finally persuaded to climb a tree and knock down an indescribable something that was hanging in its branches. Lacking head, arms and legs, the destroyed body was beyond identification, save for the obvious shapely right breast.

The only female missing was Lena Panfilova, so her grieving comrades swiftly buried the corpse, on the assumption that it was their prettiest and youngest killer.

1925 hrs 13th August 1945, Tostedt Land, Germany.

Allied forces – Carleton & York Regiment, 4th Platoon, Saskatoon Light Infantry [MG] all of 3rd Canadian Infantry Brigade, 3rd Field Regiment RCHA, 2nd Platoon, 4th Canadian Field Company RCE, B Battery, 1st Anti-Tank Regiment RCHA, all of 1st Canadian Infantry Division, Canadian I Corps, Canadian First Army, British 21st Army Group. Kommando Tostedt, Kommando Bucholz.

Soviet Forces – 4th Guards Tank Brigade, 1st Company, 79th Motorcycle Battalion, 2nd Company, 1st Battalion, 1695th AA Regiment, all of 2nd Guards Tank Corps, 1195th Rifle Regiment, 1197th Rifle Regiment, 920th Artillery Regiment all of 360th Rifle Division, Army sniper section, 1st Battalion, 2nd Guards Assault Engineer Sapper Brigade, all of 11th Guards Army, 1st Baltic Front.

Fig #35 - Tostedt Land

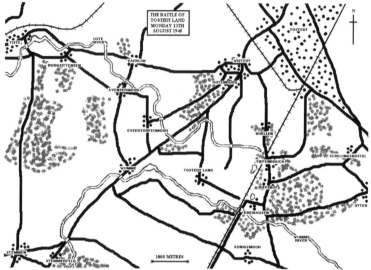

Colonel Yarishlov was extremely satisfied. The lead formations had initially walked through the enemy front line, so effective had been the artillery strike. In fact, the main issue slowing the initial advance had been the destruction to roads and tracks ravaged by shells from Soviet artillery pieces.

2nd Guards Tank Corps was one of a number of fresh units temporarily assigned to the 11th Guards Army, to bolster the attacking force in its drive south-west towards Bremen.

The infantry of 360th Rifle Division had leap-frogged his armour, and their attacks had eventually cleared out the town ahead, at the cost of decimating the 1193rd Rifle Regiment, only for the Division to grind to a halt when the Germans and Canadian forces stopped the assault just short of the bridges over the Oste and Wümme. They then counter-attacked and drove the survivors back through Rotenburg and Wistedt all the way into Tostedt. 1193rd with the assistance of relatively fresh 1197th tried at once to renew the advance,

94

but heavy casualties took their toll, and they were unable to progress alone. Yarishlov's 4th Guards Tank Brigade was ordered to support a second attempt to dislodge the enemy, and to open the route to Stemmen, Lauenbruck and Scheeßel for the rest of the Corps.

Already the timetable was falling well behind, and so there was no time for the niceties of complex planning, even though his men were more understanding and proficient than most. But neither did that mean that the tank Colonel was going to just hammer in, regardless of casualties.

A cursory look at the map was sufficient for Yarishlov to appreciate the risks of his attack, and to plan accordingly.

Fig #36 - Tostedt Land dispositions

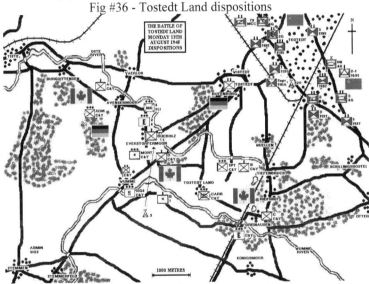

According to reports from the competent commander of the 360th, the only bridge intact on his right flank seemed to be that just east of Everstorfermoor, the defenders having brought down all but one of the bridges west and south-west of Rotenburg. The man believed that the water barrier was easily enough forded by infantry in places, but had not tested the possibility as yet. He was now on his way to the rear, his

95

war cut short by a simple stumble that left the man with a painfully dislocated right knee. Yarishlov assumed command of all forces in the area and assembled his officers for a swift and simple briefing.

Unable to take a chance that the Oste River might be fordable and not having the time to do proper reconnaissance, Yarishlov looked to a more southerly approach for his main drive, hooking around through the hamlets of Riepshof and Tiefenbruch and following the rail line through Dreihausen, crossing over the Wümme River by the rail bridge that was apparently still standing.

He described the line of march with his hands, examining each officer's reaction as he looked for a sign of weakness or doubt. None was forthcoming, and the tank Colonel was encouraged as good questions were asked, confirming that the men of his command understood their business.

The area between the rivers, centred on Tostedt Land, was of great interest to him and he drew his men in closer to the map, outlining a possible change of plan, should circumstances proved favourable.

The young Major now commanding the roughly-handled 1197th Regiment moved closer and examined the map, suggesting a small modification to Yarishlov's move westwards through Tostedt Land, leaving a smear of blood on the Wümme river line between Wümme and Dreihausen. The modification was a good one, and the artillery commander confirmed the change was an improvement. Devoid of ego, Yarishlov always encouraged and welcomed the input of his officers, and he openly commended the man, which went a long way to overcoming the pain of the Major's wound.

When he had finished his briefing, watches were synchronised, and then the officers were dismissed to their commands, but not before he ordered the wounded Major to get some attention to his damaged forearm.

Suddenly finding himself alone in the school room that presently served as his headquarters, Yarishlov stretched and lazily searched his pockets for a cigarette.

96

A knock on the door startled the Colonel out of his daydream, the more so as the knocker didn't wait for permission to enter and just kicked the door open.

Starshina Stefan Yurievich Kriks almost ran through the doorway, his hands full of huge enamel mugs brimming with obviously scalding hot liquid, his cries of distress growing in volume with every step.

"Ay-yay-yay-yay-yay!"

The mugs hit the table, each spilling a quantity of the dark brown liquid. The NCO was more interested in his hands, licking each in turn, feeling the heat on his tongue.

Colonel Yarishlov drew himself up to his full height and adopted a formal voice.

"Starshina Kriks. Look at my door, you thug! What have you got to say for yourself?"

Kriks noted the displaced hinge and cocked an eyebrow. Maybe he had kicked it a bit hard after all.

"Comrade Colonel, I was bringing you tea and I could not delay. Had I waited for you to answer the door, then I would now be on the way to hospital with burned fingers, and I would be risking a charge of self-inflicted injury from our revolutionary brothers in the NKVD."

Yarishlov sniggered.

"Good answer, Starshina, good answer."

The two men shared a grin, the sort that men who have endured hell together exchange; one that requires no words.

Kriks popped out some English Players cigarettes and the two relaxed in each other's company, away from the rigours of military formality.

Smoking and sipping alternately, there was no need for words until an ambulance passing by the window ground its gears noisily, breaking the reverie, and making both look up, its woeful cargo immediately apparent.

Kriks pointed his mug at the vehicle.

"The 360th boys did their best today, Comrade. They took a beating, but they are still up for a fight. I've seen nothing but an excellent spirit from them. I'm surprised they aren't Guards yet."

Yarishlov nodded in acknowledgement, both of the wounded men and of his NCO's words, and raised the drink to his lips again. Kriks, the man with the asbestos throat, finished his, exposing the maple leaf on the bottom of his mug.

"Capitalist cigarettes, capitalist tea, capitalist mugs. What are you doing to me, Stefan?"

Kriks turned his mug over. On the underside was the outline of a maple leaf, the British War department stamp and, in pencil, the name 'Wainwright'.

The Starshina shrugged.

"Comrade Colonel, it was Canadian tea or nothing. This is the fault of my tank commander."

The twinkle in Kriks' eyes was very evident.

Replying as evenly as he could, Yarishlov kept a straight face.

"I am your tank commander, Comrade Starshina."

Feigning surprise, Kriks proceeded.

"Quite so, Comrade Polkovnik. So, I regret to say, it is your fault alone. Had you not directed your brand new command tank through the treacherous Germanski undergrowth, without need I might add, then you would still have good Soviet tea. Whereas that tea, my smoked sausages, and certain other items of high value, are now hanging on some damn bush somewhere, to be found by some undeserving rear-echelon beauty whom, I might add, I desperately hope chokes on the fucking sausage!"

As time was short, Yarishlov could only call a halt to the NCO's diatribe by raising a hand.

"And speaking of my new command tank, has Lunin sorted the problem yet?"

"Indeed he has, Comrade Polkovnik, and you will be surprised to learn that it was not a transmission fault, just a gear linkage problem, so our beast is up and running again."

The Colonel finished the last of his tea and thumped the mug on the table.

"Well, we have it so that I can write a report on its combat usage, so let us go and see how it fights, shall we?"

98

Slapping his senior NCO on the shoulder, he picked up the map and walked out into the evening sunshine, casting a professional and appreciative eye over the T-44/100 the Corps Commander had presented to him over a month ago.

The men of Kommando Tostedt were tired. Having fought alongside the Canadians in the defence of their home town, they had reluctantly fallen back, only to turn on their pursuers and deal them a heavy blow, combining with their new allies to drive the Russian infantry back through Rotenburg and Wistedt, where they now waited for the inevitable next assault.

The Canadian Company Commander had tried to persuade them to fall back to the river line but they refused, offering to cover the withdrawal for as long as they could.

Now they were all alone, sticking out like a sore thumb, the Canadians having pulled back to more defensible ground.

Numbering less than one hundred and eighty capable men, the Kommando sat astride the four roads that ran south-west from Rotenburg and Wistedt. Whilst they could not bring themselves to quit their homes quite yet, their pragmatic leader ensured that he could withdraw his unit over the Everstorfermoor Bridge at any time.

Alfred Dœring-Beck was a veteran of both world wars. The elderly silver-haired Colonel of Infanterie affected a monocle, a clue to the fact that he had learned his soldiering in a different age, when cutting-edge tactics dictated lines of infantry sweeping down on defensive positions strewn with barbed wire and covered by machine-guns and artillery. Such ways were of little use in 1939, and he was forcibly and very publically retired by the then Divisional Commander of the 24th Infanterie Division, Generalleutnant Friedrich Olbricht. During the invasion of Poland, Beck's 32nd Grenadiere Regiment took unusually high casualties during the Polish counter-attack around Bzura in mid-September 1939, something which his inconsolable second in command reported instantly and directly to Olbricht.

Beck, embittered by his public humiliation, crowed long and hard when Olbricht was executed by firing squad, payback for his part in the failed assassination attempt of 20th July 1944.

Commanding his unit in defence of the town had not been particularly challenging, more a question of standing fast as the Russian wave broke over him. Relic of a bygone age he may have been, but he was a man of great courage, a fact attested to by several Great War decorations.

As the Russian barrage grew in intensity, he moved forward and observed Soviet infantrymen and armour massing on the outskirts of Tostedt. He recognised the danger immediately.

'If the Canadians are not in position now, then God help them', he mused.

Calling his second in command to him, Beck told the man that there was no point now in remaining in situ and instructed the former Luftwaffe Artillerie Captain to evacuate all but the first section immediately, the first section being formed of the older men who had served their rifle time in Flanders fields.

They would buy as much time as possible for the unit to withdraw.

The man saluted and scurried away.

A shell landed nearby and the screams of the dying immediately filled the air. An elderly medic rushed over to do what he could. Normally the local doctor, the medic had once been a Major in Füsilier-Regiment 80 'Von Gersdorff', and had served at Verdun, the Somme and the Aisne. His intimate knowledge of shrapnel wounds, combined with his medical experience, enabled him to understand that all five men were beyond help. Easing the pain of the two men remaining semi-conscious, he moved on to where the Soviet artillery was providing him with more work.

Moving further forward, Beck entered a large house on the edge of Wistedt, once the home of the local apothecary.

He settled in alongside the man with the binoculars, waiting until the NCO finished scanning the enemy positions.

"Well, Hüth? Are the Garde-Füsiliers ready for the enemy?"

The former Hauptfeldwebel of the 3rd Garde-Infanterie Division was used to the baiting, as he and his three comrades had endured it most evenings in the bierkeller, when war stories and tall tales flowed as freely as the chilled Beck's.

100

"We will hold until we are relieved of course, Herr Oberst."

The man relaxed the binoculars and looked at the Kommandofuhrer, the resignation on his face at odds with the weak attempt at humour.

"Mind you, Herr Beck, I rather suspect our communist enemy has a different end in mind for us."

He coughed violently and spat a gobbet of bloody phlegm against the wall, wheezing as he often did when the lasting effects of his exposure to French gas made themselves known

"I have ordered everyone back, except first section."

Hüth turned to look at Beck and nodded gently. Neither he nor his fellow ex-Garde needed further explanation.

Turning back to the window, he spoke rapidly, pausing only to duck involuntarily when a shell landed particularly close.

"We have tanks and infantry on either flank, and they don't seem positioned to attack us at the moment."

"Yes. I saw them from back there a few minutes ago."

"Still building up, as I see it. Here."

Hüth handed the binoculars over, indicating where Beck should look.

Tanks and infantry were gathering on both flanks of Tostedt, seemingly oriented to by-pass their position. Beck calmly noted that there were many more than he first thought.

"Well, we can't do anything about them, Hüth. However," sweeping along the landscape he stopped and focussed on the area directly opposite, "I do believe that they are not intending to leave us alone after all."

His eye had caught movement, and he passed the binoculars back.

"At the railway track there."

Hüth's eyes were still keen and he swept the line of the railway that prescribed the edge of the town. He could see numerous helmets and other signs betraying the presence of Russian infantry forming behind the slight rise of the tracks.

Soviet mortar rounds started to drop around the Apothecary's house, and the occasional lump of metal pinged off the brickwork or embedded itself in something softer. Adler, the

101

oldest of the Garde, received three small pieces as he went to grab more stick grenades. Bleeding profusely from his buttocks, he was tended to by one of his comrades, but wasn't spared from the man's heavy-handed humour.

Such wounds attracted such humour.

A mortar shell struck an old Citroen lying wrecked in front of their position, causing it to burst into flames

Hüth carefully raised himself up and nestled the binoculars back in position to check the enemy.

At the very bottom of his vision, from a position halfway between Tostedt and Wistedt, the old NCO saw a flash next to Bremer Straβe and knew what it was immediately.

It was a sniper firing.

Beck was behind and to the right and the reflection of the fire on his monocle was all the sniper had needed for an instinctive shot.

It was a few moments before Beck realised that he had been lucky. The bullet had passed down the right side of his face, clipping a perfect U section out of his ear, before destroying an extremely large and valuable piece of Meissen porcelain on the dresser behind. Everyone in the room jumped when the vase disintegrated, not realising the reason for its destruction.

Dœring-Beck looked back to the front and felt the pain in his ear. He slapped his hand to the wound as the blood started to flow.

The second bullet caught him in the side of the jaw, removing half his face from chin to eye socket.

The elderly man dropped to the ground, temporarily paralysed by the pain and shock, bleeding his life out.

Adler, bandaged and angry with pain, rolled across the floor and tried to reassemble the awful wound so he could bandage it.

The screaming started, the awful high-pitched squeals of a man in the extremis of suffering.

Beck had broken his left arm as he fell and his right scrabbled for his weapon, seeking the butt of his MP40 sub-machine gun.

Hüth understood immediately, and ordered Adler to move back.

What the sniper had started, he finished with one shot from his Kar98k, putting a merciful end to old Beck's torment.

A shout from one of the others prevented him from pondering his horror at the necessary deed.

The Russians were moving up on both flanks. Mortars were now dropping smoke in front of Wistedt, so it was most likely that infantry were already closing in upon them. The bonus of it was that the sniper's line of sight was now masked.

Quickly moving out of the Apothecary's residence, Hüth checked with those members of first section on either side, ensuring the order spread to all twenty-six men who now defended Wistedt. And the order was simple.

Stand and fight.

Returning to his own position, he checked the machine-gun crew in the bedroom were ready, dropping off the last of the ammunition he had grabbed from the section stockpile. It was an old First World War MG.08, but it could still do its job and kill.

A mortar shell hit the corner of the house and a new hole opened up, providing an improved firing position for the NCO. He occupied it as soon as the rubble settled, gathering up grenades and his former commander's sub-machine gun.

He heard the Russian 'Urrah' as the infantry surged forward, and he shouted out to his men to fire as soon as they saw a target.

The smoke was clearing slowly as the mortar crews had changed to HE only and shifted aim to Wistedt itself, seeking out the defenders.

The .08 opened up, its 7.9mm bullets pumping out at four hundred rounds per minute, dealing death to the first Russians through the thinning smoke. The crew had to be careful and nurse the machine-gun, as its water coolant jacket leaked profusely, requiring the loader to fill it with water from a number of old beer bottles laid out specifically for the purpose.

Hüth could not yet see a target, but he could hear the effects of the machine-gun firing from upstairs, as the sounds of men in pain reached his ears. Seeing a blur in the smoke, he threw a hand grenade and was rewarded with the sight of one of his enemies being propelled forward by the blast. The man landed and bounced forward like a child's doll, lying still, never

103

to rise again. Three others had been wounded by the same grenade, and their screams joined the rising sound of battle.

The Russian infantry did not lack courage and plunged on, even when another grenade extracted a similar price from the assault group.

Rifle fire now erupted as the last of the smoke disappeared in an instant, enabling all the defenders to engage.

Enemy soldiers dropped to the ground, some hit, others to seek cover. The MG continued its deadly work, steaming as it was when water was poured into the jacket at regular intervals.

Adler was dead already, a victim of one of the attacking units covering DP machine guns, which were being increasingly effective.

The Soviet infantry were chivvied to their feet by a young Lieutenant, who led them forward. Hüth dropped him with his first shot, but the impetus of the attack did not falter.

One Soviet sergeant threw a grenade at the MG team on the first floor. It landed amongst the bottles, where it exploded, adding a thousand lethal shards of glass to the shrapnel that cut the men to ribbons, and silenced the .08 permanently.

The old NCO took aim but someone else in Hüth's group put the sergeant down, so he switched targets to the next in line, killing a submachine gunner with a shot through the chest.

The action of his rifle stiffened as brick dust gathered upon it, and he worked it hard, chambering the next round before sending it on its way, missing a running soldier who dropped into a shell hole.

Working the near-rigid bolt once more, he searched for another target, and saw a head pop up from the shell hole, firing more in reaction than calm aim. None the less, Hüth hit the target, blowing the top of the man's head off and sending the ruined helmet flying.

Two riflemen and an officer were charging straight at him now, and he discarded the empty Mauser in favour of the MP40 and sent a stream of bullets at the running men, missing badly with the unfamiliar weapon.

The three were on him in an instant.

The leading rifleman lunged with his bayonet, which Hüth parried with the submachine-gun and shoved the man to the

104

ground, using the Russians' forward momentum against him. The second man had no bayonet and swung his rifle like a club, a blow glancing off the German's shoulder.

Squealing with pain, Hüth fired his weapon again, this time pumping seven bullets through the man's abdomen at point blank range. As he fired, the recoil pushed him back, causing him to lose balance. Hüth fell to the floor on top of the first assailant.

Before he could move, the officer shot him dead.

Not one man from First Section survived the battle.

Yarishlov watched satisfied as the 1st Battalion of 1195th Rifles swept into the village, and then turned his attention on the advance of his left flank units.

1197th Rifles had quickly reformed, its butchered second battalion being absorbed into the other units bringing both up to nearly 70% strength. Reports from reconnaissance teams operating in advance of the main force indicated enemy positions at Riepshof and Tiefenbruch, which information has already cost them two BA-64 armoured cars.

One company of 3rd/1195th had walked into Quellen without opposition and now waited for further instructions. The other companies were pushing to the south of Quellen, intent on capturing Tiefenbruch. 2nd/4th Guards Tanks provided some close support, but they were under orders not to become closely engaged so as to be ready to attack in depth when the enemy line was broken.

Further south-east two companies of tankers from the Guards had delivered their grapes of rider infantry from the 1195th into Otter, again undefended, whilst the 1st/1197th motored down the Dreihausen road, intent on delivering Yarishlov's intended left-hook, supported by the rest of the 4th's 3rd Tank Battalion. 1st/1197th was quite mobile, its enterprising regimental commander having acquired, stolen, requisitioned or captured numerous vehicles, from American Studebaker lorries through to a once pristine Wanderer W23 Cabriolet.

By accident, the Russian Tank Colonel had aimed his first effort straight into the weakest of the Canadian infantry units in front of him, Carleton & York's C Company having been badly handled during its defence of Tostedt.

The situation had seemed stable enough to Lieutenant-Colonel Lascelles, although his five mile frontage was considerably more than accepted practice it was manageable because of the river lines.

Neither river was broad but days of heavy rainfall and considerable efforts by engineers and service personnel had made it into an obstacle that was more than enough to deny tanks and vehicles access and certainly deep enough that any infantry would be seriously slowed up swimming across it. A few mines scattered on the home banks also helped to make him feel secure.

The Carleton & York's were bordered on the north-west by the Royal 22e Regiment, the famous Van-Doos of the 3rd Canadian Infantry Brigade. They were anchored in Tiste and maintained a contact with Lascelles' own 'A' Company, whose flank extended to Burgsittensen. To the south-east was the Loyal Edmonton Regiment of the 1st Canadian Division's 2nd Infantry Brigade, positioned at Konigsmoor, and running all the way to Luneburg heath and beyond.

The arrival of most of Kommando Tostedt had been a boon, as he had been expecting them to be lost in the hopeless defence of Wistedt. He assigned them a reserve position in Tostedt Land, where the carrier Platoon was also situated.

His perception changed, and the situation now seemed less than stable, as a report from 'B' Company indicated a large number of Russian infantry with tank support pressing hard against their positions around Tiefenbruch.

Lascelles had little idea that his whole battalion would be but a memory within two hours.

Yarishlov had halted the advance west from Otter on nothing more than intuition, sensing rather than knowing that he was missing something.

106

Calling his officers together for a brief orders group, he laid a map on the ground and dropped onto his haunches to examine the land once more.

Before he could address the group, the 4th's Communications officer interjected, barely controlling his breathing from his run.

He passed over a message form that confirmed Yarishlov's intuition.

"Comrades, we have an opportunity here, and I intend for us to grasp it."

Passing the message back to his signals captain, he continued.

"The 79th Motorcycles has found Tiste unoccupied and the bridge over the Oste intact."

Officers leant over and checked the map, developing immediate understanding of the enemy omission.

Such errors happen in war, and the Royal 22e's had been withdrawn on orders, a mistake that left the Carleton & Yorks vulnerable.

"I am going to order," he looked up to check that pencils were hovering over notebooks, "79th Motorcycles, my 1st Tank Battalion, and the Guards Engineers south over this Bridge."

He checked the name on the village he was looking at.

"The engineers will occupy Burgsittensen and these woods, and hold."

Moving down the map, he tapped a point approximately 1500 metres north of Stemmen.

"I want 79th to set a screen here running from these woods across to the river. This bridge," he indicated the apparently intact bridge north of Stemmerfeld, "I want this under observation so we can drop artillery on them if they gather to cross it. That will be a priority target, Mayor, clear?"

The artillery officer nodded his understanding.

"1st Tank Battalion and its grapes will sweep up the river line and into Wümme. No further forward than that for now. I want anyone in this area to be an enemy," he placed his hand over the land between the two rivers centring on Tostedt Land."

"1st will take Everstorfermoor under fire and prevent westward movement."

107

Checking the unit markings closely, Yarishlov made a quick note before speaking to the Infantry commander. He looked up and noticed the young infantry officer standing next to his temporary Divisional Commander, noting with satisfaction the new bandage on the recent arm wound.

"Your wound is treated satisfactorily, Comrade...?"

"Zvorykin, Comrade Polkovnik. Yes, thank you."

Yarishlov grunted by way of reply and moved on, addressing the senior man, illustrating his words with gestures at the map.

"I want this unit, 2nd Battalion of your 1195th, to head to Vaerlon as quickly as possible, and then push south. I wish to test the possibility that the river can be forded. If it can then I want them in Avensermoor and no further. If it cannot then harass from as close to the river as they can comfortably achieve."

The Infantry Lieutenant-Colonel understood perfectly.

"These units opposite Everstorfermoor, I want them noisy and harassing the enemy but no more for now. I want to keep them interested and confident in their positions."

The acting Divisional Commander of the 360th smiled.

"Yes, Comrade Polkovnik, we can do that."

The man, so often let down in the past by fanatics, whose ideas were no more than 'charge and die', found it wholly refreshing to be under the command of someone who was extremely competent.

"I want half of my 2nd Battalion here as soon as possible, leaving the other half to support the infantry around Tiefenbruch as before."

Looking at his watch, he did the mental arithmetic.

"Units near Tiste must go now, so get those orders out."

Two men hurried away to the radio to pass on the new orders.

"I want to start knocking on the door very soon, so I will go with what we have here, and the 2nd Battalion will have to catch up."

Catching Major Zvorykin's eye, he continued.

"You suggested the artillery change in case the enemy had defences on our flank here," tapping the bloody mark the young man had left some time before.

"I shall give you an opportunity to test that. Your infantry will take the Dreihausen Bridge and hold it. Then you will take a force down the river on the south bank, linking up with my tanks at Wümme."

The young officer kept his expression fixed.

"If there are enemy forces there, where you suspect, I want you to bring our artillery down on them. I want nothing of note on my left flank while I am pocketing these British clear?"

"Yes, Comrade Polkovnik," a grin finally splitting his face.

"Right then, Comrades, any questions?"

The artillery officer chipped in with two suggestions on additional targets and offered some rapid fire plan call signs, but that was that.

"Then we will go now and pull the enemy in towards us. The trap can shut on a fat bag of Tommies. Good luck comrades.

An under-pressure Lascelles started to receive reports as the Russian plan swung into action. Artillery and mortar fire had intensified all along his front, and troops had appeared opposite most of his positions.

It seemed that only the ends of his line, namely 'A' and 'C' Companies, were not affected at the moment, so he focussed his attention elsewhere. The bridge at Everstorfermoor had not yet been blown, despite the efforts of a platoon of engineers. Orders went out to ensure the job was done.

Support Company reported their bridge ready for destruction and Lascelles immediately gave the instruction to drop it into the water, especially as Soviet infantry had appeared on the road from Rotenburg.

His strongest unit, 'B' Company, had already dispatched some Soviet recon troops, but now they were coming under increasing pressure in Tiefenbruch and Riepshof.

The presence of Soviet armour to back up the infantry caused him concern, so he ordered the carrier platoon to move across to assist. That would give them an opportunity to employ their newly acquired knowledge. Ex-soldiers in the Bucholz Kommando had shown the carrier platoon how to use the Panzerfaust, and each carrier had a load of six weapons. As a sensible measure, Lascelles had also agreed with the Bucholz KommandoFührer to release a dozen men to the carrier platoon, in exchange for one of the Vickers machine-guns, ammunition and two boxes of grenades. Lascalles now smugly felt it had been a fair swap.

Artillery fire was being mainly directed at the enemy forces opposite Everstorfermoor, and Lascelles was loathe to switch it to support 'B' Company until the Oste bridge was blown.

He rolled the unlit Cuban cigar between his fingers rapidly, a sure sign to his staff that all was not well.

Lascelles, not raising his eyes from the map, spoke to no-one in particular.

"Get on the line to Charteris and tell him to get that flaming bridge blown!"

The radio burst into life immediately as the operator requested acknowledgement from the engineer platoon.

"Sunray, Sunray, Forest-two-six receiving."

Nothing but static returned.

The operator repeated the message, with the same result.

"Keep trying Barrington. Kevin."

Lieutenant Barrington turned back in to his operator and placed an encouraging hand on his shoulder as Acting Major Kevin Roberts, temporary OC of 'D' Company, stepped forward.

Making sure that the reliable Roberts was paying attention, Lascelles pointed at Everstorfermoor.

"Grab the RSM and his merry men. Get over to here and get it sorted please Kevin."

The pristinely turned out young officer saluted as if on a parade ground.

"Sah!"

Lascelles found the moment of humour lightened his feeling, which was the Major's intention, for Roberts was no parade ground warrior. Immaculate he may be but his chest showed that he was a fighting soldier, sporting the DSO and MC, won in hard fighting on Sicily and in Europe.

The moment of humour passed as the radio burst into life.

"Forest-two-six to Sunray, come in."

"Sunray, go ahead Forest."

"Lieutenant Charteris dead. Sergeant Parks dead. Under enemy sniper fire. Charges not complete. Need support. Over."

Every face in the room swivelled to Lascelles.

"Who is that?"

The operator made the request for information.

"Forest-two-six to Sunray. Corporal Harris, over."

"Tell him help is on its way, Barrington. Tell him the bridge must come down. It must come down."

The message was sent.

"Acknowledge Forest-two-six, acknowledge."

A few moments of static, then nothing.

"Acknowledge Forest-two-six, acknowledge."

Silence.

Corporal Harris knew very little except that the pain was extreme. The bullet had taken him in the upper chest as he raised his head over the sandbags, the heavy impact throwing him backwards. Unfortunately for him, he now lay on top of Parks, his platoon sergeant, the extra height raising him subtly above the cover line provided by the sandbagged firing position. Another bullet thudded into his left side, but there was little pain of note, a strange coldness and numbness being the worst of it.

His head lolled over to the left side and he could see no enemy the other side of the river. The body of Charteris lay strangely posed, knees on the ground, backside in the air and what was left of his face flat to the road surface, the corpse almost perfectly reflecting an Arab at prayer. By the Lieutenant's side lay the firing cables he had been trying to mend when he had been shot.

All around him lay two dozen still forms from the engineer platoon and the German Kommando, men who had tried their best and died.

The radio continued to call him but he was past caring. *'Cold, so cold.'*

Starshy Serzhant Olga Maleeva was also cold, but her coldness was within her mind. So far, her spotter tallied her at nineteen confirmed kills for the day, and it was extremely satisfying. The British deserved it of course, but she felt more joy when a German died, enjoying the vision thru her PU scope.

Sergei stirred her to greater efforts.

"He's still alive. You're slipping, sweetheart."

That would have earned him a playful blow, and might still do later, but concealed as they were, it would not pay to make quick movements and attract the enemy's gaze.

Admitting to herself that she had hurried the last shot, Olga took more care, ignoring Sergei's jibe.

The sights settled on the face of a man in pain but she felt no sympathy for the wounded corporal.

Steadying herself on target, she released her breath slowly and pulled the trigger at the optimum moment.

The instantly ruined head jerked, Maleeva grunted in satisfaction, and Sergei searched for other targets.

The leader of Kommando Bucholz watched as the man he had summoned dashed in an ungainly fashion across the open space between buildings and fell headlong into the old Gasthaus on the edge of Everstorfermoor.

He moved to the top of the stairs and looked down upon the panting figure.

Never a man to beat about the bush, the impatient ex-Captain of Armoured-Infantry hollered at the man who had just dived into his position in response to his Kommandoführer's urgent summons.

"Erwin, get up here, first floor, and bring your secret weapon!"

112

Despite his disability, the new arrival took the stairs two at a time and formally presented himself, saluting at the attention, resplendent in his German army uniform.

"Jawohl, Herr Hauptmann. What can I do for the Herr Hauptmann this evening?"

Choosing to ignore his old friend's mock formality and the huge grin on Schultz's face, he pointed the man towards the rocking chair in the corner of the room. Once Schultz was seated, he spoke quickly but softly.

"The pioniere's have had a hard time of it. We spotted two of the sniper's, and they're dead, but it cost us too."

Schultz had noticed the five bodies placed reverently outside, at the rear of the old gasthaus.

"So you need Irma and me to sort the problem out?"

Balancing on his good leg, Müller kicked a broken stirrup pump that lay amongst the rubble on the bedroom floor.

"Indeed I do, Feldwebel Schultz, but only if you are up to it obviously."

"Depends if you are going to play the damned hero part whilst I work, Herr Hauptmann."

Nearby members of Kommando Bucholz were unsurprised by the exchange, for the two were old comrades, members of the 'Grossdeutschland' from its early days until they were both seriously wounded during the Battle of Michurin-Rog. Each had lost a leg in the action, Hauptmann Müller in the act of destroying two tanks that threatened to overrun his company headquarters, and Feldwebel Schultz in reflecting the same achievement, and also in rescuing his wounded officer, whose leg had been blown off by a mortar shell. However, Schultz had also used an MG34, Müller's Walther, and a bag of hand grenades to drive off the Russian infantry company accompanying the four tanks, leaving over forty dead as they retired from the field.

Equipped with prosthetic limbs, neither had been fit to return to active duties and had trained replacements until dismissed from service in late April to return to their homes.

Both men wore their field uniforms, each man's decorations mirroring the other's, save for the Knights Cross dangling lazily at the throat of the junior man, courtesy of the

113

senior's recommendation for his actions at Michurin Rog that bloody day.

"There is no cure for throat ache now, Herr Hauptmann, so keep your head down and pull whatever stunt you have to pull."

Müller laughed, but it died quickly, for the throat ache he felt was the absence of the Knight's Cross, which most in his old machine-gun unit felt he had earned a score of times on the Russian steppes.

"Just make sure that you and Irma do the job first time clear?"

Placing his ST-44 assault rifle carefully in the corner of the room, Schultz pulled the secret weapon off his back and removed the blanket in which he always lovingly wrapped it.

The light playing on glistening wood and metal, Schultz unveiled an object of deadly beauty. 'Irma' had formerly been part of a Soviet Guards infantry unit that Grossdeutschland destroyed in 1942. Having been ripped from the frozen hands of its former owner, 'she' became the personal weapon of choice for Feldwebel Schultz. Indeed, Müller had provided him with a signed document confirming his permission to bear the weapon and preventing any overzealous officer from taking it away.

Over time, Schultz had acquired and hoarded ammunition for the Mosin-Nagant sniper's rifle. He doted on it, oiling metal and wood, keeping the weapon in pristine shape and prime killing condition.

When the rifle had been produced in a Russian factory it was firing-tested like all rifles, and the Soviets always set aside the best of them for further conversion to snipers rifles. The weapon Schultz had liberated was the very best of the best, its 4xPEM sight perfect, and not a blemish to be seen on the whole length of the weapon.

Conservative estimates credited Schultz with killing over one hundred and fifty enemy troops with the weapon but his speciality was in killing snipers themselves, and up to sustaining his amputation, he had been officially been accredited with twenty-two such executions, high value kills that meant that many German boys still breathed.

"So, where are they hiding?"

114

Müller grabbed his chin, half contemplating the stirrup pump, half preparing his answer.

"The other side of the river. Other than that, I don't really have a clue, Erwin."

"Fuck."

"I agree entirely, Feldwebel," grinning from ear to ear as his plan took shape, "But we'll kill the bastards, just the same."

Muller showed Schultz a hole in the wall. It was covered with a large pillow, and an old blanket sat next to it, ready for use.

The former officer knew how Schultz liked to operate and had made the necessary extras available.

"I thought that would be suitable for you?"

Schultz liked the height. He could comfortably lie down and the pillow would be handy to prevent the brickwork scratching Irma. He checked the area behind the hole. It was dark enough to be safe, and he settled himself down, ready to adjust Irma's sights.

"Range to the target? Best guess?"

Muller drew in the dust on the floor, sketching each item in turn until dramatically marking his final position with a cross.

"Roughly two hundred metres to the bridge. They're not there. I think eight hundred metres to the tree line, but they're not there. I think they're in the middle ground, Erwin. My gut says on the road line. You know there's a ditch either side. Probably about.....here"

Schultz considered the matter and resolved it immediately.

"I will set for five hundred metres then."

"I see no advantage in firing from elsewhere, especially as I've found such a perfect spot for you here, Erwin."

Schultz mumbled a reply, his mind already coming into focus for the job in hand.

"Excellent. Now you have a few minutes while I get set up. You'll like this."

The officer grinned with unconcealed glee as he picked up the old stirrup pump and worked at separating it from the perished hose.

115

His own preparations done for now, Schultz held the rifle between his knees and reached for his cigarettes.

"Time for a smoke, Herr Hauptmann?"

"You are way ahead of me, aren't you? Carry on, Feldwebel."

The puzzled man sat more upright and eased his false limb into the right position, lit a cigarette, and watched his commander and friend set his trap.

Schultz had finished his cigarette at the same time as the trap had been prepared. When Müller had finished, he stood back and admired his handiwork.

"You are a fucking sneaky bastard, Herr Hauptmann, if you don't mind me saying so!"

Muller half-bowed in mock appreciation.

Schultz stretched himself out on the floor, again checking the area behind him, and brought 'Irma' into position.

Taking hold of the blanket he pulled it up over his head to prevent any light showing through when he extracted the pillow.

Before committing himself Schultz stuck his head out and looked up at his leader for the command.

With an unlit cigarette in his mouth, Muller checked everything was ready.

"Let's do it. Alles klar, Herr Feldwebel?"

"Alles klar, Herr Hauptmann," said Schultz, as he and Irma retreated into their personal darkness.

"What a fool. Olga, an easy kill for you, sweetheart."

Maleeva had slid down into the ditch where she was enjoying a few sips of water before resuming her work. The whispered summons brought her slowly sliding back into position.

"Stop calling me sweetheart, you uncultured ass wipe," the words were hissed with mock venom, for she and Erinov were more of a team than was militarily permitted. Soon she would have to declare that she was pregnant, but not who the father was, or the two would not serve together again.

"Where?"

116

"The building nearest the bridge. The man hides but yet he reveals himself. Can't you see?"

He waited as the sniper swept the zone.

"The smoke, Olga. First floor balcony, yellow door to the left of centre. Slightly open. You can see him breathing out his smoke and the very tip of his helmet."

Maleeva settled and concentrated on the yellow door. There. A breath of smoke blossomed at an average man's head height from behind the slightly open door, and as Sergei had said, the very tip of a helmet was in view.

"Fool indeed, Comrade."

"Four-seven-five metres I think."

Maleeva just hummed 'uh-ha', her rifle already set to four hundred and her ability to make the adjustment herself not in question.

Carefully, she assessed the point at which the smoke made itself known around the door, using the helmet tip to make a judgement as to where to place the shot.

One more puff to make sure.

The rifle kicked into her shoulder and Sergei saw a hole appear in the door at precisely the spot he would have fired, had it been his turn to rifle this day.

Another stream of smoke escaped, and the helmet remained.

Ego is often a dangerous thing, especially if you are a sniper.

For a sniper, ego can be a terminal affliction.

Shocked that she had got her calculations wrong, Maleeva adjusted without sparing a thought for any other possibility.

She breathed out and fired, Sergei immediately marking the disappearance of the helmet tip and noted Olga's grunt of satisfaction.

Ignoring the familiar 'zip' sound of a passing bullet, Erinov turned to congratulate his lover, to be greeted by the vision of her lifeless eyes as she slid back down towards the bottom of the ditch.

Within seconds he joined her, a Mosin-Nagant round taking him just in front of his left ear and blowing off the larger portion of the right side of his skull.

"Done."

The rifle was withdrawn from the hole, and the pillow put back to stop up the gap. Immediately Schultz emerged from under the blanket, he started to run a rag over Irma's body, removing any dust.

Müller let the end of the fire hose drop to the ground and, having spat and wiped away the dirt that had accumulated on his lips from blowing smoke down it, he concentrated on enjoying a second cigarette, free from the taste of soot and rubber.

Looking across at his old comrade, he appreciated the man's professional examination of his brain wave sniper trap.

The old fire hose secured to the door at head height, with the wooden shelf jammed in behind it on which the helmet had proudly sat before the second shot sent it spinning away.

"You are one perverted soul, Jochen Müller. I have to hand it to you on that one. The Devil will welcome you to his domain with open arms, you do know that?"

Müller guffawed loudly.

"Oh, what a comfort! Danke, Kamerad. At least I won't be alone."

Schultz acknowledged the point with an accepting nod and a grin.

The light moment evaporated as professionalism established itself once more.

"Same position or do you need to move?"

Schultz gave it a moment's thought.

"I can go from here again I think. It was only the one sniper, wasn't it?"

"Yes it was. So, when you're ready, we shall see whether we will get any more customers for our contraption, although I think the Russians will be coming in larger numbers soon."

As they had started their deadly game, the artillery and mortars had picked up their firing rates, a reasonable signpost for an imminent attack.

'C' Company had been very badly mauled in their defence of Tostedt, which was why Lascelles had shuffled the pack and dropped them back into Dreihausen, where they could quickly sort themselves out.

Only eighty-seven men had made it out of Tostedt, and then, only by the skin of their teeth. Behind them lay numerous dead and wounded, accompanied by a few volunteers to tend them. Many Canadians had been summarily executed before Zvorykin brought order.

Those eighty-seven survivors suddenly found themselves in a maelstrom of fire, as Soviet T34's and rider infantry charged down the road from Otter and crashed into their hastily prepared positions. Some 2" mortars coughed defiantly, a few rifles, and one Bren, got off a few shots before the position was overrun by dismounted submachine gunners.

The young 2nd Lieutenant who now commanded the unit was beaten to the ground as the company command post was overrun.

In less than ten minutes, 'C' Company had been wiped out, over half its survivors surrendering without a fight, too exhausted by their previous exertions to offer resistance.

Through the gap, Zvorykin led his own tired men, but victory has a habit of giving soldiers energy, and they were on top of the Carleton & York engineers before they could do more than manage a few desultory shots.

Dreihausen Bridge was intact and secure, and Major Zvorykin set about the second part of his orders.

It was 'B' Company who got the warning out, suddenly aware of enemy attacking from their south, as more Russian infantry and tanks pressed in on Tiefenbruch and Riepshof from the east.

119

The carrier soldiers and the dozen men from the 'Bucholz' found themselves attacked by tanks coming from Dreihausen.

Panzerfausts taught the tanks a harsh lesson and four T34's flamed in as many minutes. The Soviet infantry again dismounted and charged.

Some carriers were destroyed by tank shells, but five were captured as a brief close combat ended with the defenders overpowered. The Canadians, for the Russians now knew who they faced, were organised into a party and marched off to the rear at speed.

The five surviving members of the Kommando Bucholz's Panzerfaust group were summarily executed as partisans.

Part of Yarishlov's force was drawn into the fighting with 'B' Company, the Canadian perimeter swiftly became a circle as the unit was surrounded, along with the greater part of the Support platoon.

Radio messages screaming for support arrived in the battalion command post but the pot was empty.

'A' Company reported enemy infantry in Vaerlon and also in Burgsittensen.

Some good news came from the Admin Platoon stationed in the woods south-west of Avensermoor. They had spotted tanks to the south, probably coming from Stemmen, which had to make them friendly but that bright spot was tempered with the fact that efforts to make contact with the new force had failed, and so they were of limited value at the moment.

Enemy troops were pushing hard at Everstorfermoor and still the bridge was standing.

"Where is Roberts? Get him on the radio. I need him to sort that bloody mess out!"

The strain was beginning to tell as it became obvious that the Carleton & York's were in big trouble.

"Any response from Brigade? I must have tanks and artillery support. Where's my artillery support? The Russians are coming. Where is air eh? Where is my air?" The cigar rotated fiercely in his hand; a hand trembling with the strain.

120

In truth, a calm and rational officer could not have saved the battalion from the fate Yarishlov had prepared for it, but Lascelles' obvious decline affected everyone, a feeling of near-panic spreading through the entire battalion headquarters.

Brigade Headquarters had heard the reports and had responded, both by radio and by dispatching physical support, but nothing they could do would salvage the situation.

Looking at the cigar, his psychological prop, he snorted and threw it onto the map table.

Lascelles slipped under the waves of despair and was engulfed by panic and terror in equal measure.

Through the mists of desperation he heard a voice shouting outside the command tent.

"Tanks! Fucking tanks!"

These were obviously the tanks Admin Platoon had seen, and a wild-eyed Lascelles dashed outside to make contact. Inside the tent, a shocked 1st Lieutenant tried hard to bring order to the chaos caused by his commanding officer's rapid breakdown.

Lascelles' mad dash caught the attention of the tank commander and he gave the contact report, his hull gunner easily locating the running figure and dropping him with a short burst. Lascalles died without understanding Admin Platoon's error.

The majority of 4th Guards' 1st Battalion swept up and into Wümme, fanning out to the north-west and enjoying the target laden environment laid out before them.

The Carleton & York's mortar platoon had been pumping shell after shell across the Oste in an attempt to stop that assault and had no time to reorient before direct fire from a dozen T34's swept their position, killing one in five of the men in a few seconds.

From Burgsittensen in the north-west through to Dreihausen in the south-east, the Canadians were being slaughtered.

Some 6-pounder anti-tank guns from the 1st AT Regiment had been turned to face westwards, and they lashed out at the tanks in and around Wümme. The others started to seek targets in the area around Tostedt Land, finding it hard to distinguish between friend and foe in the failing light.

Zvorykin had under-estimated the distance and it had taken him longer than he had expected to move silently up the south bank of the Wümme River.

To his dismay, he witnessed one enemy gun find a target and spared a horrified, yet fascinated moment to watch the destroyed vehicle burn.

Checking his map he consulted his pre-noted coordinates and called for his radio.

"Sem'ya-Two-Zero, Sem'ya-Two-Zero, this is Brat-Three-Krasnyi over."

The radio crackled with a response.

Rechecking his map, Zvorykin looked at the scene in front of him and satisfied himself that he was calling it in correctly.

"Sem'ya-Two-Zero, Sem'ya-Two-Zero, target koza, repeat target koza. Brat-Three-Krasnyi over."

The operator on the other end repeated the order and waited.

Zvorykin waited too.

The sound of approaching shells gained precedence over the other sounds of battle, and Zvorykin was rewarded with a grandstand view of a regimental artillery strike on a position one kilometre in length.

"Sem'ya-Two-Zero, Sem'ya-Two-Zero. Confirm koza is on target. Brat-Three-Krasnyi over."

The exhausted Major relaxed with a cigarette as he watched the enemy anti-tank gunners destroyed by artillery fire of his making.

Technically, it was all over, although there was still more dying to be done.

The Canadians had been overrun and wiped out.

'A' Company had folded and surrendered, outnumbered and surrounded, Avensermoor knocked into a total ruin around them.

Admin platoon had suffered a similar fate, although in less honourable circumstances, dropping their weapons and raising their hands without a fight, much to the disgust of the tough Soviet engineers who swept in for the spoils of war.

Kommando Bucholz and the MG platoon of the Saskatoon's had gone down fighting, inflicting hard losses on the 1195th Riflemen, and even knocking down a few of the engineers who moved tentatively down from Avensermoor.

'D' Company suffered few casualties, but there was no dishonour in their surrender. A ring of tanks and infantry formed round them, and artillery and mortars commenced to pound them long after day had become night.

A wounded Canadian officer was brought forward, and he agreed to negotiate with the 'D' Company survivors to save further loss of life.

Illuminated by a searchlight from the 1695th's AA unit, the wounded man stumbled forward, clutching his white flag, until he reached 'D' Company's positions.

As Acting Major Roberts organised the surrender of 'D' Company, Yarishlov busied himself with inspecting the enemy headquarters.

Arranging for the two dead bodies to be removed, he let his officers descend upon the wealth of intelligence found inside the holed tent.

As usual, Kriks appeared magically with a hot drink, and he and his colonel watched on as the Canadian headquarters was picked clean by the locusts, sharing a particularly fine Cuban cigar in silence.

Everstorfermoor was in ruins, no building untouched by the ravages of war. The civilian inhabitants had departed long before the battle commenced, so Everstorfermoor was also silent, save for the background sounds of fire consuming wood, and the occasional cacophony of brickwork crashing to the ground.

123

The Russians, conscious of the light of burning buildings and allied air power in the night withdrew, leaving the small village with only its garrison of dead.

Only lifeless eyes witnessed a cellar door slide cautiously open, and two shadowy figures move off into the night, their curious wooden gaits apparent in the flickering light of the flames.

Be not afraid of greatness: some are born great, some achieve greatness, and some have greatness thrust upon them.

William Shakespeare

Chapter 61 – THE BRIEFINGS

<u>Tuesday, 14th August 1945, 0805 hrs, the Kremlin, Moscow, USSR.</u>

Both men sat drinking their tea in smug silence, the reports of success from the ground war almost universal. Some minor irritations of stubborn defence, but the spearheads were on the move and driving deep into the German heartland.

Success indeed, but it was being bought at high cost in men and materiel, something the reports from Zhukov stated openly and something that they patently ignored, despite the continuing number of formations permanently lost from the order of battle.

There were negatives, but neither man worried too much, such was the euphoria of the achievements to date. The Allied air forces had gained control of the night sky and, in truth, the day was a delicate balancing act of who could get what assets where and when but, in the main, the Soviet air force was holding its own during daylight hours.

Again casualties were heavy, particularly on the Shturmoviks and light bomber regiments, but the Allies were suffering equally badly as the figures illustrated only too well.

Beria and Stalin did not understand that some commanders were inflating the effectiveness of their missions, claiming more kills and more ground targets destroyed than were actually hit. The airman often exaggerates, and Beria had built in a compensation for that, but casualties amongst the Allied air fleet and ground forces were nowhere near as bad as was being suggested.

The Atlantic war was a sideshow for both men but it was delivering surprisingly excellent results, with many enemy warships and transports sent to the bottom by the Elektrobootes of the Soviet Navy. Even the Pacific fleet had a notable success, one of its diesel-electric boats having sunk HMS Unicorn, a light aircraft carrier, sailing close inshore to Honshu, Japan.

Serious dents had apparently been made in the US reinforcement stream coming into Europe, with major losses reading like a who's who of important sea-going craft.

The submarines off America had done particularly well, with some serious successes against oil tankers as well as troopships.

A clandestine operation using a Swedish-flagged vessel was already underway, intending to visit each of the clandestine bases. The Trojan horse's holds were stuffed full of torpedoes and the other necessary chattels of submarine warfare. More manpower too, divided into two groups. Mainly seaman, but also a few of the secretive and quiet types who served a more sinister purpose.

The junior man broke the silence.

"I believe the group in Madrid will be ready to act very soon, Comrade General Secretary. I have not yet given the preparation order. Should I give such an order?"

Stalin, filling the bowl of his pipe with rough cut tobacco, paused and looked at the NKVD Chairman.

"Is there some reason that I should not, Lavrentiy?"

"We have guaranteed Spanish neutrality and yet they send men against us. None the less, they are few in number at this time."

Beria added a note of caution.

"What is planned could incite their nation to greater efforts, Comrade General Secretary."

The dictator struck a match and pulled thoughtfully on the modest clay pipe. Beria continued.

"Because of our links with old comrades in Spain, we can be assured of good information at all times, and I am sure that we can undermine Spanish unity."

The match burned down to Stalin's fingers as he drew on his pipe, bringing a snarl as he discarded the end into the ash tray and licked his fingers gingerly, the heat of the flame still apparent on the tips.

126

"It must be done, Lavrentiy."

The NKVD Chairman nodded. He had expected no other resolution, but had decided to cover himself just in case.

"It shall be done, Comrade General Secretary."

Replacing his porcelain cup into the exquisitely decorated saucer, Beria decided to tackle a problem head on.

"Things with the Germans have not gone as we had hoped, Comrade General Secretary."

Such a statement required clarification and Stalin's unimpressed look drew him further.

"My own and the GRU agents have done well and disrupted the formation of these German Republican units."

The glasses came off and the handkerchief commenced rapidly polishing.

"It seems likely that they are about to put ten divisions at the disposal of the Capitalists."

Stalin's eyes narrowed, and Beria understood he needed to sweeten this bitter pill as soon as possible.

"We cannot assess the effectiveness of these units, but we do know that the Allies kept their prisoners of war under suitably harsh conditions, so it is likely they will be less effective than we have previously encountered."

Soviet Liaison officers had seen the hell holes of the Rheinweisenlager for themselves and reported back on the disgraceful conditions, conditions that met with the full approval to the Russians.

"So what exactly did your agents achieve, Comrade?"

Stalin had a unique capacity to speak normal words and have them fall upon other's ears full of threat and venom.

"Many German officers have been taken out of the equation by our agents, alleging war crimes, denouncing them as Nazis; there were even deaths from in-fighting. Anything which could spread disaffection and undermine their unity has been tried."

Replacing his glasses, the NKVD Chairman rallied.

"Some of our men will have gone with these new units so their usefulness will be appreciated soon enough. Others will continue to spread disaffection amongst the German soldiery behind the lines."

127

The General Secretary puffed deeply on his pipe, filling the space between them with a thick fug.

"I had expected more Lavrentiy, much more."

Beria's smugness had now departed and he bought himself time by pouring more tea for both men. He decided to stand his ground.

"As did I, Comrade General Secretary. However, we must not believe that operations are over. Far from it."

A gentle cough to clear his throat and steady himself, and the NKVD boss carried on.

"Each agent is under orders to undermine relations between the German and Western Allied factions. We have yet to see this in action, as the German units were not yet formed. Each agent knows that Senior Allied commanders are to be eliminated where circumstances are favourable. We have yet to see this in action because the circumstances would not yet have existed. Each agent knows to sabotage but, yet again, they will not have been able to do so without the means and the freedom of operation. Obviously, betrayal of tactical plans and dispositions will happen when units reach the front line."

Surprisingly boosted by his defence, Beria concluded.

"Comrade General Pekunin and I both agree that the effectiveness of our various agents will increase, and that results will only improve."

Stalin, not wholly comfortable with Beria's robust approach, shifted in his seat and leant forward, planting both elbows on the solid tsarist desk.

"Comrade Marshall, you and Pekunin assured me that you would disrupt the formation of any German units. And yet I now hear of ten divisions of their troops being made available to the Capitalists. That doesn't sound like disruption to me; that sounds like failure."

This time the venom was very real, and the threat decidedly meant.

"The pair of you had better come up with some results soon, or someone will be counting trees."

Even though Beria knew it was impossible for his boss to do such a thing to him, and more to the point, Stalin knew he couldn't do such a thing to his Chief of NKVD, the threat was

128

very real. Stalin could not move Beria, as the Marshall had certain files that would prove 'embarrassing' to the General Secretary. He knew where all the bodies were buried and, as he had assisted in Stalin's intrigue's and plotting throughout the Georgian's rise, he was privy to all the dirt.

What concerned him a lot was that, in the past, such people tended to disappear.

Beria fully intended that, if it came to it, it would not be he but Pekunin who ended up in a Katorga being worked to death.

Eisenhower had been up for some time. Technically he hadn't been to bed, having fallen asleep in his comfy chair downstairs. His staff reduced their noise levels and let their boss sleep, knowing full well that the coming day would bring more pain and heartache.

A generous breakfast of Belgian waffles with eggs and bacon fortified the body, whilst coffee and nicotine boosted the mind for the trials of the day.

Ike knew that it would be a very difficult day indeed.

Already he had cut orders to newly arrived or reformed units, sending them not to front but to rear-line positions, making them ready to hold, hold, and hold.

His Generals were doing a magnificent job. Even Patton, hard-charging and impetuous, had his army in controlled retreat, hanging on to those either side and keeping the front line intact.

Hamburg still held, or at least some of it. McCreery's boys were working miracles in defence and, by all accounts, giving Ivan one hell of a bloody nose.

And yet, a few miles from this excellence, a huge problem had arisen.

The 1st Canadian Division had been sundered west of Luneburg Heath, permitting what looked like a whole Russian Army Corps to move through the North German Plain and bear down on Bremen.

The Canadians, by dint of superhuman effort, threw in a counter-attack and halted one of the thrusts, that between Westerholz and Scheeßel, at the cost of half of their armour.

Despite this, the Division was withdrawing again, but this time showing an unruptured front to the hard pressing enemy.

Air had played their part too, inflicting casualties on the advancing tank columns and reducing the deficit in the balance of forces.

None the less, McCreery's front still looked the most stable, certainly compared to the horror's being visited upon Bradley.

The British General had sought and gained permission to use one of the German infantry units from Denmark and this was moving south to stiffen the line, freeing up other forces to bolster the Hamburg defence. It would be a close run thing.

Having spent the night preparing, Guderian had assured Ike that the German Republican Army would commence its move towards the Ruhr at first light. Reports confirmed that to be true, with two divisions moving swiftly ahead of the rest to secure the area.

This German commitment had allowed Eisenhower to free up resources, banishing his warring voices for the moment.

Whilst the situation was still dire, there were occasional glimmers of light in the darkness of retreat.

Although of limited use in the immediate, the promise of further support by Brazil was encouraging, as was the unexpected offer from Mexico to employ some of their divisions on security duties in the Caribbean, releasing more American units for the frontlines.

The Spanish Division promised by Franco had yet to materialise, and General Grandes had been embarrassed to report that it probably would not cross the frontier for at least another seven days, possibly more. That obviously meant that the Spanish Corps would be delayed for a far greater time and Eisenhower forced it from his thinking.

Again the British had come up trumps, finding that thousands of returning POW's volunteered to go to the front again. This meant that many under strength infantry units

130

received a trained influx, albeit of men who in many cases needed more meat on their bones after time in captivity. It was also enabling the British to form some new divisions that would be available in a relatively short time, again an extremely positive piece of news.

The French too followed suit, although their men had been in captivity longer and were less aware of the rigours of modern combat. None the less, manpower was always welcome.

Conspicuously absent was any talk of another force in preparation by the French, and Eisenhower, not officially knowing, could not ask on its progress or availability.

His two selfs surfaced momentarily.

'Now why is it we don't argue about those suckers?'

'Beats me, General.'

A word to Colonel Hood should secure him the information he needed on the ex-SS Foreign Legion units.

'Later.'

For now, Ike could see the same Thomas Bell Hood hovering with Captain Foster, both looking fit to burst.

Lighting up and taking a deep draught of his coffee, he beckoned both forward, unaware that a forty year old mother of three was about to set before him the information needed to start stopping the Russians.

"Good morning Anne-Marie, Thomas. This will have to be brief as I have…."

"Sir, Captain Foster has something very interesting and you are going to want to hear it."

Colonel Thomas Bell Hood was a southern gentleman and not prone to interrupting his Commander in Chief.

Unusually irritated but curious, the under-pressure Eisenhower held his tongue and very deliberately extracted a cigarette before inviting the information.

"Sir, my apologies. It is just that this is gold dust, Sir."

"OK Thomas. Things are a little fraught around here so let's move on. What have you got for me?"

"Well Sir, you directed me last week that I should look at Soviet capabilities, particularly their trained manpower."

"Indeed I did, Colonel, and I assume you have found something of note?"

131

Hood could have swung into the presentation but he wasn't that sort of man. Foster had sniffed it out first, so he deferred to her so she would get the credit.

"Sir, Colonel Hood tasked a number of us with looking at availability, behaviour and losses of the various speciality branches of the Red Army."

She laid out five reports before her General.

Indicating the first report she continued.

"This is low-level intelligence report originating from 12th Group. It gave me my first real indication, Sir."

Inclining her head so she could quote from it she placed her finger under the relevant section.

"Soviet bridging units seem slower to respond than expected, sometimes appearing after some hours or not appearing at all. This causes inevitable delay for the Soviet advance."

"OK Anne-Marie. I got that. And?"

"This is an extract I obtained from the interrogation report of the German General Karl Burdach, commander of the elite 11th Infanterie Division in Russia."

Again she found the passage and read it aloud.

"Soviet engineers were numerous, as well as being extremely effective and competent. Temporary bridges to get infantry across water obstacles could spring up in a matter of minutes and more substantial ones in a few hours. They should take much credit for the rapid Soviet advances, for as quick as we could knock them down, it seemed they were putting them up just as quickly and continuing the advance."

Not stopping Foster reached across for the third document.

"Here we have some rough timings that I have gathered from intelligence reports. It appears that water obstacles are causing unexpected delays to the Soviet advances. This information has been out there all the time; it was just a question of bringing it all together."

This time the woman did not recite, permitting her General to scan the list.

Eisenhower's interest had already been aroused but he was now looking at evidence that the blowing of bridges was having a huge impact on the Soviet advance.

132

"Is there more, Anne-Marie?"

"Yes Sir. Intercepts which have been partially decoded seem to indicate that Soviet bridging units are now, in the main, Army Group assets at the very least. This would limit their availability, and could explain why there is a delay when they do arrive on site."

Ike lit another cigarette, his mind working overtime.

"However, Sir, it is in behaviour that I find unusual activity which could be the biggest clue of all."

She slid the last piece of paper under Ike's gaze.

"This is a post-combat report from the British 605 Squadron. They had been tasked with an attack on a Soviet engineer bridge laid over the Fuhse River at Groß Ilsede."

She realised her omission immediately but was swiftly rescued by Hood, who grabbed a small map and pointed out the location. The military importance of maintaining a bridge there was immediately obvious.

"Thank you, Thomas. Proceed, Captain."

"Well Sir, they failed to bomb it because it wasn't there."

"I'm sorry?"

"The engineers had packed it up and moved it off, and as far as we know, there is still no bridge at Groß Ilsede, which has to be causing logistical difficulties for them."

Eisenhower looked at the map, and back to the RAF report, moving on over each piece of paper in turn.

His officers stood back respectfully to await his response.

"So you are telling me that the huge Red Army is running out of bridges?"

Captain Foster cleared her throat.

"Sir, what I believe is that the Red Army is conserving its bridging assets, be that bridges, qualified personnel or both. That is a departure from their norms. According to the German interrogations this is unusual activity, again not the norm. They have changed the way they are controlled for a reason."

Again, a nervous cough.

"Combat reports indicate that water obstacles are more of a problem to the Soviets, even those which should be

133

relatively easily overcome. We have a report that assets in place are being recycled prematurely, affecting their logistics, probably in favour of maintaining the advance."

Colonel Samuel Rossiter USMC was waved down and immediately responded to Eisenhower's hand-signals.

"Sam, I want your opinion of this. Again, if you please, Anne-Marie."

Consuming another cigarette, he stood back and listened to it all again as Rossiter received the full brief.

"Well Sam, what do you think?"

"Can you give me two minutes please, Sir? I have something that can contribute to these proceedings."

"OK Sam. Quick as you can please."

The Colonel almost bounded out of sight, and Ike fired off more of his hand signals, this time encouraging a steward to bring coffee for the four officers.

Rossiter was back before the coffee was finished, so Ike calmly indicated the Marine's own full coffee cup.

"Right. Before you give me that," he indicated the paper in Rossiter's hand, "Sam, what is your take on this?"

"She sold me, Sir."

"As she has me. Well done Anne-Marie, well done."

The smile on her face was worth the wait for Rossiter's bombshell.

"So now then, Sam, what got you running?"

Rossiter's identity as head of OSS was still not known but he had, in his own right, recently been established as part of the Military Intelligence liaison team within SHAEF, and it was wearing that hat that he brought his information into open discussion.

"Sir, as you know, the Soviets do not trust the Polish Army and have placed them in occupied Poland, where they will only be called upon to defend their own country from seaborne invasion."

"Indeed Sam, and I also know you and the British have numerous agents in place reporting back. Might I assume one of them is responsible for that piece of paper?"

"You may, Sir. This is from the Brits and it came in this morning. The report comes from someone within the 4th Polish

134

Engineer Brigade. He speaks of turning over any and all bridging equipment to the Soviets on the 3rd August. He also speaks of how his unit is being employed to dismantle selected engineer bridges in Northern Poland. These are then transported to the west. He describes how volunteers were sought to do engineering duties behind the front lines in Europe."

Something lit up in Eisenhower's mind.

"The 3rd? You say the 3rd?"

"Yes Sir, although the preparation order to do so came through some time before that," and finding the information he sought, Rossiter looked straight into his commander's eyes, "On the 23rd July, Sir."

"Good god. They were stripping bridging assets out before the combat losses, so they were obviously short prior to starting this goddamn mess, as well as being prepared to risk Poles putting up their bridges. Short on qualified personnel too possibly?"

Neither Colonel ventured an opinion.

The captain had no such qualms.

"I believe that they are short on both assets, Sir."

"Explain please, Anne-Marie."

She took the plunge.

"My apologies, Sir. I presented what I knew. I left something out and I was going to explore it more when time permitted."

"Go on."

"I have not seen one report of assault bridging engineer works in combat, and yet the Soviets are trained for it, and most certainly are renowned for it. It struck me as odd at the time, Sir."

Eisenhower exchanged looks with both his Colonels, looks that carried both questions and answers.

'Bingo.'

"I have a feeling you may just have found what we needed, Anne-Marie. A very big well done."

Pausing to get his thoughts in order Ike took the plunge.

"I want copies of the paperwork compiled and sent out to every senior commander immediately. I want them to know what to look for and what to go after, clear?"

He got the nods he needed.

135

"Furthermore, I want Air to recon this possibility as a priority, and to produce a plan to knock down as much of their bridging infrastructure as possible if it's correct. When we have done here, Thomas, ask Arthur Tedder to join me straight away."

"Sam?"

"Sir, that report needs sanitising." He indicated the one from the Polish agent.

"If it goes out as it is there is too much information if the enemy gets a sniff of it. Need to protect the British agent, Sir."

"Agreed. Get it done and get this information out to my Generals."

The three officers came to attention.

"Oh, and Thomas, please cut me the paperwork for the promotion of Captain Foster. I think Major is the least we can do to the lady who may just have pulled our coals out of the fire."

"Yes Sir."

The three left, one grinning from ear to ear with satisfaction and pride.

An Air Force Lieutenant stepped forward and indicated the telephone.

"Sir, General Bradley, sir."

Eisenhower settled down in his chair with a fresh cigarette and took up the receiver.

"Eisenhower, and good morning to you, General Bradley."

Ike listened for a moment and then interrupted his senior man.

"Well as it happens, Brad, we may have just come up with something."

A pause as Bradley made some quip and then Eisenhower dropped his bombshell.

"It's all a question of rivers."

Many miles away, in the underground headquarters facility at Nordhausen, Marshall Zhukov was also talking rivers.

"So where is the new equipment we were promised eh? Where are the trained personnel? The new units? Govno!"

136

Zhukov took in the stark surroundings, seeking some solace in the map-covered concrete walls and finding solely the obligatory picture of the General Secretary to break up the monotony of military paraphernalia.

Making direct eye contact with the highly stylised portrait of Stalin, he repeated his questions more fiercely, a fact not wasted on Malinin.

Zhukov's Chief of Staff referred to a report he had prepared on the matter of Soviet bridging engineers.

"We have now stripped virtually all the assets from the Poles, and 75% of the equipment from the interior forces, plus the Crimea, and Iran."

"Your order to recycle equipment has meant that we have maintained our advance. It has caused us some logistical problems as you are aware, Comrade Marshall, but we are coping."

The word 'just' was left unsaid but well understood by the Commander in Chief, who also knew that Malinin was not criticising, just stating fact.

"It has been necessary to replace some crossings where the logistical issues were insurmountable."

Marshall Zhukov pulled out his chair and sat, making notes as his CoS carried on with his brief.

"Losses in personnel have been heavier than anticipated, meaning that some of our bridging units are less effective than they look on paper, Comrade Marshall."

Zhukov took up his tea and listened to his right-hand man confirm his worst suspicions.

"Our projections are not as accurate as they could have been, for a number of reasons."

Consulting the figures closely, Malinin enlightened his Commander.

"As of 1800 hrs yesterday, our equipment losses are running at 50% over expectations, personnel losses at 65% over."

"The order to limit combat engineering has saved lives and equipment but has had a negative effect on combat operations, particularly time wise, which is partially why we are running behind schedule."

Sounds of mumbled discontent drifted over from the bald Marshall.

"I obtained this interesting report from the Far East command, originating from Polkovnik General of Engineers Tsirlin to Marshall Vasilevsky."

Malinin rose and passed a document over, referring to his own copy as he drew his chief's attention to the damning sentences.

"In referring to his new influx of engineer officers, you will note that Tsirlin complains of low training standards and competence across the range of duties."

"On the second page he speaks of low-quality equipment, with higher than acceptable failure rates."

Producing another report for Zhukov, Malinin moved on.

"That is reflected in the second part of a report from Mayor General Perhorovich regarding the failure of his August 12th assault into the south of Hannover over the Leine River, on the Waldhausen-Ricklingen axis."

Malinin thumbed straight to the third page and précised the meat of the report.

"Perhorovich lays the blame for the failure squarely on the shoulders of the commander of the 2nd Battalion, 7th Pontoon Bridge Brigade, attached to him from 1st Red Banner's reserves."

"The commander of 70th Guards Heavy Tank Regiment was killed along with four of his crews, and valuable vehicles lost, when the bridge collapsed due to apparently faulty engineer work."

After a pause to let Zhukov digest the information, Malinin concluded.

"Perhorovich had the commander of the 2nd Battalion, Mayor of Engineers Pavlov, arrested on the spot. The NKVD took the officer away and hanged him by the roadside, complete with a placard damning him as a saboteur. Subsequent investigations discovered defective manufacturing in the ropes and low quality metal fixings and welding work on the pontoons."

Zhukov looked up puzzled, his hand suddenly touching one of his awards as a memory flickered into life.

"Pavlov of the 7th? Didn't I..."

His voice trailed off as restrained nodding from Malinin indicated his memory was correct, and he had indeed presented the young Major Pavlov with the Hero of the Soviet Union award during the Patriotic War.

Zhukov recalled the enthusiastic young officer who had led a combat bridging assault with incredible bravery and skill.

"Perhorovich acted precipitously, and we have lost a good officer."

"I agree, Comrade Marshall. Do you propose action on the matter?"

Zhukov considered his options quickly.

"Send the General a copy of Pavlov's service record and commendations. Request of him a written explanation of his actions," and pausing to finish his latest cup of tea, he ended with a flourish, "Marked for my personal attention. That should focus his mind, Comrade."

Sampling a sweet biscuit from the tray, Zhukov waited whilst his CoS made the appropriate notation.

"So, I assume shortcuts were being made in the engineer officer training?"

"Yes, Comrade Marshall. The programme had been adapted to circumstances. It is now back to its original form."

Nothing more could be said on that point.

"What steps are being taken regarding the equipment?"

"All bridging units have been ordered to check their equipment against these noted failures, Comrade Marshall."

"Good, there must be no repeats."

More tea was poured by the senior man.

"NKVD Quality control teams are on their way to interview the factory managers of the facilities that produced the defective items."

There was an unspoken understanding that such interviews would inevitably end with more executions for sabotage and the like.

139

"Personnel and equipment shortages have obviously been caused by combat operations, but particularly heavy losses have resulted from enemy air action."

Malinin halted and accepted the full cup that Zhukov pushed across the table at him.

Taking a deep draught, he cleared his throat and continued.

"Thank you, Comrade Marshall. Some examples of this. Two full bridging brigades were badly mauled when Allied bombers attacked the Vessertal concentration site near Suhl. Marshall Bagramyan reports his available heavy bridging capacity down to two companies of the 106th Engineers, both of which have seen combat and have limited equipment, as a result of ground attack by the RAF."

Another swallow of tea brought needed moisture to a throat drying out, not just from speaking but from genuine horror at the unfolding situation.

"Karelian Front is sending its own bridging assets to 1st Baltic, but this will have an effect upon our intended Norway operations. A necessary evil, but one that Bagramyan and Govorov shared with us only when they were already committed to the move."

The criticism was genuine. Although the move made sense, it had not been approved, having been sorted out between the two front commanders alone.

"We will sort that out in good time, Comrade, even though that wily old Armenian kept us out of it. For now it is a good arrangement on their part and we would have supported it immediately, would we not?"

A point Malinin conceded immediately.

"Marshall Malinovsky is desperate for more assets. He reports that the 112th Pontoon Battalion is his sole intact bridging unit with good capability, the others having little equipment left. He also states that casualties amongst his experienced engineers have been punishing. You will recall that you instructed that the latest batch of replacements went straight to him?"

Zhukov nodded, understanding that Malinin's tone indicated that had not been straight-forward.

"A partisan ambush derailed the train carrying the engineer troops at the Bode River Bridge, near Hedersleben, resulting in heavy casualties."

Zhukov looked quizzically at Malinin.

"Apologies, Comrade Marshall," and orienting himself on the table map, he swiftly indicated the precise location of the attack.

"Our comrades of the NKVD?"

"Were effective after the event, and destroyed the partisan unit that carried out the attack. Additional patrols are now being mounted and hostages have been taken from the local communities."

Neither man found it necessary to give voice to the thoughts that such reprisals were standard chekist fare.

"I will send a report to Comrade Beria shortly, and also request additional vigilance from his units. We cannot afford these losses. They are unnecessary and avoidable."

Malinin flourished a handful of paper.

"These reports all indicate either higher than expected casualties in our bridging units, higher rates of consumption of specialist equipment, or both," and in an attempt to add something positive before the crunch arrived, Malinin added brightly, "Your order to marry dedicated anti-aircraft support units to bridging units is being carried out, and we should see a reduction in casualties from air attack as a result."

The Chief of Staff cleared his throat and delivered his most important line.

"We have a problem here, Comrade Marshall."

A document was produced from a separate pile and placed before Zhukov.

"We seem to have sufficient assets to take our forces through to Phase four, provided we do not see repeats of the partisan ambush and also replacements come at the promised rates, both in men and equipment."

"And at an acceptable standard."

Zhukov's comment was under his breath, but still reached the CoS's ears.

"Yes, Comrade Marshall."

141

Zhukov grunted, his eyes taking in the projections Malinin had prepared.

"That includes the assets we have removed from the Poles. We have not asked for Polish volunteers as yet, Comrade Marshall?"

Spoken as a question, his words received a shake of the head from Zhukov.

"Not at this time. They are about as trustworthy as a bag of snakes."

And, by way of confirmation of the decision, Malinin read a paragraph from a report by the Chief Engineer Officer of 1st Baltic Front.

"It appears likely that not all apparatus requested has been made available, and that considerable amounts of that which has been reassigned from the Poles, as well as the equipment recovered by the Polish engineers, appears to be excessively worn, even damaged."

Receiving nothing more than a knowing look, he continued.

"NKVD is not acting at this time, for obvious reasons, but we may not be able to ignore the issue for much longer. Bagramyan has requested a large number of their armoured vehicles as replacements for his own force. That will give us a further indication as to loyalties."

"Indeed Comrade. Enough of the Poles for now. What is your conclusion on the matter of bridging engineers?"

"We simply will not have the assets to successfully cross the Rhine as matters stand."

That was guaranteed to get the Commander-in-Chief's attention. Silence ensued as Zhukov reread the figures.

"I agree. Vasilevsky?"

"His assets were depleted at the start, Comrade Marshall. If he loses any more, his ability offensively will be greatly reduced."

Wiping his bald pate with his right hand, Zhukov considered the problem.

"One for STAVKA to ponder, Malinin. Have the written request for more resources prepared immediately."

The CoS made the appropriate record in his notes.

142

"Anywhere else we can get assets from?"

Malinin shook his head as he spoke.

"We have stripped out Central and Southern areas to the absolute bare minimums, to nothing in some cases. On my authority, all units are being circulated with orders to remove any officers or men with bridging experience from their roster and transfer them to Army command from where they can be appropriately allocated."

"Good work, Malinin. That should give us something extra to work with, although I hope it doesn't disrupt the parent units too much."

The CoS shrugged as the priority now was bridging engineers, not tanks or infantry.

Zhukov stood and tugged down his tunic.

"I will be flying back to Moscow this afternoon and I will bring this to the attention of STAVKA. Make sure those reports," he indicated Malinin's written list, "Are ready as soon as possible. Maybe I will return with more positive news?"

Malinin tidied up the papers and hurried away to get the necessary orders drafted.

As he reached the door, he was almost bowled over by a staff Lieutenant-Colonel.

"Apologies, Comrade Polkovnik General."

"Well what has got you so excited, Garimov?"

The man brandished a message sheet.

"I need to see Comrade Marshall Zhukov, Sir."

Malinin stepped aside, allowing the excited officer to enter the room.

Snapping to attention in front of his commander, Garimov offered up a radio message slip, which Zhukov took and read.

The Chief of Staff silently enquired of Garimov, his probing look seeking out the nature of the news that was making his commander smile.

The Lieutenant-Colonel addressed him with equal formality.

"Sir," heard a satisfied Malinin, "Marshall Bagramyan reports Hamburg has fallen."

143

Zhukov took his place on the aircraft, a genuine lend-lease American C-47, and immediately felt it lurch as the aircrew received clearance for take-off, right on the appointed time of 1230 hrs.

He checked his watch and did the maths. His briefing for the General Secretary scheduled for that evening.

'Four hour time differential. A six and a half hour flight, briefing and then flight back.'

He would be absent from his command post for a number of hours but would be back before the central European day fully awakened.

Onboard with him were his travelling personal staff of four officers, plus a number of others from various branches of the Red Army, returning to Moscow for reasons ranging from attending Communist party meetings to sorting out the logistics of total war.

The combat soldiers amongst the passengers were easily discernible, as they quickly fell asleep, observing the soldier's maxim of 'get it while you can.'

Zhukov grinned.

'Old soldiers never lose that ability'.

Within a few minutes, only four Political Officers, an NKVD Major, and the GRU Lieutenant-Colonel sat opposite him were still awake, the first five being involved in a theoretical political debate that reminded Zhukov why he avoided such inane matters. The latter was deep in thought, studying a number of reports.

The Commander of the Red Banner Forces of Soviet Europe took time to observe the GRU officer more closely and before he drifted off into a deep sleep he had posed himself the question of how a GRU Lieutenant-Colonel had won the Hero of the Soviet Union award.

His prolonged snore interrupted the GRU officer's line of thought.

Putting the folders back in a small pigskin briefcase, Nazarbayeva decided to get some sleep to help her prepare for her briefing with the General Secretary that evening.

Settling herself down, she eased the boot on her damaged foot a few centimetres for comfort, and was asleep in an instant.

Nazarbayeva woke to the sound of urgent muffled voices opposite, and her senses quickly cleared to take in what was happening.

An Air Force Lieutenant was in the process of explaining the reasons behind a diversion to a different airfield to an unhappy Marshall Zhukov. The small military strip at Ostafievo was now their destination.

Enquiring of the harassed man as he returned to the cockpit, Nazarbayeva established that Vnukovo was closed indefinitely due to a ground incident.

"Govno!"

A chuckle came from the seat opposite, Marshall Zhukov amused that such a beauty was capable of combat soldiers language. But then, he mused, he should not be surprised at all, as the woman had obviously once been a combat soldier herself.

"As you say, Comrade PodPolkovnik, as you say."

"Apologies, Comrade Marshall, but my transport will be waiting at Vnukovo and I have an important briefing to give in Moscow."

Zhukov was not normally disposed to acts of charity but something about the female Officer interested him, and it was not her extremely obvious beauty and charms.

"I too am going to Moscow, and there will be vehicles waiting for me at Ostafievo. Perhaps you would like to accompany me and give me the GRU's impressions of our campaign to date?"

"Thank you, Sir. I'm sure I can assist the Comrade Marshall"

Something about her simple reply puzzled Zhukov. She seemed undaunted by his seniority, a rare attribute in the Red Army.

"Excellent. I am called to the Kremlin for 8pm", taking an automatic look at his watch, "For a meeting with the General-

145

Secretary, so we should have time to drop you wherever you need, Comrade?"

"My appointment lies in the same place. I am ordered to brief the General-Secretary and Marshall Beria. As is normally the case for me, I have no time allotted, so I suspect I will simply follow you, Comrade Marshall."

Zhukov nodded, his respect for the woman increased as no fools ever crossed that threshold more than once, and his understanding of her calm acceptance of his offer of a lift was complete.

'If she can stand before those two, then she certainly won't be worried about sharing a car with her Commander-in-Chief.'

"Excellent Comrade, PodPolkovnik. Now, before we land perhaps you might give me your name and tell me how you came by that pretty trinklet?"

Zhukov pointed a finger at her Gold Star.

"Yes Comrade Marshall. I am PodPolkovnik Tatiana Nazarbayeva of Polkovnik General Pekunin's personal staff, and I got this on the Kerch."

Zhukov felt strangely, and for him, worryingly at ease with the female officer as she spoke modestly of her combat operations.

So much so that their conversation shifted smoothly into the GRU assessment of the present combat operations and the first he knew that they were on the ground was the hard bump of a poor landing from a fatigued pilot.

Zhukov and his staff swept off the aircraft, speeding towards two ex-Wehrmacht Horsch 108 staff cars, sat idling on the apron.

Nazarbayeva assembled her files and briefcase, and then moved swiftly after the hurrying group, her limp becoming more noticeable as her pace increased.

Despite the promises he made to himself as he hurried from the aircraft, something made Zhukov turn and beckon the GRU officer into his car, turning her from the second vehicle to which she had been heading.

The conversation struck up again, the woman's analysis excellent, her observations reasonable and well thought out.

146

Only when the Horsch halted at the gates of the Kremlin did the exchange of views and information cease.

Dismounting from the vehicle, Zhukov wished her well and formally took his leave, receiving an immaculate salute from Nazarbayeva.

Striding up the stairs, his staff keeping pace behind him, he wondered if he would ever see the woman again, not knowing that his life and hers were, from that moment, inextricably linked.

Zhukov had given his presentation to the GKO, and received assurances as to replacement weapons, materiel and personnel across the board. The failure to adhere to the assault timetable had been explained and, unusually, accepted without histrionics and threats. The normal vitriol was directed against those who were behind the lines, and whose failures contributed to the engineering and equipment shortages, plus those who were failing to ensure safety in the logistical tail.

That meant that the bald Marshall had the rare pleasure of seeing Beria hounded by the General Secretary for the failure of his NKVD security force to protect rail lines and bridges. Such pleasures were best sampled without showing satisfaction, as the wounded Beria was a beast to fear.

The meeting was closed and the GKO dissolved, some to instigate the decisions of the meeting, others to their homes and beds, leaving solely Stalin and Beria with Zhukov.

Beria, still smarting from the admonishments he had recently received, sat silently and obviously deep in thought.

The General Secretary hid his amusement and ordered more tea.

"Comrade Marshall, the GRU will be giving us a briefing shortly. It will be of interest to you I have no doubt."

"Yes Comrade General Secretary, I travelled here with the GRU officer in question. I gave her a lift to the Kremlin as our plane was diverted and she had no vehicle."

"Ah, so you have met our Nazarbayeva. Your thoughts?"

Zhukov didn't need to think.

"A remarkable woman for sure, Comrade General Secretary."

Stalin waved his pipe stem at the still silent Beria, a moment of rare humour surfacing.

"Marshall Beria seems to think so too."

The eyes flicked up to look at Stalin and quickly went down again, but Zhukov saw enough to understand in their coldness that Nazarbayeva had an implacable enemy in the NKVD chief.

"Let us see what she brings to us this evening. Lavrentiy."

The Generalissimo motioned his man to the phone and felt satisfaction that he was obviously still hurting.

The summons was issued and Beria slipped back into his seat as Stalin beckoned Zhukov to a chair by his side, the three sat together almost as judges in a court, a sight which caused Nazarbayeva a moment's pause as she entered.

Stalin, strangely affable, motioned the GRU officer forward with his pipe.

"Comrade PodPolkovnik. I understand from Comrade Marshall Zhukov that you are already acquainted?"

"Yes Comrade General Secretary, that is correct."

"Excellent. Formalities over. Please begin."

"GRU sources in London inform us that the British will shortly be able to field a new force of a minimum of four full Infantry and one tank division formed from men who were, until recently, prisoners of the Germans. They can also rejuvenate existing divisions by bringing units up to full strength."

This was not news to anybody in the room and had been anticipated.

"Our information is that in basic infantry terms the British will profit from the fact that they made few technological advances during their war years, and so we should expect the new formations to be as effective as their existing ones are proving."

Zhukov could understand that, and an almost imperceptible nod gave Nazarbayeva encouragement.

148

"Unless the British use older vehicles, the new tank division will probably not be ready for deployment for some time to come. We cannot assess that precisely."

Neither had the NKVD report Beria had submitted some hours before.

Nazarbayeva moved immediately into a thorny area.

"Comrade General Secretary, we have uncovered a problem. RAF losses, indeed allied air losses in general, are not as reported."

A moment's pause as the information was absorbed.

"Go on, Comrade," Stalin's voice bereft of its usual cutting edge for once.

"A GRU officer gained valuable paper intelligence from an RAF base the army overran, and we have compared that to our own air force's claims. Allied losses were actually just over half of what was being submitted in our Regiment's reports."

Zhukov replaced his tea cup and spoke bluntly.

"An isolated case, Comrade?"

The GRU officer shook her head as she spoke.

"Unfortunately not, Comrade Marshall. Once this came to light, I ordered a further examination of captured enemy air force records and compared them with our own stated claims. From memory, the best case was a claim of ten, when the real number was eight shot down. On one occasion, a regimental commander claimed ten enemy aircraft destroyed when the RAF record clearly states solely one loss due to air combat."

Pausing for a moment, Nazarbayeva delivered a killer line.

"There were no instances when our claims were equal or less than recorded allied losses, Comrade General Secretary."

Zhukov remained silent, absorbing what he had just been told. Beria remained silent as his report had made no mention of this possibility whatsoever.

Stalin spoke first.

"Propaganda, Comrade Colonel?"

Zhukov was impressed. Many officers would hedge their bets at this point but not this one, the reply bold, clear and unequivocal.

149

"No Comrade General Secretary. These are Squadron and, in one case, Wing records. These would be a true reflection of events. To do otherwise would be lunacy."

Zhukov took the lead, although he suspected he knew the answer to his question.

"So, if that is true, what does GRU think is the present status of the Allied air forces?"

"Comrade Marshall, intelligence has seen a marked reduction in enemy air activities over the course of the campaign. I believe we have allowed ourselves to ally this reduction with the figures our air regiments have quoted for their losses, rather than think through the whole situation."

A soft cough and Nazarbayeva ploughed onwards.

"Our attacks on the 6th caught them by surprise, and we caused great casualties, as well as inflicting damage to facilities. Clearly the effectiveness of the allied air forces dropped. However, I believe we have overstated the casualty effect and underestimated the disruption effect. They are sorting out their logistics and organisation, and I believe that this is why we are now seeing an increase in the tempo of their air operations, combined with new units arriving almost daily."

Selecting a single page document, Nazarbayeva produced three copies, handing over her own to Zhukov and proceeding from memory.

"Comrade General Secretary, these figures were received an hour before I left Headquarters. On the left-hand column you will see estimates of enemy air strength based upon claims from our Regiments. On the right you will see the figures supplied by a GRU agent within the RAF."

The figures were, if true, a disaster in the making.

"We have claimed that in air and ground combat over 50% of the enemy aircraft available on 6th August have been destroyed, and that reinforcements have been slow in arriving, boosting that overall figure to no more than 55% remaining."

Zhukov was only barely listening as the figures were in his hand and screaming at him.

"The reality is that their air force is presently between 75-80% of 6th August figures. It is important to remember that this figure also includes large numbers of heavy bombers, so the

150

equation between fighters, fighter-bombers and light to medium bombers is more favourable than it would otherwise have been."

No-one there failed to understand that these figures were disastrous, if true.

"And your source, Comrade PodPolkovnik? How accurate are these figures? Could your agent be playing games for both sides here?"

Beria leant back again, observing that his questions had given the woman a moment's pause.

"This agent provided us with accurate information throughout the German war. He is well placed and trusted. More importantly, he is an ideological agent and does what he does because he believes in our common cause. If he were compromised, I am certain he would use the appropriate code and inform us."

No give at all in her position. Zhukov, whilst pained by the revelations, could not help but be impressed by Nazarbayeva's straight-forward delivery. At the same time, there was a dangerous naivety to her approach.

Stalin made his directions.

"One for you, Comrade Marshall," gesturing at Beria, "Get your men out to the air regiments and ensure that we get the right information in future. Punish anyone who has been in error."

He raised his hand to cut off Zhukov's objection, and paused for a moment. Softly and in acknowledgement of the Marshall's unspoken protest, he continued.

"Only those who have been grossly in error, Lavrentiy. We have lost too many experienced commanders already. Shoot only those who have deliberately lied to us."

Only Zhukov and Nazarbayeva wondered how many would die by that order this very night.

"Continue, Comrade, continue."

Acknowledging her leader with a nod, Nazarbayeva moved into the next area.

"The Spanish are having some difficulties in organising the Blue Division, and the independent brigade. It seems they will not be ready for some time. Most estimates give them two weeks before crossing the border, although one of our agents

151

within the division itself believes they could still march within a week."

Without any degree of triumph, Nazarbayeva continued.

"GRU predictions were correct, and we understand that over 180,000 ex-German and Italian small arms have been provided to the Spanish Army, complete with ammunition, as well as a large number of captured artillery pieces and vehicles. Also we can confirm that thirty-seven German tanks crossed into Spain during the Patriotic War, but we are presently unable to confirm types."

Beria examined the woman for signs of gloating at his discomfort, but could see none.

'*Very wise, you fucking bitch,*' he thought, unable to contemplate the possibility that Nazarbayeva had no intention of embarrassing him and was solely delivering her best interpretation of intelligence.

"Our government agent confirms that the Spanish plan is to re-equip their expeditionary corps initially, and then as much of the rest of their army as possible. This will have the effect of slowing their committal to battle, which is a plus for us, whilst undoubtedly making them more effective when they do arrive, which is not."

A fair interpretation to Zhukov's mind, and he already understood that Nazarbayeva stood by her agents so he would go with that.

"One other matter relating to Spain, Comrade Marshall."

He looked up, only to realise that the GRU officer was speaking directly to Beria.

"Our main agent speaks of a possible covert operation run in the Madrid area, which has resulted in the death of one of his supportive contacts, and brought unnecessary attention to his door."

Beria felt his bile rise.

'*Bitch! You dare to chastise me?*'

The momentary flash in his eyes was quickly suppressed and missed by all in the room.

'*Anyway, NKVD's contact Tatiana,*' smugly reminded himself.

152

"Apparently a woman was found brutally murdered in unusual circumstances, a woman who, we now discover, was being watched by the Spanish Secret Service because of her known communist links and open romantic episodes with certain high government officials, our agent included."

Beria's angry silence was noted by Stalin and Zhukov, although only one knew the facts that were troubling the NKVD head.

"The woman was sympathetic to our cause and willingly offered information to our agent, often giving him cause to believe that she was already working for another similar organisation."

'NKVD had one of your agents, and not for the first time, and not the only one in Spain either, my little Lieutenant Colonel.'

The faintest smile warped Beria's lips, which he swiftly hid with his teacup.

"Apparently, the woman was grossly violated after death and Spanish investigators are proceeding on the assumption that it was done to mask the real motive, and are also assuming that motive is related to her possible espionage activities. Especially as she was known to have associated with a group of strangers in a Madrid hotel on the day of her death, strangers that have since disappeared."

Silence was still the NKVD Marshall's only response.

"Indications are that the group have German origins, something that has caused a great deal confusion in Spanish investigative minds."

Both Zhukov was surprised by that, and failed to notice that neither Stalin nor Beria shared it.

"Our information does not support any involvement from the Germans, Comrade Marshall."

Beria shrugged.

"If this is part of an NKVD covert operation, it has placed GRU's highly placed agent at risk."

Finally animated, the spectacled officer leant forward.

"Do not presume to lecture me on covert operations, Comrade PodPolkovnik. You are here to brief."

153

Beria leant back again and threw an expansive hand gesture at the GRU officer.

"So, brief us, and leave your personal accusations at home."

Naïve possibly, but more really just possessing the strength to stand up for herself.

"Apologies, Comrade Marshall, but I convey the words of General Pekunin, who was very precise. This apparent NKVD operation has exposed GRU's highest placed Spanish agent to risk. That agent is now discontinuing his communications until the investigative activity has ceased. So we have lost our best contact at a crucial time."

Zhukov was sure that Pekunin would not have wished his officer to be quite so precise, and he felt wary for the woman.

Beria gathered himself for another verbal assault, but was cut off before he could start.

"Comrade, PodPolkovnik. GRU is correct to be angry that a highly placed agent may have been placed at risk. I am sure that Comrade Marshall Beria will investigate this thoroughly and inform us of his findings."

Beria nodded in deference to his chief, again finding himself put on the spot by this GRU woman.

Strangely, Stalin decided to defend his man, speaking of something that had been previously agreed would remain unspoken.

"I will tell you that events in Spain are about to take a positive turn, thanks to investigations made by Marshall Beria's men. I can say no more for now."

Stalin settled back into his chair and invited Nazarbayeva to continue.

"The Italian situation is not presently clear, despite our best efforts to understand their minds. I actually believe they presently do not know exactly what they intend to do, Comrade General Secretary."

That drew a snort from both Beria and Zhukov, the Italians being everybody's whipping boy.

"The secret offer made by the Foreign Ministry should certainly cause some division in their ranks. However, one piece of intelligence may indicate some good news for us."

154

Referring to her folder, Nazarbayeva listed the Italian formations that presently served within the Allied forces.

"The Italian government has requested that these combat groups, and all other support units under British commander Alexander, be permitted to journey to holding areas near Livorno, Florence and Rimini, with the expectation that they be returned to Italian authority, and with a view to creating an independent Italian Army."

Whilst this was not completely new information to her audience, her interpretation of the intelligence certainly was.

"By removing the Groups and the support units, the Italians are physically weakening the Allies Italian Force. They must know this. Therefore it is my conclusion that the Italians are withdrawing their fighting troops prior to declaring neutrality."

This time it was Zhukov who spoke first, challenging the impressive Amazon.

"On what basis do you make that conclusion, Comrade PodPolkovnik? Why can they not be forming an Italian Army to fight us?"

"Comrade Marshall, it would appear to be a simple matter of geography."

Nazarbayeva produced an uncomplicated sketch of Northern Italy from her folder and passed it across to Stalin.

It was minimally marked, and simply demonstrated her point.

"At a time when Allied resources must be under pressure, the Italians are expending vast quantities to bring their forces together on the blue line."

Both Beria and Zhukov craned their necks to see that the Blue line ran from west to east across Italy, running through the three cities Nazarbayeva had cited.

"To our thinking, the most natural place to assemble, given the present locations of their units, would be the triangle Modena, Ferrara to Bologna. It would also make more military sense to keep your assets nearer to the potential point of need."

Zhukov agreed for the same reasons the GRU officer had just cited; he had simply wanted to hear her reasoning and to understand if he had missed something in his swift appraisal.

"I can agree with your assessment, Comrade Nazarbayeva. It makes sense. Is there something within the Foreign Ministry briefing which would support this view, Comrade Marshall?"

Beria found himself the unwelcome focal point of attention, three pairs of eyes boring into him, one solely for the amusement of seeing him uncomfortable, as their owner knew well what the others did not.

"As you know we have offered to respect Italian neutrality if declared in good time, but have reserved the right to force combat on any Allied Divisions that fight on Italian soil. The Italian Government would, as part of the protocol, order Allied forces from their territory."

Without a conscious thought, his glasses were in his hand, handkerchief polishing carefully, almost as prop to his spirit as he spoke further.

"Discussions have addressed a number of issues. Our right of march across an area of Northern Italy to permit access to Southern France, technological assistance and reparations, in gold, for any damage caused."

He paused, breathed rapidly on both lenses and resumed his polishing.

"Repatriation of all Italian prisoners of war within two months of the declaration of neutrality."

Replacing his glasses, he chose to look the GRU officer in the eye.

"Guarantees of military aid and trade agreements, sovereignty over certain areas of Africa so recently coveted, but lost. Sovereignty over areas of Southern France once enemy resistance is broken."

Beria sneezed violently, sending three blobs of spittle in Nazarbayeva's direction.

"We have also declared a weapons-free attack zone where any forces are liable to attack by our aircraft."

He placed his hand theatrically upon Nazarbayeva's map and turned it so it was facing Stalin. His eyes did not leave those of Nazarbayeva, his words directed at Stalin and Zhukov, but his negative emotion all for the GRU officer.

156

"The zone is defined by a line drawn across their country from Viareggio to Cervia."

A swift examination of the map was sufficient to demonstrate that the rally point set by the Italian government fell on the safe side of that line.

Silence is a worrying thing, especially in a room full of powerful people. Zhukov broke into it, his mind already asset stripping from the formations that were due to crash into the Allied forces there.

"Then I can only agree with the GRU assessment here. It seems that Italy will be brilliantly neutralised by our Foreign Ministry."

"Good work, then we can leave Italy and proceed onto other matters."

Stalin drew a line under the 'Italian' assessment and lit a cigarette, noticing Nazarbayeva's pained look.

"Your wound is hurting, Comrade PodPolkovnik?"

"I can bear it, thank you, Comrade General Secretary. If I may continue to the military balance?"

A gentle coughing prohibited the Generallisimo speaking, so he managed a wave of assent instead.

"Comrade Marshall Zhukov suggested that I refer to the NKVD assessment of enemy forces, which you have already seen and which mirrors the GRU assessment in all important areas. Unless there is anything specific you require, Comrade General Secretary, GRU can add nothing to that but…."

She meant nothing by the words, save their face value, but Beria perceived deeper meaning and interrupted with unconcealed sarcasm.

"Thank you for your endorsement, Comrade Nazarbayeva. It is nice to know the NKVD can get something right to GRU's satisfaction."

"Again my apologies, Comrade Marshall, I meant no criticism."

Zhukov kept his smile to himself but he could not help but admire this woman who did not seem to waver. None the less, he decided to rescue her.

"You said but."

157

"Yes, Comrade Marshall Zhukov. The NKVD assessment of Allied forces is correct, but omits a new German force that is presently being formed in France."

When Zhukov and Nazarbayeva had arrived at the Kremlin, an officer had been waiting to hand over an urgent report to the GRU Lieutenant-Colonel, and she had scant seconds to pass on some of her new knowledge to the Red Banner Forces Commander; but not enough for him to give his two superiors any hint in his own brief.

Beria took advantage of the opportunity he had apparently been offered, leant across and selected a large round biscuit from the silver platter, quickly taking a bite and spraying crumbs in all directions.

"I assume you speak of the German Naval personnel presently forming at the French Ports? My sources inform me that even the Allies do not know how to use these assets yet. These are mentioned in our report."

"No Comrade Marshall, I refer to other new German forces in France."

Stalin sat gently puffing his pipe, as always enjoying the spectacle of his underlings in confrontation.

Beria stood but gained no height advantage over the woman. He gestured at the wall map.

"Comrade PodPolkovnik, we have reports of thirteen to fifteen German divisions assembling in France and Italy, most under the leadership of one-time General Guderian. We have more reports of German air regiments, possibly as many as fifteen, also in the making, and again mostly in France."

He picked up the NKVD report and the GRU report and dropped both dramatically onto the table.

"We even agree on the naval personnel issue, do we not?"

Not waiting for an answer, he sat down again.

"What new force can the Germanski possibly conjure up now?"

Nazarbayeva coughed slightly as the first stages of a viral infection made themselves known.

158

"Comrade General Secretary, my apologies. I received an urgent report as I attended this building, so have only one copy. If I may read it to you?"

Stalin gestured his acceptance.

"This is from a GRU agent called Leopard, whom we have undercover in the Allied Forces. He is presently with the French First Army in Southern Germany. It was he who located the fourth symposium."

The agent's credentials established, she read on.

"He reports of a clandestine assembly and training area run by the French, centring on the village of Sassy, south-west of Paris."

Zhukov, whilst aware of the punch line, took in every word of the journey to it.

In his peripheral vision, he saw Beria's dismissive wave.

"Part of the build-up we have already identified obviously. Nothing to worry about. The name is included in our list of such assembly areas."

Zhukov was puzzled by that. Beria was being very unBeria-like, committing himself without certain knowledge, apparently all because of the effect of the woman in front of him.

'Strange.'

"Unfortunately not, Comrade Marshall. GRU had made the same assumption, but it appears we were both wrong."

Stalin struck a match, punctuating the moment with an unspoken but very real full stop.

Puffing on his cigarette he leant forward, placing his elbows gently on the table, his look inviting her to continue.

"Comrade General Secretary. The Sassy facilities are run under the auspices of the French Foreign Legion. The Germans in question are to be formed into a corps of at least four divisions with support units for offensive combat operations."

Even though he had heard it before, the hasty snatched exchange with Nazarbayeva in the lobby having given him a heads-up, the full revelation still hit Zhukov like an electric shock.

"Comrade General Secretary. They are forming divisions of their Foreign Legion from the SS."

159

Beria realised that if his agency had missed this one then it was a bad error, so he wisely stayed silent.

It was left to Stalin to ask the necessary questions.

"Can this agent be trusted, Comrade Nazarbayeva? Really trusted?"

"Yes, I will stake my position on it, Comrade General Secretary."

Beria half-smiled, in the knowledge that she was staking much more than that on it, had she the sense to realise her position.

"When will they be ready?"

"According to Leopard's best guess, all units can move into action within a week minimum. He emphasises that is a guess, but an informed guess."

After a moment's pause Stalin extinguished his cigarette and leant back in his chair, his fingers stroking his moustache back into place.

"Comrade Marshall Zhukov?"

"Any division of German's is something of note to us, Comrade General Secretary. I'm sure no-one forgets how these SS bastards fought, but four divisions will do little to the balance of power. More would be a problem for sure. None the less, we will have to heed their presence, and I will be surprised if the Allies use them just to sit around doing nothing."

"Meaning what, Comrade?"

"Meaning I will be surprised if they are not employed on the assault, Comrade General Secretary. I would use the devils in such a role."

Beria ventured his opinion.

"Then they were politically motivated. Now they would not be, so would they be any better than the average Germanski swine?"

Stalin was singularly amused to watch both Zhukov and Nazarbayeva look in disbelief at the NKVD leader, the former speaking swiftly, partially to spare the latter from more retribution.

"The average Germanski reached the gates of Moscow wearing a flimsy summer tunic, and holding a weapon too frozen to fire, Comrade Marshall. The average Germanski reached the

160

banks of the Volga. He is not to be underestimated. And these men were not average Germanski."

Stalin, ever playful when it came to watching his henchman placed in an uncomfortable position, sought the GRU officer's view on the matter.

"Comrade General Secretary, I could only give you my opinion as this is fresh information."

"Then do so. How do you see this, Comrade PodPolkovnik, without frills?"

"Comrade Marshall Zhukov is wholly correct. The German is a good soldier but the SS had something extra. I see no reason to believe that the absence of political motivation from the National Socialism cause will undermine their will and ability to fight."

"Go on, you said something extra. Explain Comrade," the Dictator presiding benignly over proceedings almost purred the words.

"They had unequalled military skills, zeal, comradeship and esprit de corps, Comrade General Secretary, which combined with a fanatical belief that they were without equal militarily. That made them the very worst of enemies."

Beria rallied.

"Under German leadership remember that. Eisenhower and his cronies are lesser men as we have seen already."

"That is true Comrade Marshall. However, Leopard identified SS officers Bittrich and Knocke as part of the command group for this Legion Corps."

Beria contemplated saying nothing, but immediately understood that he would need the GRU's agent.

"In which case, we will be able to interfere with their effectiveness."

This time, it was Zhukov who was taken by surprise.

"How so, Comrade Marshall?"

"Knocke has a wife and two young girls, presently within the control of the NKVD, Comrade Marshall Zhukov."

Pausing for the briefest of moments to permit his plan to form, he addressed Nazarbayeva in a friendly tone.

"So Comrade PodPolkovnik, one assumes that you can communicate with your agent in the field? Give him orders to follow, messages to deliver?"

Nazarbayeva understood perfectly.

"Yes, Comrade Marshall."

"Then NKVD and GRU can between us," he conceded, "Affect this SS Group."

"Excellent, Comrade Marshall. Liaise with GRU and sort the SS bastards out swiftly. Anything else, comrade?"

Nazarbayeva passed the sole copy of the Leopard report to Stalin.

"No, Comrade General-Secretary."

"Thank you, Comrade Nazarbayeva. Excellent work. You may go, but wait outside so that Comrade Marshall Beria can organise the SS solution with you."

Nazarbayeva departed the room, the faintest trace of her limp apparent.

When the door closed behind her, Stalin chuckled openly.

"A formidable woman. Would that all Russian women had balls like that, eh Lavrentiy?"

Beria ignored the obvious retort.

"She is confident and efficient for sure, Comrade General Secretary. What say you, Comrade Zhukov?"

The bald Marshall ripped his eyes away from the closed doors, extinguishing the vision of the departing GRU officer.

"Would that all Russian soldiers had balls like her, Comrade Beria."

Zhukov exited the room and found Nazarbayeva scribbling out a copy of the Leopard report from memory.

She sprang to her feet as he approached.

"Relax, Comrade. Thank you for your input, but do watch Marshall Beria. You have an enemy there."

Tatiana went to reply but remained silent, the doors opening in her peripheral vision as Beria came in search of her.

Zhukov extracted a notebook and quickly penned a message. Folding the paper, he held it out to the GRU officer as Beria hung back, waiting for the Marshall to move on.

"My vehicles will leave in thirty-five minutes time. Just in case you are not with us, I would welcome your briefings in my headquarters on a regular basis, if General Pekunin can spare you, Comrade. Please give him this note."

The paper changed hands and Zhukov nodded his goodbye to Nazarbayeva, who saluted smartly.

As the military man withdrew, so the NKVD chief drew near.

"Comrade PodPolkovnik. I need you to get a message to your agent as soon as possible. I believe we can exert some pressure on our man."

A notebook appeared, and a second message was pressed into Nazarbayeva's hand.

"Simple enough, Comrade?"

She read the message.

"Yes, Comrade Marshall. I will inform Comrade Polkovnik General Pekunin, with my explanation and endorsement, and I am sure he will have it sent straight away."

"*With your fucking endorsement? Who the fuck do you think you are?*"

Tatiana meant nothing more than she would support the concept and relay events from the meeting, but Beria heard what he wanted and interpreted it in the same jaundiced way.

He counter-attacked.

"Good. I was sorry to hear of the death of your son."

The change in tack threw the woman, a fact not wasted on Beria.

"Thank you, Comrade Marshall. He was a soldier and took a soldier's risks."

"True, true. But we should look after our sons and husbands, and do all we can to keep them safe from harm."

'*Sympathy from Beria?*' she thought, '*Out of character.*'

"All we can, Comrade Nazarbayeva. You still have three sons and a husband in service to the Motherland. They should be kept safe."

"That is beyond me, Comrade Marshall. I can but hope that victory will come, and they will be delivered home to me alive."

"Nothing is beyond anyone prepared to sacrifice themselves for others."

A chill went through Nazarbayeva as she realised that the NKVD boss was examining her form, very deliberately studying her breasts through the tunic, his mind obviously on matters other than Agent Leopard.

"I will ensure the agent gets this message, Comrade Marshall."

Her hasty salute and departure broke Beria's train of thought, but not enough for him to stop imagining himself exploding hard inside the bitch and inflicting pleasurable pain upon her body.

"Sometime soon, Comrade Tatiana. You will know what happens to those who cross me."

Nazarbayeva presented herself in front of General Pekunin and handed him the notes from Beria and Zhukov.

The journey back by car to Ostafievo had been relatively quiet, Zhukov studying a new report on the military situation.

Once on board the aircraft, the two had talked for a while, until Zhukov called a halt and decided to get some much needed sleep.

Nazarbayeva did not inform him of what had transpired after he had left her with Beria.

Pekunin's chuckle roused her from her thoughts as she stood in front of his desk.

Placing the document from Zhukov on the table, the GRU commander returned to the dilemma posed by his Chinese puzzle box.

"So it appears that you have made a good impression on Marshall Zhukov, Tatiana. Do you know what this note says?"

Sliding one inconspicuous part across, the old man pursed his lips in triumph.

"I believe the Marshall wishes for a GRU raw brief at his headquarters on a regular basis, Comrade General."

"That is part of it," he paused in his attempt to conquer the box and the message was passed back to Nazarbayeva.

"Read it aloud, Tatiana. I may have misunderstood it."

She missed the grin on Pekunin's face, clearing her throat and feeling the first wave of chills as her body fought the virus.

"Comrade Pekunin, please arrange for this officer to deliver briefings at my headquarters on a regular basis. Promote her to full colonel immediately or risk losing her to my personal staff. Zhukov."

Another panel slid away, permitting Pekunin to move the final piece, exposing the interior of the box.

"No, I did not misunderstand it. I will draft the paperwork shortly. In the meantime, you look awful. Take yourself off to your quarters and I do not want to see you until breakfast tomorrow. Clear Comrade Polkovnik?"

"Yes, Comrade General, but there is the other matter."

Beria's note lay unread.

"It will wait, Polkovnik."

"No, Sir, it wil..."

Pekunin stood and moved to the door, opening it wide.

"It will wait, Polkovnik."

"Clear, thank you, Sir."

There is no victory at bargain basement prices.

Dwight D. Eisenhower

Chapter 62 – THE RETREAT

Colonel Thomas Bell Hood was exhausted, having been on the go constantly since day one of the Soviet attacks.

His shift had started at 0130 hrs, when an orderly had awakened him with his favourite breakfast tea.

By 0200 hrs, the fifty-four year old staff officer was downstairs in the centre of operations, examining the progress of the Russian thrusts.

The Allied troops were fighting hard, but the main campaign map left no doubt that the situation was dire. Five main Soviet developments were cutting through Allied defensive positions.

Around Hamburg, north and south, advances had been made. The British were performing miracles but having to give ground, their whole position weakened now that Hamburg itself has fallen.

A Soviet force had struck out north-west from Hannover whilst others reduced the city. Hood expected to have to report its loss to Eisenhower when the General was roused at 0430.

A dangerous pincer movement seemed to be forming, the northern jaw based upon Kassel, the southern part on Giessen. Bradley's command was desperately pulling their troops out of the way but it would be a close run thing.

Taking up the newly arrived mug of coffee, his eyes sought the next major threat.

The thrust could be going to a number of places, one or all of Mannheim, Karlsruhe or Stuttgart. That it was already threatening the rear of Nurnberg was a severe issue and one that Bradley was addressing by the only means available to him; giving up ground to preserve his force.

166

Hood gulped the caffeine laden drink down as he found the final problem.

Munich.

Thrusts north and south of the city threatened to surround it but it had not yet been abandoned. Fighting was severe, but the Soviets were being bled white for every yard and the commanders on the ground were optimistic that the advance could be stopped.

The situation map reflected other smaller successes for the Red Army but the five that stood out had exploded into life with their renewed offensive last Monday morning.

Two more reports arrived in front of Hood, which matters he would include in a folder for Ike's morning brief if important enough. Unless they were absolute dynamite, he would not wake his commander in Chief.

Finishing the last of his coffee, he examined the preliminary reports of RAF night attacks on numerous river crossing points on the Elbe, Leine, Main, Donau and Tauber.

Seeking out a refill, he waited as the orderly did his job. The document seemed encouraging, although initial reports of aircraft losses dented his enthusiasm. RAF Bomber Command had suffered fearful losses since the start of hostilities, from flak to sabotage, night-fighters to accidents. Losses were certainly exceeding the ability to replace, both in crews and aircraft.

USAAF squadrons would do their work in daylight. but they too were suffering high losses.

None the less, the Soviet advances were slowed by the Air force's efforts to interdict their logistic and support infrastructure, unless something hitherto unsuspected was causing the Soviets problem.

Drinking more coffee, he started to re-read the report, a useful habit he had acquired following a small error in his early staff days.

Movement caught Hood's eye, and he noticed the expansion of the Russian advance to the outskirts of Heilbronn.

'Stuttgart then?'

He posed the question without being able to confidently answer.

From the look of the allied dispositions, the Army Commander was protecting the Rhine in preference, whilst still holding as much of the Neckar River barrier as he could.

An extremely tired looking USAAF Major placed another air combat report in front of Hood, turning and walking away like a zombie.

'The staff are out on their feet here. We need to get the people rested.'

Immediately snorting at the words of his inner compassionate voice, his sensible and realistic side reminded him of a military maxim, the origin of which was lost in time.

'We can all rest when we are dead.'

In the meantime, there was a war to be won.

Hood downed the hot drink in one, hoping the caffeine rush would give him the kick start he still needed.

Skimming the new report, the Colonel noted with satisfaction that the Elbe bridges at Lauenburg were believed totally wrecked.

He assembled the paperwork and into the morning brief folder it went, and the tired officer went in search of yet more coffee.

<u>0514 hrs 15th August 1945, Heroldhausen-Eichenau Road, Germany.</u>

Allied forces – Fox Company, 2nd Battalion, 255th Infantry Regiment, Battalion HQ and HQ Battery, 861st Artillery Battalion, all of 63rd US Infantry Division, US 23 Corps, US 15th Army, 12th US Army Group.

Soviet Forces – 2nd and 3rd Battalions, Anti-Tank companies 179th Guards Rifle Regiment, 127th Guards Artillery Regiment, 59th Guards Rifle Division of 34th Guards Rifle Corps, 242nd Tank Brigade of 31st Tank Corps, all of 5th Guards Army of 2nd Red Banner Central European Front.

The soldiers of Fox Company had received the order to pull back, abandoning their positions between the two villages of Werdeck and Heroldhausen, covering the road south from

Beimbach. Despite suffering grievous casualties, the unit had not seen a single Soviet ground soldier from day one of the new war. None the less, just under half of the men alive on the 6th were still capable of carrying a rifle, the rest succumbing to air and artillery attack, either filling hospital beds or shallow graves.

Morale was low. 2nd/255th had advanced with the 12th Armored, only to be caught up in the debacle of Reichenberg, covering the retreat of the shattered CC'B'.

Yet again, with no enemy in sight, the company was ordered back.

Captain Pritchard consulted his map and drew his surviving commander's close.

"Regiment wants us back at Diembot soon as, securing the river crossing. No immediate threat is known, but they want us there by 0630 latest."

He made sure each of the six men could see where he was pointing.

"Once there, they want us to send vehicles down to here," he dabbed his finger at Eichenau, "Where some of our engineers are wiring the bridge. We bring some of them back and prep the Diembot Bridge for the same."

"I intend to go through Eichenau and pick up the engineers on our way. It's a better route and even though it's longer, we should make good time, plus we stay together. Questions?"

Five of the faces suggested nothing but compliance, all of them young and inexperienced. Only one seemed to have doubts.

"Sergeant Hässler, you don't agree?"

Long before the Russians had launched their attack, Hässler and Pritchard had hated each other.

One because he saw an incompetent officer who would some day cost men their lives, the other because he saw a German from the same breeding stock as put his father in a soldiers grave in the Great War.

"No Sir, I don't. This route is far and away the quickest to Diembot. Falling back through Eichenau leaves the road south to Diembot wide open. It's simply a bad idea, Captain."

169

Tact was never the German-Moravian's strong suit, particularly when it came to Pritchard.

"Don't agree, Sergeant?" in itself a veiled insult as Hässler was a Master-Sergeant and the battalion's top NCO.

"Right then, noted, Sergeant."

The Captain turned to face the others.

"That's that covered. We do it as stated, for the reasons stated, plus, it has the advantage of getting the engineers to their work quicker."

Rolling the map up, Pritchard indicated that the briefing was over and that his orders stood.

Hässler stood his ground none the less.

"Perhaps you could consider splitting your force then, Captain? Send the artillery boys to get the engineers, and drop Fox back down the quickest route?"

"Perhaps I could, Sergeant."

Ordinarily, Pritchard would have left it at that, openly undermining his NCO, as he did at every opportunity. This time he saw an opportunity of a different sort.

"Actually, that's not a bad idea for a change. You take your track and the boys of the MG platoon, and go straight to Diembot. I will take the rest of the company via Eichenau. If you get there before us you can start digging in and securing the bridge."

His look challenged the Master-Sergeant to disagree. For his part, Hässler could see the advantage of being out from under the idiot's feet, even if only for a moment, so he nodded his agreement in such a way as that no-one there thought he agreed for one moment.

"Oustanding."

Pritchard spoke in such a way as that no-one there thought he was changing his orders for any reason other than to put the NCO out in the cold.

That gets the kraut bastard out of my sight for a while.'

"OK, let's get the troops mounted up and moved out. Sergeant, you will remain and cover out withdrawal."

Looking at his watch he made a swift calculation.

"Ten minutes from the time the rear vehicle gets out of sight. Clear?"

170

The German-American smiled without smiling.

"Crystal, Captain," and turned on his heel leading the group out from the flimsy lean-to in which the meeting had been held.

The smaller man hawked and spat as the Captain shouted orders at the top of his voice, unnecessarily harrying those that were doing their best to strip down weapons and load up vehicles.

"Oy vey, but that man is the biggest schmuck I've seen since Uncle Solomon circumcised Rollo the Elephant at the Ringling Circus!"

The comment hit the spot intended. Hässler snorted spontaneously and was forced to wipe away the products of his nasal passages.

"Corporal Rosenberg, I agree with the sentiment but for a god-fearing man you are one hell of a lying bastard!"

The wiry little Jew held his hands up in mock horror.

"Feh! Not only do I have a commanding officer who is an idiot, but the Gentile Master Sergeant is calling me a liar! I did so have an Uncle Solomon, may he rest in peace."

"And did he circumcise an elephant at the circus?"

Rosenberg's face split from ear to ear.

"Would I lie to you?"

"Damn right you would, you yiddisher bastard! The whorehouse in Marseille?"

"As God is my witness, you have a memory for things don't you? Anyway, the place was schlock. Not good enough for a mentsh like you."

"That is not what I heard, Zack, as well you know. You're lying."

"OK, OK, I am lying. It was a Rhino."

The men in Headquarters Company were used to the constant sparring of this unusual duo, a friendship between opposites sparked by the extremes of military life.

As the two continued their bickering, Clayton Randolph, the unit's junior soldier, handed out the last of the coffee and left the verbal warriors to their business. The two watched the last halftrack disappear on the Heroldhausen-Eichenau road.

Rosenberg stood 'five foot and a mosquito's dick short', or at least that was how the six foot two inch NCO put it.

Combat had moulded them into a team, and set in place a friendship that only death could sunder.

"Talk English. I don't understand your Jewish speak."

Springing to attention the diminutive figure threw up a formal salute.

"Jawohl, Herr Feldwebel."

Hässler went to cuff him playfully but the Corporal ducked away, picking up his pack and slinging it aboard 'Liberty', the half-track they had all called home since they had landed in Europe.

Cigarettes lit, no sound came from the tired men as they waited for the clock to count down.

Something didn't feel right to the Master Sergeant, so he kept his men in position beyond the ten minutes, watching and ready for action.

Looking at the watch, he decided fifteen was enough and that his senses had let him down for once.

The troops loaded up quickly, and in less than two minutes, the last vehicles of 2nd Battalion were on the road to Diembot.

M5A1 halftracks were not the quietest of vehicles, but the sound of explosions and gunfire rose over the top of the roar of 7.4 litre Red-B engines at high revs.

Hässler signalled a halt, and the four vehicles smoothly slipped into cover, leaving the road empty.

Randolph was behind the mounted .50cal, scanning the road ahead and the woods to the right. Beside him stood the American-German, both men's senses straining to the limit. At the rear of the track, Rosenberg traversed his .30cal very deliberately, checking the undergrowth beyond his sights for the slightest sign of movement.

Orienting themselves on the noise, the men in the small convoy quickly placed the shooting to their south-east.

Rosenberg spat, not turning from his field of responsibility, and threw a question at the Master-Sergeant.

172

"Pritchard?"

"You can bet your kosher ass on it."

Thus far, the 179th Guards Rifle Regiment had advanced without contact. Since the blood-letting of Reichenburg, only a few minor skirmishes had occurred, claiming a life here, two there.

Moving forward towards his allotted targets, the villages of Leibesdorf and Seibotenberg had fallen silently, so Colonel Artem'yev had split his force, sending his 1st and 3rd Battalions to Elpershofen and Hessenau respectively, with 3rd Battalion additionally tasked to push out to the south-east towards Diembot if circumstances permitted.

Employing his headquarters alongside the savaged 2nd Battalion as a reserve, he moved behind them, and to the south-east. Artem'yev intended to remain out of trouble unless summoned, or 3rd Battalion was ready to attack Diembot.

His men moved swiftly through the woods to the south-east of Seibotenberg, rapidly crossing one hundred metres of open ground before again secreting themselves in dense wood to the south of Heroldhausen.

Scouts at the head of the unit gave warning and the guardsmen deployed instinctively, moving into cover along the edge of the north-south road that cut through the woods.

Despite the hell it had endured in Rottenburg, the179th was still a crack unit and it showed, its calm veterans speedily dropping out of sight, ready to fire if called upon or to remain silent and, if necessary, let the threat pass.

Artem'yev was not at the front of the column, so the decisions were left to an experienced Captain commanding the the advance guard.

Rushing to the southernmost end of his line, the Captain assessed the enemy force.

'Ten, no, twelve vehicles.'

He slapped one of his anti-tank gunners on the shoulder. The man looked at his commander, following the simple hand signals and whispered instructions.

"Komarov, lead vehicle, stop him there."

173

The hands indicated where the officer wished the ambush to be sprung. A nod acknowledged the order and confirmed understanding. The man slipped to one side with his number two, readying the panzershreck he had proudly carried with him since liberating it at Freistadt in May that year.

A simple nod to the other panzershreck pair was all that was needed. They knew enough to hold until the first vehicle was dead before selecting another down the line. There was no time to move northwards so someone at the end of the line would have to close the door.

A veteran Starshy Serzhant was already setting in place an act to do just that.

Pritchard was everything Hässler thought he was, but of all his faults, his incompetence was the major player that afternoon.

No screening vehicle was moving ahead of the column and no distances ordered between vehicles. In fact, the whole group was moving in as unmilitary a fashion as it was possible to imagine. The sole exception was the manned .50cals on the half-tracks.

Fox Company never had a chance.

A flash caught the lead gunner's eye, and his screamed warning coincided with the detonation of a warhead on the thin strip of metal to the right of the driver's vision slit.

The driver, the Corporal in the front passenger seat and the gunner, were instantly transformed into unrecognisable meat, the remainder of the crew suffering injuries ranging from flash burns to blast effects. Only one other fatality occurred in the leading half-track, the youngest man in the company horribly slain by a lump of ragged bone from the unfortunate driver. As he coughed his life out through the gaping wound in his neck, the remainder of the crew gathered their senses and tried to debus.

Not a man touched the ground alive, as submachine guns and DPs flayed them one by one.

As the lead vehicle was being professionally exterminated, the ambushing line erupted, the halftracks being

174

destroyed by grenades, anti-tank rifles and the other panzerschreck.

At the rear of the column, the Starshy Serzhant's group had managed to get three out of six grenades into the body of the rearmost vehicle.

It, and its crew, burned fiercely.

Rifles played their part, neatly picking off the machine gunners as they tried to beat off the attack. Over half the gunners never fired a shot; the rest quickly followed their comrades into blackness without being effective.

An experienced Pfc got his BAR working and laid low two guardsmen who were closing up with teller mines. Neither was killed outright, but neither would see the following morning.

The Pfc heard the thump beside him but never felt the grenade fragments that ripped the life from him.

In the third track, the sole casualty so far was the gunner, shot through the neck and hanging from the MG ring, dripping rivers of blood down the olive green flank of the halftrack.

Pritchard knew he was going to die and his bladder and bowels evacuated as his young soldiers looked to him for leadership.

A grenade dropped into the back of the vehicle and the American soldiers were divided into two groups by the fickle nature of high explosive. One group died, the other didn't.

Those who had remained in the vehicle lived, although all were wounded. The Russian who threw the grenade had used a German stick grenade, and was what saved them. The Stielhandgranate was dependent on blast for its effectiveness although the mechanism and casing caused some shrapnel wounds in this instance.

Those who bailed out died in the act of escaping the burst, all except Pritchard, who had shown amazing agility.

His wounds were extreme, a burst of PPSH smashing across his legs as he dived over the side, almost severing both his legs at his ruined knees. A single bullet neatly amputated his left thumb and another struck his jaw, breaking the strong bone and lodging in the bottom of his left eye. The officer hit the ground

175

hard and bounced onto his back, adding a broken left wrist to the litany of injuries.

His bestial screams surmounted all the sounds of battle.

In Track 2, a young sergeant got the back door open and evacuated the three survivors, using his physical strength and harsh words in equal measure.

Sparing a quick and unsympathetic look at his commander, he organised his shocked men into action.

The comparative safety of the woods seemed closer where he was, as the undergrowth had advanced more than elsewhere, and he could fall back into the trees to the east.

"OK boys, pull your smokes and put them down"

Each man he touched and pointed, indicating where he wished the smoke to go.

"On three, ok? One, two, three!"

Four grenades sailed as directed.

Three plumes of grey smoke slowly erupted, the fourth bringing forth whitish-yellow smoke and high-pitched screams.

The man had thrown a phosphorous grenade instead of smoke. It had hit the road and bounced, and was at face level when it went off. The hideously injured and still burning Komarov added his animal cries to those of Pritchard.

Here and there, hands started to rise as shocked and stunned GI's gave up the unequal fight, all except the survivors of Track 2, who made their burst for freedom. They all fell short of the tree line. albeit by only a few feet, riddled with bullets.

Individual Russians started shooting at the surrendering soldiers, and the fighting picked up in intensity again.

One enterprising DP gunner dropped flat on the road at the rear of the column, and pumped bullet after bullet into the exposed soldiers.

Soon, only the mournful cries of the hideously wounded rent the air, and unsympathetic guardsmen moved amongst them dispatching each with a bullet or the thrust of a bayonet.

It was only Pritchard's higher piercing screams that kept the killer's at bay, so awful were they.

Colonel Artem'yev arrived, panting after sprinting forward to command his men.

176

Gesturing to one of his young soldiers, he sent mercy to the wounded American.

Two bayonet thrusts and the screams ceased, although Pritchard remained conscious for some time after, he felt no pain and slipped quietly away to answer to a higher authority for his incompetence.

That left only Komarov's cries filling the senses.

Three medical orderlies were trying to do what they could to a man with no face, and whose chest and arms had been burnt down to the bone.

A barked order and simple gesture moved them away from their charge.

Two shots rang out and one more kill was made. The screaming stopped.

The executioner lowered his head, in reverent salute to the comrade he had just granted the mercy of death.

Artem'yev calmly re-holstered his pistol and moved off to leave Komarov's comrades to do what they could to honour their friend's remains.

Every American lay dead upon the road or in the vehicles, either slain in combat or dispatched when wounded or surrendered, testament to the brutal efficiency of his warrior's.

The pride he felt at his men's conduct and skill in the ambush did not remove the awful image of Komarov, and the tough Colonel unashamedly spilt his lunch upon the ground, retching until nothing came but air.

The firing stopped, and the Master Sergeant was veteran enough to understand that the sounds of only Russian weapons closing the action meant just one thing; Pritchard had been defeated and was probably running to the river.

"No time for subtlety, let's roll!"

Performing hand signals for the benefit of the other vehicles, Hässler was thrown about as 'Liberty' leapt forward and picked up speed, the others falling in behind.

Near Diembot, all was confusion.

An ad hoc aid unit, formed of personnel from the 363rd Medical Battalion, was loading up wounded GI's and German civilians, the sounds of nearby battle lending speed to their efforts.

Security was provided by a handful of green replacements that had been destined for the 263rd Engineers, but were now officially attached to the medical group as protective infantry.

Covering one route was Private Homer Laidlaw, who manned a .50cal M2 machine-gun and imagined himself holding back the whole Soviet army for weeks, mentally seeing the red hordes buckle under his fire. He was eighteen years old, nineteen on Thursday, as he had proudly informed the nurses in the aid post.

John Evans, his number two, was an equally beardless youth, who only smoked to make his voice lower. His eyes were sharper, and his hearing more acute, and it was he who shouted a warning, readying the belt of APIT rounds the pair had loaded into their fearsome weapon.

Coming from the direction of Werdeck, an armoured vehicle burst from the woods, driving hard and fast with no other purpose apparent than to ride down the two youths.

Laidlaw's great-grand pappy had been honoured in the Union cause at Chickamauga, and the family never stopped talking about it.

Now was his chance.

The .50cal burst into life, tracers betraying his wayward fire. Showing a calm well in excess of his year, he walked the bursts into the vehicle, using the star as an aiming point and was rewarded with hits.

APITs, or Armour-Piercing Incendiary Tracer rounds, were designed for soft skinned and lightly armoured vehicles, and at the five hundred metre range at which they first engaged the vehicle, their penetration exceeded the armour thickness of the target.

The half-track slowed and wobbled, before ramming and riding up upon a tree stump, stopping abruptly, and sending one man flying forward to bounce on the unforgiving road.

178

The damaged form tried to rise, but Evans picked up his Garand. The beardless youth had spent much of his youth potting squirrels, so he found that putting a bullet into a large man was easy enough.

The two patted themselves on the shoulders until they saw three other vehicles rounding the bend.

They heard screams and believed they were coming from those left alive in the smoking vehicle. That was before Evans was propelled forwards into the earth by a body blow, as a US medical Lieutenant barrelled into him.

"What have you done? You stupid bastards! Oh fuck, you stupid bastards."

Both boys looked at the red-faced officer, and at the target,

Where once there was an enemy vehicle, now stood an American half-track.

Where once there was a red star as a point of aim, now clearly visible was a muddy white star.

As both Laidlaw and Evans started to realise what they had done, the paint started to blister as the fuel ignited by the incendiaries spread through and under the vehicle, so they failed to see the name 'Liberty' slip like molten metal off her side.

The other halftracks caught up and started to deploy to attack the enemy force, before realising that a tragedy had occurred.

No further shots were exchanged, and men sprinted to get other men out of a rapidly spreading fire.

Evans remained head down on the ground, sobbing uselessly, never to take up a weapon again in his life.

Laidlaw took off with all the vigour and commitment of his years, and plunged into the burning halftrack.

He laid hands on one olive drab clad figure and pulled him clear, the medical Lieutenant taking the dead man and dropping him to one side. Both pushed back in to the flames and smoke, each returning with a bundle of torn and burnt flesh. The flames grew even higher and the Lieutenant went no more, kneeling to tend to the unconscious and bloody Rosenberg.

179

Laidlaw took a deep breath and threw himself into the vehicle, his flesh searing and blistering as his hands sought one more soul to save.

He grabbed at something and pulled. It remained stuck. He took a better hold and pulled backwards with all his strength, freeing the man, sliding at speed to the back of the halftrack until he fell out the rear door, bringing Randolph out on top of him.

It was fortunate that the young private was unconscious, otherwise the pain of being wrenched free of his crushed and burnt legs would have been too much to bear. His arms were deeply burned where they had lain in burning fuel but his torso and face showed only mild signs of the heat that had claimed everyone else in the vehicle.

More medical staff arrived and, although some recoiled from the horror before them, they worked the miracle and kept the grievously wounded man alive.

No one saw Laidlaw throw himself back into the halftrack, determined to save one more.

Perhaps, unfortunately, rather than going on his gut instinct, the medical Lieutenant, Acting Captain Thomas Goulding, discussed the matter with his Commanding officer at the first opportunity, and received clear guidance not to make any recommendations on the matter, as the boy's conduct, brave as it clearly had been, was obviously done out of grief and atonement rather than raw courage.

"And that's an order, Goulding"

The medical unit departed the area before the halftrack had burned out, and it was left to a Soviet artillery unit to pause long enough to remove the human detritus from the wreck and slip it all into a shallow grave.

Only three men were saved from 'Liberty'.

Randolph would never have survived his terrible injuries without the instant medical intervention of Goulding and his medics. The hideously injured young man was removed to a waiting ambulance where another team set to work.

Evans had shot sure and the bullet had struck Hässler in the shoulder as he started to rise, snapping his collar bone and

180

adding to the multiple fractures sustained when his body bounced on the road. His journey from the spot where he lay on the road to the ambulance that arrived to spirit him away, was eased by numerous splints and more morphine.

Rosenberg had been propelled towards the front of the vehicle when it struck the tree trunk, his face smashing into the flat edge of Randolph's machine-gun cupola, removing teeth and crushing bone. His unconscious body had started to suffer burns, until he was pulled clear by Goulding.

Stabilised quickly, he was loaded into the same vehicle as his friend, and both left the field, heading for the comparative safety of the new American lines.

Fox Company had ceased to exist.

0958 hrs, 15th August 1945, Veersebrück, Germany.

The 49th Guards Rifle Regiment slipped through the positions held by the exhausted and bloodied soldiers of the 360th Rifle Division, and headed south to Rotenburg.

A force from 2nd Guards Tank Corps had displaced the defenders of Scheeßel, and the 11th Guards Army Commander, Nikitovich, wanted Rotenburg quickly, in order to trap whatever units the enemy had to the east. A southern approach would be made by forces of the newly-arrived second wave formation, the 4th Tank Army. Its 22nd Tank Corps was sending a force northwards to pinch out Rotenburg, closing the jaws on the enemy troops to the east.

Time was of the essence, and the Corps Commander ordered the 49th to Rotenburg by the most direct route.

It was not without risk, especially as it placed the Soviet troops on the same side of the Wümme River as their quarry. Normally a modest waterway, the recent rains had swollen the Wümme to twice the size, and defensive work on the banks, both from the previous conflict and more recent additions, had created an obstacle of note.

At Scheeßel, the newly promoted Major Deniken, now commander of the much depleted 49th Regiment, sought out the 4th Guards Tanks' commander, and requested support from the man. Despite having ground to a halt with fuel supply issues, the Tank Colonel understood the situation perfectly and made arrangements for fuel to be siphoned from a number of vehicles, providing a back up force of ten T/34's and two SPAA vehicles for Deniken's advance.

The concussion he had received at Heilingenthal was almost past, but his arm wound still ached, and the healing process was constantly disrupted by his inability to rest.

Taking leave of the Tank officer, he brought together his command group and organised the move, so that he would be ready the moment the tanks were provisioned.

Kriks saluted and stepped to one side as the infantry Major left the room, watching the man depart before he entered the HQ and offered his commander a German canteen without announcing its contents.

Yarishlov sniffed cautiously and was greeted with the sweet smell of peach schnapps. He took a small sip before handing it back to his senior NCO.

Lighting up two cigarettes, the Starshina gestured in the direction of the departing Major.

"That man looks like he knows his business, Comrade Polkovnik."

Taking the cigarette, Yarishlov could only agree.

"He has the look for sure, and he wears the Gold Star, so he has seen his combat time, and done well it seems. We just discussed his mission, and I am going to give him a helping hand."

Yarishlov extended his hand to illustrate the point, which Kriks also interpreted as an opportunity to press the canteen into his Colonel's palm again.

With a shake of his head, the offer was refused.

"A clear head is needed. Maybe later, if you manage to leave any, Comrade."

In mock subservience, Kriks crashed to attention.

"It shall be as the Comrade Polkovnik directs, Comrade Polkovnik."

"Hmmm," was all Yarishlov could muster by way of reply, as he was concentrating on the map in his hand.

182

Outside, there was a hive of activity, as officers moved to obey the order and directed the siphoning of fuel from vehicles, but only after ensuring the non-runners were well hidden and properly positioned in the event of an enemy counter-attack.

Kriks stubbed out his cigarette on the window sill as he took in the scene.

"Comrade Polkovnik. I notice your tank is being fuelled. Are you planning to go on this outing too?"

Folding the paper carefully, and sliding it into his map case, Yarishlov considered his reply carefully.

"Starshina Kriks. I have been entrusted with a brand new vehicle and have yet to use it. The Corps commander might accuse me of avoiding the action if I don't give him a report soon. And that could mean you end up with a new Polkovnik, who might be less tolerant of your little ways!"

The senior NCO smiled broadly.

"Then I will go and hurry matters along, in order to save you from such accusations, Comrade Polkovnik", and punctuated his departure with a final swig from his liberated flask, "Your health, and long may you remain our understanding commander."

The Soviet force set off south, preceded by Deniken's depleted reconnaissance unit, and flanked by special platoons thrown together for the purpose. Immediately behind came the mixed force of armour, flak and mortars that could immediately swing into the support of the forward infantry units.

The recon troopers disappeared from view quite quickly, absorbed by the woods into which they drove at high speed.

3rd Battalion, under the trustworthy Grabin, was oriented to the east of the main road, accepting slower progress south in exchange for increased protection to the flank of the main force. A battalion in name only, 3rd comprised no more than one hundred and sixty fit soldiers, taken from all parts of the regiment.

183

Fig #37 - Veeresebruck dispositions.

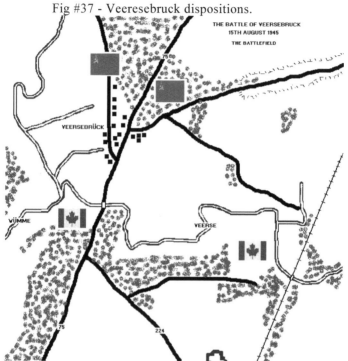

1st Battalion had been butchered during the attack on Westergellersen and its survivors were moved into the 2nd Battalion, which had fared better during its own assault on neighbouring Südergellersen and now provided the main force of the 49th Guards Rifle Regiment.

Deniken's HQ group consisted of a handful of staff officers, an automatic weapons laden headquarters infantry company, and the relatively unblooded mortar platoon, all other elements having been destroyed, or their remnants absorbed into 3rd Battalion.

From what Deniken could gather, his division would not be called upon further once this mission was out of the way, and a time of recuperation and reinforcement would follow. Not before time, as 36th Guards Rifle Corps had suffered horrendous casualties since the start of hostilities.

184

The sudden crack of a high-velocity weapon reached their ears over the drone of vehicle engines, telling Deniken that the dying was not yet over. Deeper explosions and the rattling of automatic fire followed.

Lead elements of the 2nd Battalion had reached the main body of the woods and immediately deployed from their vehicles, securing the edge, and ensuring the units behind could safely advance.

Deniken's arrival with the 2nd coincided with the erratic return of one of his remaining BA-64 armoured cars.

The Lieutenant commanding the recon troop pointed out that his radio had been destroyed, lifting a bloodied arm as best he could to indicate the entry hole of solid shot in the hull front. He dropped to one knee and spread out the map he was holding, rapidly relating what had happened to the lead unit.

Deniken overhead it all as he strode up, the wounded officer's voice loud, accentuated with pain and the excitement of battle.

The upshot of it was that the other armoured car had run over a mine and that the infantry had gone to ground either side of the road, receiving casualties from enemy machine-guns as they deployed.

The surviving BA-64 had manoeuvred quickly, but an anti-tank gun had made a hit, destroying their radio and wounding the driver, who was being retrieved from his vehicle even as the young officer passed on his information.

Not wishing to interrupt, Deniken stood back and let the Captain from 2nd glean all he could.

Consulting his own map, he listened in, making his own notes on likely anti-tank positions and machine-gun nests.

Without doubt, the enemy were sat astride the bridge in some strength, and had no intention of moving.

Walking away to his own command group, the growing racket of an armoured vehicle distracted him and he looked up to see the Tank Colonel approaching.

The tank, he wasn't sure exactly what type it was, halted and the officer dropped swiftly to the ground, followed by a submachine gun toting NCO who adopted the position of bodyguard.

Exchanging casual salutes, Deniken briefed Yarishlov in on the latest developments.

A moment's silence passed as each looked at the alternatives.

"The rail bridge, Comrade Polkovnik?"

Yarishlov could only agree with a nod.

"Get your other infantry element mounted up on my tanks and I will rush it. I take it you will do a set-piece holding action against the bridge here, Mayor?"

"Yes, I think so, Comrade Polkovnik. I will get my men in position as quickly as possible, get some mortar rounds on them, and pin them in place. Command have been very specific about the time we are to have secured Rotenburg by", and with more than a hint of sarcasm, "Although less specific about the enemy sat in our way."

With a disarming smile, Yarishlov ventured his opinion.

"That is why we frontline soldiers take our precautions, is it not?"

It was Deniken's turn to nod.

Returning to his map, Yarishlov considered matters further.

"I suggest you start immediately, Comrade Mayor, as will I, once your men are aboard my tanks. When I am at the bridge, the rest of your men can push up and secure it. I will leave some support for them, say two tanks, but I will turn quickly and cut into this lot from the flank."

The Major followed the plan on his own map. It was simple but effective.

"If needed, make sure your mortars can put down some smoke to mask my approach clear? On your own initiative, or if I request it."

"Yes Comrade Polkovnik. My mortars have four smoke rounds each."

Yarishlov cocked an eyebrow at the infantry Major, impressed that the man had such knowledge at his fingertips.

Deniken almost blushed under the complementary scrutiny.

"What can I say, Comrade Polkovnik, counting mortar shells is my only vice."

Kriks, taking a sip from his canteen, spluttered, caught unawares by the man's humour.

Yarishlov and Deniken exchanged grins before swiftly moving back to business.

"Radios and codes. This one we will call Ivan," he indicated first the road bridge before sliding his finger to the railway bridge, "And this one Boris. Your radio sign is?"

"Narot. Narot-three-one, Comrade Polkovnik."

"Sable for me. Sable-seven-one."

"My radio is misbehaving, so I suggest back-up signals, Comrade Polkovnik. I have a lot of green flares at the moment, so shall we say two greens if the circumstances are right and I decide to press the position to move them off the bridge before you get there."

"Excellent, so if I need your smoke I will launch two blue as a back-up to the radio. Let my force take the initial strain here, so don't risk your men unnecessarily. My tanks...." Yarishlov ground to a halt in mid sentence, "Apologies Comrade, I know a good officer when I see one. Right, let us to the business of the day, Comrade Mayor. I will ensure 22nd Tanks know your flare signals and call-signs."

Salutes were exchanged and both officers went their separate ways as the clouds started to grow dark and drop their heavy loads on the battlefield.

The defenders were a hastily cobbled together force of Canadians from the 1st Canadian Infantry Division. A savaged company of the Loyal Edmonton Regiment of the 2nd Infantry Brigade, until recently assigned to the extreme left flank to join up to the Carleton & Yorks of the 3rd Brigade, sat astride the road bridge. They were complemented by two 6pdr anti-tank guns that they had managed to drag back with them.

Fig #38- Veeresbruck assault.

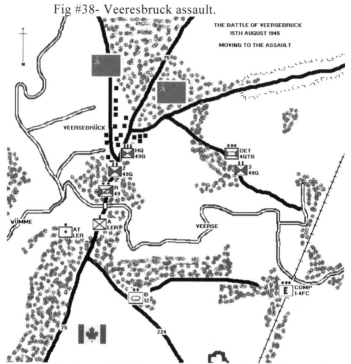

At the rail bridge was a scratch force of men from the 1st and 4th Field Companies, engineers who were tasked with ripping down the structure with their expertise alone, explosives being a medium of distant memory.

Supporting the two defensive points were five Shermans of the French-Canadian 12th [Three Rivers] Armoured Regiment, vehicles that all showed the scars of recent combat.

Each bridge had one tank close-in, the three vehicle section dwelling in between, ready to respond to wherever the crisis was worst.

Deniken's mortars started to bring down their barrage on the Canadian positions, accompanied by machine-gun and rifle fire. A 6-pdr anti-tank gun spat shells back and wiped out a Maxim crew, just before two mortars shells dropped from the sky, wrecking both gun and crew.

Visibility dropped dramatically as the weak sun disappeared and the murky day became a rainstorm of monumental ferocity.

Deniken pushed his lead elements closer to the Veerse River so that they could continue to bring down fire on the defenders who, for their part, were just as decisive in defence. After a while, the two forces had closed up to within one hundred metres, with the swelling river in between, and still not close enough to truly see what each was firing at. Casualties still occurred on both sides, as speculative shots found warm flesh, more against the Soviet infantry by dint of their larger numbers.

Yarishlov's group, skirting the woods and advancing slowly, suddenly found the going getting very heavy.

'Too slow, too damn slow!'

The experienced tank colonel reacted instinctively, switching his force to the railway line, accepting the disadvantages of a column formation and off-setting them for the advantages of getting closer quicker. The violent downpour helped the Soviet force deploy undetected, even at the relatively modest distance of three hundred metres, the sound of the rain successfully obscuring the noise of approaching armoured vehicles, at least until it was too late.

Engineers labouring in heavy rain dropped to the ground as the leading tank's hull machine gun found targets.

Even then, some of the troops clustered around the rail bridge did not fully understand the nature of the sounds that were reaching their ears.

The Sherman tank crew, woken from their slumber by a soaked and agitated gunner, got their tank ready for action, as their commander tried to understand what he was hearing and seeing.

Grey shapes in the rain materialised into enemy tanks, and he quickly called range and angle bearings for his extremely unhappy gunner before alerting the central tank troop by radio.

Taking his angst out on the enemy, the dripping Lance-Corporal Blanc made sure his first round hit the target, stripping away the front hull hatch that had been opened to permit the now-dead tank driver to see where he was going.

The T34 slewed quickly and stopped, sending its infantry riders flying, and leaving the offside completely exposed to the second round. Wheels and pieces of track flew off as the armour-piercing shot wrecked the rear drive sprocket and severed the track.

Other T34's sought out the Sherman and the commander decided to move off before the gunner could get a third and decisive hit.

Dropping back and right to the secondary position he had spotted only that morning, hasty shots flew into the former hiding place, marking the quality of his decision.

If anything, the rain had intensified, and the damaged Soviet tank could only just be observed from their second position. The young sergeant received a timely reminder that observation is a two-way thing when the T34 got off a well-aimed shot, the glowing metal striking the side a glancing blow before flying off into the field beyond.

His own tank halted in its new firing position and he gave the order to fire.

The delay was such that he repeated his order and looked across to his gunner.

"Just getting it right, Maurice. Watch this and give me a medal."

The 75mm gun spat out its shell and it tracked in through the driver's broken hatch and exploded within the tank.

"Viens m'enculer, Guillame!"

Sergeant Revel leant across and slapped his gunner on the shoulder.

Lance-Corporal Blanc wanted to bask in the moment but couldn't, as other indistinct shapes clarified into Soviet tanks that pushed past the dead T34.

"Merde!"

There was nothing the Canadian tankers could do to stop the massacre of the engineer troops on the bridge, except to try and kill as many T34's as possible.

Blanc took a deep breath and engaged the latest target, muttering as his round sailed closely past its turret.

A deafening clang took away the Canadian crew's senses, as an 85mm shot clipped the turret side.

Shaking his head, Revel tried to focus but couldn't, as much a product of the shells effect on his ears and brain as the damage it had wrought on his commanders optics. Blanc retained sufficient sensibility to successfully engage the leading tank, which halted immediately, the surviving two crew members debussing straight into small arms fire from the surviving vengeful engineers.

Another loud clang indicated a Russian hit, this time clipping the front of the tank on the edge above the hull gunner position. The shock caused him to partially evacuate his bowels, but he stuck to his job, although petrified, bursts of .30cal seeking out the Russian soldiers hopping from position to position.

The rain intensified but grew patchy, sometimes hiding the Soviets completely, other times offering up enough of a view for a 75mm shell to follow.

The Sherman relocated for a third time, the new position almost hugging the western edge of the rail track.

A second T34 was hit and knocked out, a small fire apparent as the crew bailed out, all surviving the reduced small arms fire from the beaten engineers.

Revel regained his senses and noted the damage to his optics. Opening his hatch, he stuck his head out and brought his field glasses up to his eyes.

"Take the one by the carrier, Guillame! Left turret a few degrees!"

The turret traversed a small distance and locked on the target tank.

The turret crew became aware that the tank was turning as the driver started to panic.

"Non! Arrête!"

Blanc swivelled his turret, ready to loose a shot once the damn fool driver had finished jinking the tank, whilst Revel spoke gently down his intercom, trying to calm the young driver.

The Sherman stopped dead, nearside flat on to the enemy.

Both guns fired together and both shells hit their intended target. The 75mm shot struck the glacis plate and ricocheted off into the rain clouds above, leaving a gleaming silver scar on the brand-new tank.

The 100mm shell struck the side of the Sherman immediately to the left of the driving position, entered the tank with ease, before exiting almost millimetre perfect through the same position on the offside.

Its path took it directly through both driver and machine-gunner.

The smell of tortured metal and burning competed with the sickly smells of blood and gristle, all invading their every sense.

"Get out, everyone get out!"

Revel pulled himself up through the hatch and rolled onto the rear deck, scrabbling around to lie in the lee of the turret. Blanc rolled on top of him and dropped to the ground below. Henchoz, the loader, desperate to escape, misjudged his exit and cracked his head on the unforgiving metal rim, the impact filling his eyes with blood and dropping him stunned to the floor of the vehicle.

The strike of another Soviet shell threw Revel onto the ground and silenced the cries of the petrified blinded man left in the tank.

Both survivors watched as the enemy tank moved on over the bridge to engage the three Sherman reinforcements that Revel had summoned, wincing as it killed each in turn, shaking off hits without sustaining any apparent harm. The final vehicle it destroyed burst into flames immediately, and the two Canadians witnessed a blazing survivor running blindly around the battlefield as his flesh dropped off, until a merciful burst of bullets from the enemy tank put an end to his misery.

192

They were broken men, reduced to pitiful creatures by the death and destruction all around them.

Safety was their prime concern, their only concern.

Revel and Blanc slithered across the sodden ground and slipped under their knocked-out tank, seeking both a respite from the driving rain as well as cover from whatever horrors the Russians would bring next.

Yarishlov saw no need to bother his infantry commander with flares as the rain was doing an excellent job in masking his approach.

A single Canadian tank was withdrawing rapidly, laden with men desperate to escape the inevitable.

Two shells from Yarishlov's T44 turned it into a fiery beacon that burned for many hours.

Caught between the guardsmen north of the river, and the newly arrived armoured force, the fight went out of most of the Canadian infantry.

Hands were raised, and only a few stalwarts scampered away to fight another day.

Major Deniken led his men forward, detailing some to take the prisoners under guard, whilst others were sent in search of intelligence.

An extremely well camouflaged position was located, betrayed mainly by the sounds of pain coming from within. The dry and warm first aid post contained the Canadian wounded, and Deniken ordered that all Soviet wounded and medical supplies should be brought to the same spot. Within minutes, a Russian doctor and a Canadian doctor were operating side by side, fighting to save the life of a sergeant who would, despite their extraordinarily skilled efforts, never see the shores of Canada again.

Yarishlov surrendered to the latest offer of the schnapps, having just reoriented the 22nd's units, sending them westwards to provide security whilst his tanks and the infantry sorted themselves out.

"Five kills, Comrade Polkovnik. Your report on the worth of your tank should make interesting reading."

193

Kriks took the flask back and swigged another mouthful, belching in satisfied fashion, as the fiery liquid disappeared into his belly.

"That gun, Stefan. Would that we had had the beast when the German Panteras ruled our world eh?"

The Starshina could only nod.

"I thought your gunner did excellently well, Comrade Polkovnik. Perhaps immediate leave as a reward?"

"You are going nowhere, Starshina Kriks." Yarishlov spoke with mock sternness, and his face split into a tell-tale grin, which he accompanied with a hearty back-slap, spilling some of Kriks' precious liquid.

"You did do well though, so maybe the General will consider it when I write it up, eh?"

Yarishlov stretched, suddenly extremely weary and aware that he had not slept for many hours.

"Do we have enough fuel to do the rounds?"

"Barely enough left to manoeuvre if they counter-attack, Comrade Polkovnik."

"In which case, I will beg a vehicle from our infantry cousins, go and check the men at the rail bridge, and then find time to sleep before the fuel trucks arrive."

Yarishlov wandered out to locate Deniken, only to find the infantry officer with a few of his men, tinkering with a Canadian jeep that had seen better days.

As the Colonel was about to speak, the engine roared into life and a very smug looking Senior Sergeant emerged from under the bonnet to the accompaniment of cheers and much back-slapping.

The Major acknowledged the approach of his superior with a casual but respectful salute, returned in the same fashion by Yarishlov.

"Comrade Mayor! I was about to ask if you had a vehicle I could borrow to go and see to my men by the rail bridge. Seems that you have one ready for me."

Deniken recognised the comments for what they were.

"Unless the Comrade Polkovnik intends to pull rank on me, might I suggest we go together?"

194

Yarishlov dropped his backside into the front passenger's seat without another word.

The Major whispered to a tough looking Starshina who nodded and disappeared off on whatever mission Deniken had entrusted him with. Two other men were selected with the wave of a hand and climbed into the back of the jeep, their PPSH submachine guns providing security for the two officers.

Deniken graunched the gears, causing his superior officer to cast an enquiring glance at his new driver.

"Have you driven one of these before, Comrade Mayor?"

The grinding of anguished metal indicated another gear shift.

"Never, Comrade Yarishlov. We can discover its capabilities together."

Yarishlov punched Deniken's arm in a comradely fashion, very much approving of the infantryman's humour and style.

"It's your capabilities that worry me, Comrade!"

The jeep leapt forward, almost losing the two security troops over the back, bringing the sound of barely-controlled oaths questioning the parentage of their leader. The canvas roof and sides that normally kept the weather off the passengers had been removed by its previous owners, so all four were lashed by the downpour as they bore down on the rail bridge.

The jeep hit a small hole and literally flew out the other side, crashing down on its tough suspension, and firing mud in all directions as the wheels sought traction. The vehicle was sliding now, its rear almost racing with the front, heading sideways towards a stout tree stump.

Yarishlov, as befitted his rank, said nothing and contented himself with reciting a silent prayer.

Deniken crashed down a gear and the jeep surged away, resuming its progress towards the bridge.

"Do you have any driving credentials, Deniken?" his blanched face betraying his concern.

Deniken grinned from ear to ear.

195

"None worth speaking of, Comrade Polkovnik!"

Regaining his composure, Yarishlov struck back.

"That I can believe, Comrade Mayor. I was safer at Kursk!"

Fig #39 - Veersebruck - Key positions.

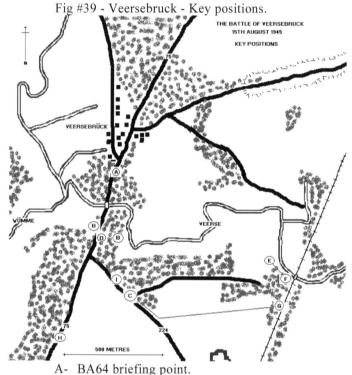

A- BA64 briefing point.
B- 6-pdr anti-tank gun.
C- Three tank reserve. Initial position.
D- Single Sherman for road bridge defence.
E- Revel's Sherman. Initial position.
F- Revel's Sherman. Final position.
G- Three tank reserve. Deployment.
H- Road bridge defence tank destroyed in this position.
I- Camouflaged first aid post.

196

Grabin greeted the arrivals, unsure what was giving the two senior officers their lively, almost excited air, and conducted them to a simple wooden structure that provided some shelter from the rain. Here he made his report before Yarishlov moved on to check out his two tanks.

Deniken and he had already agreed that the armour would remain with Grabin's unit until the 2nd Guards moved off again.

Returning to the jeep, the rain suddenly intensified to a previously unseen level and Yarishov ran quickly to a tree, under whose spreading branches he sought cover.

A previous tenant had installed a small waterproof sheet in the low lying branches, and its protection was welcome.

Sufficiently sheltered, he took the option of a quiet cigarette by himself. He inspected the knocked out Sherman tank from the relatively close distance, promising to have a better look once the rain had abated.

Leaning up against the main trunk and using a secondary growth to support his back, he relaxed. Drawing the rich smoke into his lungs, he silently reflected on the past hour, past day, past week, past...

He fell asleep.

Revel was in his mother's close embrace, but all was not well. Hugging him tightly to her body, she was scrambling through a sodden rabbit warren, ever decreasing in diameter, jamming her son's body between her and the wall of the burrow.

The water ran in strong streams, washing up over his face, causing him to cough, as it prevented him from breathing, or shouting, or crying.

His mother gripped him more tightly, battling further into the warren, ignoring its decreasing dimensions, plunging on to the safety it offered her and her son.

She pushed on, seemingly unaware that she was pressing the breath from her son's body.

197

The glistening brown walls of the warren seemed to press in of their own accord, further restricting Revel's capacity to draw breath.

'Maman! Maman! Je ne peux pas respire, Maman!'

He woke up.

Yarishlov became aware of a high-pitched scream; a strangely strangled and watery scream.

Without a doubt, it was the scream of someone experiencing the extremes of terror.

He was immediately wide-eyed and grabbing at his pistol holster.

The rain was still falling heavily but seemed to be striking the soil softly; either that or the sounds of panic took precedence in his mind. He dropped to one knee and surveyed the scene around him.

Nothing.

'Check again, you fool'.

He looked around once more, trying hard to locate the source or even direction of the strangled screaming.

'The tank?'

Standing, he swiftly checked that the sounds of running feet behind him were friendly, before taking off towards the tank, confirming with every step he took that the source was indeed the enemy tank.

Revel and Blanc had taken refuge underneath the wreck and both, totally exhausted, had fallen asleep, not knowing that their failure to stay awake would condemn both of them to a horrible death.

The rain had turned the ground into a quagmire, on top of which sat over thirty tons of metal, gently and inexorably sinking.

Revel had awoken as the floor of the Sherman pressed him gently into the muddy ground, enough to wake him, and enough to hold him in place as the tank dropped lower still.

In full and horrified understanding of what was happening, Yarishlov shouted for help as he ripped the spade

198

off the Sherman's hull, immediately starting to dig at the front of the vehicle.

As other Soviet troopers started to arrive, they too dug, with helmets and hands, entrenching tools and rifle butts, reinforcing the effort at the front and starting another dig at the back.

Deniken sent a young runner away to bring back more men and tools, and then plunged back again to his frantic digging.

"Can you drag the bastard off, Yarishlov?"

The efforts of digging started to tell, each phrase punctuated by a deep breath and another use of the spade.

"Not a hope, Deniken. No time, ground's got no fucking grip, fucking useless. He has to come out now."

"The jeep? Drag the poor man out?"

"Give it a try, but we have no time."

The infantry officer looked up and found Kriks, who nodded and ran like the wind.

Blanc was slipping into unconsciousness, the side of the tank under which he lay having dropped lower than Revel's. His terrified whimpering ceased and the gunner drowned silently as his head was pushed face first into a puddle of muddy water.

Revel's panic grew as his inability to take a proper meaningful breath increased, the flat bottom plate of the American-made tank pressing him tightly to the ground, restricting all but the tiniest movement.

The increased sounds of rescue reached him, and he tried harder to scream his presence, now unable to muster anything but a breathless squeal.

Deniken and Yarishlov worked side by side, desperately trying to manufacture a small trench into which they could try and drag the unfortunate man, or to at least move earth from under him and buy more time.

A hand suddenly appeared, moving as frantically as the restriction allowed, seemingly detached from any body. A second hand emerged and waved, both now scrabbling at the mud and water.

The two officers exchanged looks and nodded swift agreement.

Deniken leant in and took hold of the man's left hand; Yarishlov took the right.

Both men took a firm grip and pulled, the disembodied hands pulling against them to double the effort.

One of Deniken's guardsmen dived in between them to continue the digging work, others took hold of their officers and pulled.

Again and again, they exerted their collective strength, and were rewarded with a gain of no more than two inches.

Both Yarishov and Deniken ignored the pains inflicted by their own men.

The jeep backed up to the wrecked tank, and men started to attach lines, preparing an effort to drag the man clear using the power of the little 4x4.

Kriks slid into the hollow, holding the ends of two lines, waiting for the word from behind him. He ordered the spare men out, leaving just the four of them to battle for the life of the unknown enemy soldier.

His lines would remain unused, as the battle was already lost.

It was hopeless, but neither officer conceded or halted their effort until the hands they held grew soft.

Feeling a gentle squeeze, Yarishlov replied in kind, providing a presence to the unknown man dying a horrible death a few unconquerable feet from where he lay.

Deniken shared the last moment's too, the man acknowledging his grip with his own until he died, suffocated and crushed under his own tank.

Both officers were reluctant to release their hold, even when all work ceased and the other would-be rescuers stood back.

Yarishlov and Deniken sought eye-contact, and the two exchanged unspoken words. With a mutual nod, they released the lifeless hands, sliding backwards out of the digging area.

Deniken knelt down and picked up his SVT, slinging it over his shoulder, before accepting one of the numerous cigarettes being held out to him by his respectful soldiers.

A number of canteens were passing round the muddy group, none of them containing thirst-quenching water.

Yarishlov took a full swig of brandy and spoke quietly, loud enough for all to hear, but soft enough to carry his soldierly feelings and his humanity.

"Well done, Comrades. No way for a soldier to die but we, his enemies, tried to save him. I'm proud of you all."

A few words of thanks fell almost unheard as the group broke up and returned to their business.

Deniken threw his cigarette butt into a puddle and set his peaked cap properly on his head. It was the sole piece of his personal gear that was not thickly caked in dark brown mud. Saluting his equally muddy superior officer, he said his piece.

"Comrade Polkovnik, it has been a privilege to serve with you. Good luck, Sir."

Yarishlov's salute quickly turned into an extended hand and Deniken reciprocated. Two hands that had held a dying man were shaken in mutual admiration of the qualities of the other.

Betrayal is common for men with no conscience

Toba Beta.

Chapter 63 – THE MESSAGES

<u>Wednesday, 15th August 1945, 0723 hrs [Moscow Time], the
Kremlin, Moscow, USSR.</u>

Beria had received the message on his arrival at his office, and was immediately driven to the Kremlin to inform the General Secretary.

He sipped his tea, watching Stalin like a hungry hawk watches a wolf; respectfully, and without challenge to the latter's predatory skills.

Holding both the message and the proposed replies, the Soviet Generallisimo seemed strangely reluctant to make a decision.

'Assassination or maskirova?'

Stalin focussed on the NKVD chief, sensing there was something else to the matter, not knowing what it was.

'What advantages lie here, truly? Why do we not kill him and have done with it?'

That was simple, but something ingrained in the psyche of the Soviet people always relished the opportunity for sleight of hand or, as in this case, the misdirection of a nation.

"And your recommendation is?"

Beria chose to promote his own agenda once more, whilst skilfully withholding his commitment for the benefit of the microphones.

"We can do nothing, Comrade General Secretary and all will be as we first wished it to be or," he indicated the report and reply, "We can send that and possibly achieve better results."

Stalin nodded gently, removing the pipe from his mouth with his free hand.

"Is 'possibly' enough Lavrentiy? We could have done with him once and for all if we let it run. Does the alternative offer us real advantages if it goes as we hope?"

202

'*Careful,*' screamed his inner voice.

"By removing the dictator, we risk a similar man in place, set against us because of our own actions, as we do not yet have suitable friendly candidates in place. By using this variation, we can possibly turn him and those who would follow him."

Stalin puffed gently on the cigarette that had magically appeared in his hand.

"Would the new man not be grateful to us for his, err," he searched for the right word, "His promotion?"

"These are matters you have previously reconciled, Comrade General Secretary. Your reasoning seemed sound then, and I see nothing substantial has changed to call your decision into question."

'*Nicely done,*' the voice purred with some smugness.

"As I recall, you championed this change, Lavrentiy, did you not?"

"I represented the facts and options as I saw them, Comrade General Secretary."

The cigarette was violently stubbed out, sending a deluge of ash across both table and reports.

Another was lit immediately.

"And you have other assets already suitably placed, if things do not go as we expect?

The 'we' was not wasted on Beria.

"Another team would be activated immediately you authorised it, Comrade General Secretary."

Beria knew he had his man.

Stalin promised to discover what other issue was in the man's mind but, none the less, committed himself.

"We do not have the luxury of time. Send your message, Comrade Marshall. If it doesn't work we can always do what was first intended later."

Stalin slid the papers across his desk, both being neatly caught as they slipped off the highly polished top.

The ash cloud he generated settled gently across the lap and arms of the NKVD chief.

Beria indicated the phone and received a nod from the puffing Stalin.

Requesting a connection to his communications officer in the Lyubyanka, he started to feel uncomfortable under the scrutiny.

A distant voice came on the line.

"PodPolkovnik Lemsky."

"Ah, Lemsky. As discussed earlier regarding file 'Brutus', you will present messages 'B' and 'C' to the Chief Signals Officer for immediate transmission to the stated recipients. Repeat the order."

"File 'Brutus', messages 'B' and 'C' for immediate transmission to stated recipients, Comrade Marshall."

"Proceed as ordered."

Replacing the receiver with studied care, Beria felt nothing for those he had just condemned to die.

Stalin, studying his man, noticed the faint smile and knew he had been right.

Beria was also working to another agenda.

In the major Headquarters on both sides of the line, all was activity. At Nordhausen, the Soviet reinforcements were being realigned with the penetrations, such basic manoeuvres made all the more difficult by the increase in the tempo of allied air raids. Formations that should have been relieved were left to bear the casualties of the attack. Those who should have moved up were contained by destroyed roads and bridges or a lack of the vitals of military movement; a sign of significant ground attack success by Allied aircraft. In short, increasing damage to transport infrastructure was causing huge logistical problems to harassed Soviet staff officers.

Air Force intelligence indicated that some Allied squadrons were presently undertaking up to six sorties a day per pilot, a rate that was consuming both the physical and material reserves of the Allies, as well as grinding the pilots slowly into the ground with exhaustion.

Soviet units were still advancing, but slowly, much slower than the plans allowed for.

The differences between this war and the German War were becoming more defined each hour. The Luftwaffe had been a mighty organ, but it had been eroded by casualties over the years, as well as being constantly divided by the needs of other theatres.

Here, on this battlefield, the USAAF and RAF squadrons were more numerous and focussed solely upon one front.

Also, the allied inventory included numerous highly efficient aircraft designs, many of which had capabilities way beyond those of the Luftwaffe encountered in the skies of Russia.

That was painfully true with the heavy bombers, a force that had been almost disregarded in some ways, and that was now throwing so many plans and timetables into disarray.

More and more of the Soviet Air Force assets were being employed to defend military columns or important communication centres, less and less in support of offensive operations.

Night operations were done at great risk, the Allied night fighter force having chopped most of their counterparts from the sky.

The larger numbers of ground formations overcame some of the problems, carrying territory by sheer weight of numbers, often at a cost made more expensive because of the lack of air cover or associated issues caused by interruptions to supply. Profligate expenditure of anti-aircraft ammunition brought regular rewards in downed airplanes, but air to air victories were growing fewer every day.

It didn't take a genius to understand that the Soviets were losing the air war.

Certainly their Allied counterparts in Versailles thought that was the case, but the problems of constant withdrawal, and defeat after defeat, were more paramount in their minds.

The important decisions for the Allied ground forces now lay within the remit of officers in faraway places, be they Corps Commanders keeping control on their dwindling resources or battalion CO's skilfully giving up ground at great cost to the advancing enemy.

In many ways, the battle was out of Eisenhower's hands, the orders having gone out to Bradley, McCreery and the like, their leadership and generalship skills being tested as they strove to create order from the chaos.

Eisenhower busied himself with providing the means for his Generals to fight.

'Trying to provide the means', Ike thought, as he often felt he was failing in that regard.

Newly arriving units were organised and sent forward, savaged units were swiftly reinforced and rested on or nearby to the Rhine.

He harried the Germans and the Spanish, anyone who could provide him with more of the most essential tool of war; manpower.

Politically, he encouraged his civilian leaders to produce and deliver everything from tanks to bread, and more importantly, to get it to Europe in as short a time as possible.

The success of Japanese forces in China and the Pacific undermined his efforts with his own government, and he constantly saw assets he desperately needed dispatched to Slim, Stilwell, Nimitz and MacArthur's commands. The British were more Europe-focussed but had fewer resources, having been burned out by six years of war.

An innovative approach to the German POW's in the Americas might prove useful, based on the Council's suggestion, although again, time played an important part.

Regardless of the momentary joy brought by news of a new formation now available, Eisenhower fully understood a simple truth.

The Allies were losing the war.

---

182 Squadron's Blue Flight was on its second sortie of the day, all four aircraft in the air with a full load of rockets, and tasked to take out the bridges and railway in and around Luhdorf.

Flight Lieutenant Johnny Hall and the youthful Pilot Officer Andrew McKenzie each had a new pilot in tow, recently arrived replacements for comrades lost since the 6th August.

Turning to port over Garstedt, enemy light anti-aircraft fire reached up at the RAF ground attack planes, filling the sky with angry metal.

The eight Soviet Lavochkin fighters that had been tasked to overwatch Luhdorf had problems of their own, self-preservation being their only goal, as twelve Mk XVIe Spitfires of 603 Squadron RAF harried them. 603 had been due to disband in Scotland but had reassembled and returned to Europe the day before. Despite being configured as Lf versions for low-altitude work, the needs of the moment detailed 603 to act as interceptor/escort fighters for this operation.

The Soviet pilots had been fighting day in day out since hostilities started, and it showed. The fresher RAF pilots hacked three of them from the sky in as many minutes, and knocked important pieces off three more.

182's Typhoons were unopposed as they approached their target.

The main road bridges running west out of the town were still ruined, having not been repaired since the devastating heavy bomber attack.

The rail bridge to the south of them, and the small bridge two hundred metres below that, were the targets for this raid.

Hall lined up the road bridge and quickly thumbed off his RP-3 rockets, all eight completely missing the bridge and doing nothing but chewing up the riverbanks, soaking Russian anti-aircraft crews desperately serving their weapons.

To add insult to injury, Hall's Typhoon took a few hits in the port wing as he turned away, inducing a light flutter until he pulled out of his turn.

Pilot Officer Rawlings, former POW and new addition to Blue Flight, went next. He also failed to hit the bridge but inflicted more than a mere soaking on the Soviet gunners.

Two 40mm Bofors positions on the east bank were destroyed in an instant.

McKenzie lined up his target, and was about to fire, when his line of sight was obscured by a Soviet fighter. Hauling hard on his stick and pushing on pedals, the young Canadian skilfully managed to avoid the Lavochkin but almost struck the pursuing Spitfire.

The swift destruction of the Russian followed, but his attack run was ruined and he swept back into line, his rockets still in place.

Sean Dwyer was flying his first mission, having been with 182 for only two days since leaving his training squadron. He lined up the target and drove in hard through the flak, but his attack failed completely as he was unable to release his weapons, the safeties still on as fear and excitement took precedence in his mind.

His comrades were already formed up for a second sweep, but he was so thrown by his failure that he banked right by mistake.

The Russian M1910 Maxim was an old weapon but it was still in use in great numbers, as it was a reliable and effective weapon capable of six hundred rounds per minute. The Russians used them in a number of ways, and one particularly effective method was as the Quad AA weapon mounted on a Gaz truck or similar vehicle.

The Soviet 39th Anti-Aircraft Division boasted a large number of these weapons, of which eight were presently sat on the main highway north of Luhdorf, waiting their turn to cross the river by way of the damaged bridge at Roydorf.

Dwyer had banked right and was now lined up perfectly for the Soviet gunners, who made the most of their opportunity.

The Typhoon slowly disintegrated as scores of bullets struck home. The armour plating kept the aircraft flying, protecting many vital parts but nine bullets were already lodged in the most vital part of the aircraft and, with lifeless hands on the stick, the smoking aircraft rolled lazily into a right hand turn and crashed into the fields two kilometres east of Luhdorf.

Blue Flight commenced their second run, as Hall strafed the flak positions around the road bridge, successfully ripping a gun crew to shreds with his Hispano cannon.

Rawlings bored in and was rewarded with two hits on the bridge, either of which would have doomed the hastily repaired structure.

The remnants collapsed into the frothing water below.

McKenzie held his rockets back, contenting himself with a short burst of cannon fire, before falling back into formation again, ready to attack the second target.

Flight Lieutenant Hall led once more, his cannon again successful, a fixed 20mm quad position, once of Luftwaffe ownership, instantly destroyed with those who crewed it.

Rawlings, elated by his success, shot up the river, churning the water to foam with his cannon shells. Banking left he sustained a few hits from previously silent machine-guns hidden around the hedges and fields, a thousand metres west of Luhdorf.

Mackenzie's ordnance was already boring in, inexorably eating up the yards before striking the rail bridge in three places.

The structure had been badly damaged during the big raid but had been swiftly and expertly repaired, enabling trains to use it, albeit at slower speeds.

The bridge still refused to die, shrugging off the RP-3 hits, seemingly unscathed, save for the obvious twisted rails reaching dramatically skywards.

Despite hitting his target, McKenzie cursed his failure as he rejoined the flight, taking formation for the journey home.

Stelmakh sat quietly with his crew, listening and watching as the Engineer Captain ripped into one of his Lieutenants.

The unfortunate man had opened fire with a DSHK machine gun, mounting one of Stelmakh's IS-III's to shoot at an allied aircraft, and in doing so, encouraged others to open fire too.

Corporal Stepanov spat in contempt and grabbed for a cigarette.

"What's the fucking point in hiding away if some fucking idiot officer fires off the damn guns and shows the fucking enemy where we are?"

His young CO took the proffered Belomor and lit it before replying.

"These engineers have had the devil of a time with the British air force, Stepanov. Over one in three of them have gone already, and they haven't seen a ground soldier yet. He just wanted to hit back that's all. Be kind."

The tank driver snorted in disgust.

"He missed the fucking thing by a kilometre too!"

"Maybe so, but this time there is no harm done, and he will have learned."

Both their conversation and the engineer's admonishment were interrupted by the swift approach of aircraft engines.

Three Spitfires flashed overhead, one trailing a thin wisp of smoke, evidence that they had not had things all their own way with the Lavochkin Regiment.

Stepanov idly played with a Y-shaped scar on the tank's flank, product of the brickwork collapse during the air raid.

The sound of Spitfires decreased, until the steady patter of raindrops on camouflage nets took over.

"Anyway, Comrade Kaporal, just leave it and keep out of the way. I'm off to see what the new Regimental Commander has in mind for us."

Hall and McKenzie could do nothing.

A kindly WAAF Lance-Corporal had pressed mugs of tea into their hands, and the obligatory cigarettes had been provided by the remaining members of Yellow flight.

In silence, they all watched as fire crews gradually gained control of the inferno that had engulfed XM-S when it crashed on landing. Unknown to the pilot or his watching comrades, a single bullet had clipped the port tyre. The impact of the aircraft on the tarmac had burst it immediately, throwing the Typhoon violently to the left. The undercarriage gave way, resulting in the aircraft cartwheeling for a hundred yards before coming to rest upside down and exploding.

The brave fire crew fought hard to hold back the flames, and were rewarded as the rescue crew finally broke through into the cockpit area, dragging out the parts of Pilot Officer Rawlings that the fire had not yet consumed.

210

Alive, but extremely badly burned, the young flier was loaded into the ambulance and whisked away to the base hospital, where the business of saving his life could begin in earnest.

Hall and McKenzie said nothing; there was nothing to say that hadn't been said a hundred times before by fliers from all sides.

Handing back empty mugs to the horrified WAAF, they went to be debriefed on their mission, suppressing their horror and sorrow at the loss of another comrade.

*When your time comes to die, be not like those whose hearts are
filled with the fear of death, so that when their time comes they
weep, and pray for a little more time to live their lives over again
in a different way.
Sing your death song and die like a hero going home.*

Tecumseh

Chapter 64 – THE AMBUSH

Thursday, 16th August 1945, 0620 hrs, Palace Hotel, Madrid.

They had all been up since four-forty a.m.

The hotel night receptionist had apologetically rung the
room two minutes prior to that, waking Mayakov from a light
sleep. Explaining, the receptionist said that the caller had been
insistent that the message was passed immediately, but the man
still baulked at waking paying guests at such ungodly times,
especially for a message that could obviously wait until daylight.

None the less, he informed the sleepy voice at the other
end of the phone that 'Señor Juan Flores, with regret, would not
be able to join them until Saturday.'

"Is that word for word?"

"Si, Señor. The gentleman made me write it down."

"Thank you."

Mayakov immediately roused his team on the basis of
this urgent instruction. 'Juan' was a confirmation of the plan, as
agreed with the Rezident, 'Flores' being the imperative of a strike
this very morning. 'Saturday' referred to the next contact, which
would be made at the safe house arranged by the local NKVD
station.

'With Regret' meant at all costs, the sort of order old
men give younger men with monotonous regularity.

The receptionist continued reading the morning paper,
still finding Senor Flores' German accent laughable, despite its
hideous strangulation of his mother tongue.

Upstairs, the six spent their time checking the weapons
they had checked just a few hours before, making breakfast, and

212

ensuring that each man knew his job for the task ahead. The plan was simple, as are all good plans, with alternatives if required.

Their escape had been laid out by Vaspatin, the NKVD Rezident, the same man who had distributed cyanide capsules to each of them on the orders of Moscow.

By 0625 hrs, the room had been cleaned thoroughly and the group was on its way down the stairs to their vehicles, and a rendezvous with violent death.

At 0635 hrs, two shadowy figures stole into the hotel by a rear entrance and made their way up to the recently vacated rooms.

Twelve minutes later, having completed the task assigned to them, they exited by the same route, re-entering the hotel more openly and making their way to a fifth floor suite, having resumed their identities of the Marquis and Marchioness of Bodonitsa; Greek nobility holidaying in the Spanish capital.

A creature of habit, Francisco Paulino Hermenegildo Teódulo Franco y Bahamonde left his official residence precisely at 0730 hrs, slipping into his official presidential car for the fast drive into Madrid.

As was normal, elements of the Spanish Army and the Guardia Civil were stationed along his route, positioned to discourage attempts on the Caudillo's person.

One such team of Guardia Civil, complete with one of the newly supplied American jeeps, waited alertly at the convergence of the Avenida de la Guardia and the Avenida del Palacio.

"It is time, Comrades."

The jeep mounted a .50 cal Browning machine-gun, which was their killing weapon of choice on this warm summer's morning.

Elsewhere, the other three members of the NKVD assassination team played their own important roles.

The simple plan swung into action.

213

Four loud explosions rent the air, as the military base on the eastern side of the Avenida del Palacio was engulfed in smoke and flames. Beyond that, a six man army section stationed on the junction of the Pardo al Goloso and the Pardo a Fuencarral came under fire, killing or incapacitating every man in seconds.

Instantly, everything was bedlam, as troops and civil guards raced towards the action.

A quick-thinking civil guard officer waved the Caudillo's car and escort away, barring the day's intended route down the Del Pardo a Fuencarral, deflecting the presidential cavalcade down the Avenida del Palacio.

President Francisco Franco gently sipped his fresh orange juice as the sound of the explosions still echoed through the palace.

"German Bastards," he announced to no-one in particular, although the meeting room contained many ears waiting for his orders.

Major Mayakov was the first to die, a marksman's bullet taking him full in the chest and wrecking his heart in an instant.

The machine-gunner was next, less than half a second behind, flung from his position by the double impact of bullets in the chest and neck.

The other Soviet 'Guardia' was killed within a few seconds, the whole ambush team slain without firing a shot. Presently sweating in the back of the presidential limousine was retired army corporal Jose Luis de Messia. Franco's double was used to taking the risk, but today was clearly different. Buildings had been blown up, shots had been fired. He did not know that Death had already visited itself upon a dozen people and was not yet satisfied. He just knew enough to be petrified.

The quick-thinking officer who had altered the cavalcade's route was actually Serzhant David Meyer, the group's other German by birth. Acting according to the plan, he deflected the Caudillo down the ambush party's path. Confused by the lack of activity from Mayakov's group, he had hung around longer than he should have. Spanish uniforms almost surrounded him, confused voices seeking instructions and direction. Meyer ordered the growing group to follow the route taken by the President's car. Taking the opportunity offered by their swift departure, he quickly heading off to where he had secreted a motor-cycle.

He pulled the tarpaulin off the Steyr-Daimler-Puch motorcycle and mounted it in one easy motion.

Almost instantly, Meyer found himself propelled off the bike as the impact of a rifle butt knocked him sideways.

He saw a vague shape through clouded eyes and went for his pistol holster. Slowed and disoriented as he was by the blow, he never reached it. A studded boot pressed down onto his right arm, fixing it in place.

A heavily accented voice shouted in the language of his youth.

"Oh no, you German bastard, none of that. We want a word with you!"

Rough hands grabbed Meyer and dragged him towards the main road, where a vehicle stood waiting.

With his hands quickly bound, he was thrown into the back of the small truck.

As his captors boarded, he tried to flick the capsule out from his cheek but it had gone, forced from its hiding place when the rifle butt took him in the head.

With fear and courage in equal measure, Meyer pressed his neck against a seat stanchion, cutting off the blood flow in an attempt to commit suicide.

Flushed with their capture and talking of the horrors that awaited the spy, none of the soldiers noticed that their captive no longer cared.

Unfortunately for Meyer, the suicide attempt failed, his unconscious head rolling to one side, restoring the flow of blood.

To the east, the NKVD bomber arrived breathless at the car, the earth and dirt where he had crawled up to the buildings apparent on his uniform.

"Clean yourself off quickly, Vassily, quickly," the young officer pointed out the mess and turned back to watch the road, his eyes flicking to the firing spot from which he had slain the army unit, and where he had left the deadly PPSH.

Although he was puzzled by the absence of fire from the ambush party, Oleg Nazarbayev concentrated on his own and Vassily Horn's successful evasion.

Snatching up his Star Z45 submachine gun, he heard the approach of a heavy vehicle from the north, presently obscured by the dust and smoke from the burning military buildings.

"Get your pistol working, Vassily, follow my lead."

Dropping into cover behind the bonnet of the Peugeot 402, he fired two short bursts in the direction of the concealed firing point from where he had made his kills.

Horn understood immediately and triggered off three shots of his own, coinciding with the emergence of a military truck from the smoke.

The 1935 Chevrolet truck braked violently and halted in the road.

Nazarbayev fired another short burst and waved frantically at the lorry, indicating enemy in the direction he had fired.

The infantry commander understood and deployed his men immediately, a dozen riflemen swiftly oriented to flank the suspect position.

Both Russians fired again until the Spaniards were too close for comfort.

Reloading their weapons quickly, they watched as one of the infantrymen handed a PPSH to his officer, who waved it dramatically to his two 'comrades' on the road.

Nazarbayev acknowledged the man's wave and indicated two more approaching trucks.

The first infantry officer ran to the road and within an instant a second, larger group of soldiers was on the hunt for the assassin's, moving to the south of the road junction and immediately spotting the slain men.

216

The rearmost truck deployed its cargo, setting up a road block which faced in both directions, part of the Spanish plan to trap the enemy agents.

Almost immediately a fire fight broke out with the first group of soldiers, at least one going to ground hard. Such was the confusion of the hour that another party of Spanish soldiers had clashed with their own forces, with the poorly named 'friendly fire' claiming three quick victims, and providing a focal point for more units to in on in order to avenge fallen comrades.

Grasping the opportunity offered, the two Soviet officers immediately started their Peugeot and set off southwards and back towards Madrid.

By the time the Spanish had sorted out their mistake, thirteen of their number lay dead upon the field.

Akim Igorevich Vaspatin had never played poker, but his face was ideally suited to a game that requires no evidence or expression for the opponent to read.

His glass was empty, so he placed it on the crisp starched table cloth and waited for the bastard opposite to speak, the footsteps of the officer who had brought the verbal report still echoing on the marble floor.

"It would appear that we are in your debt, Colonel Vaspatin. Thank you for the timely warning."

"I am glad that I could be of assistance, Generalissimo. Thankfully our intelligence service detected the plot in time."

The Spaniard laughed the sort of laugh that does not have humour at its heart.

"Don't be too modest, Colonel. Your role in my country is well known."

For a man wearing many dangerous hats, such statements can be very worrying, and Vaspatin felt a momentary icy stab in his heart.

"You are Soviet Military Intelligence, this we know well, Colonel."

Franco looked at his guest with genuine puzzlement.

"You didn't think we didn't know did you?"

Vaspatin smiled and shrugged, relieved that only part of his clandestine world was known.

"Now, we will see if any of the German swine have survived, and what they might tell of us of their reasons."

The GRU/NKVD officer went to speak but was cut short by an imperious hand.

"We know what you have told us, at the behest and direction of your superiors of course."

The last of Franco's juice disappeared, and a waiter attempting a third refill was waved away.

"We want to hear what these assassins have to say for themselves."

An aide walked briskly in and whispered in the Dictator's ear.

"Good."

Rising from the table and slipping into the jacket held by one of his personal valets, Franco concluded the discussion.

"One of the assassins is still alive. We will question him. If things are as you state, then Spain will not get involved in your war, Colonel Vaspatin. Thank you again and good day."

Franco left the room at speed, leaving behind a worried man. A man who had not expected any survivors to interfere with the plan to take Spain out of the war.

As the Caudillo's car swept out of the Presidential Palace, this time containing the genuine article, another car parked inconspicuously some miles away, pulling into a concealed shady spot on the Calle del Sur in Majadahonda. Two men in civilian clothing walked briskly to the railway station intent on boarding the next northwest-bound train.

Their Peugeot had been dumped, pushed into the Arroyo de Trofa River before the men had used their 'clean' vehicle to drive to the ten kilometres to the station. The second 'clean' vehicle had not followed the Peugeot into the water, despite the contingency plan, both men wishing to give any surviving comrades the best possible chance.

Nazarbayev and Horn both knew something had gone wrong, in the same way as they both now accepted that no-one else from the team was coming back.

Despite the large number of people travelling that day their compartment was empty, save for themselves. They were able to talk about events softly in Russian, and more loudly about the weather in German, on the occasions that someone strolled past the glass between them and the corridor.

Both took it in turns to have a nap as the stations rolled gently by. The pair were both wide awake by the time that Valladolid materialised out of the sunny haze.

Dismounting from the train together, they quickly oriented themselves, drawing on the briefing they had received, and, identifying the main entrance, proceeded out through the arches into the Calle del Recondo, their eyes adjusting to the strong sunlight.

Moving a few metres left to the end of the main entrance they waited in a return, where the front recessed back, indulging in cigarettes as they waited for their contact.

Both were still alert and took in their surroundings with practicised eyes, noting objects and people, ticking off possible threats as each was processed through their brain.

Neither man saw anything except that which it was intended that they should see, although perhaps they should have noted that the shoeshine spent all his time on the left foot of his customer, and that the same customer had his newspaper on his lap rather than reading it or indulging in conversation.

The man and woman with the pram stood side by side, facing the station and gazing down at their silent child, Nazarbayev was just starting to ask himself questions when he spotted a huge man holding a white suitcase starting to cross the road.

Their contact halted to let the Spanish Army truck move past and then mounted the pavement, making directly for the two agents.

"Excuse me, Señors, can you tell me the time of the next train to Madrid?"

He delivered a perfectly executed pass phrase.

219

"So sorry, Señor, We don't know. We are from German Nationals from Corunna, here on business."

Satisfied with the reply, the man placed his suitcase on the ground and stepped back. It had only taken ten seconds but a lot had happened whilst the two were distracted.

Where there had been a shoeshine and customer there were now two men holding pistols. The husband and wife had similarly transformed into armed threats, both covering the Russians with their handguns.

The Army truck disgorged a dozen men in half as many seconds.

Both Soviet agents no longer had weapons and were faced with an unpalatable decision. Nazarbayev reached into his jacket pocket for his papers, expressing his indignation in the chosen language of the mission.

Suddenly both men were on the ground, as their legs were wrecked by bullets from the four Spanish Intelligence Service officers. The soldiers quickly descended upon the stricken pair, checking them for weapons, before roughly picking them up and slinging them aboard the truck.

Shocked onlookers were being encouraged to move on, even as the two medics in the truck started to work on their charges, tasked only with keeping them alive for what was to come.

Nazarbayev and Horn lay side by side, the pain increasing as the vehicle bounced on the rough roads, picking up speed on its way to the military hospital.

Horn attempted to rise but felt a stab in his side as an eager young soldier used his bayonet to dissuade him.

He rolled his head towards the moaning Nazarbayev, who nodded his goodbyes to his comrade.

Within seconds, both men had used their tongues to free the capsules Vaspatin had given them.

Horn bit on his capsule and ingested a small dose of Potassium Cyanide. This entered his digestive tract and reacted with his stomach acid, producing fatal Hydrogen Cyanide. He jerked a few times as the poison penetrated his system and then settled, dying within ninety seconds.

Oleg Nazarbayev, twin brother of Vladimir, and youngest surviving son of Yuri and Tatiana, dropped into unconsciousness and failed in his act of self-destruction, the shoeshine boy sliding rough fingers into his mouth and hooking out the suicide pill.

Horn would take his secrets to the rough grave in which the Spanish later threw his body, whereas two of his comrades remained alive to be tortured and interrogated at painful length about the German raison d'être for the attack on Franco, as well as to answer questions on incriminating evidence found in their hotel room, from planning notes of El Pardo in German through to Maria Paloma's personal diary graphically detailing her earthy expectations for few hours of romantic liaison with a handsome young German.

After local medical treatment, Oleg Nazarbayev was flown from Valladolid to join Prisoner Meyer in an innocuous building next a military airbase in the Cuatro Vientos ward of Madrid. Dwelling within an overt military security wall, the small building regularly entertained enemies of the state.

Three days later, a Spanish soldier distributed lunch according to the normal routine but, acting under instructions from his NKVD paymaster, also gave each man new means to end their lives.

Nazarbayev, suffering badly from his wounds, was tended by physicians, anxious to nurse him back to health.

Meyer, in a bad way, his recently fractured skull bringing as much pain as the torture, had already told all he knew. That the team spoke only spoke in German or Spanish, that four of the agents had arrived separately to his group, and a female agent had delivered their uniforms. He had screamed out the details of the ambush plan as his genitals were subjected to a crushing attack by weighty pliers.

The agent managed to wait the requested time, a delay to permit the guard to be out of immediate suspicion, consuming his deadly dose of Potassium Cyanide during the mid-afternoon siesta, before the Spanish Captain could start work on his remaining testicle.

Alarm bells rang and other men immediately ran to Nazarbayev's sick bed, intending to stop a repeat performance. At the first sound of running feet, Oleg, weakened by a systemic infection, had instinctively known that his comrade had taken his own life and followed suit, convulsing on his bunk as keys rattled in the door.

Sat in his office, Beria read the Rezident's report, sent 'Eyes only' the previous evening.

It seemed that the decision made by Stalin and himself had done all that was desired, as Spain was about to openly declare her neutrality, on the basis of the recent German-sponsored assassination attempt on the life of the Caudillo.

Rather than simply cut off the head, the reasoning had been that it could even be possible to turn Spanish views around, and make the country more sympathetic to the Communist cause, particularly in the light of the excellent assistance provided by the Russian Intelligence Services in foiling the recent plot.

Six men's lives had been lost, plus a very useful female asset; all in all, a fair price for the advantage gained.

If it continued to work then all was well; if not, four more agents languished in a safe house outside Malpica, awaiting instructions.

The identities of the agents had been known to him before he ordered their betrayal, and he had found himself relishing the opportunity to break the news to the woman when next he saw her, and experiencing an almost sexual excitement at inflicting yet another crushing blow *'on that GRU bitch'*.

*There must be a beginning of any great matter, but the
continuing unto the end until it be thoroughly finished yields
the true glory.*

Francis Drake

Chapter 65 – THE LEGION

General de Brigade Christophe Lavalle was not a man to
be easily impressed. He read the reports prepared for him by his
sub-unit commanders, be they old Legionnaires or ex-German
military, and found himself on the border of incredulity and
pride.

In the five days since his arrival at the fledgling camp,
the numbers of men in uniform had nearly tripled, bringing the
size of his force to just over twenty thousand.

A combination of old legion NCO's, mainly German he
conceded, a few recently arrived French Legion officers, and the
efforts of the ex-SS NCO's and officers, had already formed the
mass into recognisable formations.

Readiness levels, signed by men he trusted, indicated his
units would be available well ahead of the projected dates.

Another report lay open on his desk, this one a return on
his own submitted to Army command.

French pragmatism seemed to know no boundaries as
his suggested command structure and order of battle was
approved without alteration or adverse comment.

So surprising was it, he even considered contacting De
Tassigny to confirm that he had actually read the submission.

But he didn't.

For a number of reasons.

The Brigade he had been promoted to command, an
anticipated group of no more than ten thousand troops in small
formations, was a growing monster, deserving of higher rank and
more staff. Never a man of ego or military ambition, save to

223

prove his worth as a soldier and leader, he found himself in command of a force of elite fighting soldiers and he did not wish for it to be taken away from him before he had an opportunity to employ it in battle.

The anticipated structure of the Legion Corps D'Assault had been filled and all of the four major constituent formations were being expanded to cater for each day's new arrivals, as well as creating a holding unit from where replacements could be drawn once combat operations started to take their toll.

His officers had laid out TOE's for each unit, and it was anticipated that further formations would be a possibility, as more and more ex-SS troopers made the journey to Sassy to answer the call to arms.

Bittrich, Lavalle's Chief of Staff and de facto second in command of the Corps, worked miracles on an hourly basis, creating organisation from nothing, and it was mainly down to his work, and that of the sub-unit commanders, that the Corps was organised and almost ready to commit.

One major worry was tank spares, and so Lavalle had sanctioned a scavenging group to go as far afield as possible to collect what they could. He had placed one of his best tank commanders in charge of the party, ably supported by Major Cyrille Vernais, Regimental Sergeant Major of the Legion. The small Swiss had been assigned to the 1st Legion Chars D'Assault Brigade and had immediately fallen foul of his comrades' humour, prejudices, and misconceptions about height, size and capability. Several ex-Waffen SS soldiers learned the difficult way that Vernais was as hard as nails, and that the rank of Legion Major is not earned by one's ability to count paper clips.

In a very short period of time, the diminutive Legionnaire had the respect of his troops, and Lavalle was sure that Vernais was one of the reasons that the 1st, the unit named for the legions greatest action of Camerone, was the best of a group of extremely good units under his command.

Two other of the reasons were its commander, the famous Ernst-August Knocke, and the officer in charge of the tank regiment, Rolf Uhlmann. Colonel and Commandant respectively, the two brought something special to the 1st and

224

had forged an instantly successful professional relationship, which a soldier like Lavalle could appreciate.

Uhlmann was leading the scavenging party, supported by Vernais, who had conceded that the German was almost good enough to serve in his beloved Legion, which translated meant the man was bordering on officer perfection.

Lavalle smiled to himself as he recalled another reason for the 'Camerone's' special edge. Uhlmann's senior German NCO Braun had bonded with Vernais, forming a solid partnership. The two were often seen prowling round the 1st's lines, inflicting themselves on the unwary. The pair were obviously hard men, apparently fair men, and certainly competent men. And according to the feedback Lavalle had from Bittrich, the two were hugely respected by their soldiers. That counted for a lot in his book.

Lavalle poured Bittrich and himself a coffee, passed the busy German his drink, and took station at the large window. Consuming his slowly, he examined the hustle and bustle of the camp set out before him.

One thing the Legion and the Waffen-SS had in common was a love of song, and more than one melody could be heard through the glass.

It was one of those songs that was popular on both sides of no man's land, a large mixed group of Legionnaires and Germans singing, each in their own language, one side's 'Ich hatt einen Kameraden' rising above the other outnumbered group's version of 'J'avais un camarade'.

Lavalle enjoyed the moment, particularly some wonderful harmonies from the ex-SS.

A dispatch rider caught his eye, slowly moving in between the soldiers on the camp main road, heading towards the headquarters building.

The sight of the man returning to his motorcycle coincided with the sound of approaching boots as one of his French officers brought the dispatch upstairs.

Bittrich, afforded the rank of Général de Brigade, stood up and threw his pen onto the table, stretching as he shook off the stiffness his body felt after hours of solid staff work at the desk. Lavalle still could not get used to the uniforms of his new command. His CoS was clad in American combat trousers with gaitered British army boots, topped off with a German officer's shirt, the Knights Cross hanging proudly round his neck. On the back of Bittrich's chair was a French officers' tunic, complete with the new Corps badge on the upper left arm, the flags of France and Germany either side of the Legion's grenade emblem. The badge was laid out in that fashion in order to cover up or replace the German eagle insignia on the original uniforms, a position it also now occupied on French uniforms. Completing the new uniform were Bittrich's personal awards, de-nazified as per orders, and the new armband, again produced to replace the old Waffen-SS cuff titles. The dark blue band, 35mm wide, boasted two scarlet parallel lines, each set 4mm in from the edge. In white text, the words 'Legion Etrangere' were bold and striking, the whole armband representing the colours of the Tricoleur.

The concept behind it was well understood; the preservation of the espirit de corps of the old Waffen-SS, maintaining the differences, the marks of distinction that set the German SS soldiers aside from all others.

Picking up his coffee, he moved to the window next to Lavalle.

The dispatch arrived and was accepted by Bittrich, who immediately passed it on to his commander.

Finishing the rest of his coffee, the German noted the obvious surprise as Lavalle read the message.

"More coffee, Sir?"

"Yes please, Willi," and the Frenchman passed over his empty mug without taking his eyes off the paper.

By the time Bittrich had refilled both mugs, the message had been read.

"This is a warning order, Willi. How's your French now?"

The German exchanged Lavalle's mug for the order.

"We shall see, Sir."

The German scanned the paper, checking a couple of words with his commander before surrendering the document.

"When? Where?"

226

"It doesn't say. Nothing specific. Just...," Lavalle searched for the relevant part and, on finding it, read it word for word, "... Prepare to move your command by rail to a location in Eastern France on receipt of a verbal order with written confirmation to follow."

"Last time I heard something like that it concerned Vienna in '45."

A matter of which Lavalle had no knowledge at all, but that didn't stop him from understanding exactly what Bittrich meant.

"At least they have included rolling stock capacities. That will enable us to plan that side of things, Willi."

"We need to know where we are going too. That would help."

The grumbling continued as the two sorted their way through the whole document.

As they concluded, agreeing that senior officers were the same in all armies, 'La Camerone's' Commanding officer arrived.

Knocke, despite his own version of the mixed uniform, looked every inch the perfect soldier; clean, smart and professional.

Like Bittrich, he wore boots and gaiters, although his were of German origin. His trousers were American issue olive drab, crowned with his black Panzertruppen jacket, Death's Heads removed from the lapels in favour of the French rank markings of a colonel. The famous black tunic was sporting all Knocke's awards and displayed the new Corps badge and armband. However, his armband carried the legend 'Camerone' instead, to denote his unit affiliation. In truth, there were few such unit armbands as yet distributed, but, as more became available, the whole unit would eventually carry the distinctive markings.

On his head he wore his old M38 side cap, again the eagle exchanged for the new insignia. Whilst Haefeli's kepi had been an honour granted by an officer of La Legion, Lavalle sought guidance from higher authority before permitting its general use, a stance that Knocke understood perfectly.

227

Saluting Lavalle, and being honoured in return, he removed his cap and silently enquired for news.

"I assume your antennae just twitched then, Ernst?"

Bittrich grinned at the Panzer commander, handing him the drink he had just poured.

"I saw the dispatch rider leaving. Plus, I have some requests to submit, Sir."

Lavalle put Knocke in the picture as best he could, which gave the man only headaches and no answers.

"I will expect that your brigade will be first away with a cadre from my headquarters. Once we know when and where, we will write proper orders. Until then, make sure you are ready to implement a full unit displacement."

"Yes Sir."

"How long until you can implement?"

Knocke considered the matter for the briefest of moments.

"I can move up to the ramps and commence within the hour. I would expect to have my whole Brigade loaded within five hours, if the stock is in place Sir."

From another man it might have seemed like a wild claim or bravado. Both senior officers accepted it for what it was; a fellow professional who knew his men and his business inside out.

Lavalle failed to hide his smug look and moved on.

"You have requests you said? What do you need, Ernst?"

"At the moment, my maintenance crews are working miracles, and everyone one of my tanks is running. That cannot last, Sir."

Lavalle looked at Bittrich, who understood perfectly, and moved to his table, seeking a particular folder.

The French officer gestured Knocke to continue.

"Sir, I know Uhlmann and St.Clair are out and about scavenging for parts, and that will help. But my need is also for personnel, trained maintenance personnel, or I risk having the tanks and the parts but no one capable of marrying the two. My engineering crews are out on their feet Sir, and mistakes are starting to be made."

228

Lavalle asked the most obvious question.

"How many men do you need, Colonel?"

"If I had another forty trained personnel the problem would be gone, Sir."

That drew a smile from the Frenchman.

"That I cannot do but," and he nodded his thanks to Bittrich who had provided the necessary document, "There are eleven panzer maintenance personnel on their way here as we speak, 17th SS Panzer-Grenadiere Division prisoners taken by the Resistance in Normandy. They ended up languishing in a civilian prison, forgotten or ignored. Either way, they should be here tomorrow or the day after."

Lavalle returned the document to Bittrich.

"That is a start, Ernst," and looking at Knocke's expressionless face, he felt compelled to continue, "Not enough but a start."

"Thank you, Sir. The movement preparation order may make things difficult, as we may not be here tomorrow or the day after. But I have an idea for now, one that should provide a long term answer."

"Your solution?"

"Is there any reason why non-SS cannot serve here? Unless I am mistaken there is not."

Lavalle pondered but remained silent, encouraging Knocke to continue.

"In which case, seek volunteers from the forming German units and the existing camps around here, requesting trained personnel and organise their immediate transfer."

"And?"

"Personnel who have mechanical experience can be of use, to do some of the heavier manual labour. I do not doubt that such people can be found in a range of places and units, Sir."

"I do see a problem, Ernst. The orders."

Knocke conceded with a nod.

"I had not anticipated a movement order, Sir, but we may yet have time to bring in some new personnel from the local camps to help my mechanical engineers."

229

Lavalle had absolute trust in the judgement of the man in front of him and made sure he demonstrated that whenever possible.

"I will get you some more men, Ernst, you may count on it."

Knocke stood, putting his empty mug on the side table.

"Thank you, Sir. I will return to my duties and get my unit ready."

Replacing his side cap, he gave a smart salute and left.

1315 hrs, Thursday 16th August, Headquarters of the Legion Corps D'Assault, Sassy, France.

Back in the less than impressive hut that presently served as the headquarters of the 1st Legion Chars D'Assault Brigade 'Camerone', Knocke called together his officer group, less Uhlmann and St.Clair, who were still out scavenging.

Frenchmen, Germans, and a smattering of officers from a kaleidoscope of nations, answered his summons and received the warning order on the Brigade's movement.

The questions, when invited, were predictable.

"Menschen, you know what I know. It will be Eastern France and we will go by rail. That by itself is information from which we can glean much."

Turning to the map pinned on the wall between the two windows, Knocke stepped to one side so that the majority could follow his reasoning as he fingered the map.

"The new siding is not yet complete, so we will have to load up at le Bas de Pont."

A French officer cut in, complaining that the loading ramps there were not yet finished either.

Knocke, sensitive to the nature of his new command permitted the man to interrupt without sanction, whilst the German personnel present felt uncomfortable at the breach of military protocol.

"Capitaine Thiessen, the works there are fit for purpose. I inspected them myself this morning when the heavies were practising their loading procedures."

230

The legend's tone brooked no argument, and he continued conjuring up possibilities on the map.

Quickly he turned back to the man.

"Although perhaps we should check that the Schwere Panzers haven't undone the good work, eh?"

His grin was infectious.

Different fingers traced different rail lines on the map, each route examined and either accepted or rejected in turn.

Abruptly Knocke stopped

"My best guess is Strasbourg, Meine Herren. French First Army area, good access, west of the Rhine. Maintains flexibility of deployment. Thoughts?"

A chorus of agreement from the assembly and Knocke rapped out his orders.

"Each man to be issued with four days rations immediately, not to be consumed without orders."

"Full battle order for the march. All weapons and fuel, air spotters and security deployments. I want no surprises catching us with our pants down, Kameraden."

Checking his watch, Knocke looked impassively at his officers.

"This Brigade will be ready to move off at 1600 hrs, Kameraden. Advance guards away at 1540 hrs. Klar?"

Eyes dropped to watches and immediately realised the enormity of the task ahead.

The 'Oui's' and 'Jawohl's' mingled together without further comment, as there was no arguing with the schedule.

"Very well. Dismissed. Sturmscharfuhrer, stay if you please."

Try as they might, the ex-Waffen SS often slipped back into the natural way of things, and Knocke was no exception. Braun held the French 'Major' rank, Vernais' equal as Regimental Sergeant Major. He also rarely used the French ranks when dealing face to face with former comrades.

"Before you help Hauptsturmfuhrer Pöll get things organised, get a message to Uhlmann and St.Clair to return by 1800 latest please. Don't say too much over the radio obviously."

"Jawohl, Standartenfuhrer."

Knocke's deadpan face betrayed nothing.

231

"And try to use the French ranks, Braun."

"Zu befehl."

No hint of expression.

"We must remember that we are French soldiers now."

"A vos ordres, mon Colonel."

Knocke's grin betrayed the humour of the moment, and his slapped the NCO's shoulder playfully.

"Braun, wipe that look off your face and go and get him back here."

1433 hrs, Thursday, 16th August 1945, Headquarters, Red Banner Forces of Europe, Kohnstein, Nordhausen, Germany.

Zhukov listened impassively as Malinin read back the request he had just dictated.

"Let us hope that our leadership sees the sense of the request and gives us the men we need."

Malinin nodded gently, his mind processing the proposition as it had been doing since the first moment he and Zhukov had approached the concept.

Released Soviet soldiers who had been prisoners of the Germans were regarded with huge suspicion, more often treated as traitors and institutionally ostracised, falling to the most menial of jobs. Many were sent eastwards to work in cruel conditions as punishment for their failings. Some were even shot.

After all, the Soviet soldier was expected to die in combat rather than surrender.

The losses inflicted upon the Soviet Army during the ten days of the war had been worse than projected, but unusually heavy on certain key specialists, not the least of which were the highly skilled bridging engineers, despite orders to limit the dangers to these key personnel.

The request Zhukov intended to submit to the GKO was a plea to permit all qualified bridging troops to return to the ranks as soon as possible. A reasonable idea to overcome the present worrying shortage of trained engineers.

Nearly five million Soviet soldiers had fallen into captivity during World War Two, of which over one and a half

232

million were still alive, having been liberated during the Red Army's advance.

One major issue was the state these men were in, most having existed under the harshest of regimes with little sustenance, meaning they were not capable of being effective soldiers for some considerable time to come.

A discussion had taken place prior to the start of hostilities, during which the fate of the POW's was discussed. Then, without apparent imperatives, there had been no change in the harsh policy that the State and Party applied to the liberated soldiers.

Now that such an imperative existed, Zhukov hoped for some understanding from his political leadership.

Even so, he had used some standard ideological concepts to try and sway the men in power, such as employing the men in Shtrafbats, as Stalin had set up the penal units under Order 227 in July 1942.

"Get it tidied up and I will sign it immediately."

Malinin saluted and swiftly vacated the room, leaving Zhukov alone with his thoughts.

Michel Wijers leant back in his chair and enjoyed a bask in the Italian sun as he watched the little Ukrainian at his task.

Beside him sat a snoozing corporal, who had long since become bored with watching Ostap Shandruk moving through the prisoners of the 14th Waffen Grenadiere Division der SS, the infamous Galacian Division.

The 'corporal' would have looked more at home in the uniform of a US Marine 1st Lieutenant but, like Wijers, Solomon Meyer was in his role as a member of OSS.

Making up the threesome was a serious looking Polish Captain, there purely to smooth the way with the Camp Commandant once Shandruk had completed his task.

Polish II Corps controlled Rimini, and therefore the Galacians were their responsibility, or more accurately, problem.

Already a decent number, Wijers estimated about seventy men, were sat in an area designated by the camp commandant, ready for their part in Rossiter's plans

Shandruk, having been plucked from Sassy in record time, had met quickly with Rossiter for a briefing before moving off with the two OSS agents on a task of great importance.

Which task brought him to sunny Italy in the uniform of an American infantry Master Sergeant in the presence of men from his old division. A dozen of the segregated men had fought in his old Pioniere unit and he knew their worth well. The celebrations that should accompany the reunion with old comrades could wait for now, as Shandruk understood the need for haste.

Explanations could also wait and, in a testament to their respect for the former officer, men held their questions back.

Dusk was falling before the task was completed and one hundred and ninety-eight Ukrainian SS had volunteered, satisfying Rossiter's criteria.

The Polish officer sorted out the matter of release with the mystified Major commanding, backed up by the presence of a full colonel of the Dutch Princess Irene Brigade, for that was Wijers' role for the duration, adding weight to the cover story the Poles had been spoon fed.

His 'rank' also guaranteed cooperation from the Italian transport company from which he had commandeered truck and drivers, trucks which would shortly carry the 'volunteers' to the military airfield nearby.

The ten C47 aircraft that waited were well beyond his ability to obtain, having been approved by a much higher authority in Versailles.

It was gone midnight before the group began their long flight to Paris, and shorter second leg to their final destination of Camp 5A on the shores of Lough Neagh, a few miles east of Cookstown.

Cookstown was in County Tyrone, Northern Ireland.

Set aside for German prisoners of war, the OSS had appropriated the 5A facility for their own purposes two years beforehand, and few of its present inhabitants were American or British by birth.

Officially, neither the camp nor its inmates existed.

War does not determine who is right, only who is left.

Bertrand Russell

Chapter 66 - THE LUNATIC

1300 hrs, Sunday 19th August 1945, Hurlach, Germany.
Allied Forces - 4e Compagnie, 2e Battalion, 152e Regiment, and
disorganised remnants of 12e Dragoon Regiment, all of 14e
Infantry Division of French 1e Army, Remnants of 2833rd
Combat Engineer Battalion, 540th US Engineer Combat Group,
of US 7th Army, 522nd[Nisei] Field Artillery Battalion, all of US
6th Army Group.

Soviet Forces - 3rd Battalion, 11th Motorised Rifle Brigade, and
1st Battalion [less one company] 186th Tank Brigade, all of 10th
Tank Corps, and Special Tank Company, 44th [Motorised]
Engineer Brigade, and 76th Guards Mortar Regiment, all of 5th
Guards Tank Army.

The deluge had been constant since night had turned into
day, deadly objects of all shapes and descriptions dropping from
the sky onto the positions occupied by Lieutenant Mercier's
grandly named '4th Compagnie Battle Group'.

A grandiose term for a modest group consisting of the
survivors of his own 4e Compagnie, 2e Bataillon, 152e Infantry
Regiment, swollen by stragglers and remnants from other units of
the doomed 14th French Infantry Division plus thirty leaderless
US engineers from the 2833rd Combat Engineer Battalion..

He was supposed to be acting as a mobile reserve for his
battalion, blessed as he was with a number of American trucks
and 'liberated' civilian vehicles.

Instead, Soviet artillery and ground attack aircraft had
pinned him in place, his casualty list growing, seemingly every
minute bringing a report of more casualties.

The radio had been active, but none of the urgent
messages were for his unit. Requests for orders were rebuffed or
ignored.

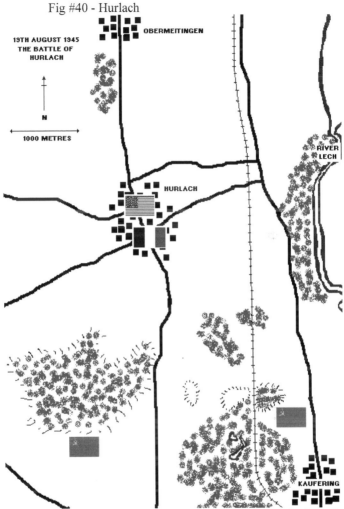

Fig #40 - Hurlach

19TH AUGUST 1945
THE BATTLE OF
HURLACH

N

1000 METRES

OBERMEITINGEN

RIVER
LECH

HURLACH

KAUFERING

Mercier was one of the few 'proper' soldiers in the unit, or indeed, the division. It had been formed from mainly FFI elements as France was liberated and the powers that be wanted to be seen to contribute more manpower to the destruction of Nazi Germany. In truth, the French Military probably never imagined that the weak FFI based units would ever see real

237

action, and certainly not of the type visited upon them by the battle-hardened Russian troopers.

In Southern Germany, they had been virtually welcomed as bordering on Liberators at times, the alternative of Soviet Occupation being far too horrible for most to contemplate.

Now things were very different.

On the 9th August, his division had found itself in the front line and on the receiving end of heavy Soviet ground and artillery attacks.

The 14th Infantry disintegrated under the pressure, some stalwarts managing to form defensive positions as the Soviets flooded past them, others running as fast as their legs could carry them.

US Cavalry and French armour had arrived and temporarily halted the attacks, but they had recommenced, displaying even more fury, and the defences were constantly breached and pushed back.

What was left of an organised 14th Division had been concentrated in the area between Hattenhofen and Fürstenfeldbruck, holding a frontage of ten kilometres. They had been bolstered by the addition of two battalions of the 2e French Armoured's 3e Regiment de Marche du Tchad, competent motorised infantry, sadly now without much of their transport following heavy combat and air strikes.

The remnants of the 12e Regiment de Curiasseurs had been organised into a large company and were positioned around Adelshofen, ready to counter-attack when necessary.

The Soviet attack fell upon the forces gathered along the Augsberger Straße running south-east from Mammendorf, vast quantities of high-explosive being delivered by the artillery of 5th Guards Tank Army.

10th Tank Corps, new commander in place and logistical issues sorted, drove hard and fast into the French lines.

2e French Armoured Division, anchored to the 14e at Mammendorf had to give ground, or be outflanked.

To the south, a composite team from the 45th US Infantry Division, covering from Fürstenfeldbruck to Gröbenzell, similarly folded back, but not before a company of M-10's from the 645th Tank-Destroyer battalion savaged the flank of 10th

Tank Corps advance, knocking out twenty of the 186th Tank Brigade's T34's in as many minutes.

Despite this success, the 45th had to give ground.

10th Tank Corps flooded through, pushing hard and quickly, overrunning the artillery and support units behind the lines.

River crossings over the Amper at Schongeising and Grafrath were captured intact and without a fight, as the 10th raced on to its target of Buchloe, some forty five kilometres beyond the front line, intent on outflanking Augsberg.

A desperate attack by USAAF Thunderbolts ravaged the lead Soviet formations, leaving hundreds of men from the 11th Motorised Rifle Brigade dead and wounded in their wake, although not without unaffordable cost to the ground-attack unit, which left five of its precious aircraft behind on the field.

The 11th thundered on and bounced the River Lech at Landsberg am Lech, a town made famous by the prison in which Hitler had written 'Mein Kampf'.

A handful of men from 2e French Armoured's 97e Quartier General, a motor transport unit, were cut down as the motorised infantry pushed hard.

Soviet recon troops entering Kaufering found the bridges still down, having been destroyed by the Germans during the previous war.

Meanwhile, Lieutenant Mercier was still asking for instructions, desperate for information, not even beginning to imagine how close he was to destruction.

A French officer from the 2e's Fusiliers Marins Tank-destroyer unit had decided to dig his heels on the Lech, just east of Klosterlechfeld, and bloodily halted the unsupported Soviet infantry before they crossed the river.

The Soviet commander made a swift appreciation of the situation, and ordered units from Landsberg to move north, in order to drive into the flank of the French tank-destroyers.

Lacking good intelligence, he decided to order the Katyushas of 76th Guards Mortar Regiment to drop their rockets on likely defensive points on the road heading north, paying particular attention to Hurlach and Obermeitingen, both on the road to Klosterlechfeld.

3rd Battalion, 11th Motorised Rifles, was tasked for the attack, directly supported by a tank company from the 44th [Motorised] Engineer Brigade, with most of the 186th Tank Brigade to follow as soon as it caught up.

The 76th's twenty-seven surviving Katyushas punched out their rockets, and, as was expected from such a veteran unit, they arrived on target.

In truth, few men were killed outright, and casualties were relatively light considering the amount of high-explosive that arrived in a short period of time.

However, the shock value was immense, especially to troops that had sustained a constant moderate barrage for some hours, and many a former FFI warrior messed his pants and cried for his 'mère.'

The 11th Motorised, although a unit that was tried and tested, also contained men who had seen little by way of proper combat.

Such a man was Major Vsevolod Skotolsky.

A French machine-gunner opened up as the lead units of the 3rd Battalion drove out of the cover of the trees and into full view. The sole casualty was the Battalion Commander, a popular officer who believed in leading from the front. Blood and brain matter splattered all over the panicky Skotolsky, and he turned his formation to the west, exposing the flank to further fire, as he desperately tried to regain the cover of the tree line to the west of the road.

The French were using an old Hotchkiss M1914 machine, unusually equipped with the 250 round belt, and the young Frenchman using it had no compunction about firing off every round, the shock of the Katyusha strike wearing off with the pleasure of retaliation.

One more man was injured in the hailstorm and all vehicles made it back into the woods.

Skotolsky, conscious of the passage of something unspeakable down his face, snatched up the microphone and called in a report.

By the time the unhinged de facto commander of the 3rd Battalion had finished, those listening believed that half the Allied Army was fortified within the confines of Hurlach.

240

The 76th's Katyushas, already lined up for the next strike, were retasked, and let loose again on the small German village.

186th Tanks were redirected to take advantage of the west approach, intent on hooking up through Schwabmühlhausen and round the west flank of the Hurlach defences. More elements of the 11th were to accompany them as infantry support.

Unfortunately for Semenchenko, the new Commander of 10th Tanks, he received a call from Colonel General Poluboiarov, who had recently taken over from the terminally-ill Volsky.

The man was impatient for news of success and, on being informed of the hold-up, ordered instant action, regardless of losses.

Perturbed, the normally calm Semenchenko quickly considered the options and made contact with the commander of the 44th Engineer Special Company.

Orders given and acknowledged, he moved on to Skotolsky, pinning him in place until the 44th had arrived and then ordering him to support closely.

In the short period of time he had been commander of the 10th, he had not been able to acquaint himself with all his unit leader's, so was unaware that Skotolsky was not the normal commander, otherwise he might have acted differently, especially as the 11th's commander was close at hand in Landsberg.

But he didn't, so he left the battle in the hands of an inexperienced engineer Captain, and an incompetent, panic-stricken wreck of a Major.

Mercier listened attentively as an NCO reported on the Soviet forces, although the evidence was in front of his eyes.

They had stopped, and more than that, had stopped in a fixed position.

Such things are the recipe of disaster.

He beckoned his radio operator forward, detailing the unit he wanted to contact.

There was no reply.

"Merde! Try another."

Fig # 41 - Battle of Hurlach

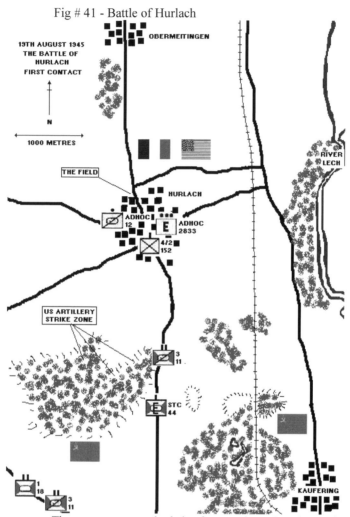

The operator consulted the frequencies, altered to suit, and again transmitted.

Nothing.

A third try and the set chirped into life as an Oriental accent acknowledged the cry for help.

"Tell him to stand by," shouted Mercier, fumbling with his map.

He wrote down the map reference details and the coordinates and relieved the operator of the handset.

"Roger that, Emile Two-Four-Alpha. Shot on the way."

Lieutenant Mercier had no idea what the 552nd was equipped with, but judging by the ranging shell that arrived and ploughed into the woods, it was very large and very deadly.

"Raleigh Two-Six, fire for effect, repeat, fire for effect."

Ten OT-34/85's of the Special Tank Company, 44th [Motorised] Engineer Brigade leapt into view, driving hard in column until they cleared the edge of the woods, then shaking into line.

The young Captain in charge went by the book, organising his tanks as if back in Officers School.

An experienced officer would have contacted the infantry, ensuring they were advancing with him but he was carried away by the moment.

An experienced officer would have spotted that the infantry were rooted to the spot and halted his advance, diving for cover as quickly as possible.

An experienced officer might well have destroyed his command in the doing, as the 155mm and 8" Howitzers of the American battalion placed their heavy shells right on the money, wrecking tree and vehicle in equal measure, transforming the former into lethal splinters that decimated the motorised troopers and converting the latter into funeral pyres for their occupants.

Men died ten times over, tossed and smashed by the heavy barrage, buried alive or driven mad by the relentless assault. The US artillery strike coincided with another salvo by the Katyushas falling full sqaure on the French positions.

FFI soldiers who had risen to enjoy the view of the artillery, succumbed in large numbers as the rockets crashed down.

The radio operator and his equipment became victims immediately, and Mercier could no longer speak to the American artillerymen miles to the rear.

243

This was unfortunate, as the Soviet armour approached his position in a steady line.

Had he fought the T34 before then he may have noticed the difference, but he hadn't, so the surprise was as complete as the horror they brought to the battle.

OT34's were modified for Engineer use, the hull machine gun removed and an improved ATO42 flamethrower installed, which flamethrowers now started to spit fire at the French positions.

It was too much.

Some ran, some stood and stared, some surrendered, and some died in the most horrible way.

Two American engineers lurked with explosive charges, waiting for a moment to dash out and destroy a tank. Two ATO's found them and transformed them into living torches, thrashing blindly in the ruins until they were dispatched by a sympathetic burst from their corporal's grease gun.

Skotolsky's unit had started to move by themselves, a handful of vehicles and men moving out of the artillery death trap to close on the relative safety of the village.

Crying like a child, the Soviet Major was curled up in the back of his M3 Scout car, the driver having moved forward of his own volition, in search of safety, and to hell with the idiot in the back.

The young Corporal, sat opposite Skotolsky, spat in contempt. The only other conscious survivor in the vehicle, he shouted at his officer, cursing, swearing, trying to stop the man's shocked babbling.

Making the road, the M3 ground forward, all four tyres punctured and coming apart, finally surrendering to the inevitable as the vehicle ground to a halt close by the first fiery barricade.

Too close as it happened. Paint started to bubble immediately and petrol from a holed fuel container set fire to the nearside front.

The Corporal grabbed his PPS and screamed at his Major, pointing at the growing fire.

Skotolsky saw the flames and reacted, throwing himself theatrically over the side and landing face first.

244

The shock of the fall, and of the facial impact, seemed to calm him, and he rose shakily to his feet.

Bleeding from both nostrils, he drew his Tokarev automatic and staggered into the village.

The 44th's flame-throwing tanks had set fire to over half the buildings, and acrid smoke filled the air, stinging eyes and torturing lungs.

French resistance was broken.

Survivors from the motorised infantry had closed up and had started herding the French survivors into a small field, west of Meitinger Straße.

The Major saw two of his men supporting a French soldier, the man's foot blown off at the ankle, carrying him to the collection area.

The Tokarev fired and the prisoner dropped lifelessly away from the shocked men's grasp.

"No fucking prisoners! No fucking prisoners!"

He continued repeating the order as he staggered unsteadily up the street, shooting an already dead body he passed on the junction with BahnhofStraße.

By the time he got to the small field he needed to reload, having shot another live prisoner and wasted bullets on four dead bodies.

Twenty-one battered and dazed prisoners were sprawled in the field, some being tended to by medical orderlies from both sides.

"Get away!" he shouted at the medics, "Go and tend to our own men, you bastards!"

The two Soviet medics rose and moved off to where their own casualties were being collected, well looked after by the newly arrived battalion medical section.

Skotolsky, his eyes now wild, turned to the young Captain, Pryskov of Armoured Engineers, who had dismounted from his tank to share a cigarette with his crews.

"Kill them. Kill them all."

The engineer officer swallowed hard, exchanging eye contact with his men.

"They are prisoners, Comrade Mayor. No threat now."

245

Skotolsky dragged his eyes away from the Frenchmen and spoke in a hiss.

"Kill them now, or I will kill you, Comrade Kapitan."

The tank's gunner slipped his hand towards his own holster, unnoticed by the mad Major.

"No, I cannot do that. In conscience, I cannot do that, Comrade Mayor."

The Tokarev barked twice and Captain Pryskov was dead before his body bounced off the side of his tank.

The gunner struggled with his weapon and also received two bullets, dropping him to the ground, screaming in agony.

"Conscience? Your conscience counts for nothing, you scum!"

Another shot silenced the scream of pain at his feet.

The Tokarev moved to threaten the next in line.

"Kill them, now soldier; now!"

The hull gunner fumbled with his holster and turned towards the nervous Frenchmen.

"Not with that, you fucking idiot! With that!"

The hull gunner climbed the front of the tank and slid inside to where Skotolsky pointed, attracting more attention from the nervous prisoners.

Those guarding them understood and increased the distance between themselves and those about to die.

No gout of flame satisfied the Major's lust for blood and death.

He shouted in through the open drivers hatch.

"Kill them, you bastard, or you are dead meat. Kill them!"

The petrified gunner had no more petroleum jelly and tried to explain to the mad man, drawing nothing more than point-blank bullets and instant death.

Skotolsky dropped off the front of the OT34, turning to the other tank nearby, waving at the Sergeant in charge.

"Starshy Serzhant, kill them now, or you will get the same. Move!"

The sound of running feet made the man turn, and the Medical Officer from the battalion aid section arrived, with two men in tow.

246

"What in the name of the Rodina are you doing, Comrade?"

Looking at the Captain with crazy eyes, Skotolsky raised his weapon and fired.

A PPS ripped the relative silence, smashing the lunatic officer against the tank. The bloody form dropped onto the roadway.

Helping the wounded Doctor to his feet, the two orderlies with him applied pressure to his radial artery and hurried him away to the aid station.

The young Corporal driver replaced his half-empty magazine and moved to the tank.

Skotolsky was dying, his body rent by over a dozen bullets, his life blood spilling onto the concrete beneath him.

He looked up at the familiar face and smiled.

The familiar face sneered and spat at the dying man, casually aiming his sub-machine gun.

Then, they both died together.

Acting on their last orders, and in the absence of contrary ones, the 76th's Katyushas fired another full volley into the French defences.

Skotolsky, the mad man, hadn't stopped them.

Pryskov, the novice, hadn't stopped them.

Semenchenko, the new commander and devoid of proper knowledge, hadn't stopped them.

Five of the valuable OT34's were lost in that strike, along with many of their crews.

The survivors of the 11th's 3rd Battalion, gathered in the town but not hidden in cover, suffered badly. After the battle, the battalion was broken up and used to fill gaps in the 11th's other units.

The medical aid station had ceased to exist.

Two of the American engineers managed to cling to life for a few hours before slipping away, the efforts of the surviving Soviet doctors in vain.

Three French prisoners survived the strike, and two of them lived out the day.

A desperately wounded Corporal of the Regiment du Tchad, who would eventually succumb to infection in the second week of September, and a dazed Lieutenant Alain Mercier, whose broken arms seemed a small price to pay to survive such carnage.

Choices are the hinges of destiny.

Pythagoras.

Chapter 67 - THE POLES

<u>0800 hrs Monday 20th August 1945, Headquarters of SHAEF, Trianon Palace Hotel, Versailles, France.</u>

"Well, you sure are a sight for sore eyes, Walt."

The welcome was genuine, the handshake firm.

"Glad to be back, Sir."

Major General Walter Bedell-Smith had served as Chief of Staff to Eisenhower during the German War, returning to the States immediately after the end of hostilities.

"Are you well, Walt?"

"Very stiff but my brain still works, Sir"

"There is work for your brain here and then some, Walt."

Eisenhower looked at his watch and did a quick calculation.

"Get yourself settled in. Have some chow and prepare yourself, Walt. Theatre briefing is at 1000 here. See you then."

A further handshake was exchanged and Smith was escorted away to a suitable room, where he could shake off the rigours of his awful journey from the States.

Smith had been onboard a Douglas C-54 Skymaster, which had departed Newark AAF, New Jersey, on the morning of 8th August, for the short hop to RCAF Greenwood on Nova Scotia. Having dropped off an RCAF Wing-Commander and his staff, involved with the Tiger Force 'Very Long Range Bomber' project, the C-54 was scheduled to deliver its remaining passengers to RAF Northolt, UK.

From there, they would go their separate ways, or at least that had been the plan, which failed the moment the crippled C-54 belly-landed in the Gulf of Maine, thirty miles from anywhere dry.

249

The survivors, eleven in total, were picked up the following day by a Catalina of the hastily reconstituted 5 Squadron RCAF.

After a period on hospital, Smith again made the transatlantic attempt, his aircraft having to make an emergency landing at RAF Belfast as a fuel leak robbed the C-54 of its legs.

He found a ride to Paris in a C-47, and spent the time chatting with one of his co-passengers, a USMC Lieutenant Colonel, who was extremely knowledgeable about the European situation.

Both men travelled together, all the way to the Trianon Palace Hotel, where they went their separate ways.

0912 hrs Monday 20th August 1945, Headquarters of French First Army, Room 203, Hotel Stephanie, Baden-Baden, Germany.

Naked, and steadily dripping water and soap bubbles onto the expensive wool carpet, his still-damp fingers tainted the thin paper, as he examined the written message that the hollow-handled knife had surrendered up. The breakfast tray had been brought to his room by a new man he only knew by sight, the precise staccato sequence of knocks causing him to rush from the bath in the full knowledge that it was not just food that was being delivered today.

Any reply he made would be collected with the dirty crockery, exactly fifty minutes after the tray had been delivered.

The message was comparatively long, directing a course of action that would undoubtedly place him in extreme danger.

He swore in the way he had taught himself to do.

"Skurwielu!"

'*Govno!*'

1000 hrs, Monday 20th August 1945, Headquarters of SHAEF, Trianon Palace Hotel, Versailles, France.

The briefing kicked off with the horrendous developments in the area of French First Army, where the

250

remnants of the 14th Infantry had simply disappeared, and the powerful 2nd French Armoured had been all but annihilated, opening up a huge gap.

"And De Lattre says there is no chance of a recovery?"

Bedell-Smith shook his head.

"Then I see little choice, Walt. We have to acknowledge that we are now split, and move our units accordingly."

Major-General Smith eased his aching back, both hands pushing in on his sides, his eyes not leaving the situation map.

"I understand, Sir. They have guaranteed Swiss neutrality, and we could use the border to ease our situation some."

Eisenhower knew his man. There was a 'but'.

"Sir, can we trust that? What if they decide to drive through Switzerland and into France or Italy beyond?"

The Allied Commander drew deeply on the cigarette and composed his reply.

"If we try and hold the line, what damage will be done, could be done? If we prepare to fall back now, then we can gain ourselves some breathing space, some time to establish."

Ike moved closer to his Chief of Staff, who spoke candidly.

"Munich is lost, that we must accept, but we can form a line... Stuttgart to Ulm... and south on the Iller River to the border," he pointed at the map, sweeping imaginary lines to better convey his words, "Dropping back onto the Austrian Border where natural defences will help us."

Eisenhower could see that possibility, but the question of time was crucial and he put the question out there.

"That depends on who we can put in harm's way to stop them, Sir."

Ike shook his head.

"Not a lot immediately. We have one hell of a problem with the French."

The CoS understood the 'French' issue only too well, but misconstrued the problem.

Eisenhower continued.

"Some of their units are simply not up to the job. The ones they formed from the FFI mainly."

251

Smith could only nod as he had stated his reservations about the worthiness of these units in March, even with Germany in its death throes.

"Not only that but they changed the designation of one of their units, two to five, so we thought we had an additional armoured division because they didn't make it clear."

Smith was not a great lover of the Gallic allies.

"What else is coming to the party then, Sir?"

"The Germans, but they are not there at the moment."

Eisenhower looked around before whispering conspiratorially.

"The Spanish, but again, not at the moment."

General Smith frowned in surprise.

"I thought that was..."

He trailed off, reading the look in his commander's eyes.

"I will bring you up to date on that one later, General," stepping back as a written report was offered to him by a newly-promoted Major.

Eisenhower cast a swift eye at the report, intending to properly examine it later, but stopped in his tracks.

"Anne-Marie, is this accurate?"

Turning back to Eisenhower, the CWAC officer smiled.

"With regard to targets hit, the reconnaissance photography has not yet been done. With regard to the friendly casualties, wholly accurate, Sir."

Eisenhower nodded, sharing her smile, and passed the report to Smith.

"According to that, our British cousins sent out seven hundred and sixty-four aircraft last night and all but six of them returned home. Six!"

By the standards of the German War, it was incredible. By the standards of the present conflict, it was the firmest indication yet that the night now totally belonged to the Allies.

Smith broke the momentary euphoria.

"What do the Swiss say, Sir? Do they trust this guarantee?"

Momentarily off track, Eisenhower looked puzzled, then realised that his CoS was back on subject number one.

"Yes they do Walter. Historically, no-one touches Switzerland, as you know, and it is the devil of a country to cross in peacetime, let alone with the Swiss Army nipping at your heels."

Smith grimaced.

"It is a risk but if they do try it, the journey will be long and hard for them, giving us time to prepare something."

The grimace seemed set to the man's features, drawing concession from Eisenhower.

"If we cut out two of the newly arrived divisions to babysit the western Swiss border, that should be sufficient for us to take whatever risk this poses."

"And our German Allies? What do they think of the possibility of more land in communist possession?"

On that Ike could speak with direct knowledge.

"They are already reconciled with the main defence line on the Rhine. They understand that we have to concentrate our assets as soon as possible, and need a secure defensive line from which to operate."

"So, I must ask again, Sir. What else can we bring to this now?"

Smith's uncompromising approach had served Ike well in the past and he welcomed the support the General brought to his headquarters.

"OK Walt. I can move 92nd Infantry, in fact they are already moving. The Brazilians are very keen to get involved for political reasons back home I think. They too are moving as we speak."

"There are two tank-destroyer groups that can get there quickly and I am sure I can shake loose some armor support from both Devers and Alexander."

"Can we trust the foot soldiers, Sir?"

"Truth is, I'm not sure, Walt. The Brazilians did well but were not badly tested. The 92nd did ok but, again, not as they will be tested now."

"We need to give them some back-up then, Sir. What's in the back pocket?"

253

"The Brits are moving two division but they won't be quick enough. Our dough's the same, unless I take risks and move in someone already tasked."

Smith checked the map before he spoke.

"And the Eagles?"

It was Eisenhower's turn to grimace. The 101st was the only unit in 18th Airborne Corps that was at full strength and had not seen any fighting in this war.

"I was keeping the 101st up my sleeve for offensive ops, Walt."

Smith remained silent, pursing his lips, as much in a sign to Ike as it was a marker that his brain was working the problem.

Eisenhower pre-empted him.

"Is this where you tell me that if we don't nip this in the bud, we may not have the offensive option?"

Major-General Smith enjoyed an excellent relationship with Eisenhower, but that didn't mean he was going to push it too hard.

"The Eagles would have the ball for a week tops, Sir. After that, we drop them back into 18th Corps and rest them, ready for whatever you have in mind."

Ike wondered if his CoS knew he had nothing presently in mind offensively, and had been talking in general and future terms.

"I think we may have told those boys something like that before, but," sighing deeply, the decision made, "Ok. Cut the orders and get the machine working. Group the three divisions and hand them to Devers. I will speak with Jake directly."

Smith started to wind up, dragging staff officers towards him as he began translating Eisenhower's wishes into proper orders.

<u>1125 hrs Monday 20th August 1945, Camp Châlons, Mourmelon le Grand, Marne, France.</u>

A telephone rang in the headquarters office of the 101st US Airborne Division, the legendary 'Screaming Eagles'.

254

Within four minutes, telephones all over the camp were sounding, as the order was relayed from the top, cascading down through all levels of command.

The noise level increased as a camp of troops engaged in training and lectures transformed itself into an airborne division about to go into combat.

The new commander of 2nd Battalion, 501st Parachute Infantry Regiment replaced the receiver and took a deep breath.

Of all of his division, he was the only 101st trooper that had seen combat since hostilities began and lived to tell the tale, and his experience had been close-up and personal with Soviet Paratroopers.

Major Marion J Crisp was going back to the war.

1355 hrs Monday 20th August 1945, Cuxhavener Straße, Two Kilometres North-West of Buxtehude, Germany

The drive forward from Lühdorf had started with fourteen running tanks, in various stages of disrepair, lights knocked off, fenders ravaged, external items destroyed. Only one of the IS-III's had not sustained damage.

As the advance progressed, tanks fell out as mechanical difficulties took their toll. The unreliability of the IS-III was its its greatest downfall, and on this line of march, it claimed tank after tank.

By the time the 6th [Independent] Guards Breakthrough Tank Regiment entered recently liberated Buxtehude, there were only seven runners left, the others decorating various points of the road from whence they had come, engines and transmissions failed under the strain. Admittedly, the newly appointed regimental commander's tank had not broken down, but that was no comfort to the dead man, killed with his crew by a German Panzerfaust on the approached to Elstorf.

Command of the unit now fell to a Captain, who organised the survivors into two platoons of four and three, himself in charge of the former, the latter falling under the command of Acting/Senior Lieutenant Stelmakh.

255

Fig #42 - Battle of Nottensdorf- the battlefield.

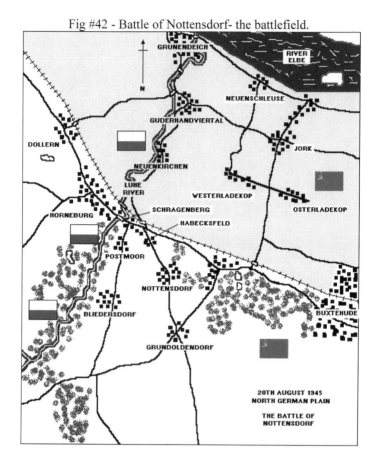

1400 hrs Monday 20th August 1945, Northern Plain around Nottensdorf, Germany

Allied forces - 1st Polish Armoured Regiment of 10th Armoured Cavalry Brigade, and 1st Polish Highland Battalion, and 2nd Platoon of 1st Polish Independent HMG Squadron, both of 3rd Polish Infantry Brigade, and 1st Polish Motorised Artillery Regiment, and A Squadron of 10th Polish Mounted Rifles Regiment, and 2nd Radar Section of 1st Polish Light Anti-Aircraft Regiment, all of 1st Polish Armoured Division, and

256

Fallschirmjager Batallione 'Perlmann', all of British XXX Corps, and 209 & 210 Batteries of 53rd Medium Regiment RA, all of 21st Army Group.

Soviet Forces - 1st and 3rd Battalions of 46th Mechanised Brigade, and 2nd Battalion of 376th Howitzer Artillery Regiment of 21st Breakthrough Artillery Division, and 72nd Penal Company, and 1st and 2nd Companies of 517th [Separate] Tank Regiment, and 3rd Battalion of 66th Engineer-Sapper Brigade, all of 11th Guards Army, all of 1st Baltic Front, and 6th [Independent] Guards Breakthrough Tank Regiment [Temporarily attached to 11th Guards Army], of 2nd Guards Tank Army, 1st Red Banner Central European Front,

25-pounder and 105mm high-explosive rounds commenced dropping on Nottensdorf and its environs on the stroke of 1pm precisely.

Formed up in the small German town were elements of the 11th Guards Army, about to launch their own attack, timed for an hour later.

The Soviet Mechanised battalions were arranged in line, which meant that the forward 1st Battalion bore the greater brunt of casualties. The tank-riding infantry were particularly badly hit, and frightened men ran in all directions seeking shelter from the barrage.

The battalion's tanks, T34/85's suffered less as they dropped back to the back edge of the town, leaving only two of their number behind.

After ten minutes, the artillery stopped abruptly, encouraging the infantry to emerge from their hiding places and seek out their wounded and dead comrades.

3rd Battalion, positioned in the woods behind Nottensdorf, watched on in horror as two groups of aircraft arrived overhead, one clearly fighters intent on protecting their charges, the other more concerned with attacking the targets on the ground.

The next group of Allied aircraft swept down to the attack, discharging their mix of rockets and 500lb bombs on the first run, then circling around and attacking with Hispano cannon.

257

Fig #43 - Nottensdorf - Dispositions.

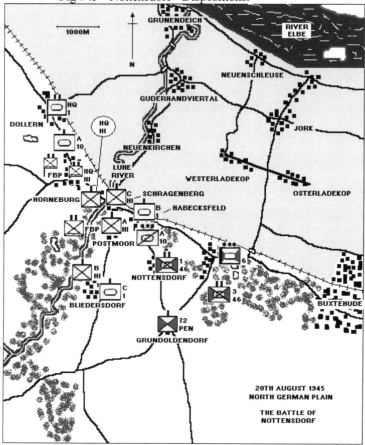

The fighters, Spitfire Mk XIV's of 41 Squadron RAF, immediately clashed with a Soviet fighter regiment, the XIV's proving more capable than the outnumbered and outclassed Yak-3's.

The Yak's jettisoned their bombs before contact, and tried to use their superior low altitude performance to escape, but 41 Squadron splashed five in quick succession, driving the Soviet Air Regiment from the field.

The RAF had very few Hawker Tempests capable of ground attack, but losses meant that the highly capable fighter aircraft were so employed this day. Twelve Tempest V's of 486 Squadron RNZAF were tasked with blasting a path for the Poles, instead of sweeping the skies for enemy fighters.

The 46th Mechanised Brigade contained six triple DShK anti-aircraft machine-gun mounts, each fixed on Gaz lorry, all of which pumped 12.7mm rounds into the air.

Two of the valuable Tempests were hit, one driving hard straight into the town, adding its fuel and weapon load to the fires already burning there. The second aircraft hit seemed to stagger in mid-air and started burning immediately. The pilot jumped, too late for his parachute to open.

As per the air battle plan, 486 Squadron then withdrew to safer height to police the battlefield. and prevent Soviet ground attack units from interfering.

The Polish artillery then opened up once more, walking the barrage from Nottensdorf, straight down the Cuxhaven Straβe, intending to batter the outskirts of Buxtehude.

Again, Soviet soldiers moving in the town were caught unawares and incurred more casualties.

The Polish attack force started moving up, and was clearly seen in the fields behind Bliedersdorf, as well as emerging from Horneburg.

Colonel Rumyantsev, the Brigade commander, wisely decided that he was outgunned, his assault a non-starter, and that defence was his sole option for now. From his position on a small piece of rising ground behind Nottensdorf, he ordered the 1st Battalion into some sort of order and directed the howitzers of the 376th Artillery Regiment into action.

47th Mechanised was fortunate to possess a large number of lend-lease vehicles, and Rumyantsev profited from having a roomy M3 half-track as his headquarters vehicle.

He ordered his liaison officer to get the assigned Shturmovik Regiment to hit the enemy artillery positions as a priority.

Assessing the approaching enemy forces, he oriented the 1st mainly against those emerging from Horneburg, dispatching half of the 3rd Battalion down the road towards Grundoldendorf,

259

where a short company of penal troops had already been defensively positioned. The other half of the 3rd, he retained as a reserve.

A message sent to the seven tanks of the 6th Guards Tanks asked them to move up immediately, in order to take advantage of their heavier guns and range, a message that was not received.

The Allied air battle plan had a final twist up its sleeve.

Successfully employed by RAF Coastal Command in an anti-U Boat role, three Mosquito FB Mk XVIII Tsetses had been pressed into service for ground-attack. Today was their first official use in this role, and they were accompanied by another Mosquito with purely observers onboard, tasked with an evaluation of the performance. The Tsetses were allocated to ground attack on enemy vehicles, giving the final close support to the attacker's.

T34's and a handful of Zis-3 anti-tank guns opened fire at the lead elements of the Polish armour, being immediately rewarded with two very clear hits at long range.

Unfortunately for them, the Soviets were not using smokeless ammunition, and professionals with binoculars noted positions on maps whilst others talked into radios, passing on details to the Tsetse pilots circling over Ebersdorf.

The Mosquitoes approached from the south-east, confident in the cover provided by the circling Tempests above.

The Soviet DShK gunners waited patiently for the enemy to come into range, watching, assessing, as the British aircraft from the recently reconstituted 235 Squadron approached slowly, angling in from a height of three thousand feet.

At a range of about one and a half miles, the lead Tsetse opened fire.

The Tsetse's carried a kick that was new to the Soviets, and the fuselage mounted 57mm Gun came as a nasty surprise. Normally equipped with twenty-five rounds, ammunition shortages meant that each aircraft carried only eighteen,

The first two shots missed a stationary T34, the third ploughed into the top of engine compartment, wrecking the power train and starting a small fire.

A gentle easing on the stick brought more joy for the aircraft, three shells smashing another T34 with more spectacular results. A further three shells badly damaged a Zis-3, incapacitating the crew.

The Mosquito flicked to port and applied power, rising into the sky as angry tracers from the DT's followed behind.

The second aircraft in line used ten rounds of 57mm and followed its leader, leaving another T34 and an AA/Gaz lorry in ruins behind it.

Lining up in leisurely fashion, the final Mosquito took out another tank but did not escape unscathed. A machine gun from the penal company scored hits, severely wounding the navigator. A bullet clipped the pilot and, instead of escaping safely to port, overflying the advancing Poles, the damaged plane lurched to starboard. The exposed underbelly attracted more fire, and pieces flew off the tail plane and starboard engine, and other bullets punctured the fuselage, releasing the navigator from his suffering and adding to that of the pilot, as a heavy calibre bullet destroyed his left calf.

Flight-Lieutenant Erskine, one of the few home grown New Zealanders in the squadron, accentuated his turn, applying power in an attempt to evade and gain height in the same manoeuvre.

The other two Mosquitoes, seeing their comrades in difficulty, returned to the attack, both claiming fresh kills as they discharged the rest of their 57mm rounds.

Erskine, in a display of great courage, conducted a second run, approaching from the south-east.

Spotting Soviet tanks on the edge of the woods, he thumbed the firing button, only to be greeted by silence as the damaged 57mm refused to fire.

Flicking the selector to cannon, he spared a sustained burst for two camouflaged vehicles sat on high ground between the woods and Nottensdorf, before his aircraft started to shudder and his most pressing concern was staying airborne.

The Mosquito flight disappeared over the Allied lines, two undamaged aircraft riding shotgun over their less fortunate comrade.

Senior Lieutenant Pan, senior surviving officer of 1st Battalion, grimacing as a sympathetic but heavy-handed Sergeant bandaged his wounded legs, tried the radio again.

There was no reply.

Neither would there be.

The Brigade headquarters group had been hammered by the final pass of the twin engine aircraft that had hit 47th Mechanised so hard.

Colonel Rumyantsev was not dead, but would not last the hour out. The command group now consisted of a handful of shocked men trying to do their best for the wounded and dead contained in the two destroyed half-tracks.

A GAZ staff car containing 3rd Battalion's commander halted at wreckage. Major Pugach could do no more than encourage the survivors in their efforts and say a soldier's goodbye to the dying man who had been his leader for over two years.

Taking command of the 47th's forces on the field, he went with Rumyantsev's plan, handed 3rd Battalion to his deputy and moved up into Nottensdorf to command the battle.

The Polish attack had hit problems. An over eager Major had pushed his units hard at the lightly defended Grundoldendorf, and, in the overextended advance, had exposed his left flank to fire from the Soviet tanks and anti-tank guns in Nottensdorf.

The central attacking force had not advanced in a coordinated fashion and was only just entering Habecksfeld. This had permitted the Soviets to concentrate their defensive fire against the southern force.

Sherman tanks of the 1st Armoured Regiment's 'C' Squadron engaged T34's to the north-east of Grundoldendorf, as well as those on the edge of Nottensdorf.

The artillery officer from the 376th called in salvoes on and around Dohrenstrasse and Nottensdorfer Strasse, where he could see the Polish tanks and infantry struggling forward.

All momentum was lost as the casualties amongst the tanks and support vehicles mounted, and the Polish Highland Infantry's 'B' company went to ground in search of cover.

Machine guns of the Independent Company, positioned on the edge of Bliederdorf, tried to suppress the defenders with little success, the range being too great for effective work.

The heavy Vickers machine-guns tailed off as the order to cease fire was relayed, but not before some errant bursts had claimed seven of their own amongst the Polish infantry to their front.

Seven Sherman had been knocked out or disabled so far, in exchange for only three T34's. 'C' Squadron attempted to push forward once more, partially as a response to the screaming and shouting over the radio from the Lieutenant Colonel commanding, and partially in an attempt to get out from under the barrage of artillery fire.

The Soviet M-30 122mm howitzers were pumping out five rounds a minute, successfully lashing the Poles struggling towards Grundoldendorf.

Behind the allied lines, the lessons of the previous days were being put into practice by the radar section of the Polish Anti-Aircraft Regiment. Experienced eyes checked maps and trajectories and found four suitable areas, relaying the coordinates to the two waiting batteries of 5.5" medium guns.

Ordering two full salvoes on the nearest possible location, the Royal Artillery officer waited for reports of slackening enemy fire.

None came, and the failure was emphasised by the distant but none the less spectacular destruction of a Sherman, blown apart by a direct strike on the turret roof.

Fire was switched to the second location, eight hundred yards behind the first and more high explosive was dispatched, but again, no lessening in fire resulted.

The Artillery Major from the 53rd Medium regiment examined the latest data and realised that the trajectory information had been misinterpreted.

Looking further afield he identified an area just east of route 141, beyond the range of his weapons standard ammunition.

However, in 1944, the British Army had introduced a super charge shell for the 5.5", capable of reaching out to over eighteen thousand yards. His orders sent four salvoes of these 82lb shells into an area fifteen hundred feet wide by a thousand feet deep.

The effect was instant.

At the front line, Soviet artillery fire immediately halved, dropping away further as each salvo arrived on target.

The Soviet M-30 howitzers were being hit, but worse still were the casualties to their crews. Men were being obliterated as the effective counter-battery fire did its grisly work.

Hardly a shell failed to kill or wound, injure or destroy, but the Soviet gunners, inspired by their fearless commanding officer walking through the steel storm, strove hard to hitch up their charges and get the guns out to another location.

The Polish troopers in the southern prong stubbornly clung to their ground, but now lacked the strength to advance until reinforcements arrived.

1507 hrs Monday 20th August 1945, Horneburg, Germany

Polish infantry Lieutenant-Colonel Micha Krol, OC of the Highland Battalion, was in a blue funk. His attack had gone to pieces, the southern prong exposing its flank and then being battered into immobility by enemy artillery, his central force finding it unexpectedly hard to pick its way through the rubble of Schragenberg and Habecksfeld, the northern force slowly crawling through unexpectedly boggy conditions above the rail line.

Faulty reconnaissance work had failed to spot that the ground, whilst capable of supporting the Humber armoured cars of 10th Mounted Rifles advance element, would not take the medium tanks of 'B' Squadron, 1st Armoured Regiment.

There was no opportunity to chastise the officer responsible, as 'A' Squadron of the Rifles Reconnaissance Regiment had taken casualties and ground to a halt within Habecksfeld, its commander's vehicle gently burning on the main road.

264

His own 'A' and 'HQ' companies were badly strung out between the two villages and under fire from Soviet mortars.

Whilst the German Paratrooper unit was in the woods behind Postmoor, and could have been sent to stimulate the southernmost prong, he decided to sort out the main attack first. Prejudice and hate had played their part in his positioning of Perlmann's unit, and both continued to do so, excluding the experienced unit from his thinking.

The company commanders of the Highland Infantry's 'A' and 'HQ' companies received forceful reminders to push forward in support of the tanks and he ordered more artillery to suppress Nottensdorf again.

1509 hrs Monday 20th August 1945, Schragenberg, Germany

'B' Squadron's tanks were getting nowhere fast, and Major Pomorski decided to switch back to firmer ground, moving his command's axis of advance to the rail track.

Immediately they made better progress, despite Soviet anti-tank guns bringing them under fire.

The lead tank was a relatively new M4 Sherman Firefly with a 17 pounder high-velocity gun, flanked by two 75mm equipped versions of the famous American medium tank. The nature of the terrain, boggy on one side with a small stream to the south, ensured that the armoured triangle was tight.

Pomorski's 'C' Company pushed up with the tanks, successfully swatting aside Soviet infantry who had pushed out in advance of the main positions, losing only one vehicle as the combined force pushed on.

The force was made swift progress and quickly found itself level with Nottensdorf, screened from the town by trees.

The southernmost 75mm boomed, and a small hut disappeared, complete with whomever it was that had been stupid enough to show themselves as the tanks approached. The Sherman's hull machine gun rapped out small bursts, lashing each clump of bushes or section of hedge with .30cal bullets.

The lead tank stopped and its turret moved almost imperceptibly. The gunner had responded to the commander's orders and sought out the target that had been called. He found the squat shape immediately.

"On target!"

The commander, a battle-hardened old Sergeant, wasted not a moment.

"Fire!"

The tank bucked and the breech threw itself backwards.

"Driver forward and right...," the smoke of his own gun obscured his view, so he quickly tried to remember the terrain ahead, "In behind the hedge to our right front, Jan!"

The tracks rode over the rails, bouncing the tank, as the driver located the spot he had been directed to.

The gunner rotated his gun to try and keep it pointing in the direction of the enemy tank. Another shell was already waiting in the weapon.

Sergeant Grybowski did not like what he saw through his periscope.

"Shit! There are three of the bastards!"

The gunner, Lance-Corporal Nowicki, had eyes solely for the one in his sight.

"On target!"

Grybowski gave the order as his periscope filled with light.

The 17 pounder shell grazed the gun mantlet of the Soviet tank, distorting the end of the co-axial machine gun before rocketing skywards without penetrating.

The armour-piercing shell from the IS-III's 122mm gun struck on the base of the Sherman's turret, instantly tossing the huge lump of steel and its human contents upwards and backwards. The two hull crew members, shocked, stunned, disoriented, looked back into unaccustomed daylight, albeit slightly blurry with smoke, and marred by fresh red stains, and a pair of trousers still containing the lower half of Lance-Corporal Nowicki.

Captain Evanin had split his small force, sending the group commanded by Stelmakh north, whilst pushing his own

266

group of four tanks into the woods at Fischerhof, and it was Stelmakh who had destroyed the Firefly with his first shot.

The other two tanks fired at the accompanying Shermans, achieving one first time hit that transformed the notorious 'Ronson' into a fireball, from which the crew were lucky to escape.

The other Sherman dove to the right, spotting a track in the woods heading south.

Two minutes later, it ran headlong into one of Evanin's group, and died.

Back on the assault route, 'B' Squadron tried hard to press home the attack, and accompanying infantry debussed into the woods, charging forward to threaten a flanking movement on the monster Soviet tanks.

Evanin may have been relatively new to combat himself but he was nothing if not efficient, and Stelmakh's group profited from the close support of a full platoon of sub-machine gunners and a section of engineers.

Casualties amongst the Polish infantry were modest but enough to halt their efforts to get around the IS-III's.

Understanding the problem's, Stelmakh ordered his unit to move forward slowly, not wishing to find himself under artillery fire, orders which he passed on by hand signal to the accompanying infantry. The tremors in his hand went unnoticed.

A number of small and extremely bitter combats broke out in the woods as the Poles were slowly rolled backwards.

More Shermans were transformed into scrap metal for no loss, the enormous armour protection of the IS-III's being impervious to anything the 75mm and 76mm guns could throw. The 17 pounders might have had a chance but, for reasons known only to the commander of 'C' Squadron, the remaining Fireflies were at the back of the advance. In truth, he had preserved his main gun tanks, as he expected solely infantry and anti-tank guns in defence, and had been supported in his view by reconnaissance photos taken that morning, photos that had singularly failed to spot any of the tanks of 47th Mechanised or 6th Guards Tank.

There was nothing the IS's could not kill, and their heavy guns fired repeatedly, claiming hit after hit.

Stelmakh's tank, 'Krasny Suka', was leading the advance, and therefore was the most vulnerable and vulnerable.

Spotting enemy infantry close by on the left, Stelmakh ordered his gunner to traverse the turret and spray the woods.

The weapon immediately malfunctioned as the first two bullets jammed hard in the distorted barrel.

Vladimir squealed in fear as an enemy shell struck below his hatch, the shaped charge PIAT round failing to explode, skipping off to drop beside the heavy tank.

Driven by self-preservation, he hauled himself up through the hatch and swivelled the heavy 12.7mm DShK machine-gun mount.

A second PIAT round whistled past him and he sent a stream of heavy calibre bullets into the group of Polish anti-tank soldiers, killing and wounding all six men.

A number of bullets pinged off the turret armour as both riflemen and machine-gunners attempted to cut down the foolish Soviet tank crewman.

He ducked back down inside the relative safety of the IS-III, his neck wet with blood from a metal splinter hit and his trousers again damp with the product of his bladder.

Fear ate at his insides as he tried to remember his training, a fear he overcame, pressing his eyes to the periscope again.

Regaining his composure, he once more started to direct the crew of 'Krasny Suka' in the fine art of killing.

Evanin's IS-III's had engaged the lead elements of the reconnaissance unit from their hidden position in the edge of the wood at Fischerhof.

Yet again, the Allied tanks were no match for the leviathan's, and the Cromwell's of the 10th Mounted Rifles were knocked out in quick order, the last two survivors falling back between Postmoor and Schragenberg, leaving the infantry component clinging to Habecksfeld.

Captain Evanin pulled his unit back five hundred metres and set about resupplying main rounds to his greedy tanks.

268

The IS-III carried only twenty-eight main gun rounds, which in modern combat was a distinct disadvantage and one the 6th had practised long and hard to overcome by constant exercises with their supply element in close support.

Elements of the supply company also awaited an opportunity to restock the other group, but the intensity of the fighting prevented then getting close in safety.

Whilst the heavy tank unit had remained unscathed, that could not be said of 47th's tank units, numerous oily columns of smoke marking the position of dead T34's.

The main group of IS-III's moved back once the swift restocking had been completed, and immediately ran into problems.

Artillery started to arrive on Evanin's position and he kicked himself for returning to a previously registered position, regret that turned to anguish when one IS-III was struck by a heavy artillery shell, transforming the tank into silent wreckage from which no-one emerged. The remaining three tanks swung south-west and skirted the edge of Nottensdorf, looking to deal death and destruction to the Poles struggling around Bliedersdorf.

Five Shturmoviks appeared, survivors from a full regiment tasked with supporting the intended Soviet attack.

Selecting the most advanced group of allied tanks and infantry, the vee of aircraft swiftly attacked and dropped their PTAB cluster munitions over the southern prong of the Polish attack with devastating effect, killing tanks and halftracks as well as men.

High explosive transformed a few acres of Northern Germany into a place of death, and flames and smoke gave credence to the thought that the very gates of hell had been opened.

The 1st Armoured Regiment retained four Crusader AA tanks in its order of battle, and these were disposed in a line between Bliesdorfer and Postmoor.

The Soviet ground attack aircraft chose to turn hard starboard, intending to reverse course and return at low level, following the Elbe, which course took them right over the waiting twin 20mm Oerlikon's of the AA Platoon.

269

One Shturmovik staggered as two AA tanks successfully found their target, the heavy 20mm cannon shells destroying the port wing, knocking off the aileron and wing tip, before they progressed further, chewing lumps from the fuselage on their way to damaging the tail plane and removing the rudder.

Uncontrollable, the Ilyushin aircraft rapidly lost height and crashed into a Polish anti-gun position halfway between Horneburg and Neuenkirchen.

A second Shturmovik was badly hit, rapidly falling behind its comrades. The struggling aircraft eventually fell victim to a roving RAF Mustang fighter.

Fire from the three IS-III's under Evanin's command was sufficient to break the nerve of a few of the Polish soldiers, whose panic became infectious, and soon the whole southern prong was retreating back into Bliedersdorf and, in quite a few cases, well beyond.

The central force, now aware that their comrades had been badly beaten, halted, and then started to give ground, moving back to occupy and defend Habecksfeld.

<u>1522 hrs Monday 20th August 1945, Horneburg, Germany</u>

Major Pugach enjoyed the sight of the withdrawing Allied forces, but lacked the strength to push forward and make use of the advantage gained in the repulsing of both the southern and central assaults. To the north, the sounds of heavy fighting now became overpowering, particularly the boom of the big tank guns, and he ordered a further company of his infantry up to support the 6th Regiment's tanks.

His opposite number, Lieutenant-Colonel Krol, was incensed that the Polish attack had ground to a halt.

Quickly consulting the map, he summoned up a possibility that had been discussed earlier that morning, and swiftly set his men to the new task.

Pulling back two troops from 'A' Squadron, a Firefly-heavy troop from the stalled 'B' Squadron, and adding in his own HQ tank troop as well as a troop of Stuart light tanks, Krol ordered a rapid movement to the north, hooking round through Neuenkirchen and then eastwards towards Jork, the plan being to secure the latter before driving south and into the unprotected rear of Nottensdorf.

Infantry support came from the carrier platoon, as yet unblooded, and 'A' Company's 3 and 4 Platoon's, also unscathed.

Perlman, the Fallschirmjager Major, who had recovered sufficiently from his ordeal at the Hamburg Rathaus, was unsure what to think. The Poles had started badly but now seemed to be reacting well to the crisis, still planning to attack.

He waited for a break in Krol's orders, or as he started to think, when the Pole actually decided to take a breath.

He seized his moment as the harassed Polish officer lit up a cigarette.

"Oberstleutnant Krol, may I offering my mobile platoon for some measure?"

Krol's knee-jerk reaction was to decline, but the professional in him decided he could not refuse thirty well-armed experienced men, experienced soldiers who also carried a number of the excellent panzerfausts in their vehicles, two SDKFZ 251 Ausf C half-tracks and one of the later model Ausf D's. The additional firepower of the vehicle mounted MG42's would also be welcome.

Again he consulted the map, drawing the German forward.

"Get all of your men up to Guderhandviertal immediately, not just the mobile platoon, and be prepared to act as my reserve force, Perlmann."

"As you order, Sir. I will forward Hauptmann Schuster's mobile platoon immediate and following with the rest of mine men in the lorries." His nod to the Hauptfeldwebel was sufficient to set the man moving to the task.

1541 hrs Monday 20th August 1945, Dorfstrasse [Horneburg – Jork Road], Germany

The HQ light tank troop had pressed forward swiftly, performing a standard leap-frogging advance up Route 140.

The route was less than ideal. The coastal plain was normally boggy, without the recent rains. The additional water ensured that nothing but a man on foot could move far from the roads.

'*Almost like there isn't a war on*', thought the Sergeant in charge of the lead vehicle, right up to the time that a relic of the previous war exploded, the Stuart swinging off the road, its broken right track flopping uselessly out both behind and in front of the immobilised light tank.

The column of recon vehicles moved slowly past the stricken tank, continuing the leapfrogging style, an occasional cat-call or laugh aimed at the hapless crew as they dismounted to effect repairs.

Bazyli Czernin, an experienced NCO, dropped to the ground at the back of the tank, his feet positioned neatly on the soil disrupted by the intact track.

"Watch out, idiot!" he shouted as Kondrat, the clumsy new boy, landed heavily and nearly knocked the sergeant over. Kondrat and the other one weren't bad soldiers. They were just new to the game and had much to learn.

"Careful boys, if the bloody cleaners missed one, they could have missed more."

He stepped carefully around his vehicle, examining each blade of grass and stone as he went, satisfying himself that there was no further danger from mines.

Mazur, experienced driver, excellent soldier, and quite the most ugly man ever to inflict his visage upon the planet, had dismounted at the front, stepping onto the sanctuary of a fallen tree trunk. From there, he surveyed the ground at the front of the Stuart.

The other new boy, Rakowski, fed up with waiting on the glacis plate, gingerly stepped across onto the wooden refuge and slipped, his hand shooting out to steady himself.

Both he and Mazur went tumbling, falling either side of the trunk.

Czernin heard the crack and scream as Rakowski's leg, held firm by a rigid branch, snapped at calf level. The bone ripped through flesh, exiting into daylight. Blood spouted, but the screaming stopped abruptly, as the young trooper smashed his head face first into the ground.

272

On the other side, Mazur landed heavily, winded, but unblooded.

Czernin called for the First Aid kit and saw Kondrat climb up into the tank in response.

Aronowitz, the tank's experienced gunner moved quickly to assist Mazur.

Click.

Even with the noise of the passing vehicles, the small sound was recognised for what it was by the experienced men, and Czernin locked eyes with Mazur for the briefest of moments, a microcosm in time during which both men read fear in the other.

The German S-Mine was one of the most effective anti-personnel mines ever invented and this one, a 1945 version, had been put in the ground a few weeks before the German capitulation.

The initial charge fired the mine upwards where another ,more deadly charge, delayed for a few seconds, exploded and sent the contents of the mine in all directions. This mine did not contain the standard steel balls, as it was one of the last produced. The desperate Germans had filled it with old rusty nails, screws and waste metal shards.

The mine exploded at precisely three foot above the ground. Aronowitz was shredded by unforgiving metal, his lower and central portions instantly transformed into a bloody mulch.

Mazur received dozens of fragments, none of which killed him outright, although the totality of the damage gave him less than two minutes to live before his system drained of blood.

New boy Kondrat was struck in the right shoulder as he emerged from the turret and immediately dropped inside, screaming as blood from a major vessel pumped over the interior of the tank.

Rakowski's open fracture, exposed to the mine, was flayed by metal, severing the leg at the site of the wound and causing more damage all the way to the knee and beyond.

Only Czernin was unscathed, his quick reactions allowing him to use the tank as cover.

Raising his head, he saw his senior crew members were beyond help, and that young Rakowski was mercifully still

273

unconscious. Pulling off the boy's belt, he fashioned a tourniquet to staunch the flow of blood.

The screaming in the tank had dropped to a low animal moan and he saw Kondrat hauling himself out of the vehicle, the covering of fresh blood making him seem almost demonic.

The fortuitous appearance of one of the infantry's ambulances saved him moving, and he gesticulated at the orderlies, sending them to the tank first.

Reaching around and under his wounded comrade, Czernin staggered to his feet, surprised that the explosion seemed to have robbed him of his balance.

He took a moment to steady himself and draw a deep breath before picking up Rakowski, surprisingly lighter than he expected until his mind factored in the missing part.

Clutching the badly wounded boy to him, the veteran Sergeant carried him towards the waiting ambulance.

Click.

1610 hrs Monday 20th August 1945, An der Chaussee [Heitmanshausen – Jork Road], Germany.

Leaving behind his two running mates, Acting Senior Lieutenant Stelmakh acted on a hunch.

The enemy forces to his front had withdrawn to holding positions and hunkered down, not even engaging his small force.

Artillery started to fall and he reoriented his unit to avoid further loss.

He could only guess that a flanking movement was in progress. Communicating with Kapitan Evanin, he received permission to investigate, as well as the welcome news that his commander would send one of his own tanks back to help.

Ordering a squad of the accompanying infantry to board 'Krasny Suka', he moved back down Cuxhavener Straße into Heitmanshausen and turned northwards to cover the road from Jork.

As he found a suitable position, Stelmakh was surprised to find one of the 3rd/47th Mechanised's 76mm anti-tank guns arrive, complete with a T34, and a full platoon and headquarters group from the 3rd Battalion, 66th Engineers.

274

The Kapitan in charge sought the tank commander out.

"Greetings, Comrade Mladshy Leytenant," Stelmakh's temporary rank not apparent to the engineer, "Onipchenko..."

His brief introduction was cut short by a coughing fit, during which the Engineer Captain extracted his map and spread it on the turret roof.

Stelmakh's quizzical look drew a response.

"September 43, Germanski bullet in the lung, Comrade, liberation of Bryansk."

The younger man could only nod in acknowledgement as Onipchenko looked down at the map, orienting himself quickly.

"Command structure is shot, Comrade. Enemy aircraft have hurt us badly. General Skorniakov is wounded and out of the fight. Colonels Polunin and Rumyantsev are dead. It falls to my Brigade commander to sort this mess so," he found what he was looking for, "Colonel Khozin has decided that we will envelop the enemy force."

The engineer swiftly indicated two lines of advance drawn in red on his map.

"This axis is aimed firstly at Bargestadt and Harsefeld, part of that force will then head northwards."

Using both hands, he described a classic pincer movement.

"Our force will move up to Jork and then push hard towards Stade."

Steklmakh's obvious comment died on his lips as the coughing started again. He waited but Onipchenko anticipated the tanker's objections.

"More units are coming, Comrade Mladshy Leytenant. We have been sent here to get things moving but there will be more on the ground to come, plus artillery and guards mortars in time."

Stelmakh nodded.

'Fair enough'.

"Nothing tricky here, Comrade. Your tank is our ace if we come across enemy heavy armour, I will have the rest of my battalion and two companies of Tridsat Chetverkas here within ten minutes, but we are not to wait, Comrade."

He looked across at the only other tank present, a wornand battered T34 bearing the name of a distant battleground.

"Our comrades in 'Polotsk' can lead the way with the main force until our armoured cars arrive. We will advance quickly, and in close order, until I say otherwise, Comrade."

Again, Onipchenko prescribed the route of advance, singling out the separate route he expected the IS-III and its support units to take.

"Are you ready to move, Comrade?"

"Immediately, Comrade Kapitan."

"Good, then drop in behind the lead elements and let us find the enemy together."

A swift salute and the man was gone, shouting at his men, as he headed to the T34 to issue a similar brief.

Three minutes later the small battle group started to move off in the direction of unoccupied Jork.

1619 hrs Monday 20th August 1945, An der Chaussee [Heitmanshausen – Jork Road], Germany.

Both sides hammered away at each other with artillery, causing casualties, yet both sides were unaware that the emphasis had switched to a number of insignificant tracks north of Nottensdorf.

That was about to change.

The Sergeant in charge of 'Polotsk' was less than happy to be placed at the lead of the column.

His nerve was placed under more and more pressure, the nearer his tank got to the crossroads at Westerladekop, his jitters transferring to his crew and unsettling them all.

In fairness, they had been through hell in the last two weeks, subjected to allied air raids, artillery, even shelling from some Allied naval vessels inshore.

This first taste of ground combat since they had overcome the Germans pushed their resilience to the limit, and in the case of the Sergeant, beyond.

"Pull off the road and stop! Stop the tank!"

276

The driver did as he was ordered, although he was puzzled at the instruction, especially as 'Polotsk' was still about a kilometre from the turning.

"Engine off."

Again he obeyed, but now he understood that the Sergeant's nerve was completely gone now.

Standing clear in the turret the frightened Sergeant had sufficient composure to wave the following vehicles past, shouting at an enquiring Lieutenant about how the engine had given up.

The lead elements of the Soviet advance ground past until Stelmakh's IS-III drew level and dropped off the road in front of the silent T34.

In an instant, the young officer was out and boarding the other tank, suddenly aware that something was not right.

The squad of infantrymen remained huddled on the hull of the heavy tank, watching impassively; just thankful that whatever it was would keep them from the maelstrom for a few minutes longer.

The sounds of whispered voices arguing rose to meet the tank officer as he climbed aboard the T34.

"Stelmakh here. What's going on lads?"

He wasn't prepared for the response.

"Fuck off, you child. Go and play with the British."

Taking the briefest of moment's to decide how to proceed, he took the plunge.

"Starshy Leytenant Stelmakh here. Give me your report. Why have you stopped here?"

"Tank's fucked Comrade. We will have a look at it shortly, Sir."

"Let us look at it together…now, Comrade?" Vladimir's tone not betraying his nervousness.

"Sergeant Chelpanov."

"Comrade Sergeant Chelpanov. Now."

The Sergeant rose from the turret, straight into the barrel of Stelmakh's Tokarev automatic.

"Now, now, Comrade Leytenant, no need for that."

"I will decide that, Comrade Sergeant. Now, what appears to be the problem?"

277

"Engine gave out, Comrade."

"Get the grills open and we shall see."

The moment the young officer had produced his pistol, his own crew had sprung into action, and the watching tank riders started to get more interested in events.

The IS-III gunners had stayed in place, watching to their front, in case the enemy decided to interfere, whilst Corporal Stepanov had armed himself with a PPD and moved to support Stelmakh. Three of the infantry squad dropped casually to the earth and moved to back up Stepanov.

Stood at the front of the tank, but out of the arc of the hull machine gun, Stepanov spoke loudly, so he could be heard by all.

"Problem, Comrade Starshy Leytenant?"

"It appears our comrades have an issue with their engine, Comrade Kaporal. We shall help."

Stelmakh intended to say more but picked up on a hand signal from his driver.

Stepanov tapped on the driver's position, the large hatch folding outwards immediately, exposing the face of a clearly worried tanker.

"Start your tank, Comrade Driver."

The engine turned over without the merest suspicion of firing up.

"Excellent effort. Now Comrade," his eyebrows adopted the position of a school teacher making a final attempt to deliver a vital lesson, "Let's try it with the fuel switches on."

The look from the driver confirmed Stepanov's suspicions, and when the 12 cylinder diesel engine roared into life there was no more to be said.

The Sergeant and his crew knew their lives were forfeit.

Stepanov looked at his fellow tanker, maintaining a neutral expression. "These engines can be very temperamental, Comrade Driver. An air lock perhaps? Something lodged in the filter for a moment?"

A squad of heavily armed engineers drew up alongside, an old and experienced Starshina quickly stepping out.

"Comrades, can we help?"

278

Stelmakh straightened, his rank suddenly apparent, the Starshina saluting impressively, also now aware that the tank officer was holding his automatic.

"Comrade Mladshy Leytenant. Can we be of any assistance?"

Stelmakh slipped his pistol back into his pouch as he stared into the eyes of the tank sergeant.

"No help needed, thank you, Starshina. The Tridsat's engine died but has now loyally rejoined us, ready for the advance."

The Starshina did not relax his grip on the PPSh, his eyes flicking between the pistol and the white face of the tank sergeant.

As if suddenly realising he was holding a pistol, Stelmakh laughed.

"I had to threaten it of course, Comrade Starshina."

Slipping the Tokarev back into its holster, Stelmakh dropped to the ground.

The men exchanged further salutes, the Starshina's look informing Stelmakh that he understood only too well what had come to pass. He climbed back into the captured Opel blitz and accelerated away.

Chelpanov stepped onto the front hull, sitting on the leading edge of the turret and exchanging a look of relief with his driver.

The Lieutenant turned and spoke softly to the tank Sergeant.

"We are all afraid, Comrade, but we must go on."

The Sergeant looked shocked, still coming to terms with the fact that he was not going to be summarily shot.

"I don't want to die. I've done my share, Sir. I just want to go home."

Stelmakh looked at his own driver, who could only shrug.

Turning back to the Sergeant, he could only speak from the heart.

"We are all soldiers of the Rodina, and she has called us to fight against aggression once more. Many have done their share, Comrade, and yet they still go forward. Can you or I hold back and hide when such men continue to do their duty?"

The sergeant replied with resignation.

"It is fine for you, brave and unblooded. You have no idea, Comrade, no idea what it is like to be so afraid!"

Stepanov had been slowly climbing up to the turret but heard the tankman's words and bounded forward, grabbing the man by the lapels.

"You useless fucking prick! You think you are the only man who is scared on the battlefield? Fucking idiot!"

Calming himself, he let the sergeant go and adjusted the slipped strap of his submachine gun.

"I've been in combat since 1941, and I have never felt brave or invulnerable. I always feel scared, as does the Starshy here," he indicated Stelmakh, climbing back up the side of the tank, who suddenly realised that he had not fooled his crew one iota.

"But he goes on, through his fear; and he fights!"

Stepanov answered Stelmakh's unspoken question with a shrug and a half-smile before turning back to the object of his diatribe.

"We are all scared, always scared. What it is important is that our courage overcomes and we do what we can, for the Motherland and our comrades, those we know by name and those we have never heard of."

The silence was broken by artillery falling to their south, far enough away not to cause concern but close enough to remind all of the trial ahead.

The Sergeant sighed.

"You are right of course. I am sorry. I ordered my crew to do what they did, and they are not to blame. What would you have me do, Comrade Leytenant?"

Stelmakh smiled genuinely, and slapped the man on the shoulder.

"Remember what this man just said, and look after your comrades. Now, I believe you are supposed to be up there?" he indicated the distant houses.

"Thank you, Comrade Starshy Leytenant."

"Oh, and Serzhant. We will say no more about this unfortunate...?"

He looked at Stepanov, seeking the words.

"Filter blockage, comrade Starshy Leytenant. I have no doubt that on next maintenance, the driver will be able to produce evidence of a blockage."

That message was received by the man in the front of the T34.

"We will say no more of this blockage, Comrade Serzhant. Good luck."

The Sergeant saluted and dropped into the turret, deciding to get his tank moving before the officer changed his mind.

The two riders dropped off the tank and watched as it sped away.

"Nice speech, Comrade Driver."

"Thank you Sir. Sorry about...well... you know."

"No problem, Stepanov. True words."

They reached the IS-III and mounted.

"Mind you, Comrade Starshy Leytenant, I have heard a rumour that half of all medals are won by someone retreating in the wrong direction."

The turret crew heard the laughter but missed the joke, both driver and commander settling in to their places with smiles on their faces.

Stelmakh's smile disappeared as a thought overcame the humour of the moment.

'Was it a joke?'

He put it from his mind to concentrate on the job ahead.

"Tank, forward."

The battleground was narrow and flat, with next to no room to manoeuvre, so much of the surrounding ground sodden and impassable, or full of irrigation ditches.

Firepower would rule, unless some other intervention could turn the day

Fig #44 - Flanking attack at Jork.

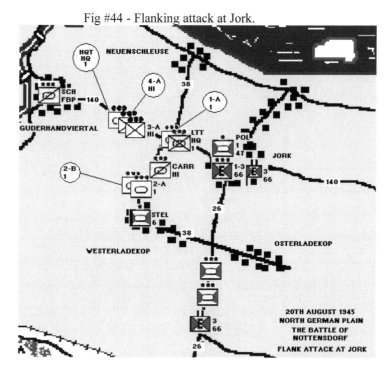

1645 hrs Monday 20th August 1945, Jork, Germany.

'Polotsk' caught up with the lead elements, or more accurately, found the lead elements gone to ground on the western edge of Jork.

Chelpanov ordered the T34 to pull over, where an infantry officer was waving to get his attention.

The Sergeant dropped down from the turret and the Engineer Captain immediately took the tank commander to a gap between two houses.

No field glasses were needed to see that a sizeable enemy force was declaring itself on the road to their front, slowly pushing towards their current position.

"One of the bastard's hit a mine some distance back and it's slowed them up. You need to slow them up more, Comrade

282

Serzhant. I will keep the infantry off you, but you have to stop the tanks."

"I will do what I can, Comrade Kapitan."

The Engineer officer coughed violently but heard and acknowledged the reply.

Quickly peering over the fence, Chelpanov immediately spotted what he was looking for.

"That's my prime position, Comrade Kapitan. Get your men out of the way of it and I will fight from there at first."

"It is done. Good luck Comrade."

Captain Onipchenko moved off towards the position Chelpanov had selected, shouting and waving his arms at a group based around a Maxim heavy machine gun.

Returning to his tank, Chelpanov quickly briefed his men and the T34 moved out from its position into a small hollow behind a pile of blackened bricks that was once the country retreat of a member of the local Gauleiter's staff.

The move was seen by the lead M5 Stuart, which broadcast the contact report immediately.

However, Route 140 was a narrow road and the ground either side not suited to armoured vehicles, restricting movement and escape options, vital to the survival of light tanks.

The Soviet 85mm spoke first, the solid shell tearing virtually straight up the road and missing the US light tank by a coat of paint.

The Stuart could do nothing to harm the T34, even if it had stopped to fire accurately, its armour piercing capability insignificant. Neither did it possess a smoke shell to create some sort of cover. What it did possess was engine power, and the twin Cadillac engines gave the Stuart an excellent top speed. In this case, all they did was drive the vehicle closer to its end.

'Polotsk's' gunner did not miss a second time, although the shell killed neither the tank nor the inexperienced crew inside, smashing into the front offside, removing the drive sprocket as neatly as a surgeon with a scapel, and sending pieces of the track flying.

The crew debussed rapidly, before the T34 could fire another shot.

The Maxim crew, still annoyed at being turfed out of their lovely firing position, vented their rage on the American tankers, 7.62mm bullets sending them to ground in search of whatever cover the bare soil could provide.

'Polotsk' sought and found a new target. It was dispatched with a single shell, a second Stuart tank burning readily along with most of its crew.

Other Stuarts were moving back, their commanders and gunners tossing smoke grenades out of their hatches, desperate to cover their withdrawal.

They were replaced by three Shermans from a troop of 'A' Squadron, one of which was a deadly Firefly.

Lieutenant-Colonel Krol was already raging, the slowness of his recon advance the first cause, losses in light tanks the second.

Ordering one squadron of his Shermans forward, he immediately switched his axis of advance southwards from the crossroads, intending to bypass Jork to the south, using route 38 through Westerladekop before rejoining the '26' to drive down to Cuxhavener Straße and into the rear of the Soviet defences.

Unfortunately for him, as he made his decision, forty-five tons of Soviet tank was already driving hard up Westerladekop, heading westwards.

Behind 'Krasny Suka', another IS-III, as promised by Evanin, drove hard to reinforce the Soviet effort, pushed along the road by the impending presence of two T34 tank companies and a battalion of lorried engineers.

Unfortunately for the Soviet forces, two events then took over and delivered a disaster.

In the first instance, the IS-III was straining hard to avoid holding up the faster moving troops behind it, and the strain told as the engine noisily ripped itself apart, the smoking and crippled tank coming to rest in the middle of the road, with the column behind closing fast.

In the second instance, the tanks and lorries started to bunch up on a straight road, which coincided with the passing of aircraft from the two light carriers, HMS Argus and HMS Queen, steaming off the coast of northern Holland, sending their Naval aircraft out in support of ground operations.

The former had recently been recommissioned and sent to sea, carrying 822 and 853 Royal Naval Air Squadron's, Fairey Firefly I's and Vought Corsair Mk IV's respectively.

The latter brought the experienced Seafire F/VX's of 802 Squadron RN, along with 848 Squadron RN's Mark III Grumman Avengers.

The Seafires of 802 were leading the mission, seeking out enemy fighter responses to the Fleet Air Arm excursion.

Intent on bombing the railway line north of Scharnebeck, the new target was bypassed by 802 and 848.

822 and 853 were to support the attack, but were permitted to attack targets of opportunity, and it was the considered opinion of Lieutenant-Commander Steele, officer commanding 822's Fireflies, that fifteen enemy tanks and well over twenty-five trucks were suitable for their undivided attention.

A solitary ZSU-37, in the rear of the tank column, put up its shells in an effort to ward off the attacking aircraft, failing to even damage one before it became a victim.

Sending Yellow and White sections into the attack, Steele remained with the rest of his squadron, half watching the attack, half seeking out threats in the unfriendly air space.

Six Fireflies swept down and discharged their weapons, each aircraft capable of firing a salvo of sixteen RP-3 rockets, twice the normal payload of Allied ground attack aircraft.

Aiming at the stalled column of seventeen tanks was child's play, and each attack was greeted with explosions and secondary explosions as the two Soviet tank companies were ripped to pieces, as well as massive casualties inflicted on the lead elements of the engineer battalion.

Behind them came Red section of 853, backed up by another two Corsairs from the reserve section.

No organised fire opposed them as they swept over the sky above the remaining lorries, from which tumbled scores of bewildered Soviet combat engineers.

Each aircraft dropped its load, each adding two aerodynamically shaped containers to fall erratically but unerringly to earth amongst the Soviet troops.

Twelve containers discharged their awful contents and turned the sky yellow in an instant, as fire flew in all directions, consuming everything in its path.

Napalm.

The casualties were horrendous; the lucky ones killed instantly, those for whom luck played no saviour's role ran amongst their comrades screaming, the sticky napalm ensuring that fire destroyed them despite their efforts to escape it.

It was war at its most horrible.

The Fleet Air Arm aircraft went on their way, satisfied that their intervention had helped their ground colleagues, and knowing that they had given Ivan a bloody nose.

In reality, 3rd Battalion of the 66th Engineer-Sapper Brigade was wiped out, save the few men that Onichenko had with him in Jork. The survivors on the road were either wounded or so shocked as to be out of the war for some time to come.

Surprisingly, four of the 517th's T34's were still runners, although their crews were similarly in shock.

The lone IS-III did not survive; its turret lay blackened some hundred yards from its smashed and twisted hull.

1658 hrs Monday 20th August 1945, Westerladekop, Germany.

Stelmakh was distracted by the events to the south, firstly by the explosions, and secondly by the wall of flame that sprang up so awfully.

He suspected that the reinforcements were having a hard time but had no time to consider it further as he reached the corner at the same time as an M5 Stuart tank of the Polish Mounted Rifles.

The enemy tank fired first, the range a ridiculous thirty yards at the most.

The puny 37mm hard shot hit the turret of the IS-III and flew off into an adjacent building, one of the few left undamaged by the passage of the previous war.

286

The recon tank threw itself into reverse in an effort to survive, the driver skilfully performing the task without losing a track or fouling the debris lining the road.

A second shell missed the Soviet leviathan but struck one of the infantry group as they were jumping off their mount.

The distorted body was thrown back, coming to rest hanging upside down from a small balcony on a ruined house behind the IS-III.

The 122mm gun boomed out and the Stuart virtually disintegrated as the heavy high-explosive shell detonated on its front plate, killing the whole crew instantly.

Pulling into cover behind a pile of building debris, Stelmakh keyed his radio, intending to inform Evanin that half the Allied Army was coming down the road towards him. The message was not received as his commander had been forced to evacuate his tank when it was immobilised by enemy fire.

One of the infantry section sprinted up the side of the road, bent double, in an effort to be as small as possible. He disappeared thru a battered doorway, re-emerging ten seconds later without the satchel charge he had been carrying.

His sharp-eyed Sergeant had spotted another US light tank hiding behind the building, and sent the soldier on a mission to destroy it.

An explosion threw a mixed load of debris up and out from behind the building, some of which was clearly identifiable as parts of a vehicle, indicating a successful kill.

Stelmakh had no time to do anything but fight his tank, his vision filled with a force of enemy tanks strung out on the road in front of him. Approximately five hundred metres to his front the road curved, exposing the side armour of the Allied vehicles, but also permitting more than the front tanks to bring their guns to bear.

He selected a tank with a bigger looking gun and ordered the killing to start.

The shell streaked past the stationary vehicle, its own 17-pounder returning fire instantly.

The APDS shell clipped the side of the turret close by where the first hit had been sustained, again ricocheting off.

287

The IS-III fired again and was rewarded with an immediate explosion and fire in the target vehicle, a Sherman Firefly of the Polish Armoured Regiment's 'A' Squadron.

Flashes from the roadway indicated more enemy shots but none struck the heavy tank, although infantry that had been close by in support decided to exercise discretion, moving further away from the object that was attracting so much attention.

Selecting another target, Stelmakh yelped with fear as a shell clanged heavily off the turret, again failing to penetrate the thick armour.

His bladder held and he ordered the shot, being rewarded with yet another 'kill' as the armour-piercing shell easily bit through the hull armour of a Sherman to their front.

Smoke started to thicken in his line of sight and he swiftly popped his head out of the open hatch, noting that the Allied troops were either throwing smoke grenades or small calibre mortars were putting down a screen.

In fact, both things were happening, as Krol tried hard to get his men to keep pushing.

The smoke was a good idea, as it screened the Poles from the deadly 122mm, but it also did the reverse, and Stelmakh swiftly ordered Stepanov to relocate forward.

The IS-III slid into the newly selected firing position and waited for the smoke to disperse.

It didn't, seeming to continue to grow rather than dissipate.

An unearthly squeal marked the arrival of artillery shells, hammering the corner of Westerladekop where the IS-III had just moved from.

The Soviet tank crew appreciated that their youthful commander had acted quickly and saved them from the dangers of the artillery.

However, the Polish artillery claimed four of the infantry section, one shell bursting within the huddled group and leaving no identifiable trace of their existence.

Out through the smoke came two Shermans, side by side, charging like Napoleonic lancers.

Both 75mm's fired together and their shells landed commendably close to where their gunners intended.

288

White phosphorous shells burn but also produce smoke and the two shells landed near the IS-III, one to the front and one to its left side.

Both tanks disappeared in the new cloud almost immediately.

"I can't see!"

The gunner was strangely calm, perhaps because he was in one of the most heavily armoured tanks of the time, or perhaps because he had faith in his commander.

"Shift your aim to the bend, right of the smoke, see it?"

"Yes, Comrade Commander."

The turret moved until the long gun was pointed at the spot Stelmakh had selected.

"If you have a target and can hit it, fire without my command. Clear?"

No answer came for two seconds, and then the breech flew backwards as the 122m lashed out again.

One of the Shermans lay askew, its offside running gear in ruins, track in pieces.

Bravely the crew stayed with the vehicle and got off another WP shell.

"Are you still sighted, Yuri?"

The gunner noted the use of his name.

"Yes, Comrade Commander."

"Then kill him."

Again the monster gun boomed and a shell streaked off into the smoke, disappearing quickly from view. The other side of the screen of chemical smoke, the heavy shell drove into the base of the tanks turret, killing the commander and gun crew. The hull crew abandoned immediately.

Off to the right edge of his vision, Stelmakh noticed a small movement.

"Gunner, machine gun, target right, infantry on foot."

"Comrade, the machine gun is useless."

In the heat of the moment, Stelmakh had forgotten.

"Govno! I forgot! Engage any tank you see on the road without my order."

He popped his head up through the hatch, exchanging the smoky, propellant tainted air of the interior for the phosphorous smoke outside the tank.

Grabbing for the machine-gun, he became aware of 'insects' buzzing round him, deadly insects fired from a Bren gun supporting the small group of infantry.

He cocked the 12.7mm machine-gun, feeling a tug at his collar as a bullet passed close.

Again he conquered his bladder's desire, controlling his fear and focussing on the task he had set himself.

The heavy DShK machine gun hammered out its bullets, throwing up earth and stones as he directed his first burst wide of the target.

Stelmakh adjusted, but felt the sting of pain before he fired again, a bullet clipping a lump of flesh out of his left forearm.

His fear left in an instant, replaced by a professional anger and his finger pulled the trigger again.

The Bren gunner, waiting whilst his number two set a new magazine in place, was the first to die, three of the heavy calibre bullets striking him and claiming his life instantly.

The loader was struck in the wrist as he placed the new magazine on the machine-gun, both hand and magazine flying away, leaving him screaming in pain.

Next to die was the radio operator, four bullets making a perfect line across his back as he turned to run.

The artillery observation officer was next. One bullet was enough.

Two of the supporting infantry were the last to die, one instantly, one eventually, as he had both femurs smashed by the heavy calibre rounds.

The remaining three men went to ground and decided to stay there indefinitely.

Stelmakh ducked back down to grab more ammunition as the main gun barked once more, smashing into a Firefly distant on the bend but flying off acutely, the angle of both the armour and the vehicle positioning defeating the heavy shell.

Another whoosh, and a metal clang told the crew that one more enemy shell had come close.

Quickly wrapping a cloth around his bleeding arm, he pulled the ammunition pannier up and rose up once more, only to find the DShK gone, the only sign of its presence being a small sheered metal bracket where it had once stood.

'Govno!'

"Machine gun has gone," he announced, matter of factly, as he dropped back down again, a sudden trembling present in his hands.

The loader finished ramming home a shell.

"Comrade Commander, we are low on ammunition."

The IS-III had been born low on ammunition, being provided with twenty-eight rounds at best.

"How many, Viss?"

"Eleven, and only three armour-piercing."

'Oh fucking hell!' thought Stelmakh.

"That's enough to do the job," said Stelmakh, portraying a confidence he did not wholly feel.

The gunner called a warning, and the big gun fired again.

Another Sherman burned.

"There are more targets than I have ammunition for, Comrade Starshy Leytenant," said Yuri the gunner, the edge in his voice showing that he was also just in control of himself.

"Maybe, but they don't know that do they, Yuri?"

Stelmakh was coming of age.

"Pile on the pressure, Yuri. Save the armour piercing for the big gun tanks but I'm sure our HE will do the job on their Shermans."

"What's in the gun now?"

"AP." The loader had the last AP round ready to load following the next shot.

"Give me HE from now on, Viss."

The loader slid the component parts of an AP shell back into the rack. The 122mm was a powerful beast but had its drawbacks, split ammunition being but one of them.

"Firing!" came the warning and the IS-III dealt out death once more, although the shell missed it's intended target it struck a bren gun carrier behind, wounding every man aboard.

291

More WP shells arrived bathing the area in a dense cloud of white smoke.

"Driver, relocate to previous position."

The big tank was reversing within two seconds, the skills of Stepanov now apparent as he moved the vehicle backwards using solely his memory, before stopping and driving forward into the prime position again.

"Nice work, Ovy!"

The IS-III crew were doing extremely well, products of the training programme that Stelmakh had conducted.

But, despite intensive training, costly mistakes can still be made and such a mistake nearly cost the loader his life.

"Firing!" was the warning from the gunner, as he sent another shell on its way.

The breech crashed back but this time found something soft in its path. Flesh and bone stood no chance against steel propelled by explosive force.

Mercifully, the impact had also smashed Vissarion Gushko's head against the wall of the turret, knocking him out at the same time as his shoulder and upper left arm were shattered by the unforgiving breech.

Stelmakh could only pull the injured man out of the way and stand in his stead, loading the two parts of the HE shell as quickly as he could.

The gunner had missed his previous shot and was determined to make up for his error.

He took the track off a Sherman and was pleased to spot the crew abandon immediately, fearful of sitting in an immobilised tank in front of the IS-III's awesome gun.

The tank next to it suddenly blossomed into flame as a shell penetrated it and set it alight, roasting the crew alive.

One of the surviving T34's had made it up to support, even though the crew were still a little shocked from their near-death experiences.

Their first two shots had missed, and Stelmakh and crew weren't even aware that they had help on hand until the T34's third shell struck home so spectacularly.

Another HE shell was rammed home and the last light tank in view came apart with the explosive force of the huge shell.

The fight went out of the Poles and they started to melt away, still laying smoke to cover their withdrawal.

Soviet artillery had started up a few minutes beforehand, called in by Onipchenko from his positions in Jork.

<u>1716 hrs, Monday 20th August 1945, Nottensdorf, Germany.</u>

'Polotsk' had survived the encounter intact, albeit scarred by hits and near misses. Six enemy tanks lay in front of their position, testament to their solid defence.

An engineer Corporal scaled the tank glacis plate to offer shares in his personal vodka stash, so impressed was he with the tanker's performance.

Three men from the Maxim crew had become casualties, one of which was fatal.

In Westerladekop, Stelmakh, Stepanov and Ferensky had pulled their beast back into cover and carefully extricated their wounded comrade, laying him on the engine deck until an ambulance came to take casualties away.

Stelmakh found himself still unable to make radio contact with anyone, so contented himself by talking with the infantry officer, gleaning as much information as he could about the wider battle.

Perversely, the Red Army had undoubtedly won the ground exchange, stopping each Polish advance in turn, causing more casualties than they sustained at each point.

None the less, the advantage gained had been lost by the badly timed arrival of the Royal Naval air squadrons, and the success of their attack.

It would have been no comfort to the soldiers on the ground to know that the RN aircraft had suffered 30% casualties in their attacks, falling foul of Soviet anti-aircraft guns in numbers.

Fig #45 - Nottensdorf - relevant locations

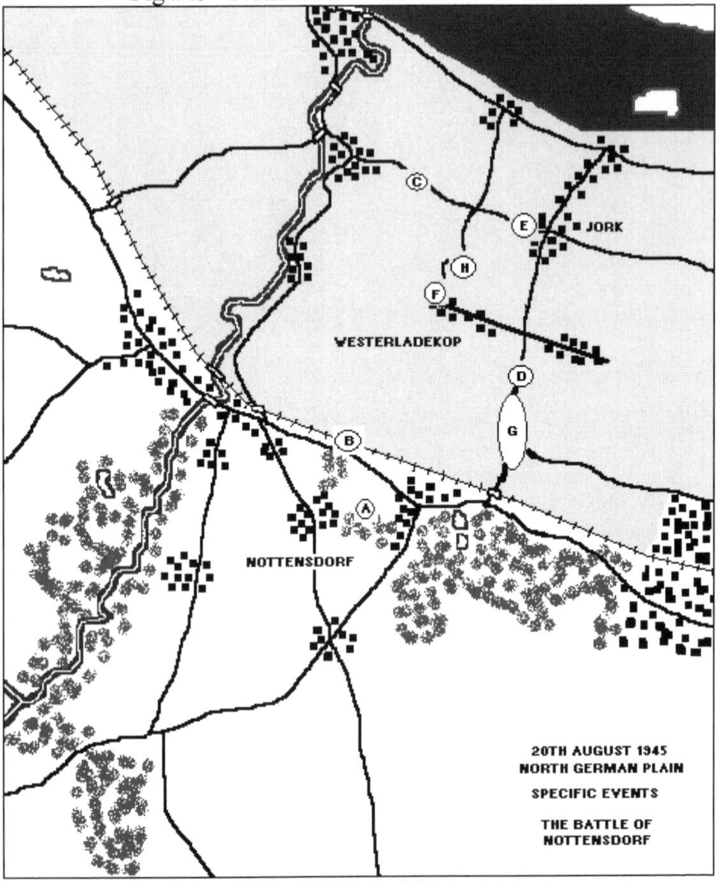

A - Rumyantsev's last position.
B- 'Krasny Suka' blunts Pomorski's attack.
C- Czernin's tank hits the mine.
D- 'Polotsk' has engine failure?
E- 'Polotsk's' defensive positions.
F- 'Krasny Suka's' defensive positions.
G- Royal Naval air attack on 3rd/66th Engineer and 517th Tanks
H- Polish artillery observer group's last position.

294

The loss of the engineers and tanks had stopped the intended northern route attack, firm Polish resistance halted the southern force's progress, and further air attacks and artillery exchanges meant both sides settled down in their start positions, no ground lost or won, save the previously unoccupied Jork now in Soviet hands.

Losses in senior personnel had been bad for the Poles, but much worse for the Soviets. 47th Mechanised Brigade was now under the command of Acting Lieutenant Colonel Pugach, 66th Engineers under Captain Onipchenko and the remaining five IS-III's of 6th Guards Breakthrough Tank's were led by Acting Senior Lieutenant Stelmakh.

Both sides had their 'investigations' into the debacle.

The Soviet one resulted in blame being fixed on the dead, partially because the naval air attack had been unpreventable.

On the Allied side, the buck stopped at the door of Lieutenant Colonel Micha Krol, who was relieved of his command and sent to less onerous duties.

Nearly two thousand men had become casualties during a battle that had made no difference whatsoever to the overall military position, save to remove a number of significant formations from the Order of Battle on both sides.

He who has lost honour can lose nothing more.

Publius Syrus.

Chapter 68 - THE PROPOSITION

<u>0534 hrs Wednesday 22nd August 1945, Rastatt rail sidings,
Germany.</u>

The trains had thundered eastwards and brought the
whole of 'Camerone' to Rastatt, where men and machines
debussed for the short journey to their holding area in and around
Muggensturm and Waldprechtsweier, Germany.

The journey through France had been uneventful, the
strangely clad legionnaires hardly raising an eyebrow amongst
the few civilians that examined the troops passing through their
area. An occasional old soldier made the connection but, in line
with the view taken by de Gaulle, his people generally cared only
that units of the French Army were on the move and paid no
attention to the detail.

When 'Camerone' debussed at Rastatt, things were very
different. Whilst no SS insignia were in sight, the very nature of
the men who quietly and efficiently disembarked, forming into
their combat units with practised ease, was obvious to anyone
who had been in Germany in the last decade.

Despite the seriousness of the situation facing their
Fatherland, some of the population were less than enchanted to
see the Schutzstaffel marching once more, albeit under the flag of
the legendary Legion Etrangere, and more than one passing
German gave voice to their fears.

Not all were so disposed, and word quickly spread
amongst the townsfolk, with many braving the early Wednesday
morning to witness the sight.

Ernst-August Knocke and his staff saw every unit off
their transport and on the road to their temporary base.
Camerone's commander was everywhere, chivvying up a unit
that took too long to disembark here, praising efficiency in

assembly there, and often using names of even private soldiers, a gift of memory that was granted few commanders.

As quickly as the units formed for the march they moved off, anxious to be safely quartered in the woods east of Muggensturm before any Soviet aircraft found them.

0857 hrs, Wednesday 22nd August 1945, Chencun, China.

It was bound to happen eventually, and in many ways, Nomori Hamuda was surprised that it had taken this long.

The Soviets had supplied the captured German vehicles and manuals for their maintenance. They had also provided qualified manpower, in the form of captured German Panzer-Pionieres, who had little choice but to conform.

At first, the Germans had been confused.

They had been captured by their deadly enemy and then shipped half a world away to service their own tanks, which were now in the possession of their ally, Imperial Japan.

Initially, they had applied themselves and the Panzers had run smoothly, despite the difficulties of operating in a climate for which they were not designed.

American prisoners were suspected of sowing the initial seeds of mass discontent, informing the Germans about the new world political map, and, more importantly, that Imperial Japan was no longer their friend.

The quality of work was hit first, and the tanks started to drop out of line. Fully half of Hamuda's First Company was strung out on the road back to Guiping, none lost to enemy action, engine failures robbing him of their firepower.

He had tried to encourage the mechanics, failing to secure any noticeable improvement.

Today, he would try a different tack.

Arriving at the temporary service point at Chencun, just east of Guigang, the lack of industry was immediately apparent, despite the presence of two of his precious Panthers, one with a serious transmission problem.

297

With the Marquis Hirohata by his side, and a squad of infantry led by Kagamutsu at his back, Hamuda approached the leader of the German mechanics, a Captain Bauer, formerly of the panzer maintenance company, 19th Panzer Division, until his capture in 1944.

Previous conversations between Hamuda and Bauer had become increasingly strained, not assisted by the fact that their only common language was English.

"Good morning, Captain," Hamuda always addressed the Germans by their rank, and in the case of Bauer, he gave the courtesy of a salute.

"Good morning to you, Captain Hamuda," the absence of a salute being wholly deliberate and intended to convey the German's position.

"I need my tanks back. When will your men have this two ready?"

"Three days I think, certainly not sooner."

"That is not acceptable, Captain."

"That is reality, Captain Hamuda. The Bergepanther is fucked," gesticulating loosely at the recovery tank sat under camouflage with its engine sat on the rear hull.

Hirohata shifted like a dog straining at his leash. His command of English was superior to Hamuda's, but he had a different job this morning.

"What is reality is that you and your men is failing. When we start, a transmission was being doned in a day," Bauer shrugged, "A day maximum, Captain Bauer. Now my tanks are disappeared, left by the roadside, and your crews go back to mends them and are not seen for days."

Bauer looked up from the report he was reading and made eye contact.

"We do the best we can with what we have. We don't have enough spare parts now and we have to manufacture many items ourselves. It all takes time."

Hamuda looked around the maintenance site, noting the men in various stages of activity. He was no fool and very quickly understood that there was little being achieved.

"That man there," he pointed with his cane, "He has undo that bolt and then tighten it twice since I have stood here. Explain."

Bauer took a look at the man and turned his head back.

"Perhaps he finds your presence daunting and is put off, Herr Hauptmann?"

The look on Bauer's face crossed the threshold of insolence in an instant.

"Captain Bauer. Understand this," and Hamuda raised his voice so that any other English speakers amongst the prisoners could hear his words, "Your usefulness here is centres around these tanks. Your existence is centres around these tanks. You will keep them running or we will have no use for you. Can I make me any clearer?"

Both Hamuda and Hirohata detected a few reactions amongst the German audience.

"I rather doubt that you will kill any of us, Hamuda. We are too valuable to you. Who else would mend the tanks eh? Your men? They couldn't maintain a fucking hard on in a brothel. We do what we can, as quick as we can."

A number of sniggers came from the listeners, further proof that others listening could understand his words.

The die was cast.

Hamuda took a moment to calm himself.

"Very well. You leave me no choice."

Moving off to one side, the tank Captain raised his voice, drawing all attention to himself.

"You men are been treated well and want for nothing. All we have asked is for your most work. Once we were Allies, but that has now changed."

He sought eye contact with one of the senior NCO's from the prisoners but the man refused it, dropping his eyes once more to the engine he was 'servicing'.

"None the less, we has being decent to you all, and you repay us with your laziness and," he turned to a grinning Bauer, "Your contempt."

The grin seemed to sharpen further, becoming a full blown sneer.

"Enough. It stop now."

299

He emphasised his point by slapping his cane against his boot, producing a sound not unlike a gun shot.

The German NCO looked up in time to witness the pre-planned act.

The slap was the signal that Hirohata had been waiting for, as well as an attempt to ensure everyone's attention was fixed on what was about to happen.

Hirohata's katana was out, flashed across the intervening space, and parted Bauer's head from his shoulders in the blink of an eye.

The body dropped to the ground and the head, still bearing its sneer, rolled away, coming to rest in the middle of a group of mechanics that had been stripping down a dismantled engine.

Hamuda looked around for the surviving senior man and picked him out with a stab of his cane.

"Lieutenant, you is now responsible for my tanks," and pointing at the headless corpse, he emphasised the point, "In the same way as he is responsible."

He let that sink in before finishing up.

"Both of them will be back operational by tonight or I will return."

Spinning on his heel, he nodded to Kagamutsu, who ordered his tough looking group to spread out into positions from where they could monitor the mechanics as they worked.

Hirohata wiped his blade and slid it back into the scabbard with more than usual ceremony, his face lacking any visible emotion, and he followed his commander away from the scene.

Both Panthers were ready for combat by 1800 hrs.

1200 hrs, Wednesday, 22nd August 1945. Headquarters, 1st Legion Brigade de Chars D'Assault 'Camerone', The Rathaus, Waldprechtsweier, Germany.

Now that the French officers from First Army had left, Uhlmann had taken the opportunity to report to Knocke on his unit's readiness, and the two had enjoyed coffee together as they went over the details of the move and the recent 'acquisition' of the nineteen ex-Wehrmacht Panzer-Pionieres who had been willing to join 'Camerone'.

The men, mainly ex-21st Panzer Division, had welcomed the opportunity to serve with the ex-SS, although Uhlmann later admitted to his commander that he had 'forgotten' to tell the men that they had a choice.

Most of the new arrivals already sported the insignia of the German Legion formation, a decision that had been taken by Knocke to encourage the 'unit' to take root in each man's psyche as soon as possible.

Lavalle had promised that every member of the Corps would have their insignia before the end of the month and, from the consignment that had met them when they arrived at their present location, it appeared that he was holding to his word.

Both men had been up all night, and both were dead on their feet, in need of sleep.

By mutual agreement, the meeting drew to a close and Uhlmann departed, passing on Knocke's request not to be disturbed for two hours.

He saluted to the Polish Officer who had been chatting to one of the Brigade's staff officers, and left to find some rest in his own billet.

The staff officer knocked on the commander's door and received permission to enter, the tone of the reply indicating that Knocke was clearly less than happy with the immediate failure to observe his wishes.

After a small exchange, the Staff Captain emerged and ushered the Polish Major in to see Knocke, closing the door behind him.

Salutes were exchanged, and Knocke motioned the new arrival towards the seat, still warm from Uhlmann's occupation.

"Coffee, Herr Major?"

"Not for me thank you, Sir."

A second's hesitation before Knocke decided that more caffeine was probably a good idea, and so he poured himself one before sitting opposite Major Kowalski.

"Captain Weiss tells me that you wished to speak privately on an urgent personal matter."

"Yes, that is true, Herr Standartenfuhrer."

301

Knocke held his hand up immediately, failing to stop the word tumbling from Kowalski's mouth.

"No longer of the SS, Major Kowalski. I am now Colonel of the Legion if you please. Now, what do you want of me?"

"Your compliance in a small operation that I am overseeing for my superiors."

Alarm bells were ringing but no-one could hear them except Knocke, the tone and poise of the man opposite giving cause for immediate concern.

"But first, allow me to introduce myself. I am Sergey Andreyevich Kovelskin, Kapitan in Soviet Military Intelligence, and here to give you a message, Herr Standartenfuhrer."

The Soviet agent sneered his way through Knocke's former rank adding, "Oh yes I know, now a Foreign Legion Colonel. Well, not to me. Once an SS bastard, always an SS bastard as far as I am concerned."

Kowalski/Kovelskin was holding a Walther PPK in his right hand, a fact that Knocke had only just become aware of.

"This is just to ensure that you listen to what I have to say, Knocke."

His own Walther was still in its holster, attached to his belt, the same belt he had taken off a few minutes beforehand when he expected to get some rest. It sat in his line of sight immediately behind the Russian, taunting him with its nearness and yet infinite distance.

"You have my attention. Say your piece."

Knocke's mind was working hard, different parts looking at alternatives, planning and processing options.

As Kovelskin spoke, that all changed, every cell in his brain focussing on the simple statement that preceded the Russian's business.

"Greta and your daughters say hello."

1207 hrs, Wednesday 22nd August 1945, On Römerstraße, south-west of Baiswell, Germany.

Being able to see out of only one eye was an inconvenience at the best of times. A clod of earth and grass had

302

been propelled by an artillery shell and hit him directly in the left eye. Marion Crisp was finding it hard going but there was nothing he or the medics could do to restore his sight at this time, so he bore it as best he could.

Anyway, it was the least of his problems, as the 101st US Airborne was bleeding out trying to stem the Soviet advance.

2nd Battalion, 501st Parachute Infantry Regiment, Crisp's command, was still in reasonable shape, but other units throughout the division were shadows of their former selves.

In fact, the situation was so fluid that the division, indeed all the divisions in the area, had started to lose their cohesiveness, units out of place and fighting alongside comrades wearing different insignia and sometimes national uniform.

At the moment, Crisp was withdrawing from a perfectly good position at Baiswell, forced back to Eggenthal by Soviet advances to the north and south.

The handful of trucks he had remaining were loaded up with the wounded, and an advance guard briefed to start setting up a defensive perimeter at Eggenthal; all had set off an hour beforehand.

As Crisp pushed his men hard down the road, the grim wrecks of two of his trucks gave testament to the activities of Soviet ground attack aircraft, both vehicles' passengers still aboard, having been either too wounded or too drugged up to be able to save themselves from the subsequent fires.

The paratroopers had heard the air attack behind them as they were driving off the Soviet infantry in the last enemy attempt at capturing Baiswell.

Now, they had handed the insignificant German village to the enemy for nothing, high-tailing it back to the next defensive point as fast as their legs could carry them.

Just off the road lay a shattered Soviet aircraft, an Li-2, the Soviet copy of the DC-3.

His senior non-com had organised a small group to check out the wreck, although it wasn't fresh and had probably been down since the start of the Russian attacks.

The Master-Sergeant dropped back to Crisp's group with his report.

"Three enemy dead aboard her, Major. Stinking to high heaven, so been there a'while. Preacher Manley found this and I confiscated it before he did his thing." They exchanged grins, conjuring up a scene of fire and brimstone centred around the devout Christian Manley and the devil of alcohol.

"Anyway, now is not the time."

Crisp took the extended bottle and examined the label. None the wiser, he handed it on to Captain Galkin for translation.

"Moscow Crystal vodka, Major. That's as good as it gets in Mother Russia."

Galkin's father had served with the White Russians and escaped to start a new life in Oregon, USA.

The bottle passed through hands again before coming to rest back with Master-Sergeant.

"When we get settled later, share it around, Rocky," no-one could remember how Baldwin had acquired the name, but it was his none the less.

"Yes Sir. Left a little present in there for our red friends."

"We will steer clear then. Now, get the boys moving Master-Sergeant."

2200 hrs, Wednesday, 22nd August 1945, Europe.

Eisenhower had retired early so that he could be up early enough to listen to Operation Gabriel, so Bedell-Smith satisfied himself that all was in motion for tonight's big plan involving the RAF and the following dawn's effort by the USAAF. It was an innovative idea and it had to be tried, if only the once.

An orderly presented him with his usual 10 o'clock coffee, the General's eyes straying to the large clock to confirm the time.

At 2200 hrs, in a dimly lit white church in Eggenthal, Major Marion Crisp discussed the tactical position with his officer group, having already walked the defensive lines, touching base with all his units and assessing the morale of his troopers, noting the now empty vodka bottle in Fox Company headquarters, now acting as a vase for some colourful weeds, courtesy of some wag.

304

Major Kowalski, his Polish persona now back in being, sat in the officers mess, consuming a modest Riesling, and pretending to read the latest version of 'Stars & Stripes' whilst not registering a word as he processed the day's events. A mess steward presented himself with another glass of wine. Kowalski produced a fountain pen and signed the chit. The steward took away the empty glass, the chit and the pen containing a simple message. The pen was returned to him by an apologetic orderly as the clock lightly chimed out ten o'clock.

Kowalski checked his wristwatch, noting with surprise that the mantle clock was out by four minutes.

In his billet, Ernst-August Knocke sat alone, no longer needing to present a normal front to his men, now able to think long and hard about the Russian's proposal.

'They are alive!'

War is cruelty. There's no use trying to reform it, the crueller it is the sooner it will be over.

William Tecumseh Sherman

Chapter 69 - THE RAID

Operation Gabriel had been underway for some time, as aircraft rose from airfields across Allied Europe, intent on closing in on a modest area of Northern Germany and transforming it into a wasteland, consigning anyone and anything in the area to a sustained hell of high-explosives and fire.

The original idea had been floated on the basis of Allied night time superiority. It had been a sound idea and the planners and senior officers had seized on it. The concept grew and the overseers bastardised it into a gigantic beast, a beast that required over half the bombers in the RAF and its Commonwealth squadrons, from the lighter Mosquitoes to old Stirlings hastily serviced and put back into action.

Allied recon had improved in the last few days, the most successful missions being those late in the day, trading lower resolution photos for survivability, at a time when the day transited into night, and the dark skies were ruled by the fighters of the RAF and USAAF.

Tonight, hundreds of bombers were targeted on a specific location, but not on a city, a town or a village; not on a bridge or a viaduct, a road or a canal. They were all targeted on a point on the map, representing a large number of living beings, assault divisions of the Red Army identified to be preparing for an attack.

Operation Gabriel, conceived as a modest area bombing strike to destroy specific enemy units behind the lines, had blossomed into five hundred plus aircraft modern Armageddon, about to fall upon the prime assault units of the 1st Red Banner European Front gathered around Celle.

306

Army officers had assisted in the planning, including some German officers from the new German Republican Army, using their hard-won knowledge to assist the target planners, applying their understanding to work out where the Russian would hide and camouflage his materiel.

Tons of high-explosive were targeted according to their intuition and expertise and if all went to plan then the Red Army would lose a significant part of its forces for little Allied loss.

0224 hrs, Thursday 23rd August 1945, the night skies of over Northern Germany.

The Squadron motto was 'To strive and not to yield', a sentiment wholly appropriate for a night illuminated by a full and bright 'bomber's' moon when one engine had already packed up and the starboard inner, all important for its contribution to the aircraft hydraulics, playing up and misfiring.

The crew of UM-V had only recently arrived at the squadron's home base at RAF Wickenby in Lincolnshire, survivors of a submarine attack on their ship, the Aquitania, which claimed the lives of a number of their comrades.

Transferred into 626 Squadron RAF to replace heavy casualties, this was their second mission, the first having been a doddle over the area east of Lübeck.

In the gleam of a brilliant moon, it was easy to spot all sorts of Allied aircraft, flying in one direction, for a single purpose.

UM-V was a Lancaster Mk I, a venerable aircraft that had seen its fair share of action already, passed airworthy after strenuous tests, and handed to a green crew, fresh from training in Canada.

626 had been allocated an area immediately north of some green and yellow markers, indicators accurately laid by RAF Pathfinder mosquitoes to indicate the line of Route 214.

The large area earmarked for the bomber's attention that night had been divided up into zones, beacons of different colours giving the aircrews a ground visualisation of the plans each aircraft had been issued with, permitting each bomb aimer to understand his target completely.

Pilot Officer Cecil Black had spent his war on the ground, being a late transferee into flying duties.

Now he was at eighteen thousand feet over Northern Germany, wrestling with an unresponsive and failing aircraft, desperately trying to get his charge to the right point to release the bombs and then get her home.

Other aircraft had already attacked, and the ground appeared to be moving, mainly because of the shadows that danced so lively on the earth, stirred to greater efforts by each further explosion.

It was also moving because of what looked like ants, spilling from hiding places, desperate to find cover away from the storm.

Briefed to look out for the right colour group, it was the radio operator who spotted the green/yellow markers, with the purple to the north-west and red/yellow to the north-east.

Black lined up the aircraft and checked the bombing height was at the correct eighteen thousand feet. Then the bomb-aimer took over.

Experienced pilots knew better than to let their attention wander but not Black, the absence of enemy activity and clarity of vision causing him to miss a vital instrument's warning.

The bomb-aimer called him from his reverie and Black had control as the bombs dropped from their rails, a full load of 500lb general-purpose cookies and four Small Bomb Containers, each holding two hundred and thirty-six 4lb charges.

The aircraft from 626 Squadron targeted on the area unloaded on top of the intact Soviet 1091st Gun-Artillery Regiment, weapons, vehicles and crew all secreted in a small wood just north of Route 214, to the north-west of Hambühren..

The results were devastating, and the 1091st would take no part in any combat action from that time forward, the few survivors being sent to other units to try and make good some of their losses.

However, Black's inattentiveness had condemned him and his crew, despite him finally noticing the defective altimeter, now reading fifteen thousand.

308

He opened the throttles, only to be greeted by sounds of destruction from the starboard inner as something vital came apart under the additional strain.

Correcting the sudden dip of the starboard wing, Black tried to feather the engine, without success. The prop refused to be adjusted, throwing the aerodynamics out, challenging and exceeding the skills of the new pilot.

More height was lost.

The Canadian mid-upper gunner had hardly moved to key his mike when the five hundred pounder he had belatedly spotted, dropped from a sister aircraft that was bombing from the correct height, struck the port wing immediately to the rear of the inner engine.

The bomb did not explode, but carried sufficient energy to remove the engine and bend the wing at the point of impact.

Black ordered his crew to bail out as he struggled with the rapidly falling aircraft.

Three minutes later, Lancaster UM-V added itself to the wasteland below, carrying Pilot Officer Black with it.

The whole crew slowly descended by parachute, but not all survived, as bombs dropped by their colleagues above and vengeful Soviet soldiers below took the lives of all but two of them.

UM-V was one of only seven aircraft lost on the night, the Soviet Air Force being notable only by its complete absence.

Once daylight permitted, Allied photo-recon aircraft took off to record the results of the night raid.

Soviet interceptors rose to meet them but quickly backed down, as swarms of fighters formed a barrier to protect their unarmed charges.

Two small skirmishes ensured, resulting in the loss of two RAF spitfires and no loss to the Soviet Air force, but the RAF and its cohorts owned that bit of airspace and none of the precious photo-recon birds were lost.

On return, the films were hastily processed and the interpretation commenced.

By 1500 hrs it seemed clear enough that a large part of the Soviet assault formations of the 1st Red Banner Central European Front had been ravaged in the raid. Undoubtedly, those that had survived would be very shaken up, and it seemed likely that no large scale offensive operations would be carried out by 1st Red Banner for the foreseeable future.

A good plan violently executed now is better than a perfect plan executed next week.

George S. Patton

Chapter 70 - THE FARM

The dispatch rider had brought a great deal of paperwork from units all around the Army headquarters at Baden-Baden.

Important mail, particularly that destined for senior officers, made its way quickly to the right hands.

The general mail was passed into the system, sorted and either sent out to be delivered by hand, or placed in pigeon holes for the appropriate person to pick up at leisure.

One nondescript letter sat in the slot dedicated to Major Kowalski, a standard military envelope addressed to Major Kowalsky. Such an error was understandable and would draw no comment or suspicion whatsoever, which was precisely why the Russian had instructed Knocke to change the last letter to a 'Y' if he was prepared to act to save his wife.

The letter contained a formal response to Kowalski's fictitious enquiry, Knocke had the presence of mind to continue the spelling within, supplying some nondescript administrative information and inviting the 'Pole' to revisit the Legion unit as soon as possible, complete with a signed special pass to assist his passage.

Pausing at the orderlies' station, he asked for lunch to be delivered to his room at one o'clock, figuring that would give him enough time to prepare his report for his GRU superiors.

A familiar face betrayed no emotion as Kowalski discussed the luncheon menu options with the attentive orderly, hearing but not openly acknowledging the simple request for an additional bread roll, which coded phrase told the orderly that there was important information to be passed.

She was an unremarkable vessel, at least at her launch in 1928, merely solidly built, destined as she was for trade routes in cold climes.

It was the fervent hope of every man aboard her now that she retained her unremarkability, even after weeks of alterations and conversions, creating an ugly swan from an ugly duckling.

At her launch, the mother of the local party chief had named her 'Dmitry Karbyshev', after a Lieutenant-General of the same name, a hero of the Great War.

As the darkened hull had slipped her Murmansk moorings and departed, she left the persona of 'Karbyshev' behind, the dawn light casting its rays on the Swedish merchant vessel 'Golden Quest', or at least a passable effort to look like the soon to be launched Scandinavian ship.

The real ship was intended to ply its trade between Sweden and North America, which latter destination was exactly where the heavily-laden Soviet vessel intended to make its second landfall.

Soviet Naval aviation had scored few triumphs thus far, but this mission was intended to announce their presence in style.

Intending to draw resources away from the attack aircraft, Soviet regiments noisily demonstrated against allied positions on the west coast of Denmark and Northern Germany, sideshows that claimed the lives of twenty airmen and half as many valuable aircraft.

But they worked, and the attack force slipped through unnoticed, skimming at wave top height towards their target.

312

HMS Queen was already recovering her aircraft, circling as they were, anxious to land after a sortie in support of 7th Armoured Division below the Danish border.

HMS Argus, steaming in line less than a mile to the starboard was burning and landing had ceased until the fires were extinguished.

A Fairey Firefly had made a total dog's breakfast of its approach and was now a funeral pyre for her crew, along with three naval ratings who had bravely tried to extricate the unfortunates.

Two explosions had already been witnessed by Queen and her escorts, and a third drew their attention as yet another of the unexpended rocket munitions exploded.

All aircraft were now under orders to return with unexpended wing munition, given the shortages some squadrons were experiencing, although the orders did not yet extend to returning with bombs aboard.

The air patrol, three Seafires from Queen, flew lazily around some miles to the east, but close enough that the pilots could see the trouble experienced by their running mate.

It also proved a distraction and gave the 51st Mine-Torpedo Regiment aircraft an opportunity to close.

Despite all the warnings their intelligence officers had issued, the Seafire pilots relaxed at the sight of A20 Bostons in US colours until their attitude and direction burned through the lethargy and made the radio report to their carrier more urgent.

"Snow White, Snow White, this is Sneezy Red One, ten unidentified aircraft closing your position due east at sea level, ten miles and closing for a torpedo attack."

The naval Lieutenant said 'unidentified' to save on initial explanations.

"Roger Sneezy Red One, intercept and identify."

Now was the time

"Roger, Snow White. Aircraft are A20 Boston's in US markings. Diving now."

Some of the aircraft returning from the support mission moved to help, but a combination of good tactics, luck and poor decision making on the part of the Spitfire pilots had put the 51st in prime attacking position, and all ten Bostons put their torpedoes in the water, five for each flat top.

Three of the Bostons were hammered into the water by fighters, a fourth manoeuvred violently and drove itself into the waves without receiving a hit.

One of the original air patrol Seafires received a full burst from a dorsal turret weapon, turning the fighter into a funeral pyre that swiftly extinguished itself in the cool waters of the North Sea.

HMS Trafalgar, a Battle class destroyer, was a design specifically created for anti-aircraft work, from her stabilisers to provide a suitable gun platform, through to her enhanced AA armament of 4.5" and 40mm Bofors.

Two of the escaping Bostons flew too close and were knocked from the sky simultaneously, their wreckage mingling as they disintegrated on contact with the water.

The remaining four Boston's sped away as fast as their Wright Cyclone engines could power them, their turret gunners all shouting joyously as their torpedoes bore fruit behind them.

The fire caused by the crash on HMS Argus had been all but extinguished but it was of little concern now, as three torpedoes ripped the starboard side open, allowing water to enter and explore the ships vitals, the carrier soon to be betrayed by her origins as a civilian vessel.

HMS Queen evaded all but two, but they were enough. Her main engine room flooded within minutes and power for fire fighting was lost. Some escorts tried to close and supply water, and HMS Magpie, one of the Black Swan class sloops succeeded.

The explosion that followed sunk both HMS Queen and HMS Magpie in seconds, bombs and other explosives falling victim to unchecked fires within the carrier's hull.

There were fatal casualties on a number of other vessels, with blast effect, pieces of metal, wood and other matter claiming lives up to a thousand yards from the explosion, both at sea level and in the air.

314

Nine hundred and sixty-three men had died in a heartbeat.

The shock wave rocked the Argus too, hastening her end, although her crew were able to escape in numbers, only sixty-four succumbing as the ex-ocean liner swiftly sank beneath the surface.

Some of the aircraft expecting to land started to ditch, others made for nearby Heligoland or for some other safe haven, eventually adding another twenty-one aircrew to the list of dead.

Two of the Bostons returned to friendly airspace where one was shot at by friendly flak, killing the turret gunner.

51st Mine-Torpedo Regiment had been virtually wiped out, but had exacted a huge price on the Royal Navy, sinking two small carriers and a sloop, killing a thousand men and potentially removing four squadrons of enemy aircraft from the Allied inventory.

Soviet Naval Aviation had indeed announced its presence.

1500 hrs, Saturday, 25th August 1945, Eggenthal, Germany.

Allied forces - HQ, E, F, & G Companies of 2nd Battalion, of 501st Parachute Infantry Regiment, of 101st US Airborne Division, and I & K Companies of 3rd Battalion, 370th Infantry Regiment, of 92nd Colored Infantry Division, all temporarily attached to French 1st Army, US 6th Army Group.

Soviet Forces - Mobile Group Virnok, of 4th Guards Mechanised Corps, temporarily attached to 5th Guards Tank Army, of 3rd Red Banner Central European Front.

The artillery was incredible, accurate and relentless. Eggenthal was already transformed into a wasteland of rubble and shattered wood.

And yet, every time the Soviet infantry charged forward, troopers from Crisp's battalion rose up and sent them back, bloodied and torn.

Seven hundred and one paratroopers had started the campaign. Eggenthal now contained less than four hundred and

315

fifty, the remainder split in equal measure between evacuations to aid stations or left dead upon the field.

An unexpected boost was received when two companies from the 92nd Colored Division's 370th Regiment arrived with ammunition just before chow time. The Buffalo soldiers were quickly directed to defensive positions, Item Company to the north, arraigned around Route 12, and King Company in a blocking position approximately half a mile south-west of Eggenthal.

A line of T34's took position facing west towards Crisp's positions and proceeded to batter the village with direct fire, all the time supported by the relentless artillery of the 4th Guards Mechanised Corps.

Major General Turbin sent orders to Colonel Virnok, dispatching his formations to the north and south, intending to surround and reduce the pocket and preventing escape.

Now Crisp's 2nd Battalion could not evacuate its casualties, the approach roads also being bathed in high-explosives. The aid station, established in the church and appropriately marked, overflowed with damaged bodies, spilling its contents out into the grounds, bringing those close to death alongside those long departed.

However, red cross markings were notoriously unreliable protection when fighting the Red Army, and such was the case today as shells had already struck the ancient building, partially demolishing the square tower.

At 1600 hrs, a further attack was repulsed, but the momentum of the Soviet advance had carried it all the way to the American foxholes, and in two cases, beyond.

Major Crisp called an officers group and passed on his decision to bug out, received with universal relief.

The first unit out was Crisp's own George Company, a fast moving point party supported by a business-like support group, the rest of the troopers assisting wounded men to move back.

The point party came under fire and went to ground, three of its members never to rise again.

316

The Russians had closed around behind Crisp's positions, cutting off the six companies.

Soviet artillery redoubled its efforts and Eggenthal sank lower into the maelstrom.

Fig #46 - Relief of Eggenthal - the battlefield.

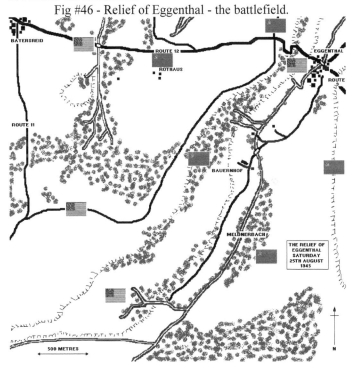

Paratrooper Generals are like no other military commander, for the very nature of their command places them in harm's way in order to be effective, dropping into enemy territory with their men.

It made for a particular breed of commander, derived from a very particular breed of man.

Maxwell Davenport Taylor had returned to Europe to resume command of the 101st, only to be pitched headlong into the defensive operations that were currently bleeding his division dry.

Reports of the encirclement at Eggenthal filtered through from 501st's commander.

One look at the map showed the experienced Major General that his cupboard was nearly bare.

He had amassed bits and pieces of the fractured and virtually destroyed 80th US Infantry Division under his command, but they were not enough to punch through to relieve the 501st by themselves. Looking at the assets available, he factored in the recent arrival of the ravaged A Company and virtually intact B Company of the 702nd Tank Battalion. Adding to the mix some of the 80th's divisional artillery elements, all Taylor was light was infantry.

Unfortunately, very few of the 80th's doughboys had escaped, and what had made it through to US lines would need some time to recover and shake out.

Taylor examined the map closely. Drawing his CoS in close, he spoke quietly.

"Route 12 is important to them, quite clearly."

Brigadier General Gerry Higgins only nodded, knowing his General was in decision making mode.

"I could order to hightail it back to Bayersried, or Obermelden..."

Higgins didn't think that Taylor intended anything of the sort. Such a manouveure would probably result in the loss of the force.

"Or I could break him out and give Ivan a bloody nose into the bargain."

As if Taylor could read Higgins' thoughts, he tapped the map in irritation.

"Light on rifles though, Gerry."

Closely examining the area around Obermelden, Taylor could see the untasked support elements of the 80th that would be itching to hit back, but he could not see doughboys anywhere, leastways none he could free up to counter-attack Eggenthal.

Higgins consulted his notes at length, referring to the map to get his bearings.

"When do you want to go, Sir?"

318

Taylor, sitting on a stool, finished his coffee before replying.

"Ideally, by 1900 hrs at the very latest. That will give the boys two hours of daylight to do the job, and offer up the night to get Crisp's boys outta the hole."

Higgins nodded, doing some swift maths before floating his idea.

"Our air is good at the moment, so we have no worries about movement. We can firm that up with Penguin Pete of course," the CoS referring to Major Peter George of the USAAF, the 101st's air liaison officer, by his accepted nickname.

"Here we have the 100th, less a company. Solid troops with halftracks. If we send them now, they can be to the line here," Higgins used a pencil to propose a start line for the counter-attack, receiving an instant nod from Taylor, "By 1830 latest, giving time for a brief."

Taylor ran his finger down the roads from Attenhausen to the start line north-east of Obermelden, calculating the difficulties as he went.

"OK. Give me more, Gerry."

"We have a platoon of the Brazilian cavalry here at Unteregg, and a company of their engineers somewhere south of Sontheim."

To the informed listener, such a conversation would be a sure sign of the disarray of the Allied defences, bits and pieces from all units scattered everywhere.

None the less, the line had held so far and the two officers had started to develop a plan to counter-attack and rescue the cut-off force.

"OK Gerry. Get Demario and Smith down here straight away, with a warning order to prepare for a move a-sap. Also, Castelli needs to be in on this, similar warning order for his artillery."

Taylor squinted at the map, finding the combination of gas light and sunlight insufficient for his needs.

"Orders out to the Brazilians, 2nd/1st Mechanised Cavalry and 1st/9th Combat Engineer Battalion to concentrate on Obermelden immediately."

Taylor grinned at his CoS.

319

"Once that is done, we will go through the niceties of letting our fellow Generals know what we are doing with their men."

Higgins grinned back at his Commanding officer, a small part of him knowing exactly how Taylor would take it if some other General started monkeying around with his boys.

'Still, needs must,' he told himself.

General Taylor sought out the information as to who might command.

"Looks like it's the 100th's ball, so get me their Colonel on the line once you have all the boys moving."

Within a minute, the radio started pumping out orders to the various units.

1900 hrs, Saturday 25th August 1945, Task Force Petersen, two kilometers south-west of Eggenthal.

The artillery of the 315th and 522nd Battalions had been working the Soviet positions for twenty minutes precisely, the mix of 105mm, 155mm, and 8" shells altering the landscape in and around the hastily scraped defensive positions.

At 1900 hrs, the lead tanks of the 702nd Tank Battalion, easy-eight Shermans from B Company, pushed forward, the Brazilian Cavalry not yet having taken the field.

Lieutenant Colonel Petersen, commander of the 100th [Nisei] Infantry Battalion, had been given a very specific brief by Maxwell Taylor; one that was unequivocal and simple.

Extract the isolated unit.

Kill everything with a Red Star.

Petersen enjoyed the looseness of the orders, as they permitted him to fight the battle as he chose.

General Taylor had been very specific on one point, which Petersen understood, and he acted to ensure no such thing happened. He had given the artillery strict instructions in order to prevent any friendly fire incidents, with either his task force or the troopers of the trapped Eagles. Such warnings cascaded down to the lowest levels, each and every man made conscious of the fact that there were also friendlies to their front.

320

Radio contact with the cut-off airborne troopers was sporadic, but the plan had been communicated and he expected the 101st to play its part in full.

With the Meldnerbach stream securing their right flank, infantry from his 'B' Company were pushing ahead along a wooded ridge line, mortars from the 100th's heavy weapons company waiting expectantly behind them, ready to overcome any resistance.

'C' Company tucked in behind the lead armored elements, and the rest of his force was stacked up, ready to deploy in line with the hastily devised plan.

'B' Company started to come under machine-gun fire and the mortars responded to the call, accurately sending round after round on target until the obstruction was eliminated.

The lead Easy-Eight, so called because of its E8 variant designation, appeared to kick on and swerve off the road, the sound of the explosion reaching his ears shortly after the visual image.

Through his binoculars, Petersen could see the tank crew abandon as tracers sought them out, fired from the Soviet positions to their front. One of the tankers disappeared in an explosion of red, struck by multiple projectiles, but the others made the relative safety of a stone wall, a few yards behind their stricken and now burning tank.

The second Sherman fired as they made it to their safe haven, a flash erupting at the top of the incline to their front.

'C' Company of the 100th oriented to the left side, and pushed tentatively forward, immediately coming under more fire from the high ground.

The US tank company brought more tubes to bear and directly engaged the defenders, beating each point down in turn.

'C' Company picked up the pace and pushed forward, dropping again when two Soviet tanks declared themselves on the ridgeline, engaging the infantry at first before recognising the presence of the American armour.

The Soviet commander had improvised with his defences, and the weapon that had claimed the lead US tank fired again. The 85mm 52K Anti-Aircraft gun was a large weapon, not normally suited to front line engagements, but the Colonel in charge had installed four on the ridgeline covering the approaches. Two had succumbed to the artillery already, but the survivors now engaged the American tanks with some success, a second E8 falling victim to a direct hit from which the crew did not escape.

The next US tanks in line were not so easily destroyed, and two hits were shrugged off by the lead Pershing, its own 90mm seeking out and killing one of the reversing T34's.

Backing up at speed, the other T34 nearly made it to safety but a 76mm shell tore off its nearside track. The disabled tank was ripped apart by numerous strikes, turret separating from hull as it exploded spectacularly.

Another 85mm shell ricocheted off the lead Pershing, a modest silver scar revealing its impotency.

The Pershing hit back, the shell passing within millimetres of the gun itself but failing to strike metal, hurtling into the sky beyond without noticing that it had obliterated two of the crew as it went.

Bathed in the essences of their dead comrades, the horrified gunners broke and ran.

The surviving 85mm engaged the lead tank, adding a second scar alongside the first.

'C' Company's mortar section dropped their shells right on the money, twisting flesh and metal with ease and knocking out the defenders last weapon of note.

The Lieutenant commanding the defending infantry ordered a hasty withdrawal, and the ridge was vacated.

The Nisei infantry pushed forward, both companies coming under fire from stragglers but keeping up the pressure, conscious of the limited amount of daylight available for their needs.

<u>1912 hrs, Saturday 25th August 1945, GuteNacht Bauernhof, south-west of Eggenthal, Germany.</u>

The Soviet commander had launched his own attacks at 1900 hrs, intending to compress Crisp's position and pushing his perimeter back further from any possible rescue attempt.

On the ridge line south-west of Eggenthal, soldiers from the 4th Guards Mechanised Corps threw a handful of the 101st troopers out of the 'Good Night' Farm, a prominent range of buildings that commanded both the ridge and overlooked the Eggenthal-Oberhelden road.

1916 hrs, Saturday, 25th August 1945, Die Rothaus, west of Eggenthal, Germany.

The modest but impressive looking Red House sat two hundred metres south of route 12, and was a vital position, whichever uniform you were wearing.

It was now in the possession of the infantry of 4th Guards Mechanised Corps, but they had paid a heavy price to displace the defending buffalo soldiers of King Company.

This was not going according to planning, as Crisp had banked on retaining the Red House, and using Goodnight Farm as a start point for his own push towards linking up with Petersen's force.

A swift orders group was called and found Crisp fired up and ready for business.

"OK, the Reds have fucked up plan A. Here's plan B."

He had pencilled in his plan on the map and used the markings to pass on his orders.

He started with the Item Company Commander from the 370th.

"Your boys simply must take it back and hold it, Abraham. We can't have the enemy sat there covering this road."

Crisp emphasised the road he meant, the one down which it was intended to evacuate all the wounded.

The wounded captain understood perfectly, his facial wound restricting him from anything other than an indistinct 'yes sir'.

Abraham Isaiah Johnson was descended from a line of black soldiers, the first of which had fought with the 54th Massachusetts, surviving the debacle at Fort Wagner, only to fall at Boykin's Mill on 18th April 1865, in one of the last engagements of the Civil War.

323

"I will give you some mortars, and you can have first call on any artillery Petersen can provide."

Moving quickly on, Crisp brought in Reeves of George Company.

"Bill, you leave a platoon behind in town to support our friends in King Company," he nodded at the black officer who sat waiting his turn.

"Keep your right flank tight on Abraham's boys and help him if he needs it ok? But, your job is to open the road here, all the way to this point," Crisp redrew a small cross in a heavier hand.

"No further forward than that. Beyond that is an artillery free fire zone. Clear?"

"Crystal, Boss."

The first time Johnson had heard the expression he wondered if it was some intended sleight but now he knew it was standard fare for the Eagles troopers. However, he couldn't bring himself to follow suit.

Captain Williamson of 370th's King Company was next in line.

"Ben, again, leave a platoon behind in your positions. Hang on tight to Bill's flank here. I want you to sweep the whole ridge up to here and not beyond. Stay inside the road line, probably best to stay inside the wood line. Support the attack on 'Good Night' from the ridgeline here, but I need you to take and hold this ground here as a priority."

Crisp tapped the gentle curve of the woods, sat next to and commanding the important link road.

"Yes Sir."

Turning to the next man in line, Crisp knew he was dealing the officer a bad hand but someone had to do it.

"JJ, you get the farm. Bring everyone you have. I will give you HQ's mortar and machine gun platoons too, but you have to take the farm."

1st Lieutenant Timmins appreciated the extra help, but Crisp was not finished.

"I will also come up to you as soon as things in town are sorted, but at the start it's all yours."

The normal commander of Easy Company was an experienced Captain, presently lying on a stretcher in the battalion aid post, both legs amputated below the knees; one by the surgeon's scalpel, the other by Soviet shrapnel.

Crisp would have preferred to use George or Fox Company but could not spare the time to reorient his forces.

That left Captain Gosling of Fox Company and 1st Lieutenant Muller, the latter placed in command of all the battalion elements holding Eggenthal itself.

"I am leaving you two with most of the transport so you can get the hell out on signal. Until then, hold the line, end of story."

Crisp relaxed.

"Rocky, you and your element are responsible for ensuring we leave nothing of value behind. Do your thing."

The grinning Master-Sergeant's grin said all that needed to be said, so Crisp moved on.

"OK then. Codeword's are the same, even though Ivan has messed with our original plan. Routes of withdrawal are the same."

Gosling proffered a lucky strike and the pause as Crisp lit it cued others in for their own smokes.

"I must remind you, we risk friendly fire here. Purple smoke on your location as soon as you breakthrough and make sure your troopers understand that Petersen's men are coming, and where their stop line is expected to be."

Gruff replies and nods showed that message was received.

"We've been handed a tough duty folks, but we will get out of this. Clearly, General Taylor thinks our scrawny hides are worth saving, and I happen to agree with him."

The genuine laughter of his officers told Crisp much about the way they were feeling, but he noted that Timmins had not joined in. The young officer's face was composed, and yet Crisp could sense the man was close to the edge.

325

Fig #47 - Eggenthal Breakout

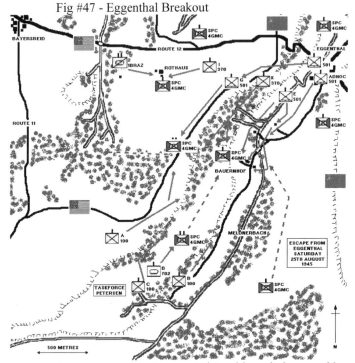

A moment's doubt crept into his mind, a sudden yearning to install another, more proven officer to command,

Crisp stayed his hand, knowing that Timmins could do the job and reminding himself that he would back him up.

"Stay within the plan. No gung-ho antics. Listen for your orders and react immediately. If things don't go to plan then we will have to improvise. No matter what, this force will be the right side of the red line tonight."

He stated it confidently, as firing erupted from the line on the edge of Eggenthal.

"Questions?"

More than one of the officers looked towards the area held by Fox Company as they shook their heads in answer.

The group synchronised watches on command.

326

"We go at 1930 hrs. OK, let's break it up and get the job done. Good luck."

Not unexpectedly, Gosling beat everyone out of the lean-to, sprinting away at top speed, anxious to find out what his men were engaging.

Crisp fell in beside Timmins and clapped the Easy commander on the shoulder.

"No problems, JJ?"

To the younger man's credit, he spoke his mind.

"Just hoping I'm up to the job, Major, that's all."

Crisp's face split into a grin that had charmed and relaxed many a man over the years.

"If I didn't think you could handle the detail you wouldn't have it. Now, get 'Easy' on the move and take that goddamn farm."

1927 hrs Saturday 25th August 1945, Eggenthal.

Crisp received the report of the Soviet attack with mixed feelings. The experienced Lieutenant making the report was a solid trooper, and his view was that it was already fading out.

The loss of Gosling was keenly felt, shrapnel cutting him down as he arrived in Fox Company lines. A medic had saved him from bleeding out, and the Captain was already installed in one of the half-tracks, ready to be evacuated.

Soviet mortars continued to drop their shells on the town, but the infantry attack had petered out almost as soon as it had started.

Crisp wondered why that was but thanked God for the reprieve in any case.

Quickly checking that the new commander of Fox Company was up to speed on orders, he decided to move off to join Easy in their attack on the farm, spurred by the sudden firing coming from that direction.

Easy Company had taken casualties and was now stalled one hundred metres short of its objective.

Three outbuildings had been cleared with sub-machine guns and grenades, particular attention being paid to the Soviet DP gunners that had exacted a high price from the assault platoon. Each of them received additional confirmation of death from the bayonets of those nearby, mainly in retribution for the killing of two highly regarded NCO's.

Major Crisp and his party moved up the line of a small stream, using the banks as cover where possible.

The Soviet infantry holding the farm started lobbing rifle grenades in their direction, and not without success, as a yelp from one of his signaller's revealed. The man hobbled on, his hand slapped hard to a bloodied hip.

In the cover of a small stand of trees, he found Timmins being bandaged by a medic.

"Why have you stopped?" the absence of Crisp's normal friendliness not wasted on anyone present.

"Sir, Sergeant Hawkes is organising some troopers with the Russian machine guns to give us a base of fire. We have no support from the 370th yet, so I figured we are going to get only one bite so we would do it right, Sir."

The unhurried calmness of the reply immediately removed Crisp's concern.

"Fair enough, JJ, but we have got to move it soon. How's his head?"

The medic spoke without stopping his work.

"Bleeds a lot, and the Lootenant will have a powerful headache come sun up, but he'll live, Sir."

Timmins smiled at his CO.

"Guess that reinforces the theory that I'm a meathead then."

"Dirty that bandage up some before you stick your turnip up JJ. Ivan will see you coming a mile off."

328

Another rifle grenade dropped nearby, shrapnel fizzing through the tree above them and dropping a smattering of twigs and leaves on Timmins and the medic.

"Right, let's get this show on the road. Take me to Hawkes so we can coordinate."

A short run across open but sheltered ground brought the group to the south-westernmost building, wherein Hawkes had placed the two captured DP's, with crews and a security squad.

The Sergeant was in animated discussion with the 2nd Lieutenant commanding the point platoon.

The one-sided discussion ended with the appearance of the unit CO.

As per the habit of a combat veteran, Hawkes saluted neither officer.

"Sir, we're set up and ready to go. The stream is good for cover up to the track and beyond. We can use it to get within about thirty yards if I'm right. At least a coupla squads, Sir."

Easy Company's second platoon had previously been posted in 'Goodnight' and Hawkes had confirmed the geography with them.

"Good work, Hawkes," the wounded officer pulled his map out and knelt beside the Sergeant.

The two others also took a knee.

"I will drop some mortars on them...here," he looked at both men for agreement, which was immediately forthcoming.

"King Company can bring some fire on the farm. They should be up by now."

Timmins thought for a second.

"Last minute, the mortars stick down some smoke across the frontage here, the squads in the stream put in a flank attack. Once the Russians are confused we go straight up through the smoke and in the front of the farm."

He got no argument from either man. As swift plans went it was as good as any.

"Get King Company on the horn."

Crisp watched the reinvigorated officer go about his business, the confidence flooding back despite the nasty head wound he had suffered.

A work party had finished policing up ammo and grenades from the dead and wounded and were distributing their spoils amongst the living.

2nd Battalion's Commander helped himself to a pair of frags and spent a moment rechecking his Thompson.

Easy Company prepared to advance again.

On the mark, the high-explosive changed to smoke and the farmhouse became a hazy shape before disappearing completely, the lack of any wind helping the plan.

Fire from both King Company and the captured DP's stopped in an instant.

The squads of Second platoon rose from the stream bed and rushed the edge of the 'Goodnight' buildings, preceded by a swarm of grenades.

They caught the Soviets looking the wrong way.

Bullets ripped into vulnerable Soviet flesh, as the mechanised infantrymen suddenly found themselves without appropriate cover.

Shouts of alarm focussed the defenders on the new perils and a volley of ill-aimed shots hit flesh before Second Platoon had found cover.

None the less, find cover they did, although there was an immediate territorial dispute as a group fell on top of a Maxim machine-gun team concealed behind a destroyed wall, silently waiting their chance to spring a surprise on the Amerikanski.

One of the Russians got off a pistol shot before all six were taken down by carbines and Garands at close range.

Hawkes reloaded his Garand, looking around but failing to locate the platoon commander.

A grenade landed next to two troopers whose sole intent was to keep their heads down out of the increasing torrent of Soviet fire.

One of them swung his rifle butt and batted it away, making himself small once again as the deadly little charge exploded out of harm's way.

'*Home run,*' thought Hawkes. A Soviet soldier threw another grenade, trying to learn from his mistake and hanging on to it a tad longer. It exploded too soon and only caused his comrades to seek cover. A small piece of shrapnel laid his cheek open to serve as a permanent reminder.

Through the smoke, dissipating now that the mortars had stopped firing, swiftly moving silhouettes could be seen closing on the Soviet positions, obviously men from the main assault force taking advantage of his diversion.

The ping of a bullet off the brickwork next to his head reminded him that not all had turned to face the main force.

The attackers had now swarmed over the first positions, and Hawkes could see some men engaged in hand to hand struggles.

"Smoke!" he shouted, pulling his own smoke grenade and arming it in one easy movement.

Five smoke grenades skittered across the track creating an effective screen within seconds.

"Move right! Charge!"

The squads rose as one and angled right, Hawkes' call being vindicated within seconds as tracer lashed through the smoke into the area they had previously been.

Picturing the scene in his mind's eye, he ran into the smoke, hoping that the unequal combat he had witnessed had not yet ended.

Emerging from the smoke, he instinctively pulled the trigger, putting down two of the Soviets that had cornered Timmins. One of the others lay with a shattered skull, courtesy of a swinging blow from Timmins' Thompson, which broken and useless submachine gun was still clutched in his hands, the young Lieutenant desperately fending off his assailant.

Sergeant Hawkes ploughed into the back of the Russian, sending him flying and into the ground, where three kicks in the face from Timmins drove his jawbone into his brain.

Both men turned and ran on, stopping at a double doorway. Dead men from both sides lay on the threshold, freshly killed, blood still seeping from multiple wounds.

Hawkes risked a quick peek and received a peppering of brick splinters for his pains, at least two automatic weapons covering the entranceway.

331

Two more paratroopers joined them and military sign language explained the plan.

A grenade went through the doorway, deliberately bounced off the door to get a reverse angle.

Timmins and the other soldier made a human chair and Hawkes stepped up, gaining enough height to see through a narrow window in the upper wall.

One of the sub-machine gunners was holding his face in his hands, grenade splinters having ruined it.

Another four men concentrated intently on the expected assault route through the door, a fifth was deliberately aiming his Mosin rifle at a suddenly terrified Hawkes.

The Garand spoke first, two bullets killing the rifleman, whose reactions were slowed by the blast effects of the grenade.

Another Russian was shot before a PPSh started to destroy the window around him, forcing him to rapidly drop from sight.

"Let's go!"

Hawkes rushed the door and rolled rapidly, his last three bullets hitting the PPSh gunner, smashing the weapon from his hands.

Not realising he was alone, Timmins having stumbled and brought down his comrades, Hawkes pointed a rifle he knew was empty at the two remaining defenders.

After two seconds they dropped their weapons and raised their hands.

Hawkes breathed a sigh of relief, not knowing that the appearance of Timmins and his two men had made all the difference.

A medic also arrived and made his way straight to the Russian with the ruined face, whose cries of pain were becoming increasingly loud and penetrating.

Detailing one of the men to ride shotgun over the medic, Timmins moved on.

In the main building, a bloody stalemate had developed.

Upstairs, heavy machine guns lashed out in all directions, even causing casualties in King Company to the north-west.

Inside, the dog-legged staircase was an unassailable barrier that had already claimed the lives of four airborne troopers in the first rushed attempt to gain the upper floor.

Occasionally, a Soviet grenade would bounce down the stairs, forcing the troopers back into cover, and scuppering any attempts to gain good positions.

Detailing a sergeant to command, Marion Crisp went off to reconnoitre the situation and come up with alternatives.

Eagles outside the building were coming under fire from Soviet soldiers upstairs, so much so that it seemed almost impossible for any more men to get up to the farmhouse itself.

Crisp turned back and almost ran headlong into Timmins.

Dropping into cover at the base of the farmhouse wall, he explained the tactical position, although a possibility had immediately suggested itself.

Both Timmins and Hawkes turned to look at the roof of the garage building that they had recently taken, checking out how it joined the main building.

"Same as, JJ. I will get you and Sergeant Hawkes some more men and you'll give it a go."

He checked his watch and grimaced.

'20:07 hrs!'

They had already fallen well behind schedule, such had been the defence so far.

'Fucking hell.'

His mind suddenly digested the picture in front of him and within seconds he had attracted the attention of a bazooka man from the HQ Company.

More sign language and within a minute the team was set up ready to go.

Eight other men from the machine-gun platoon were placed under Timmins' command and the plan was set.

On cue, the bazooka spat its rocket out, accurately entering the window nearest the garage. What damage it caused was unknown to those outside. A second rocket followed for the next window, and so on, until five had been fired, none being wasted outside of the structure.

Inside, they had caused devastation and death.

On hearing the second explosion, Timmins propelled himself out through the hole in the garage roof, and across the tiles towards the side window of the main farmhouse. The Soviet rifleman positioned there had escaped the explosions unscathed and shot the US officer down instantly, his wounded body dropping and rolling off the roof to the ground below.

Hawkes, his Garand reloaded, avenged the officer, decorating the garish floral wallpaper behind the Russian with brain matter.

He threw himself through the window and dropped into the first floor bedroom, quickly beckoning the others forward as the sounds of increased firing gave testament to the diversion organised by Crisp.

The curtains were smouldering, small red bull's eyes coming and going with every breath of wind. A small fire burned in a pile of clothes next to the door.

Two badly wounded and unconscious Soviet soldiers lay on the bed, two others, beyond help, lay on the floor.

A Soviet medical orderly came through the doorway backside first, dragging another wounded comrade behind him.

One of Hawkes' troopers smashed the butt of his carbine across the back of the orderly's neck, dropping the man on top of his dying charge.

The rest of the assault team gathered in the bedroom and Sergeant Hawkes quickly formed them ready for the attack. A quick look through the door was all that was needed and Hawkes held a grenade out for the rest to see. Resting his Garand across his thigh, he used his other hand to inform the group of his plans.

Nods and grins indicated their understanding.

334

The clip sprung off and the deadly charge bounced along the upstairs hall, coming to rest behind a group of four Soviet soldiers behind a barricade at the top of the stairs.

The weapon exploded and two of the Russians were propelled over the heavy table they were hiding behind, both men landing hard on the stairs. The Airborne troopers below shot them immediately, unsure if either was still capable, or even alive.

The other two defenders were thrown aside by the blast and their resistance ended.

Hawkes stepped through the door and immediately felt a bullet tug at his arm as it passed through the tunic, nicking the skin on its way to hitting one of the troopers behind.

Sensing, rather than seeing the enemy, Hawkes dropped and rolled, discharging his entire clip into the ceiling where he now saw an open hatchway into the loft. As he swiftly rammed another charger home, the damaged ceiling started to bleed, drops of bright red blood raining freely on the carpet below.

The rest of the assault force swarmed through the doorway, having been held up by the fallen body of their comrade, wounded by the bullet that had nicked Hawkes.

Fanning out according to instructions, two man groups moved through the upper floors, killing and wounding, their appearance behind the defenders a surprise.

The team that moved through the rooms hit by the bazooka found less resistance, much of the grisly work already done by high-explosive.

As soon as the upper hall was secured, Hawkes hollered the agreed word down the stairs.

"Geronimo!"

Identical shouts rose to meet his own, and quickly fellow troopers were springing up the stairs, confident that the way was now clear.

A rattle of automatic weapons gave them a direction in which to move, and the first four men moved to the back route to support Hawkes' men.

The next group secured the landing area, and were accompanied by a bedraggled Major Crisp, now sporting a head bandage.

335

In reply to Hawkes' unspoken question, the officer grinned the grin of a man made slightly mad by the proximity of detonating explosives.

"Someone was passing on the plan and yelled 'Geronimo' to his men."

By the way Crisp looked at the back of the Corporal positioned defensively at the top of the stairs, and the way the man hunched in shame, the responsible party was close at hand.

"I ran out and got blown up for my goddam troubles!"

The Corporal seemed to shrink further.

"No harm done, and lesson learned."

Crisp slapped his hand on the shoulder of the Corporal by way of forgiveness, although he promised himself a quieter and sterner word when the battle was over.

Lieutenant Timmins, his jacket bloodied and rent, gingerly mounted the stairs.

"Hell, I thought you were a goner, Lootenant!"

Hawkes moved forward and assisted the wounded officer through the gap in the barricade.

"Fortunately he was a lousy shot and just clipped my side. Also I fell on something soft."

His words coincided with everyone realising that something truly awful was clinging to his battledress, a realisation that was both visually and nasally challenging.

As one, the men surveyed the unfortunate man, unconsciously moving away from the awfulness he carried on himself.

Crisp couldn't help himself.

"What the fuck have you been swimming in, JJ?"

Tearing his eyes away from the apparition, Crisp acknowledged a signal from a Sergeant, indicating that his team had swept the area clean.

"A dead cow, boss."

Looking at himself, he added, unnecessarily.

"A long, long, dead cow."

The putrefaction was all pervasive, and a hand pressed to the face, seeking to seal the nose, did nothing to keep the abhorrence at bay.

336

Speaking through his fingers, Crisp issued a swift direction.

"Jesus, JJ, but go and get yourself cleaned up before the cavalry decide they don't wanna rescue us after all!"

The afflicted officer made his way back down the stairs, but the awful smell lingered long after he had gone.

However, for some reason known only to those who have shared the rigours and comradeship of combat, wide grins like Cheshire cats were everywhere, even on the Corporal who had nearly killed his commander.

"Right men," and pointing to Hawkes, "Let's get this place secured," and to his radioman, "And get me King Company on the horn now."

Finding a stepladder, Hawkes and two men prepared to check out the loft.

It contained only the dead bodies of three Soviet soldiers.

2029 hrs, Saturday 25th August 1945, GuteNacht Bauernhof, south-west of Eggenthal, Germany.

The reports were all in from Crisp's units, every objective having been carried in good time.

Fox Company had taken more casualties but the Soviets had fallen back, resorting to light mortaring, seemingly closing up shop for the day.

George Company had done their job in record time, and King Company had suffered few casualties in achieving their first objectives.

For Item Company, 370th Colored Infantry Regiment, the Rothaus has indeed proved a tough nut, earning its name as it ran with the blood of men from both sides.

It had taken three assaults to clear the position of enemy, costing thirty-eight dead and as many wounded.

Perversely, it was the ravaged Item Company that was first relieved by a unit from Petersen's force, the recon troops of the 2nd/1st Brazilian Cavalry, late to the field but now in the van.

337

Along the 101st's line, purple smoke marked friendly positions to the relieving forces as the mission moved from success to success.

Soviet artillery now started to build in its intensity, both George and King companies taking casualties.

A tank and infantry appeared to the south, driving hard straight at them, following the west bank of the stream at speed.

"Enemy to front!"

No order to fire was given but the Airborne started to lash out, Soviet soldiers dropping to cover immediately.

The tank crew were confused, expecting friendly troops in the farm ahead.

Beside them, the infantry got a DP28 working, its bullets seeking targets in the nearest windows.

The bazooka team sprang into action and moved to the stream, hugging the bank in an effort to close with the T34.

They were spotted by the infantry and both men picked off in short order.

More Soviet infantry appeared, following in the tanks track marks, coinciding with some of the arrival of the American rearguard elements from Eggenthal.

The tank, satisfied now that the enemy were ahead, started to pump high-explosive shells into the farmhouse.

The second shell started a fire on the ground floor, the smoke from which soon pervaded the whole building and made conditions awful for those inside.

The Airborne battalion's mortars were directed to hit the new arrivals but their fire was inaccurate, and the burning farmhouse and accurate machine-gun fire prevented any decent sighting and direction.

Under cover of their DP and the T34, the Soviet infantry, now swollen to about sixty in number, launched a flank attack, utilising the cover of the stream.

Crisp had anticipated this and had positioned one of his surviving .30 cal's to guard the route, supported by a squad of troopers.

The Soviet assault failed, the soldiers pulling back, leaving a dozen dead and wounded men behind.

338

As they gathered themselves for another effort, their tank took a telling hit, the engine compartment starting to burn fiercely. A second hit blew the turret off the vehicle and the whole crew perished in an instant.

Two Pershings from B/702nd had engaged the Soviet tank from behind, and killed it.

The imminent arrival of tanks and armored infantry in their rear, combined with the stubborn defence of the Airborne to their front, was too much and the Soviet infantry threw down their weapons and started to surrender.

An officer started to shout and scream, threatening his men with everything the Soviet State could throw at them, but to no avail. He sunk to the ground when he realised his men were done, throwing his pistol into the stream and hiding his head in his arms in shame.

Crisp, returning from having overseen the repulse of the stream attack, noticed an important omission and screamed at his men.

"Purple Smoke! Use purple smoke now!"

An E8 Sherman moving alongside the Pershings, had spotted movement and, even as the airborne men threw their markers, a shell was sent on its way.

The 76mm high-explosive shell clipped the corner of the farmhouse, deflecting very slightly from its course, zipped across the putrefying corpse of a cow, and into the garage.

Inside the garage was an aid station, where the wounded of both sides were being given comfort by the 2nd Battalion medics.

Twenty-one died in the blink of an eye, the highly effective shell exploding against the far wall just below a high window.

Three men were pulled from the flames, two Russians and one badly wounded Eagle.

The garage burned steadily, consuming the dead; five Soviet soldiers and thirteen US Paratroopers, along with three medical personnel, including the newly-arrived replacement Battalion Medical Officer.

339

Purple smoke wafted around Goodnight Farm, taunting the defenders and the relieving force, reminding the survivors that the damage had already been done.

Satisfied that nothing more could be done, Major Crisp occupied himself with organising the removal of the remaining wounded and getting his force out intact.

Soviet artillery was beginning to draw closer to his position, so there was some urgency to his efforts.

Hawkes and a squad had been detailed to sweep up the surrendered Soviets. Timmins was tasked with getting the men loaded on to the halftracks when they arrived.

Liaising with his unit commanders by radio, Crisp satisfied himself that all was going well elsewhere, so dedicated his efforts to Easy and the remnants of the rearguard.

Tanks and vehicles from 'Petersen' moved up, ready to get involved if any counter-attack should materialise.

The E8 remained at distance, the crew knowing only too well that they had fired on their own, albeit accidentally.

Meeting up with Timmins, Crisp noticed that the man was soaked through.

"Dumped myself in the stream, Boss. Didn't wanna mess up the infantry's vehicles."

Crisp sniffed the air and discovered that the stream had not removed the whole legacy of the fall onto the cow.

"Well, JJ, I gotta say, you are a sorry looking, sorry smelling sonofabitch."

And that was true. Grubby head bandage, faintly resembling a Japanese head scarf, complete with rising sun marking, this particular circle of red being the product of his head wound.

A medic had bandaged his side, the whiteness of the dressing noticeable through his rent jacket.

An additional wound, a split thumb web, dripped blood steadily onto the ground.

"Jeez, but you must want the Heart so badly, JJ."

Marion Crisp referred to the Purple Heart, an award mainly given for combat wounds.

"If you promise me not to stick your head up again today, I will write you up for it this very evening."

340

"I already got one, Boss," the young officer grinning from ear to ear, pausing in his discussion to show four fingers at 'Rocky' Baldwin, a cue for the senior non-com to move another unit off to safety.

A diminutive figure approached, clad in the uniform of a US Infantry Major.

"What the fuck?" The words had barely left Timmins' mouth than the short, stocky officer was on top of them.

Too experienced to salute, the new arrival contented himself with a small bow at each man before introducing himself.

"Takao, 100th Infantry Battalion."

Major Chikara Takeo was a challenging sight, businesslike and professional to the eye, every inch a combat soldier. But as always, when he was encountered for the first time, it was the sword that took the eye, even though only the handle could be seen, as it was presently slung across his back.

Obviously, the two officers were staring.

"Don't worry, I save it for the enemy."

Takeo was a member of the elite Combat Team 442, of which the 'One-puka-puka', 100th [Nisei] Infantry Battalion, was an important part.

Comprised mainly of Japanese-Americans, most of whom had been interned after Pearl Harbor, CT442 had earned a reputation for steadfastness and bravery in combat, a reputation second to none in the US Army.

'One-puka-puka' came from its Hawaiian birth, formed from various territorial and national guardsmen.

Perhaps more surprisingly, CT442 was the most highly decorated Regiment in the history of the US Armed Forces.

"Crisp, 101st," and indicating his still unsavoury companion, "Acting Captain Timmins."

Hands were shaken and Crisp deliberately ignored the surprised look on his companion's face, the field promotion dropped into conversation without warning.

Artillery was creeping closer now, and a direct hit threw a fireball into the darkening sky as a halftrack was struck.

"We need to get everybody outta here pronto, Major. My boys will hold the line while you fall back. 702nd will remain here with me until I move out."

341

As if to reinforce his words, groups of Japanese-American infantry moved forward, setting up defensively here and there, creating a barrier between the Soviet lines and the exhausted airborne troopers.

Anticipating Crisp's protest, Takeo gripped the younger man's arm.

"You have done enough, Major. See to your men and get them out. Then, I can get mine out too. OK?"

"OK Major." Crisp nodded, and to Timmins he continued, "Nothing fancy now, the 100th have the ball. Get everyone up and moving back right now. Quick as you can, JJ."

"Sir," the newly-promoted Captain Timmins scuttling away to put a burr under the ass of any trooper he saw.

As Crisp had been passing his orders on, Takeo had taken in his surroundings, the sights and the smells of deadly combat. Here, a pile of Russian dead, thrown unceremoniously together, as their medics strove to clear space for new arrivals. There, a neat row of airborne troopers laid out under tarpaulins, silently waiting their turn to evacuate with the rest of their comrades.

From the still burning garage, the sickly sweet smell of roasting flesh pervaded everything.

"Looks like you boys have had a hell of a time, Major."

Crisp shrugged, his head bandage unravelling as if to illustrate the point.

"It was a tough fight. These Russians are hard bastards for sure."

His eye had only recently started to ache and water, the swelling of the impact beginning to make itself known as it became more agitated by the smoke and fumes.

"Looks like you need a medic, Major Crisp?"

The exhausted paratrooper could only shrug.

"All in good time Takao, all in good time. For now, I must see to my men."

Crisp extended his hand and grasped that of the Hawaiian.

"Thank you and your men, Major. Good night and good luck."

342

"Just to satisfy my curiosity, Major. What was that shit on your man's battledress?"

Crisp laughed wearily.

"Matured cow," he paused for thought.

"Very matured cow."

Takao understood perfectly, releasing the handshake, and nodding at the exhausted airborne officer.

"Safe journey to you and your men, Major Crisp."

"Take care, Major Takao."

Crisp walked off, slinging his Thompson over his shoulder.

Waiting for him was a group of six of his men, three from his command group plus Baldwin, Hawkes and Timmins.

A halftrack driver gunned his engine, keen to let the passengers know he was ready and willing to depart.

Crisp stopped short of the group.

"A hard day, troops."

He got no argument on that score.

"Right, let's mount up and get the hell outta here."

The six climbed aboard and turned to help their Major up.

Crisp turned to the farmhouse and saluted formally.

The GuteNacht Bauernhof was a wreck, a burning wreck, but it would become part of the folklore of the 101st from that day forward.

A wry look set on his face.

"Good night."

The irony was not wasted on anyone.

And with that, they were away, leaving behind them a steadily growing fight, marked by the pronounced flashes from guns of all types firing in the rapidly growing darkness

---

All units of Crisp's command successfully escaped the pocket, although the Soviets did not properly reinforce their forces, assisting both the escapers and relieving forces greatly.

The Nisei infantry and 702nd tankers withdrew after repulsing one heavy attack, inflicting crippling casualties on the Soviet infantry who were so profligate with their lives.

The crew of the E8 were formally absolved of any blame for their part on the accidental deaths of the airborne wounded, although the finding could not assuage the grief and guilt they all felt at the friendly kills.

They all died two weeks later, when the 702nd was attacked by Soviet ground attack aircraft. Their Sherman was blown off a riverbank by a near-miss and propelled into the water, drowning the entire crew.

Pride goeth before destruction, and a haughty spirit before a fall.

Book of Proverbs

Chapter 71 - THE ANSWER

Passing the last of the checkpoints, the Polish officer dismounted from his jeep outside the main building.

His intelligence brain took in the military aspects as he stretched himself, hands in the small of his back, noting a Panther under a flat roof to one side, and two anti-aircraft weapons on rooftops, covering the headquarters.

Further study revealed soldiers going about their business, clad in a variety of uniforms that often betrayed their military roots, as well as indicated their present service in the Legion Etrangere.

Resplendent in full Legion uniform, a French Général de Brigade was in animated conversation with one of the new German Legion members. A senior one as far as Kowalski could make out, certainly an officer, given the jacket he wore.

Curiosity got the better of him, and he studied the pair a moment longer.

He suddenly realised that the two men were now walking in his direction, so he busied himself with retrieving his briefcase from the back of the 4x4.

He turned back as the two were almost upon him, his heart racing for a reason he couldn't quite understand.

A German voice cut through his doubts.

"Maior Kowalski?"

The German had spoken with pleasantness and the tone brought instant relief.

"Yes, I am Kowalski."

Salutes were exchanged between the three men and introductions made.

345

"Lavalle, Legion Corps D'Assault."

"Von Arnesen, Panzer Grenadiere Commander, 1st Camerone Brigade."

"Kowalski, Polish Liaison at First Army, formerly of 1st Polish Armoured Division."

The pleasantries over with, Von Arnesen took the lead.

"Unfortunately, Colonel Knocke has been detained for a short time and he has asked me to look after you until he is free."

'What's this?'

Kowalski's doubts, so recently stirred into action, then allayed, rose again for the briefest of moments.

"Thank you, Commandant," finding it natural to use the French rank.

"I will take my leave of you. Adieu, gentlemen." Lavalle offered a brief salute and disappeared inside the Rathaus that presently served as the headquarters building for 'Camerone'.

Checking his watch, Von Arnesen grinned.

"Perhaps, given the hour, I can offer you some food and a drink in our mess, Maior Kowalski?"

Part of him yearned to get close to Knocke immediately, but another part, the professional agent part, sensed that some time spent in the mess might yield some useful information.

"Lead on, Commandant, lead on."

The cooks of 'Camerone' produced great meals, especially when they could rely on foodstuffs from local producers sympathetic to the cause.

Both men had eaten heartily of a ham and onion stew, heavily dressed with potatoes and cabbage.

Whilst engaging Von Arnesen and his fellows in harmless conversation, the GRU agent discovered that Camerone was soon to be moved up to assist in the defence of Augsburg, before the rest of the Corps committed to the field for an offensive operation.

Coffee and sweet pastries opened mouths even wider and by the time lunch had drawn to a natural close, Kowalski had gleaned much worth reporting to his GRU superiors.

346

One question burned brightly; not one for his hidden agent side, but one purely of professional curiosity.

"Commandant, I simply must ask. This mess. There are common soldiers here, eating with the officers. I don't understand. Why?"

Those sat around stopped what they were doing, anxious to hear Von Arnesen respond.

"Not conventional, we understand this, but it was the SS way, Maior Kowalski. I shall explain."

Von Arnesen looked around for a suitable example.

"Ah yes. There, Maior."

He pointed out a group of six men sat three by three on a bench table, one a Captain, one a Lieutenant, the others two and two, NCO's and privates.

"Shall we?"

The legion officer rose, picking up the water jug and a stack of glasses, and invited Kowalski to follow him, moving to the spare seats on either side and sitting down with the six men, indicating that they should not rise, but continue as they were.

The first thing the Polish officer noticed was that none of the men were fazed by the presence of the senior man. They seemed to accept his appearance as quite natural, and their conversation flowed as freely as it had done before.

Von Arnesen split the stack of glasses and carefully poured, passing a full glass to each man in turn, deliberately starting with the private soldier to his immediate right.

"All that talking must be making you thirsty, Walter!"

The laughter was soft but not put on, and certainly not done to impress.

"Walter is always thirsty, Sturmbannfuhrer. His throat is the driest in the company."

"I confess, I enjoy a occasional pils, Sturmbannfuhrer."

Looking directly at his tormentor, Walter raised his eyebrows in admonishment, confiding in Von Arnesen in such a way that everyone within ten metres could hear.

"Whereas Dietmar is never dry of throat, but he does like a bath to sit in, because he talks out of his arse!"

Some playful punches were exchanged, and more genuine laughter accompanied it.

347

That Dietmar was old enough to be Walter's father, and a senior NCO, was not wasted on the visitor.

Von Arnesen then engaged every man in conversation, the first names slipping easily off his tongue.

He then went on to make his point, asking one man how another man's son was doing in kindergarten, or how his comrade's wife was enjoying her new job at the bank.

The men didn't understand what was going on but went with whatever their senior officer was trying to do.

Von Arnesen looked at Kowalski, and then returned his gaze to the young Walter.

"So, Walter, now that the Hauptsturmfuhrer's father has his new leg, is he able to walk the dog again?"

The young soldier was confused for a moment, his furrowed brow and gaze at the former SS Hauptsturmfuhrer beside him betraying him momentarily. The officer shrugged and smiled, motioning with his head in silent encouragement.

"Well actually, Sturmbannfuhrer, Herr Fenstermacher managed a full walk around the park only last week."

Now Kowalski couldn't help himself.

"May I ask something, Commandant?"

Von Arnesen grinned and gestured with his head, at the same time accepting a fruit pastry from the other private.

"Soldier, can I ask, which leg and what is the dog?"

"Herr Fenstermacher lost his right leg at the Battle of Dogger Bank in 1915, Sir. His dog is a Weimaraner called Blucher, named after his ship that day."

Von Arnesen chose his words carefully.

"Herr Maior, these men know each other, each other's families, and the history behind each man."

He looked around the quiet group.

"Each of these men has a relationship with the man by his side, regardless of rank. These men have a bond beyond that of a normal soldier."

Von Arnesen shot to his feet.

"Stillgestanden!"

The entire mess room came to their feet, rigidly at the attention. The sound of scrpaed chairs and clicked heels echoed in the mess, and then all was silent.

348

"Hauptscharfuhrer Dietmar Olsen. Schutz Walter Riedler is a holder of the Iron Cross First Class, is he not?"

"Jawohl, Sturmbannfuhrer."

Von Arnesen nodded gently as he continued.

"How did he earn the award?"

"Riedler single-handedly counter-attacked a trench that had been captured by Soviet soldiers, saving the lives of two comrades who had been captured and were about to be executed. In the process, he engaged eight men in single combat, killing three, wounding two more, and driving the survivors off, restoring the position to German control. It was his second action, Sturmbannfuhrer."

Walter Riedler was actually blushing with embarrassment.

"Who were the two men he saved that day?"

Olsen looked Von Arnesen in the eye, the faintest glimmer of a smile flickering at the side of his mouth.

"You and I, Sturmbannfuhrer."

"As you were," declared Von Arnesen, nodding at Olsen as he resumed his seat, closely followed by everyone else.

"How is your sister Lottie anyway, young Riedler?"

"Very well, thank you, Sturmbannfuhrer. I should have a niece or nephew before Christmas day."

Von Arnesen smiled at Kowalski, having just shown him a number of reasons why his men were the best of the best, with an esprit de corps second to none.

He reinforced the message.

"Political ideology plays its part at first," he conceded, "But it is always the comrades by your side, those men with whom you share everything, that inspire you. It is unthinkable to let down a comrade, even unto death, and we are all comrades here!"

Kowalski got it.

The last of the fruit pastry disappeared, and Von Arnesen showed his pleasure by licking his lips noisily.

A senior Legionnaire non-com strode purposefully into the mess and presented himself to Von Arnesen, his exaggerated salute interrupting the wiping away of sticky sweet residue around the officer's mouth.

349

"Sir, you asked to be informed when Colonel Knocke has returned. He is in his office."

Placing his serviette on the table, Von Arnesen stifled a belch.

"Thank you, Braun. We will be there directly."

The NCO fired off another salute, turned on his heel and strode purposefully away, intending to visit himself upon his Regimental Headquarters Flak section, which had incurred his wrath that very morning over the important matter of dirt on a gun sight.

1308 hrs, Monday, 27th August 1945, Headquarters Building, 1st Legion Brigade de Chars D'Assault 'Camerone', The Rathaus, Waldprechtsweier, Germany.

Von Arnesen and Kowalski walked back to the headquarters building, discussing the recent thigh wound that had given the German a lame gait, and entered through the main door, watched but unchallenged by the two legionnaires standing guard.

Inside, the uninitiated might have seen chaos, but to the two military men it was organised high-pace activity, as staff personnel laboured long and hard to get the Brigade organised and ready for its next deployment.

A female officer wearing the uniform of the Free French approached the Legion officer, proffering a clipboard for his attention.

"Excuse me a moment," Von Arnesen accepted the report and swiftly took in its contents before adding a comment and signing off on it.

Whilst he waited, Kowalski's eyes swept the room, avidly taking in details from the charts and maps on the walls, noticing the uniforms of the Legion and the hated SS melded together betraying those of German origin, and pure French uniforms indicating those who were French Army proper.

The second woman in the room was a different matter to the plain and nondescript officer who had approached Uhlmann.

350

She was a raven-haired beauty who made the uniform of a French Capitaine look extremely sexy, even when half-hidden behind a desk straining under the weight of files.

Her eyes flicked up, holding his for a second, the brief contact broken when she nodded at him and bent herself again to the task she was undertaking.

"Always important to make sure we have enough paper clips, Major."

Von Arnesen's slap on the shoulder interrupted a stirring in the GRU officer's mind, the briefest of flirtations with his memory bank.

The moment was gone.

Von Arnesen led the way through the throng and into the outer office, staffed by three legionnaires and two officers, one of each kind according to their uniforms.

"Good afternoon Capitaine Thiessen, Major Kowalski to see the Colonel, and he is expected."

Thiessen nodded pleasantly.

"One moment please."

He knocked on a bright red door and entered immediately, emerging quickly and inviting the Polish officer forward.

The door shut behind Kowalski and he found himself alone with Knocke.

Knocke, immaculately dressed as always, stood at the window, appearing to examine everything in sight with a professional eye,.

He turned sharply.

"Please sit, Herr Maior," the 'please' escaping Knocke's lips in such a way as to indicate that the German was experiencing an inner struggle.

When both were seated, the modest desk forming a 'No Man's land' between them, Knocke deliberately lit a cigarette and sat in silence, his eyes challenging the man opposite.

"I received your positive reply, Knocke. My superiors are pleased and have ordered me to tell you that all three are safe and well. They will not be harmed if you do as you are told."

Knocke sat impassively now, his emotions clearly under control.

351

"This is all about information. You provide it to me and that, plus my continued safety, ensures that your wife and daughters will continue to enjoy a comfortable life."

The GRU agent stopped, expecting some sort of response from the German. None was forthcoming, and he felt strangely uneasy.

"I will give you the details of a reporting line," he tapped his jacket pocket, "But I will also visit and take my information away in person when I can."

The feeling of unease deepened as the unblinking eyes held their line, boring into him at every opportunity.

He decided to establish his superiority.

"Knocke, I am not easily intimidated, and the silent game doesn't impress me. I hold the cards here. You would do well to remember that."

Taking a quick breath, anxious to press on, Kowalski stood.

"As a token of your compliance, I require some information now. When I leave this office, I want the full order of battle of this unit."

He moved off to the window, placing himself in the precise position the German had been stood when he entered.

As if to establish his superiority further, Kowalski recalled some conversation from the legion mess, adding almost as an after-thought, "I already know of your impending deployment to Augsburg, and of the subsequent counter-attack obviously, and more details of that will be needed before you move off."

Turning back to the desk, he resumed his seat.

Knocke finally spoke.

"I will require proof that they are alive."

Kowalski leant forward, broaching the barrier of the desk.

"You require? You require? You request is what you mean, Knocke."

The German stubbed out his cigarette and wiped an imaginary speck of ash from his sleeve.

"Require, request, whatever word you choose, Herr Maior. The end result will be the same. Without proof, my

352

usefulness to your superiors is nil. You supply irrefutable proof, and I will play your games."

Kowalski realised that he had lost the initiative.

"There is already a plan to provide you with proof, but it will take some time to implement, Knocke."

A nod of acceptance was all that was forthcoming.

"However, my superiors have needs that must be satisfied now. A token of your compliance, such as I have requested."

Knocke opened a folder on the desk in front of him and lifted out the sole document therein, a four page report detailing the precise make-up of the 1st Chars D'Assault Brigade 'Camerone'.

'How did he know that?'

Momentarily thrown, Kowalski took the document and skim read it before sliding it into his briefcase.

"Very good, Knocke, very good," the first for the file, the second most probably for the anticipation of his request.

"Proof, Herr Maior. Get me proof, or our relationship is over," Knocke's eyes carried a coldness not seen before, "And you will die."

Both men stood, their chairs scraping on the wooden floor with the speed of their movement.

"Never ever presume to threaten me, you German bastard."

Knocke said nothing; no words were necessary.

"I assume this pass will hold good for all eventualities?"

"That is so, Herr Maior."

The GRU agent went to turn away and then thought the better of it.

"The proof you need will come. Until then you will do as you are told. Are we clear, Knocke?"

The expression on Knocke's face was similar to that of an Owl about to feast upon a helpless rodent.

"Alles klar, Herr Maior."

The jeep started first time, and the Polish officer moved out of the security cordon, bumping along the road so recently damaged by the passage of a number of Legion Panther tanks.

Kowalski hardly noticed, his thoughts all-possessing.

He smiled, safe in the knowledge that he possessed irrefutable physical evidence of Knocke's treachery, and that the man was now forever entwined in his betrayal.

If the German went along with Soviet plans then he would prove useful; if he didn't, then the evidence of his betrayal would fracture the legion.

Knocke lit another cigarette as he watched the Russian drive away.

A knock on the door received the expected invitation, and the sound of people shuffling into the office broke Knocke's small reverie.

Turning around, he assumed the parade 'at ease' position, making eye contact with the three people opposite.

He beckoned them to sit, taking his own seat and moving four folders to one side.

"He asked for the order of battle as we expected."

The four others folders all contained information that the agent could have asked for.

"So, I am now a Soviet spy."

De Walle pursed his lips.

"That will be what he thinks obviously. So, he will now provide proof of your family's existence, which is what you need. But we play a dangerous game here."

Von Arnesen had nothing to add to that.

"If it all goes bad then I can just disappear from the Brigade, a victim of accident or whatever."

Knocke spoke directly to De Walle.

"But if it goes right, then we can feed the Soviets misinformation," and switching to make eye contact with the third person sat opposite, he continued, "And my family can be returned to me."

They held eye contact, Anne-Marie de Valois understanding the importance of his family, as well as his needs, his wants and his fears.

It was a dangerous game indeed.

The war against Russia will be such that it cannot be conducted in a knightly fashion. This struggle is one of ideologies and racial differences and will have to be conducted with unprecedented, unmerciful and unrelenting harshness.

Adolf Hitler

Chapter 72 - THE BOMBERS

<u>0312 hrs, Tuesday 28th August 1945, Soviet medical facility, Former Concentration Camp [Nordhausen sub-camp], Rottleberode, Germany.</u>

She awoke with a start, her eyes gradually coming into focus, the feel of a cool, damp compress on her forehead assisting her in coming to terms with the unexpected appearance of the outside world.

Tatiana Nazarbayeva had been extremely unwell, the aggressive viral infection striking her down until now, when its stranglehold had finally been broken.

She gently pushed the tending hand aside, and tried to raise herself up in bed but her strength failed her.

Forcing her eyes to open as far as they could, she tried to shake off the tiredness that threatened to send her back into a deep sleep.

"How long have I been here?"

The nurse shrugged.

"I'm not sure, Comrade Polkovnik. I am new to this hospital, but you were here before I arrived. One moment please, Comrade."

The nurse took up the record sheet, flipping the page.

"You were brought here on the 16th August, Comrade Polkovnik."

"And today is?"

"The 28th, Comrade Polkovnik."

Tatiana's mouth dropped wide open, her shock at her prolonged absence from duty wholly apparent.

"I will fetch the doctor, Please lay back and relax, Comrade."

She did so, still reeling from the news that she had been unwell for twelve days.

Taking in her surroundings, she saw little to stimulate the mind. A modest room with one window, with nothing but trees to see, although the darkness of night did not even permit her that view. A bedside table and an armchair completed the ensemble in the freshly painted white room, all illuminated by a single light bulb, also very obviously recently installed.

The doctor arrived quickly, examined Nazarbayeva, and was very pleased with what he found. He was especially pleased from a personal stand point, as a number of extremely important and powerful people had made it quite clear that his continued happiness was dependent on the female GRU officer's recovery.

The notes appeared again and he made his notations, whispering instructions to the nurse, who nodded constantly as he went.

The doctor missed the clip and the folder dropped to the floor with a slap, rousing a sleeping figure curled up on an armchair.

Tatiana did not notice and croaked a request.

"Comrade Doctor, I am thirsty. May I have a drink?"

"Of course, Comrade Polkovnik," and he nodded to the nurse, who was already filling a glass.

A hand came into Tatiana's vision, gently relieving the nurse of the task.

"Allow me, Comrade Nurse Lubova."

Tatiana focussed hard, her heart racing at the timbre of that voice.

"Yuri?"

"Tatiana."

Starshina Yuri Romanovich Nazarbayev smiled lovingly into his wife's eyes as he placed the cool glass to her lips.

Both Doctor and Nurse beat a hasty retreat.

She consumed the water greedily, coughing as her efforts took a wrong turn.

"Yuri, what are you doing here, my husband?"

357

"I was ordered to attend here and aid your recovery, my love."

"Ordered? You were given leave to come to me?"

Yuri Nazarbayev smiled the smile of a man with a secret, and turned away to his tunic. He extracted two documents, neatly folded but already heavily thumbed.

"No Tatiana, I was ordered."

She took the proffered documents and opened them one at a time, her eyes taking in the enormity of the papers in front of her.

"Oh."

There was a lot she could have said. After all, it was rare enough that a soldier received a direct written order and pass signed by the Theatre commander himself, but there it was; Zhukov's signature standing out proud on a document ordering her husband to immediately attend his wife, and providing him with authority to make the journey by any means he chose.

The second document ordering Yuri Nazarbayev to his wife's side was even more of a shock, signed as it was by Generallissimo Joseph Stalin.

'Oh!'

Yuri told the story as he used a damp cloth to wipe his wife's face and neck.

Zhukov's order had arrived first, and Yuri's Colonel was already in a blue funk trying to cope with the thought that the great man's attention had focussed on his unit. The order from Stalin almost unhinged him when it was hand delivered by an NKVD Major, who had treated it like it was unstable dynamite.

Starshina Nazarbayev suddenly became a man to fear, given his impeccable credentials, and the most powerful of friends.

Yuri was a humorous man, something that the young Tatiana had found hugely attractive when they were courting. His humour surfaced now, although it failed to mask his concern and worry.

He recovered the first letter, folding it and sliding it back inside his tunic pocket.

"Comrade Marshall Zhukov?"

358

The second received the same meticulous attention and the pocket was buttoned in place.

"Comrade General Secretary Stalin?"

He patted the pocket, almost as if checking the two messages were still there.

"So, is there something you want to tell me, my darling?"

0752 hrs, Tuesday 28th August 1945, Soviet medical facility, Former Concentration Camp [Nordhausen sub-camp], Rottleberode, Germany.

The nurse and doctor had flitted in and out through the rest of the night, but neither Tatiana nor her husband were aware of their presence, the former still tired from her illness and the latter, being a veteran soldier, making the most of the opportunity to rest.

Yuri Nazarbayev stirred a little as the door opened, his eyelids parting to take in a shape entering the room.

They closed again, seeking to promote more sleep before his brain started to bring him round, warning him that he should now be alert.

His eyelids shot open and he was greeted by the uniform of a Colonel-General stood quietly over his wife's bed.

His body responded instantly and he shot to his feet, assuming the attention position, automatically reporting to the Senior Officer.

The old general stopped him in mid flow.

"Stop now Yuri Romanovich, you will disturb your wife. At ease, Comrade."

His confusion was now complete, unused to being addressed in such a way by such a senior man.

"The doctor's tell me she has come back to us."

As if to prove the point, Tatiana provided a gentle snore for the moment.

"Yes, Comrade Polkovnik General. She regained consciousness during the night."

The older man nodded, turning to gaze at his most valuable asset.

359

"I had to come to see for myself, but I will not disturb her now she is resting. Look after her well, Yuri Romanovich, and please tell her I came to see her."

"Apologies, Comrade Polkovnik General, but who shall I say called?"

"Ah my error, Comrade. I made an assumption. I am Polkovnik General Roman Samuilovich Pekunin."

'The head of the GRU? Govno!'

Pekunin understood the silent processes taking place before him.

"Do understand, Comrade. Your wife is my very best intelligence officer, and extremely valuable to the Motherland."

Pekunin turned to leave, but halted and turned back.

"As you are most certainly aware, Tatiana also has some extremely powerful friends."

Pekunin nodded and made to leave, but he turned back yet again and grinned, adding, "I don't normally do hospital visits, you know."

No matter how fatherly the man presented himself as being, Yuri Nazarbayev was still in the presence of an extremely senior officer and could not unbend.

Pekunin understood.

"Comrade Nazarbayev. My sympathies for the loss of your son. Be proud of him."

Exchanging salutes with the Starshina, he left quickly, leaving the elder Nazarbayev to return again to the question of his wife's position in the hierarchy of the Motherland.

<u>1142 hrs, Tuesday 28th August 1945, Sector Six, Soviet Air Defense Command Facility, Butzbach, Germany.</u>

USAAF bombers had already struck hard at the important rail junction in Friedberg that morning, leaving behind a radically altered landscape and miles of ravaged track.

Soviet fighter regiments were caught on the hop, and few intercepted the American bombers. Those that did were heavily engaged by the accompanying Mustangs.

360

Reports of another approaching bomber force were examined carefully, the new enemy following the precise route of the first attack.

None the less, the Soviet air commander was not a fool, and ordered some of his interceptors into action on the line of flight, retaining the rest to protect the suddenly vital junction.

A phone call from the new Air force Commander had focussed him on the inseparable link between the preservation of the rail link and his own career.

Perhaps that was what made him retain more assets to protect Friedberg then he needed.

Air raid warnings went out, covering the line of the enemy flight, and his fighters rose into the skies for the second time that morning.

1151 hrs, Tuesday 28th August 1945. Airborne at 20,000 feet, ten miles from and approaching Limburg, Germany.

"Five miles to target, Major."

"Roger."

USAAF Major Ronald Sterland had recently brought his 401st Bomb Squadron back from Florida, settling the unit back into its old base at Bassingbourne, England.

This was the first combat mission they had flown since that return and, so far, it was an absolute daisy.

Be that as it may, having fought in the skies over Germany for two years already, he, along with his experienced crew, could not help but feel uneasy at the sight of the fighters flying above them.

Feeling similarly strange, Hauptmann Kreuger of the 16th Jagdstaffel, had often piloted his FW-190D to attack the aircraft he was now tasked with protecting, and with great success, having knocked out a confirmed eleven of the giants from the skies over the Fatherland.

16th Jagdstaffel consisted of fourteen FW-190D's, of which twelve were presently riding shotgun over the Flying Fortresses of the 401st and the other squadron's of the 94th Combat Bombardment Wing. One FW aircraft had simply refused to start, leaving its experienced pilot fuming and harrying

361

the ground crew. The other aircraft was probably still burning, having crashed on take-off, consigning Maior Dörn, the Staffel commander, to a fiery death.

The bombers were outnumbered by fighter escorts, the Luftwaffe Focke-Wulf's sharing the sky with scores of USAAF Thunderbolts and Mustangs.

The heavies settled into their bombing run, preparing to visit hell upon the area five miles west of Limburg.

Messages from the area, some from German civilians, one even received over the still working telephone system, and a radio message from a cut off platoon of Rangers, had established that the Soviets were using the wooded area bordered by Hambach, Hirschberg and Görgeshausen as a hidden gathering point. The reports indicated that units that crossed the River Lahn overnight hid up there during the day, before moving on when darkness again gave them some respite from the increasing number of fighter-bombers.

94th Bombardment Wing was the first of five USAAF bomber wings tasked with obliterating the area in which the enemy were hiding.

The Soviet air controller vectored some of his fighters in to attack, and they found the 401st in the van, already on its bomb run.

The cries of warning reached Kreuger's ears. Checking the sky and locating the threats, he oriented himself before ordering his Staffel to dive to the defence.

Identifying the enemy as La-7's, the Focke Wulf pilots knew they were facing a speedy and robust enemy.

The Soviet aircraft belonged to the 32nd Guards Fighter Regiment, so that added combat experience and skill to the mix.

None the less, the breakneck dive of the FW's deflected the Soviet regiment, even though no hits were apparent from the first pass.

Both sides jockeyed for position, the fifteen Lavochkin's favouring an approach that brought them nearer to the bombers, the FW's moved anywhere that gave them a chance to hack the enemy from the sky before they got at their charges.

Neither side were wholly successful.

362

The close escort Mustangs now had their own issues, as two regiments of Yak's appeared from the south, boring in hard on the squadrons behind the 401st.

Further Mustangs from the top cover relocated, moving to assume the close escort position.

A flash occurred in Kreuger's peripheral vision as one of the Lavochkin's fireballed, the disciplined voice of a Luftwaffe veteran calling the kill in.

Within as many seconds, two more Soviet fighters were knocked out of the fight, both streaming away with smoke pouring from them, pursued by hardened men not inclined to mercy.

An FW came apart in mid-air, its yellow impeller leading the front section forward, the severed fuselage and wing section fluttering downwards like a sycamore seed.

Two Lavochkins closed upon the flank of the B-17's, their triple Berzarin cannon seeking out and finding a target.

The Mustangs failed to intercept them, a swarm of Yaks barrelling into them as they dived.

The 'Lady Loo' took seventeen solid 20mm hits, of which six were in her cockpit, reducing the flight crew to bloody offal.

The large silver aircraft rolled over on its back and described a curve all the way to the ground, burying itself and its green 'first mission' crew deep in German soil.

The US bombers screamed out for help, but a quirk of fate had robbed the 16th Jagdstaffel of its English-speakers before they had deployed to combat height.

None the less, the language of fear is universal, the tone and pitch of the transmissions searing into the Luftwaffe pilots' brains.

Kreuger ordered his aircraft to protect the bombers, breaking off from the fighters in order to get back closer.

Another of his FW's was missing, its pilot skilfully gliding away with a dead engine, right up to the moment he dropped into a defined flak zone. Soviet anti-aircraft gunners enjoyed the slow target and plucked it quickly from the sky.

Two more Lavochkins were attacking the rear B-17 in the American defensive box, and their success was apparent as

363

the tail plane simply came away, leaving a slender upright section.

However, the B-17 was renowned for its ability to take punishment. A waist gunner underlined the aircraft's ability to resist by lashing the engine and cockpit of the Soviet fighter with his .50 cal.

The La-7 dived and rolled away, its robust design also ensuring its survival, although the pilot was made of more vulnerable material. His eyesight was taken by fragments from his instrument panel, and he flew blindly away from the combat.

Kreuger hauled his FW round in a tight arc to get behind an attacking Lavochkin, only to find another FW had got there first, selecting short bursts with its 20mm MG151 cannons.

The pilot was missing badly and the Lavochkin scored hits on the target B-17.

Yells of alarm had preceded the attack and continued afterwards, the defensive machine guns engaging both the La-7 and the FW.

Kreuger screamed into his radio, "Nicht Scheissen! Nicht Scheissen!"

An American voice excitedly replied in schoolboy German, "You shot at us, you fucking assholes!"

Responding angrily in his own language, Kreuger pulled his fighter round and up in a rising hard port turn

"He was engaging the Russian fighter!"

Air combat rarely gives a man opportunity for conversation and Kreuger had exhausted his time, flicking right as an La-7 dropped in behind him.

A comrade overshot the dangerous Lavochkin without engaging, leaving Kreuger to manoeuvre hard to shake the obviously experienced enemy pilot.

The American-German voice cut in again, this time with even more anger and urgency.

"Bastards! Stop shooting at us! You killed Woody!"

Hauling back on his stick and executing a perfect loop, Kreuger lost his tail and stole a look at the B-17's. The formation's corner Fortress was smoking badly from both starboard engines.

Thinking on his feet, he ordered the Staffel not to close the bombers but to engage the fighters further out, passing that on to whichever of the bombers it was that spoke German.

A sixth sense made him roll away, the air he had occupied cut with tracers as an La-7, probably the one he had shaken off previously, attacked from below.

The Soviet airman made a mistake and turned the wrong way, the veteran Luftwaffe pilot taking the offer of the Lavochkin's belly and transformed the sleek craft into a jumble of fiery pieces with one sustained burst.

The American-German screamed across the air waves.

"Oh Jesus, oh Jesus! You kraut bastards!"

Kreuger sought out the stricken plane, its whole right wing a mass of flames, smoke also pouring from the waist gunners hatches, as fire progressed through the crew spaces of the dying Fortress.

He also noticed that the killer was still firing.

He also noticed that it was an FW-190.

'Götz?'

"Götz! Cease fire, you fucking idiot," which OberFeldwebel Götz did, but only because the B-17 was already doomed.

It was Götz who had flown into the attack before, deliberately missing the La-7's to hit the bomber beyond.

'Bastard.'

Keying his mike, Kreuger spat out his words.

"Achtung! Götz in nine is a communist! He's shooting at the Amerikanski! Take him down immediately!"

Only two of the German pilots responded immediately, the idea of shooting down a comrade, even a traitorous one, too much for the others.

Neither was successful and Götz, showing a skill not previously witnessed, slid underneath a third B-17, walking his cannon shells along its belly, the doors still open from when the 401st other junior crew had dropped their bombs.

The La-7's were still in play, but the FW's seemed to be on top of the situation, and the whirling mass of fighters started to fall behind.

365

The three FW's now bore in on the one rogue aircraft, all seeking to preserve their new allies.

A tail gunner on 'Rock of Ages' saw his opportunity and took the wing off an FW neatly, a long burst severing it at the root.

Kreuger screamed into the radio.

"Nicht Scheissen! Friendly aircraft shot down!"

The other FW hauled off, the situation beyond him, as those he sought to protect hacked his friend from the sky.

Götz, having got off a burst at 'Rock of Ages', pulled up and rolled back right, determined to make another attack on the fortress.

By his estimation, he had very little ammo left, so he decided to close to where he could not miss.

Kreuger, approaching from the rogue FW's starboard flank, saw his opportunity and pressed the button.

Silence.

'Verdamnt!'

2nd Lieutenant Dominic Di Mattino could see the eyes of the German pilot, but was powerless to act. Both his arms had been shattered by the first attack, so his rear gun station, although perfectly positioned to knock the kraut out of the sky, stayed silent.

In slow motion, the yellow impeller came from left to right as he watched incredulously, smashing into the other FW even as it fired its cannon.

Deliberate.

Calculated.

Sacrificial.

Courageous beyond measure.

The collision took place fifty yards from his face and Di Mattino watched as the impetus crushed the cockpit of the rogue FW, bending the aircraft like a reed, as the other Focke-Wulf came apart, wings folding together like hands clapping.

The mass of scrap metal dropped like a stone. Di Mattino shifted painfully to watch it fall.

Nothing emerged from the aircraft that had fired at them, the pilot very obviously destroyed by the impact.

A rag doll detached from the second aircraft and tumbled away.

The air gunner watched fascinated, horrified, sickened, as the form descended, trailing useless cords from a useless harness.

Spiralling.

Falling.

Without hope.

The attacks were beaten off and the bomber's mission completed.

In silence, the 401st had turned and, in silence, it was escorted back by the remaining six FW-190D's of 16th Staffel.

At the allotted point, the fighters took their leave, the final words left with the senior American officer.

"Thank you 16th, and good luck."

And, in silence, the two ravaged squadrons returned to their own bases.

The mission had been a massive success, Götz aside, the only problems being caused by those Soviet Air Defence response regiments that intercepted just in advance of the bomb zone.

On the ground, units of the 3rd Guards Army had been devastated, packed tightly as the intelligence suggested.

The 87th Guards Heavy Tank Regiment had been totally obliterated, its IS-II's nothing more than expensive scrap metal. 140th Gun Artillery Brigade was so badly hit that it was withdrawn from the order of battle and its survivors used to fill gaps in other artillery units.

6th Pontoon Bridge Brigade lost much of its equipment but luck preserved over half of the qualified engineers.

However, it was the infantry of 22nd Rifle Corps that sustained the worst of it, with virtually the whole Corps written off.

In the most devastating single air raid of the war so far, the Red Army had lost over four thousand dead. The same number were wounded in various measures, but no-one who was under that attack came away unscathed, the psychological effects breaking many a hardy soul.

In the air, the La-7's of the 32nd Guards Fighter Regiment had been decimated, the other Soviet regiments more fortunate but unable to engage close their prime targets, losing three Yaks to four Mustangs.

The Thunderbolts were not engaged, much to their annoyance.

The 401st lost more B-17's than the rest of the force combined, six aircraft being lost with one, 'Rock of Ages', crash-landing on return.

Highest casualties were meted out to the Luftwaffe pilots of 16th Jagdstaffel. Including the unit commander, who crashed on take-off, seven FW's had been lost, although the Jagdstaffel Intelligence officer was loathe to record seven losses and stated six, crediting the additional kill to Hauptmann Kreuger's record before adding the simple and poignant word.

'Gefallen.'

The report of the 401st's commanding officer made its way up the chain of command and was acted on within SHAEF's headquarters, the final approval resting with Eisenhower himself.

It was then forwarded to Washington, where other minds decided to decline its approval, given the full nature of the day's events.

The matter was revisited under Eisenhower's presidency, and he set aside time during his informal visit to Bonn on 26th-27th August 1959 to rectify the omission, at which time he presented the Medal of Honor to the wife and son of the still missing Hauptmann Walter Kreuger.

The ever-thoughtful Ike also ensured that the surviving men from the B-17 'Rock of Ages' were all present, with their families, to complete the honouring of a very brave man.

Eisenhower heard the footsteps and looked up, his face carrying a pained expression.

"So, what do the council say?"

Bedell-Smith deferred to Bradley, as he had just finished a heated conversation with Dönitz.

'Or as heated as a conversation through an interpreter can be,' though Smith wryly.

"He said he wasn't surprised to find infiltrators, Sir."

Bradley eased his collar a little, reliving the confrontation in his mind.

"He says that they have identified a number of these infiltrators, and more will be found soon."

Eisenhower lit up a cigarette, knowing his man hadn't hit the headline yet.

Bradley was quite clearly furious.

"Dönitz says that we have to accept some issues, or withdraw the German forces completely, as he cannot offer any guarantees."

Eisenhower nodded sagely.

'Figures.'

He shrugged, his mind quickly reworking the problem and coming to the same conclusion it had some time beforehand.

"Well, we simply can't take them out of the line, now that they have established in the Ruhr can we?"

He wasn't asking so much as confirming his thoughts.

"What we can do, sure as hell, is make sure we don't get that sort of repeat in the air. Make sure that sort of co-op mission is avoided in future. Let German look after German, then if there is a rogue, it's them that'll suffer."

That made sense and Bedell-Smith noted it roughly on his pad, although he added, "Apparently, the German leader came good though Sir. It's only a few rotten apples, that's what the feedback says."

Ike stubbed out his cigarette, his bladder suddenly announcing its needs.

369

"Maybe so, Walt, but if we can avoid cross-national groupings until they have their issues sorted then I will be happy."

'Happier, more like.'

"Now, reports from the ground are good. Recce will firm that up for us."

Bradley was quite happy that a large amount of stuff painted with a red star was no longer his concern.

"So, before I pee myself, I am confirming the 'Go' order for Operation Casino. Let's see if we can stop them dead for McCreery."

Operation Casino, a near-copy of 'Gabriel', was an intelligence-led strategic bomber attack like that near Limburg, but on a larger scale. The full might of the RAF Bomber Command being called upon to deliver one devastating rolling attack.

There was one small problem.

The intelligence was mainly provided by a Leutnant Huber, formerly of the 21st Panzer Division, captured in Normandy by the 43rd Wessex Division, and subsequently trained and equipped by British Military Intelligence to remain behind the lines and supply information on Soviet movements during the uneasy peace.

The new war changed his status from persuaded agent to committed ally.

His Intelligence trainer and main liaison officer, posing as a Colonel in the Pay Corps, had been wounded early in the new war and the hospital he was in captured by the advancing Red Army.

He had been visited in Kirchgellersen by a senior officer of the GRU, who went away with more knowledge than she had arrived with. That knowledge now meant that Leutnant Huber spent every day in pain, responding to the whims of those who held lordship over his wife and life.

Operation Gabriel had been a huge success.

Operation Casino was to be the greatest disaster of the Allied air war.

Nazarbayeva had visited the enemy prisoner in the medical facility at Kirchgellersen and initiated the interrogation of the Military Intelligence Officer, the combination of her soft female voice and a Pentothal injection inducing indiscretion in a man already affected by anaesthetic.

All in all, the Englishman had betrayed twelve agents in place, nine of whom were now working for the GRU, the other three having made a more dramatic and terminal choice.

In the absence of Tatiana, the operation had been proposed by Lieutenant General Kochetov, using his former enemy's assets to the maximum, Kochetov combined with Zhukov and Bagramyan, designing a trap from which the RAF could not escape unscathed.

'Maximum effort' had been called for, and Sir Arthur 'Bomber' Harris had moved heaven and earth to get the maximum amount of high-explosive into the air.

Aircraft long removed from the Allied inventory were back in action, crewed by anyone qualified to sit in an aircraft. Experienced men who had seen all the air war had to offer through to beardless youths on their first mission, all were called on.

The Allied effort was concentrated on a corridor in Northern Germany, a strip of forest running parallel with the River Elbe, particularly focussing on the stretch from Bleckede, through Amt Neuhaus and onto Dömitz.

In an area roughly thirty kilometres long by three kilometres wide lay vast quantities of Soviet materiel and manpower.

Recon flights had been harried, but successfully brought back images showing tracks and camouflaged vehicles spread liberally throughout the forest.

Agents reported seeing fuel storage facilities spring up under the trees, and tanks in their scores feed greedily from them.

More reports spoke of artillery pieces, wheel to wheel in places, lined up as if on parade under the protective canopy of the large green forest.

And soldiers.

371

Thousands and thousands of soldiers.

The maximum effort of Operation Casino totalled eight hundred and eighty-nine machines put into the air, forming a huge line of multi-engine aircraft all the way from England to the mouth of the Elbe.

The cloud was patchy, and sufficient moonlight broke through for the bomber force to see the Elbe. They used it as a navigational marker to fly by until they were approaching Amt Neuhaus and its environs.

Soviet maskirova had worked, the subterfuge of dummy vehicles and temporary wooden structures doing all that had been hoped for and more.

There were no fuel facilities.

There were no tanks.

No soldiers, leastways not how they had been described in the agent's reports.

Underneath the bombers lay their target rich bombing area, an area that was virtually empty of troops and vehicles.

However, there were guns lined up wheel to wheel, and thousands of them, although they were not the artillery spoken of in the spy's reports. There was flak, division after division of it, thousands of anti-aircraft guns brought in to form the sides and end of a funnel down which the RAF and its allies intended to fly.

Mosquito NF30's swept ahead of the main body, knocking down five Soviet aircraft, a token attempt to get night-fighters into the attack.

The lead Pathfinders marked Blecklede and Besitz, the next group Hitzacker and Vielank, others marked key locations in between as the main force grew closer.

Soviet fire discipline was superb, and the only shells that rose into the night sky came from positions not involved in the secrecy and planning.

The lead bombers adjusted their turn at Lauenburg, bomb doors open, the plan being that they should drop on the line between Blecklede and Besitz, with subsequent waves advancing the bomb line to the south-east.

The Soviet plan was simple.

Shoot them down.

372

The Soviet AA Divisions reflected the full arsenal available, from the lighter 20mm and 40mm weapons, disposed to protect the others from ground attack sorties, through the 85mm AA guns, finishing with the lethal German 88mm, 105mm, and 128mm weapons, all plentifully supplied, and all directed by German radar sets 'liberated' in the Patriotic War.

Eight hundred and eighty-nine aircraft in a bomber stream stretching back to England entered the funnel and started to drop their bombs.

Arranged down the sides of the funnel were the AA guns, radar and searchlights, waiting their chance to strike back.

It had been a relatively easy call to predict the bombing run that the RAF et al would adopt. None the less, more Soviet assets had been put in place to cover two other options.

There were no chances taken.

The command was given, the guns thundered, and night became day.

Aircraft after aircraft was clawed from the sky, more than one exploding viciously as its load detonated.

Messages back to England were garbled and misunderstood, prolonging the agony.

Messages from England to the raid commander went unheeded, the man and his aircraft now on the ground and burning.

The bombers kept coming, dropping their bombs and turning away, as directed by operational orders, a route that took them over concentrations of Soviet AA guns.

Another group was bombing now, advancing the destruction, but paying the price in men and machines.

The night sky was permanently illuminated by exploding shells and burning aircraft.

Here and there a group of parachutes floated down, a crew, whole or in part, escaping death.

Searchlights had joined in, searching the target rich skies for enemy bombers, transforming the skies into a spider's web into which flies, driven by desperation and courage, continued to fly, even as their comrades died all around them.

373

Some experienced pilots dived, taking their charges down low to escape the big flak guns. So many of them perished as the 20mm and 40mm weapons joined the killing.

The worrying messages went unheeded, the bomber force's chain of command smashed as deputy and deputies were hacked from the sky.

The vast quantities of shrapnel in the air started to descend, and more than one AA gunner was killed or wounded by their own sides' metal.

More bombers arrived, the bravery of the crews incredible in the face of such fire. Courage was a common commodity that night.

A Wing-Commander made an appraisal and got an informative message off to Bomber Command, telling them of the increasing disaster.

Their reply, seeking more information, was not acknowledged, the Wing-Commander's aircraft already in a fiery dive.

It was Harris himself who acted, aborting the raid with immediate effect and calling his boys home.

Eight hundred and eighty-nine had gone out, and ashen-faced WAAF's started to accumulate details from radio messages and reports from air bases.

At RAF High Wycombe, the headquarters of Bomber Command, a stark picture was emerging.

A staff officer had organised a written display and running total that was being kept up to date in the main room. Harris and his senior officers watched in horror as the numbers altered minute by minute.

On the left were those aircraft returned to base, down on the ground, and their crews safely in debriefing or drinking away the horrors of the night.

In the middle was the number of aircraft about which no information was available. That number went down when one was added to the 'returned to base list' or, more tragically, to the third 'destroyed' list.

Harris sat watching, white as a sheet.

374

'351, 358, 180.'

Activity increased, flustered men and women reporting to the tellers, who in turn reported back to the marker, the middle-aged WAAF Company Commander, a Flight-Lieutenant equivalent, whose eyes were watery with understanding of the human tragedy behind the numbers.

'385,324,180.'

The tea had gone cold long ago but Harris sipped it as he watched.

'394,304,191.'

On the left and right walls, squadron status boards were mounted, from where up to date information was sent across to the numbers tellers.

Harris watched one WAAF replace her telephone receiver and sink to her knees in floods of tears, her board bereft of a single mark.

115 Squadron RAF had nothing left, bar its shocked and appalled ground crew, waiting in vain on a dark runway.

Other boards were similarly bare, bare of all but hope, as the WAAF's at each waited. Their silent prayers entreated higher powers for some to be spared. Most prayers went unheeded that night.

The lost figure topped two hundred and skipped to two hundred and nine within a minute.

Harris stood, his shocked entourage rising sluggishly to follow. Indicating that they should remain, the Commander of Bomber Command removed himself to his office, in order to start the painful process of informing the Allied leadership that his command had been devastated and would be out of the mainstream of combat for some time to come.

After the phone calls, Harris wrote out his letter of resignation and passed it into the mail room on his way back to see the latest numbers.

With only a few aircraft still in the sky, the board made awful reading.

Two hundred and forty-nine confirmed losses, each loss marking the death, injury or capture of a crew.

Down and safe were five hundred and ten.

One hundred and thirty bombers were yet to be accounted for.

A quick look at the squadron boards revealed five virgin white and blank, the tellers either waiting anxiously for news or devastated, having had the very worst sort.

A wave of calls flooded into the centre, as more bombers made safety, either in England or airfields through France and the Low Countries.

Air-sea rescue launches were hard at work in the North Sea and Channel, Royal Naval MTB's and the like pressed into service to help.

An incredible headache overtook Harris, and he sought out his private quarters for some rest, before beginning the piecing together the events of the night.

The true cost of Operation 'Casino' was not fully appreciated for some time.

All in all, five hundred and ninety-one bombers returned home, some untouched, some badly knocked about.

Two hundred and sixty-nine aircraft had been confirmed as lost, some over Germany or crashed in friendly territory. Some fell apart just short of their home runways, and more ditched in the North Sea, consigned to a watery end.

A Short Stirling, recently returned to operations from mothballs, savaged by flak and flying blindly, eventually succumbed to its wounds and crashed outside the German village of Marbeck. Unfortunately for the Allies, it landed on top of the 14th Nebelwerfer Regiment, part of the deploying German Republican forces. Casualties were extreme, both in men and materiel.

Another RAF bomber, a Lancaster III, badly damaged and abandoned by her crew, finally came to earth in Groningen, destroying an orphanage, and causing over two hundred civilian deaths.

Such events were not confined to the Allied side of the lines, as a brand-new Avro Lincoln I came to ground in a field on the northern bank of the Hemmelsdorfer See, destroying itself, and spreading its remaining load of fuel all over the headquarters

376

of the Soviet 22nd Army, sending the entire Soviet Army's hierarchy into a fiery Valhalla.

There were twenty-nine bombers still missing, and it was some days before several aircraft were reported as landing safely as far away as Sweden, Switzerland and Finland, where they were interned.

Eight Squadrons had been totally wiped out

After the war, RAF investigations were unable to progress all the remaining twenty-one missing and many of the unresolved losses were only put to bed by accidental discovery or the intensive work of historians, decades later.

To date, six aircraft remain unaccounted for.

Soviet losses totalled five night-fighters, sixty-seven AA guns of varying types and five hundred and sixty-three casualties.

The reactions in Nordhausen and Versailles could not have been more different.

Elation and celebration.

Shock and horror.

<u>0409 hrs, Wednesday 29th August 1945, Soviet medical facility, Former Concentration Camp [Nordhausen sub-camp], Rottleberode, Germany.</u>

Nazarbayeva awoke and stretched contentedly, her eyes taking in the dimly illuminated room and all it had to offer.

The small vase on the drawer unit, placed there earlier by a giggling Nurse Lubova, in response to a woman to woman request, its simple woodland flowers offering up the promise of rich colours even in the low light.

The top secret folder lay to one side, a single fallen petal casting its modest shadow on the label. Inside were details on the progress of her misinformation programme, and how it was to bear fruit in the skies over Northern Germany that very night.

A neatly hung uniform, that of a full Colonel of the GRU, proudly topped by the Gold Star, sharing the recently arrived clothes stand with that of a much-decorated Starshina of the Red Army.

The armchair where they had sat together, and talked of the loss of their son.

377

At the window, the silhouette of her husband, naked, toned, still damp with the sweat of their exertions.

"Yuri."

Her husband turned and smiled.

"Ah, my wife awakes. How you can just drop off to sleep like that amazes me, my sweet."

The sheet was in her hands and she raised it to her face, only her eyes exposed and full of mischief, her voice that of a new bride on her first night.

"Your exertions exhausted me, my husband. You are so powerful and needy."

He smiled again, deciding whether or not to play the game. The mischievous soldier-husband nearly won, but the needy lover-husband proved too strong.

"Needy, my sweet?"

He took hold of the sheet and pulled it gently down, liberating her face, then her shoulders, before travelling all the way and settling on the floor at the foot of the bed.

"How can I look at such beauty and not need, not want, not desire?"

His silhouette altered in such a way that Tatiana merely beckoned him forward and onto the bed, opening her legs and entwining him as he slipped inside her and they started making love for the third time.

1005 hrs, Wednesday 29th August 1945, Headquarters of RAF Bomber Command, RAF High Wycombe, UK.

Harris replaced the red receiver, breathing a sigh of relief.

His resignation was not accepted and he would be left in charge of the recovery and re-assembly of Bomber Command.

The preliminary written report was on his desk, and had formed the basis of his telephone conversation with Prime Minister Clement Attlee.

In truth, the figures were beyond comprehension.

Two hundred and seventy-five aircraft now confirmed lost, and along with them over one and a half thousand air crew, either dead, maimed or prisoners.

378

'Unmitigated disaster.'

That had been Attlee's shocked understatement, wholly accurate, but insufficient to carry the weight of the terrible events.

Whilst restoring his command was his number one priority there was undoubtedly another matter which needed addressing.

Standing up and turning to the window, he looked into a cloudless sky and asked a question of no-one in particular.

"How did they know we were coming?"

A question that was already taxing other minds across Europe.

Attlee replaced the receiver with extreme care, his face white, the news he had just been given so appalling as to beggar belief.

Not in even the darkest days of the German War had such losses, so many young men, been taken by the Gods of War.

His hands were trembling, hindering his efforts to charge his pipe.

The other occupant of the room waited silently, knowing that the Prime Minister would reveal all when he was ready.

That did not prevent Sir Richard Percival Carruthers, Attlee's personal private secretary, from acting to precipitate the conversation.

He placed a healthy measure of single malt in front of his leader, sampling his own, his concern mounting as he watched the shaken man consume his with unusual speed.

The silence continued, even after Carruthers had supplied a refill, the PM's mind occupied solely with working through the problem.

Attlee drained his glass again and positioned it neatly on the table, moving blotting pad, pen stand and all the other writing accoutrements into perfect position, squared off, symmetrical, much like his thoughts that had just been perfectly placed into position in the greater run of things.

"Richard, I need you to perform your country a great service."

Intruiged, Sir Richard Carruthers listened.

At first, in horror, as Attlee repeated all the awful details of the disaster that had befallen RAF Bomber Command.

Secondly, with concern, as the poor military situation in Europe was summarised.

Thirdly, in curiosity, as Attlee outlined an intruiging proposal.

1420 hrs Wednesday 29th August 1945, Headquarters of SHAEF, Trianon Palace Hotel, Versailles, France.

Already, the disaster was having a knock-on effect, the USAAF bomber missions for the day having been scrubbed, leaving solely fighter and interdiction sorties in place

Eisenhower had finished a very difficult briefing session with Air Chief Marshall Tedder; one that left him in no doubt that Bomber Command would take some time to recover.

An investigation had started, and had already looked at the intelligence on which the raid was based, deciding the no action was to be taken on such reports until further notice.

Whilst the loss of so many aircraft and crews was awful, other matters became more pressing as the morning wore on, reports of Soviet gains arriving, reflecting an increase in pressure across the front as a whole.

The situation map illustrated the changes, or at least, it was constantly attended by staff personnel, desperate to keep the map current as the situation started to become extremely fluid.

The Soviets were taking big chunks out of the front line and the Allies were falling back in front of them, his Generals doing a difficult job in difficult circumstances, and doing it extremely well.

Eisenhower held off calling some of his senior men, leaving them to do their job uninterrupted.

He opened his second pack of the day and inhaled the smoke, watching as a small problem became a huge problem and red arrows spread like a virus towards the Ruhr.

By the time he lit another cigarette the situation was clear; awful, but crystal clear.

380

He suddenly became aware of an USAAF Lieutenant holding out a handset to him.

"General Bradley, Sir. It's urgent."

Of that, Eisenhower had little doubt.

After a brief outline of the situation, reinforcing the visual image conjured up by the map in front of him, Eisenhower sought answers to Bradley's problems, and found none without pain.

With some reluctance, Eisenhower announced his decision.

"OK General. I get the picture and I understand your choices, limited as they are."

Ike scribbled an order as he spoke, relaying the contents to a worried Bradley.

"I am ordering the 18th Airborne Corps to be placed under your command. Use them wisely, Brad, and try and give them back to me intact. I will scare up some more assets to help plug the gap but I agree. Now is the time for Guderian and our German allies to take some strain."

He signed the document and dotted the signature so forcefully as to penetrate the paper and mark the exquisite walnut table top.

"I will contact both Guderian and Ridgeway," he thought quickly, "And in that order too, telling them to take their orders from you. Anything else you need from me, Brad?"

A few staff officers had gravitated towards Eisenhower, understanding that there was about to be a burst of activity.

Eisenhower laughed a laugh that held no amusement whatsoever.

"Miracles are not within my purview I'm afraid, Brad. One moment."

Eisenhower held out his hand to receive a report he had been waiting on. Swiftly reading it, Ike nodded in satisfaction.

Placing it on the table, Eisenhower refocused on the 12th's Commanding General.

"I will certainly tell Air to prioritise you for now, but there is a lot going on, Brad."

Obviously Bradley wanted to get about his business, now he had some extra assets to play with.

381

"OK Brad, you do that. I will tell both to contact you immediately. Get your boys in line safely, General."

He looked at his watch, his face betraying a modest calculation.

"Sure thing, Brad. Now, get it done. Good luck, General."

The written order was given up to be typed, and another two were quickly issued.

Two telephone calls were made.

Eisenhower was never quite sure why it was, but his dealings with the Germans often made him feel inferior.

'Maybe that's part of it?'

In this instance, it may have been because Guderian had expected such an order, and had started to make some adjustments to his forces already.

By the time he put the phone down on Ridgeway, the map threw up another problem.

Stuttgart was surrounded.

"Get me General Devers on the horn, please."

<u>1820 hrs Wednesday 29th August 1945, Headquarters Building, 1st Legion Brigade de Chars D'Assault 'Camerone', The Rathaus, Waldprechtsweier, Germany.</u>

Knocke and Lavalle were sat discussing a delicate problem when they were interrupted by an insistent knocking on the door.

Both men were handed seperate messages, and both men were long enough in the tooth to know what they were before they read them.

Dismissing the messenger, Knocke pulled out a map, angling it so that Lavalle could examine it with him.

The two worked in silence, making the calculations, imagining the move and all the pitfalls it held.

Finally, Lavalle moved back, pouring two Perriers, and passing one to his Brigade Commander.

"Santé, Ernst."

Knocke acknowledged the toast and took a sip before putting his glass down.

382

"Distance of about ninety kilometres to the present line, one hundred to break through?"

Lavalle concurred.

"Will they hold, Sir?"

"The Algerians are a tough bunch, Ernst. They will hold."

The order had given specific instructions on what was expected of them once they got to the Stuttgart area, but little of substance on how to get there, and what assistance they might expect.

"Right then, Ernst. Take the two ready units of 'Alma' under your command, and get your Brigade ready to move as soon as possible. I will organise some support and get the information we will need."

Lavalle took another look at the map, examining a rough route pencilled in by Knocke.

"That seems appropriate, but I think the bridges at Pforzheim are down?"

Without the merest hint of superiority, Knocke shook his head briefly.

"Back up yesterday, Sir. Two bridges, both capable of bearing my Panzers."

And without the merest hint of offence, Lavalle acknowledged the information.

'Well, he is the best, isn't he?'

"How long, Ernst?"

Taking a look at his watch and another sip of water, Knocke did a swift calculation.

"I can have Camerone rolling within the hour, Sir."

At 1925 hrs, the first units of 'Camerone' moved out of their laager and through the small town of Malsch, heading to the sound of guns, and the relief of Stuttgart.

383

On a man to man basis, the German ground soldier consistently inflicted casualties at about a 50 per cent higher rate than they incurred from the opposing British, Canadian and American troops __under all circumstances__. This was true when they were attacking and when they were defending, when they had local numerical superiority and when, as was usually the case, they were outnumbered, when they had air superiority and when they did not, when they won and when they lost.

Colonel Trevor Nevitt Dupuy, US Army.

Chapter 73 - THE CAMERONE'S.

0830 hrs, Thursday 30th August 1945, Combat Headquarters of 1st Legion Regiment du Chars D'Assault, Hauptstrasse, Aidlingen, Germany.

The movement had been swift and uneventful, save for the incredulous looks from locals, drawn to the passage of German tanks through their village or town.

'Camerone', and its additions from 'Alma', had arrived in darkness and efficiently secreted themselves, completing the task just as the first rays of the new day made themselves known.

The commander of the Stuttgart Garrison had made his plans for the breakout, and these had been relayed to the relief force.

Thankfully the man knew his job and there was nothing to criticise in his proposition.

All call-signs, fire free zones, and routes of advance were thoroughly briefed, and that left the task of the tactical break-in battle to the skills of Ernst-August Knocke and his commanders.

The mission had changed, from one of relief to evacuation, but it had come as no surprise, and made no difference to the Legion dispositions.

Lavalle had secured standing air protection for the battleground to keep Soviet Shturmoviks at bay, and even some ground-attack assets to suppress the Soviet artillery.

384

To their front lay the small town of Dagersheim, the centre of the escape route planned by the French General commanding the 3rd Algerian Division. Not just the Algerians, it was now known, as a plethora of smaller units had withdrawn into the city as the Soviet pressure built.

The Algerians, supported by some American armour, would strike towards Sindlefingen at 0900 hrs, with a view to opening up the main road out, and expanding the hole sideways as much as possible.

Once that was achieved, the Algerians would fold inwards, funnelling their soldiers out of Stuttgart to the relative safety of allied lines.

Some would stay behind, volunteers or pressed men, in order to cover their comrades' departure.

'Camerone' had merely to advance two miles and smash the outer ring of the encirclement, widening the hole to the north-west and south-east as much as possible, whilst ensuring that the flanks were held against any efforts to reseal the pocket.

Considering that the unit had been hastily put together, it was superbly equipped and well supplied.

Although Knocke was hugely responsible for that, the abilities of his officers and Lavalle had greatly contributed to the efficiency that had been quickly developed and maintained.

Inside the Rathaus on Hauptstrasse, a final assessment was being made, based on yesterday's aerial reconnaissance photos.

Cigarette smoke hung lifelessly in the air, despite the huge hole in the wall beside the large table, a product of a near-miss in some American barrage the previous April.

On the reconnaissance photos there seemed to be a few tanks in an area of interest.

"I can only agree, Rolf; where there are four there are probably more. None the less, it seems we will face mainly infantry and anti-tank guns."

The Germans were used to doing things on the hoof and with little reconnaissance and were not fazed by the likelihood of surprises.

385

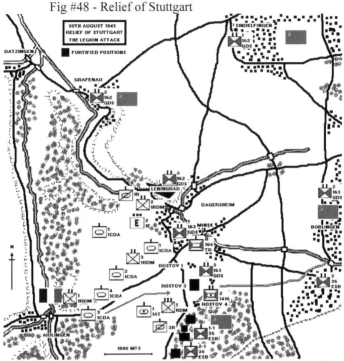

Fig #48 - Relief of Stuttgart

"We anticipated a hedgehog here," Knocke tapped an area north-west of Dagersheim, marked by a rise in the ground and shielded by a small watercourse, "And artillery have their orders to hit them hard."

It was designated 'Leningrad'.

Uhlmann nodded along with Von Arnesen, the latter being more concerned as his 1st RdM'S 2nd Battalion was tasked with clearing the position.

The tank regiment commander pondered for a moment, and his reflection brought some good news for Von Arnesen.

Uhlmann addressed Knocke with his suggestion.

"Sir, I was keeping hold of my self-propelled guns as an additional reserve. I can move them up behind the infantry's advance to provide direct support if you wish?"

386

There was never any chance that such an offer would be turned down, so Uhlmann's 5th Company of Sturmgeschutz III's and IV's was re-tasked.

Outside, some 20mm Flak weapons started to hammer out, but the firing soon ceased as whatever it was disappeared from sight.

The noise provided no opportunity to talk, so those present took the opportunity to examine the map to ensure they were fully acquainted with the plan.

The senior officer from 'Alma' wiped away a trickle of blood from his forehead bandage, a trophy of a vehicle accident during the night march.

Lieutenant Colonel Lange was an unknown quantity to those in the room, his military credentials unproven. Whilst his service in the 17th SS Panzer-Grenadiere Division 'Götz Von Berlichingen' had apparently been spectacular, it had also been brief, his war ending when he was captured by US forces during the Battle of Mortain on 7th August 1944.

His 5th RdM was tasked with opening the southern side of the breach, supported by the other 'Alma' unit, the 3rd Legion Reconnaissance Compagnie.

Knocke had also assigned the self-propelled guns of the 1st AT Battalion to support Lange, should he need them. JagdPanthers, JagdPanzer IV's, and two Nashornes would deal with any enemy tanks encountered, and the recon photos showed none whatsoever.

Knocke had retained some units under his command, ready to respond to an emergency or reinforce success, whichever one visited the battlefield that day.

A wave of relaxation seemed to sweep the officers group, as all realised that the planning was over and that their new war would start very soon.

They moved out into the main room.

It was 08:45, and the headquarters was a hive of activity; last minute checks, orders being confirmed, the mechanics of war smoothly operating prior to the attack. However, a stillness fell upon the room, as staff officers hard at work realised that the senior officers had completed their private discussion, and that

387

the Brigade Commander was now stood on the briefing podium, silently waiting for their attention.

Those who knew him well could see the tiredness and strain sitting heavily upon the man.

Knocke, resplendent as always in his crisp black tankers jacket, his medals catching the eye and confirming his quality, looked down on his men with proud eyes and, when all had stopped around him, he began.

"Meine Herren, the time is upon us when we will atone for the wrongdoings of recent years. Not necessarily our own, or those of our country, but certainly those of the political leadership."

Knocke softly gestured around the room as he continued.

"We fought long and hard, with comradeship and bravery, but we fought to preserve a political system that brought our country, and this world, to the brink of an abyss."

The pause was heavy with widespread but unspoken thoughts of comrades, men who died in furtherance of that cause, that leadership, that political system. The voice grew in firmness and conviction.

"No man here has anything to reproach himself for, as you all fought with vigour and courage."

Knocke reinforced that message with his piercing look at any who gave him eye contact.

Strongly he continued.

"But no matter how honourable we felt the cause for which we fought, or the pride with which we carried arms for our country, we must all now accept that there will be a price to pay before we, and the Fatherland, can again stand tall and take our rightful place in world affairs."

More softly, and with full knowledge of the meaning of his words, he went on.

"The stain can only be removed by the further sacrifices of our nation."

He left that statement hanging for a moment, and then raised his voice strongly once more, driving into the substance of his exhortation.

"We have been given the chance to bear arms once more, and now stand side by side with our former enemies, united with the French, British and Americans in a common cause."

"Today, we lead an attack and start the bloody process that will start to roll back the communists, and ultimately secure the future of our Fatherland, Europe and the world."

Nodding as he spoke, Knocke pressed on forcefully.

"On this battlefield a change will be made, and communism will know a defeat."

"There will be other days, in other places; hard days for us all."

A moment of silence and reflection.

Knocke nodded to himself, his mind acknowledging the future sacrifices that would be demanded of his troopers.

"But this Brigade, all of us..."

He paused to gather himself.

Every man felt the electricity of the moment.

"I," a strange crackle of emotion affected the commanders' voice, "Will not rest until the day this war is won."

The moment passed and Knocke's voice steadied.

"Some of us will die, as many of our comrades have already done on countless battlefields these last few years. But all of us will live on, remembered for what we do now, and the way we in which we do it."

Stopping abruptly, the listeners heard his words softly echo round the room as Knocke gathered himself for his final words. He gently gesticulated around the group, singling out no man, encompassing all.

"Each of us knows that this must be done."

"Each of us knows what is required of us."

"Each of us knows what it may cost."

And with a smile and real fire in his eyes, Knocke ventured.

"And yet, none of us would change places with others in safer places, eh?"

The gentle, relaxed laughter was not forced, but came naturally from men confident in their cause and leader.

389

"Now, Kameraden, truly, for the new European order, and for the Fatherland, let us do all we can, so that we can all go home again."

Knocke punched the next words out so they would have the desired effect.

"Meine Herren" and the officers, as one, shot to attention. His tone softened but remained powerful. "Meine freunde, you are the best of the best, and it is an honour and privilege to command you."

His crisp military salute was returned by the entire room.

"Good luck to you all."

Watches were synchronised and the senior officers dismissed to their commands.

Lavalle offered his hand to Knocke and, not for the first time, the two shared a warm handshake.

"Ernst, I am off to get the rest of the Corps moving. If I can offer you anything else today then I will let you know, but I doubt it."

Knocke shrugged, reconciled to the fact that the other units of the Corps would not be up for some time to come.

"Stay in touch, and good luck."

They saluted each other and Lavalle left, mounting his staff car and speeding away.

Knocke was alone, all the staff engaged on last minute preparations.

He lit a cigarette.

Blowing the smoke over the map he saw it cling and roll, gently moving over the roads and contours, almost as the smoke of a battlefield.

His mind wandered over his capture by the French and the abomination of the Rheinweisenlager. His first meeting with Lavalle, and THE conversation.

'Well, here we are now.'

When the proposition of teaching Allied soldiers had been discussed, he had agreed, expecting to be a classroom soldier until the Allies had no further use for him.

The Chateau on the 6th of August had changed that idea.

'What is it the English say? Once again to the breach?'

Stubbing out the half-smoked cigarette, he strode to the full-length mirror to check his uniform.

The new armband drew critical attention, feeling both so wrong and so right in equal measure.

He fingered his throat decorations and ensured the 'Pour-le-Merite', was foremost.

Completing the ensemble, he placed the dark blue Kepi on his head, and paused to take in the figure before him.

Nodding his approval to the reflection, he turned smartly and left the room, his command tank starting up with a brusque instruction from Lutz, his NCO signaller, when he saw the Colonel approach.

The original concept of the Legion units had been to form ex-SS troopers under the command of French Officers. The plan never got off the ground, especially as existing French officers did not necessarily have the skill sets required to direct tanks in action.

Pragmatic as ever, the French had understood that the Waffen SS leadership would do the job for them, and so the units formed under mainly German command.

The attempt to relieve Stuttgart commenced under the direction of Colonel Ernst-August Knocke, whilst the most senior French officer in the Brigade was a Major.

<u>0832 hrs, Thursday 30th August 1945, French First Army Headquarters, Hotel Stephanie, Baden-Baden.</u>

It was a simple enough task, now Kowalski had declared himself. His every move was microscopically observed and recorded, and all those he associated with, however briefly, received their own dedicated teams.

Whilst Etienne Bossong welcomed the additional clientele that visited his wine shop, he remained unaware of the scrutiny he was under, a scrutiny that became more focussed

391

when one of 'Deux's' bright sparks made the connection with the Chateau du Haut-Kœnigsbourg.

Irma Schmidt, girlfriend of the 'Polish' Major, and one-time Luftnachrichtenhelferinnen, was given a clean bill of health, but still the watchers kept watching.

The same could not be said for Georges Heppel, an hotel worker with deeply hidden but impeccable connections to the pre-war French Communist Party, nor for Heinz Rüssel, a one-armed German baker, whose father was found to be a Spartacist. Most certainly not for octogenarian ex-army Colonel Christian Löwe, who had a previously unknown and decidedly unhealthy interest in powerful broadcasting equipment.

Following his contact instructions to the letter, Heppel inserted the message in the hollow cutlery and delivered breakfast to the agent's room, knocking in the accepted manner.

In order to preserve the pretence of Knocke's compliance, the message had to be accurate.

Which it was, reporting 'Camerone's' movements and plans precisely.

It just happened to be too late to act upon the contents.

Sat in the hotel lobby, examining a magazine that pictorially and saucily depicted the latest Paris fashions, De Walle leant forward and stirred the newly-arrived coffee, noting with satisfaction the signal for success.

Heppel had eventually understood where his loyalties lay, and his sister's continuing good health depended on his ability to carry on as normal under 'new management'.

0900 hrs, Thursday 30th August 1945, Wurm River line, two kilometers from Dagersheim, Germany.

Allied forces – 1st Regiment du Marche, and 1st Regiment, Chars D'Assault, and 1st Engineer Battalion, and 1st Anti-tank Battalion, and 1st Chasseur D'Affrique, and 1st Recon Compagnie, and 1st Legion Artillery Battalion, all of 1st Legion Brigade de Chars D'Assault 'Camerone', and 5th Regiment du Marche, and 3rd Recon Compagnie, seconded from 3rd Legion Division 'Alma' to 'Camerone', all of Command Group 'A', of

Legion Corps D'Assault, of 1st French Army, of US 6th Army Group.

Soviet forces – 162nd & 163rd Guards Rifle Regiments, and 125th Guards Artillery Regiment, all of 54th Guards Rifle Division, of 3rd Guards Rifle Corps, and 1st & 2nd Battalions, 36th Engineer-Sapper Brigade, and 1416th Self-Propelled Artillery Regiment, and 12th Guards Heavy Tank Regiment, and 65thTank Regiment, and 166th Tank Regiment, all of 59th Army, of 2nd Red Banner Central European Front.

On cue, the supporting artillery units started firing their ordnance at the Russian positions, throwing up mountains of earth, and occasionally something more fragile.

A simple order rode the air waves.

"Vorwärts."

Uhlmann, his headquarters tank moving slowly behind the first two companies, remained glued to his binoculars as return fire arrived; some mortars, but no artillery as yet.

Swivelling to his left, he watched as the half-tracks and recon troops of the 1st RdM pushed forward, moving ahead of his tank line.

Pressing his throat mike, he encouraged the 1st Company commander.

"Berta calling Cäesar Zero-One."

A moment's pause before the ex-Hauptsturmfuhrer from Das Reich replied.

"Cäesar Zero-One, go ahead."

"Pick up the pace, Cäesar. Stay in line with Julius elements. Over."

"Zu befehl, Berta. Cäesar Zero-One out."

Uhlmann swivelled to watch his First tank company noticeably quicken, encouraging the trailing Second Company to follow.

Enemy artillery started to arrive but it was inaccurate and did not trouble the Legion tanks, although it was of a large enough calibre to worry Uhlmann, should the Soviets get their response organised.

393

Behind the assault wave, Knocke was focussing his binoculars, his view obscured by the occasional artillery burst as well as the mass of moving soldiery to his front.

His Beobachs Panther possessed no main gun, removed to provide extra room for more radios.

These radios were now alive with reports of targets and contacts, incoming fire, and the first casualties.

He concentrated part of his mind on the messages, the other he used to interpret the sights of battle.

On the left flank, the 1st's Recon troopers had been hit, one of the Puma armoured cars smoking badly, an accompanying half-track ablaze behind it.

Mortar men from the 1st RdM's 2nd Battalion swiftly deployed and got to work. They were rewarded with a secondary explosion right where they were told the enemy anti-tank position was, and no further fire came from it.

However, the hedgehog position was bristling with weapons, and more AT guns, supported by machine-guns, started to take a toll of men and vehicles alike.

The commander of the reconnaissance element was dead but his second took over, calmly ordering the pre-arranged smoke to fall and cover the advance.

Knocke decided to give some more assistance.

"Anton to Adler, receiving."

The air liaison officer, bouncing along in a half-track next to Uhlmann, quickly acknowledged.

"Order one parcel to strike Leningrad immediately, Anton over."

Again, the liaison officer acknowledged, immediately organising a flight of ground-attack aircraft to drop their wares on top of the hedgehog position, codename Leningrad.

As he did so, Knocke opened the network and broadcast the new information for those on the peripheries.

In the blink of an eye, four Thunderbolts swooped from the sky and deposited their rockets on the Soviet defences, immersing the enemy in more smoke.

Knocke contacted the liaison officer again, partially to recognise the professionalism, and partially to confirm what

394

support was remaining, stifling his disappointment at the limited air power available to his forces.

'I spent years without air support anyway.'

Prior to the battle, his sixth sense had told him that 'Rostov' was going to be a problem, and so his command tank had been directed to proceed favouring the southernmost route, just in case.

1st Company of the tank regiment had enjoyed some success in front of Dagersheim, a sole T-70 light tank having been quickly killed by numerous shells; a number of anti-tanks guns were similarly dispatched.

However, it had not been without cost, two of the Panzer IV's having been knocked out in return.

1st Company deployed centrally, with 2nd Company splitting up equally and accelerating to right and left, permitting 3rd Battalion of the RdM to launch an attack through the middle.

This attack was under the control of Uhlmann, Von Arnesen having elected to stay with the undoubtedly more difficult assault on the 'Leningrad' hedgehog.

With tank cover on both flanks, the 3rd Battalion swept forward and into the Soviet positions, a few men dropping here and there, but mainly without problems.

The two tank companies pushed on again, vacating ground that was struck by artillery shortly afterwards.

Both Knocke and Uhlmann noticed the increased effectiveness of the enemy artillery.

Unfortunately, 'Camerone' did not possess the appropriate equipment for effective counter-battery fire as yet, and so manoeuvre was their best defence.

From the reports emanating from the hedgehog, Von Arnesen was having the very devil of a time getting his men in close, a small watercourse having been liberally sown with mines, holding up his attack, and causing casualties amongst his Legionnaires.

'Camerone's' pioneer unit deployed a platoon in SDKFZ 251 half-tracks, bringing small bridges into position and spanning the divide. The brave engineers were swept with fire, killing both the commander and second in line as they shared the dangers with their men. Seven more men were hit and dropped to

395

the earth, the four that were only wounded being recovered by grateful infantry.

Knocke watched intently as Von Arnesen's voice commanded the air waves, hurling his men over the bridges and up into the enemy position.

The supporting Sturmgeschutz self -propelled guns had been adding to the smoke screen, but now received orders to change tactics and seek more hardened targets.

The mortars switched their fire, bringing down high explosives to try and cut 'Leningrad' off from any support.

Knocke satisfied himself that the assault was proceeding and turned his attention to the 'Alma' force attack.

The enemy artillery seemed to be building here too, and smoking wrecks marked some losses amongst the reconnaissance element, as well as the motorized infantry company that backed up the lead troops.

A movement caught his eye and he swivelled his binoculars upwards, immediately seeing the forbidding sight of Soviet aircraft.

In his ear he heard the Air liaison officer screaming for fighter cover.

Three Shturmoviks were boring in, even though two of them trailed smoke, a sign of the air combat that had already claimed the rest of their group.

The three aircraft deposited their bombs and turned for a cannon and machine-gun run.

One of the precious JagdPanthers received a direct hit from a 50kgs bomb on the engine grille. The blast dismantled the tank-destroyer, removing sections of armour plate and throwing them in all directions, causing some gruesome casualties amongst 'Alma's' Legionnaires.

A 20mm Quad mounted on an SDKFZ 7 chassis brought one aircraft down, the crew pancaking behind the lines to fight another day.

Selecting one of the Nashorne's, the leader pumped out shell after shell from his 23mm VYa cannon. He pulled up and left the field, raging at his inaccuracy.

His second aircraft selected a half-track, and was quickly rewarded with a blossoming fire, as his shells set light to the vehicle. Burning steadily, the German half-track drove on, carrying its dead crew forward in a surreal fiery assault.

The second aircraft escaped without further damage, retreating over its lines but subsequently blundering into a group of USAAF Thunderbolts, responding to the calls for assistance, who wasted no time in adding to their total of kills.

Knocke watched closely as the 5th RdM moved forward, sensing its lack of direction, all the time straining to catch some hint of Lieutenant-Colonel Lange on the radio.

He decided to take the matter into his own hands.

"Anton to Gelbkopf-zero-one over."

He was not acknowledged.

Concentrating on the landscape ahead of 'Rostov', he directed one of his signallers to continue trying to raise Lange.

The artillery plan now directed HE on 'Rostov', and sure enough, the landscape changed as shells started to land.

Machine-guns started to stammer out a challenge and men died in front of him, their bodies flung aside as bullets knocked them over.

Still, no word from Lange.

'Verdamnt.'

"Anton to all units Gelb, all units Gelb, push forward quickly," and as he was talking, he assessed the defences, "Centre on Rostov Four. Acknowledge."

Messages returned from relieved commanders, conscious of the fact that a firm hand was on the tiller.

Switching to another channel, he thumbed the mike.

"Anton to Emil-zero-one, receiving."

The 3rd Tank Company commander, a highly-experienced former Obersturmfuhrer of the SS-Leibstandarte, had already anticipated the order and was closing up.

Having acknowledged Knocke's order, the 3rd Company picked up pace, its eighteen Panther tanks churning up the soil as they strove to get up to support 'Alma'.

Binoculars up again, Knocke swept the enemy positions and saw something emerge from its hiding place, the foliage and netting cover now alight following a close strike. His brain fought to recognise the shape, and he concentrated more to bring it into focus.

397

'Scheisse!'

The ISU-122 was very bad news indeed, its main gun capable of killing anything on the field that day and, unlike its IS cousins, it carried enough shells to do a thorough job.

As if to emphasise the point, shells erupted from various camouflaged points along 'Rostov' as concealed ISU-122's opened up.

One JagdPanther received two solid hits and came apart like a dead rose head, leaving nothing but the running gear and lower hull in place to mark its end.

Another JagdPanther took a single hit, slewing to one side as the nearside track unravelled.

Two of the JagdPanzer IV's were destroyed, both equally catastrophically.

One thing about the ISU-122 was its vulnerability, a fixed mount gun carried on a modestly armoured vehicle.

All of the Legion tanks present could kill the thing with one shot, and one of the Nashorne's led the way, striking and destroying the southernmost ISU with its first shell.

The Nashorne itself was extremely lightly armoured, the thickest plate being 30mm, but it carried the deadly Pak43 88mm gun, so it was a question of gunnery.

And German gunnery was excellent, the stationary Nashorne consuming another two ISU's before it attracted any attention in the target-rich environment.

The heavy shell missed as the Nashorne had relocated.

Another JagdPanzer had succumbed, its crew dodging bullets in a successful attempt to reach a friendly shell hole.

The artillery, not to be outdone, took out another ISU, a dramatic mushroom cloud of black smoke and flame marking its end.

The infantry of the 5th RdM had reached Rostov-Four, a small hamlet lying near the Stockachgraben stream, where Knocke could see a vicious fire fight taking place at close-quarters.

A report from Uhlmann broke through his concentration, the tank officer reporting a successful breach in the lines at Dagersheim.

398

Also, the voice of Lange made itself known, encouraging his men forward.

"Anton to Gelbkopf-zero-one over."

The reply was distorted and Knocke tried again.

This time Lange's reply was loud and clear.

'Strange.'

"Anton to Gelbkopf-zero-one. What is your status over?"

Again, the response was crystal clear.

"Gelbkopf-zero-one to Anton. Have experienced communications problems. Now sorted. Am in command, over."

Knocke toyed with the possibilities and gave him the benefit of the doubt.

"Anton to Gelbkopf-zero-one. You have command. I am behind you with Anton and Emil. Ende."

'Some explaining to do later.'

Knocke's thoughts overrode the reply from Lange.

To his front, the ISU's were coming off much worse, two more of their number dying before his eyes in return for a JagdPanther damaged.

The Nashorne was methodically working the line, its lethal gun requiring only a single hit to claim a kill.

The legionnaires of 'Alma' had taken Rostov-Four and reported its fall over the radio scheme, closely followed by Rostov-Three, as they moved to join forces with Uhlmann's troopers in Dagersheim.

Von Arnesen's lead units were held up within the hedgehog, and he reported that he was going forward to 'encourage' his men.

Knocke half considered warning his old comrade to take care but reconsidered. Such advice was wholly unnecessary in the circumstances.

He turned back to watch 'Rostov', his concerns soothed by the now regular radio transmissions from Lange.

Considering that the Soviets had been occupying the positions for only a short time, they had done a fine job of making them difficult for any attacker.

Von Arnesen, his thigh aching from the exertion, had moved forward through the trenches, and discovered an increasing number of dead and wounded from his legionnaires. These casualties came in groups throught the defences, groups that marked the location of each pocket of resistance, as the Soviets gave ground reluctantly.

Ahead of him, a grenade exchange was taking place. One of his French officers, a Legion Captain, was organising an assault, seemingly oblivious to the fact that his left hand was shredded and useless.

He left the man to it, solely ordering the officer to accept the ministrations of the waiting medic.

Moving off down an adjoining trench, Von Arnesen's point man was nearly bowled over by a soldier bursting from a small gully, laden with bags of grenades, intent on supplying his comrades with the means to hold the Allies at bay.

Fortunately, the Corporal leading the party recognised him for what he was, and dropped the Russian with a controlled burst from his ST44.

The heavy bags of Soviet grenades were taken up, to be used against their former owners.

The sound of tank guns firing rose to a crescendo, as did the radio messages from the Tank companies, who were having their own problems in Dagersheim.

Von Arnesen's party moved forward again.

The trench fed into an anti-tank gun position, containing what used to be an anti-tank gun, and probably what used to be its crew, although it was extremely difficult to tell, as the bits were spread around like some mad butcher had thrown tidbits to his hounds.

Here a small aid station had been set up, and six badly wounded legionnaires were receiving attention from orderlies, the wounds testing their medical knowledge.

400

Swift questioning of the orderlies revealed the correct route to follow, and von Arnesen's party set off down the central trench. After a few minutes, they approached a growing fire fight and arrived as the Russian infantry were launching a counter-attack.

Unfortunately for the Soviet soldiers, their attempt to attack both through the trenches and over the top proved unsuccessful, Von Arnesen's group flaying the exposed guardsmen as they prepared to grenade the German legionnaires below them.

Von Arnesen risked a swift look over the edge to orient himself and dropped back down again as fire from an enemy machine gun whipped up the earth nearby.

Summoning the legionnaire officer to him, he hastily drew a plan in the damp earth floor, using a large wooden splinter.

"Lieutenant Durand, here is the gap," the original plan made a gap in the woods to the rear of the hedgehog a focal point.

"Here is the log bunker," he made a hole with the stick and drew the road in behind it, running from left to right.

"Here we are," a very deliberate thrust of the stick generated a suitable marker.

"Take your platoon around to the right and get behind the bunker to this point," he emphasised the location with another, deeper hole, "Take anyone who retreats from the bunker and prevent its reinforcement, but do not cross the road. Move now, but stay in that position until we come up to you."

Lieutenant Durand, once of the Vichy 6th REI, captured in Syria in 1941, understood his orders and sped away to get his men together.

Von Arnesen turned to his own group, and the stragglers who had joined it, briefing them in their part in the push, namely the trench assault on the bunker.

A quick radio conversation informed Knocke of his intent, and a second ordered two more companies of legionnaires into the hedgehog defensive system.

401

The group of twenty men moved off into the left-hand trench as the last of Durand's men disappeared down the larger right-hand trench.

Elsewhere in the hedgehog, submachine guns were at work, assisted by grenades. The more grisly and close work made little identifiable noise.

At the front of Von Arnesen's group there was a sudden commotion, and he could see men scattering.

An explosion and cries of pain followed, the point man having been wounded by a Soviet grenade.

The bleeding man was dragged backwards and young legionnaire took his place, dropping his Kar98k and picking up the wounded corporal's ST44 and spare magazines.

Checking behind him, the legionnaire took a quick look over the parapet. Satisfied he dropped down again and then stole a look round the corner. He shouted a warning but stood his ground, pausing to catch the thrown grenade before returning it down the trench.

A solid crump followed, followed by more screams. The legionnaire ran forwards, the assault rifle spitting bullets in short bursts.

Support quickly followed, and another section of trench was wrenched from Soviet hands.

Three Soviet guardsmen lay wounded on the ground, obstructing the way forward with their damaged bodies.

Two legionnaires dragged them backwards swiftly, immune to the extra screams from the most wounded one, his entrails catching on an ammunition box as he was moved.

Ex-Hauptscharfuhrer Höffman cocked his Colt pistol and dispatched each in turn, killing with a single shot to the forehead, his eyes cold and clinical.

"Scheisse untermensch."

The Colt was replaced and he thought no more about it.

Time was against them, so Von Arnesen pushed them on again.

402

At 'Minsk', it was mayhem.

More T-70's had declared themselves, harrying the infantry, whilst trying not to expose themselves to the Panthers and Panzer IV's of Uhlmann's command.

The battle with the ISU's had distracted him momentarily, but he saw the fight going in the Allies favour and returned to his own more immediate issues.

It was easy to see what was happening, house to house fighting going on in front of his eyes.

He pushed the Panzer IV platoons closer up, with orders to support the infantry using high-explosives and machine-guns, retaining his Panther units on the flanks to increase their killing zones.

The Panzer IV's were shelling furiously, some directed by infantrymen, NCO's and officers sheltering behind their turrets, pointing out a tough pocket here, a suspected position there.

Dagersheim seemed to be slowly melting before his eyes, the edge of the town crumbling under the assault.

To avoid artillery, Uhlmann moved his command group once more, favouring the southern side again.

His gunner spotted an ISU and sought permission to engage, but the SP gun was knocked out by another tank before he could fire.

Uhlmann spared another look at the 'Alma' units and saw them closing, much as his own infantry force, closer combat taking place in the woods and outskirts of Boblingen.

Numerous ISU's were knocked out within his field of vision, yet more marked only by a pall of smoke from somewhere in the distance.

He grunted with satisfaction as he dwelt on one of his Bergepanther's, rushing up to a disabled JagdPanther, the self-propelled guns' heavy track unravelled after a direct hit.

His ears became aware of the distinctive crack of a Panther's 75mm, and then the reports from his 2nd Company

403

commander positioned on the North side, reporting a sally by Soviet tanks.

Between the Hedgehog and Dagersheim, the ground had been shorn of trees by the artillery of both sides, both from this conflict and the last. Uhlmann's Panthers used the field of fire to its fullest extent.

A second report quickly followed.

"Dora-zero-one to Berta over."

Uhlmann faced north, watching his Panthers urgently redeploying.

"Berta receiving. Go ahead."

"Dora-zero-one, we have numerous IS heavy tanks to our front, supported by..."

The transmission cut short, coinciding with the appearance of an immense fireball topped by a slowly-rolling tank turret, tons of metal thrown skywards by the force of the explosion.

Uhlmann could imagine Schneider's baby face as the turret tumbled back to earth.

"Berta to Dora-one-one, report."

The first platoon's second in line responded professionally.

"Dora-one-one to Berta, zero-one is destroyed. Heavy and medium tanks in brigade strength to our front, range two thousand metres. Dora is engaging, over."

"Berta acknowledged. I will order Friedrich to support. Take care. Ende."

Braun, call sign Dora-one-one, now the commander of first platoon, switched quickly to his own net, more to encourage his troopers than to issue orders, his eyes glued to the command sight.

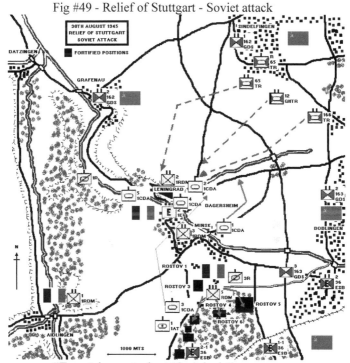

Fig #49 - Relief of Stuttgart - Soviet attack

"Target, heavy tank at 12 o'clock."

"On." The gunner had anticipated Braun's selection and was tracking the leviathan's progress.

"Feuer!"

The 75mm spat its high-velocity shell as the IS-II fired back.

The moving IS had little chance of success, and its shell passed the 75mm and disappeared beyond the target.

The Panther's shell struck the front armour and ricocheted skywards in a shower of sparks.

Braun could comfortably expect to fire off three shells to every one from the IS-II.

Their second shell totally missed the Soviet vehicle, much to the surprise of commander and gunner, although not so much as a grunt passed between them.

405

The loader rammed home a third shell and the gunner sent it on its way, striking the enemy tank on the join between turret and hull, jamming the turret in place but not penetrating.

Another 75mm struck the IS, fired from a different angle, the solid shot penetrating between the front idler and the hull.

Hatches flew open, and the tank crew fled in all directions.

Braun ordered another target as the other Panther finished the tank off.

The T-70's were buzzing around like flies but had no place in the tank engagement, their guns and armour insignificant in the confrontation between main battle tanks.

It was almost as if the Soviet commander had left them on the battlefield to distract the legion gunners, and to soak up shells that could have taken out the battle tanks.

If so, the tactic was successful.

Many of them were destroyed.

The T34's understood that their best chance of survival lay with closing, and they split into two wedges, flanking the heavy tanks and driving hard for the legion tank line.

The eight surviving Panther's followed standard doctrine, working from the edge inwards, but in this instance the doctrine was flawed.

The T34's were closing fast.

Braun hit the transmit.

"One-One calling. First platoon concentrate on the left hand group of T34's, second platoon on the heavies."

Braun's gunner traversed and selected the nearest T34.

"T34 target. On."

Braun gave the order and the tank jumped.

Satisfied that his target was destroyed, the gunner moved on.

With half an eye to his own tank and the other half on the larger battle, Braun noticed the IS's stopping.

'Verdamnt normal!'

He counted twelve IS-II's intact upon the field, and each one put a 122mm shell in the air.

An express train went past his turret, the whoosh discernable, a sound well-remembered from battles on the Eastern Front.

Another passed on the other side.

All in all, ten shells sailed past. Two hit.

The two shells arrived simultaneously, striking the hull front of a second platoon tank as it moved locations.

Braun knew better than to expect survivors.

Another two IS-II's succumbed to direct fire, joining four more T34's added to the total since Braun had claimed his last kill.

However, the tide of tanks was still flowing closer, and Braun was tempted to relocate backwards.

However, such a withdrawal would leave the forces at the Hedgehog dangerously exposed, and open up the rear of Dagersheim.

A Panther tank from another unit dropped into a position just forward and to his right, the markings clearly that of his regimental commander and future brother-in-law.

Uhlmann also saw the T34's as the greater threat and joined with First platoon in engaging them. His gunner was a fresh-faced young corporal, once of the Hitler Jugend Division. It was accepted that he was an uncanny marksman, without equal in 'Camerone', an ability he ably demonstrated by firing three quick shots, each of which hit home, stopping his two targets and sending the crews to a fiery death.

The HJ gunner was already the proud holder of the Iron Cross First and Second class, and Braun suspected he would receive more jewellery in the days ahead.

Another shell from his own tank struck a T34 on the gun barrel, bending it dramatically, rendering it useless.

However, the Soviet gunner fired in his panic and the shell detonated in the barrel.

The crew abandoned but did not make friendly cover as an MG42 lashed out from the hedgehog area.

A Panther took a hit on its turret side with spectacular results. The 122mm shell bounced away, ploughing into a small farmhouse and bringing down the gable end.

407

The welding on the Panther's turret had conceded to the kinetic shock and come apart, opening the side of the turret to sunlight. Not that it bothered the gunner or loader, as both were killed by the shockwave.

The commander, his face bashed and bloody when his head was dashed against the cupola, groggily ordered a withdrawal and the damaged second platoon tank pulled back, pursued by fire from the rapidly closing T34's.

Braun took the opportunity of a side shot on a manoeuvring T34 and wrecked its engine, leaving it side on and unable to move. The crew decided to evacuate, escaping before second shell destroyed the vehicle.

Uhlmann had organised an air strike, and three USAAF Thunderbolts swept the battlefield, sending twenty-four rockets into the stationary IS-II's, two more being instantly transformed into expensive scrap metal.

Soviet artillery was falling more heavily around the tank line, and Uhlmann ordered an immediate adjustment of one hundred and fifty metres backwards, tanks leapfrogging to rear positions.

The company's most venerable Panther tank, an Ausf D captured in Normandy, broke down as it left cover, suddenly attracting the attention of both IS-II's and T34's.

No shots struck the lame duck.

But an immobile vehicle is no place to be on a battlefield so the crew abandoned their smoking tank, a small fire having started in the engine compartment. It burned lazily for the rest of the battle.

On the edge nearest the hedgehog, the T34's were up to two hundred metres, although over half had been knocked out as they charged forward.

An 85mm pinged off the Panther's gun mantlet, a white-hot trail rising straight up into the sky; a second clipped the top of the turret, the metal glowing a dull red momentarily.

2nd Platoon's northernmost tank was forced to rotate its turret, determined to stop its flank being turned, but in so doing exposed the side to a solid shot.

To the inexperienced eye, there was little more than a hole the size of a tea cup, precisely central on the side plate.

408

Those that had experienced the horrors of tank warfare understood that the solid shot had transformed the turret into a charnel house of pieces that even a mother wouldn't recognise.

The gap needed to be filled and Braun reacted immediately, moving his tank to cover, halting, and turning one of the T34's into a metallic bonfire with a single shot.

Selecting a hollow position behind a modest bush, he kept his silhouette to a minimum and worked the flanking force, picking off another tank.

'Are the bastards breeding?'

It seemed no sooner did one tank get knocked out than another two took its place, which in fact was probably a fair description, as the Soviet Brigade commander frantically fed more of his forces into the fray.

The fields between Dagersheim and Sindelfingen seemed to be crawling with armour, well over a hundred vehicles committed to action.

Braun became aware of more high-velocity weapons firing, and was relieved to discover comrades from 4th Company moving into position.

4th Company was a hotchpotch of vehicles, which was why it had been left out of the assault.

Now, its SP's and tanks started working the field efficiently, killing and killing and killing.

The T34 drive vanished, gutted further by the arrival of 4th Company, the survivors turning and running, exposing thin rear armour to vengeful Legion tankers.

Another wave of T34's moved forward, but this time mingling with the IS-II's, the centre of the battlefield containing an inexorable wedge of advancing Soviet armour, still outnumbering the defenders.

Braun checked his watch, surprised to find it was precisely ten o'clock.

Uhlmann ordered a forward movement all across the defensive line, regaining their previous positions. The Katyusha barrage arrived as the tank companies relocated once more.

409

Two of his men lay dead, torn to pieces by a machine-gun that was covering the trench leading to the bunker. Another man had exposed himself above the parapet for the briefest of moments and was now coughing out his life as his ruined jaw and windpipe leaked vital blood into his lungs.

Sounds of combat from Durand's platoon moved further away, as the Legion Lieutenant drove his men to fulfil his orders.

Two of Von Arnesen's men equipped themselves with some grenades and made speculative throws over the top, aiming at the machine-gun.

Both failed, and one man earned a bullet in the wrist for his troubles, an alert guardsman shattering his ulna.

Reinforced by some more stragglers, Von Arnesen could still only muster two dozen men. In any case, two hundred men wouldn't be any good unless the present tactical problem could be overcome.

Höffman dropped down by the edge of the trench, accepting a Mauser rifle, its bayonet fitted and stained with recent use.

Wiping the blood away, he extended the weapon, using the reflective blade to look up the trench, assessing and planning his own move.

Returning the rifle to its owner, the fanatical NCO slid across to his commander, who was on the radio ordering mortars onto the target.

"Sir, I think I can sort this. I need a smoke grenade and the ST44."

No explanation was required, indeed, there was no time for it.

The ST44 changed hands for the third time that hour and a nebelgranate was pressed into his hands.

Ensuring the assault rifle magazine was full, Höffman moved to the edge of the trench and prepared his grenade.

"Don't do anything until I shout, Kameraden," he spoke with black humour, "If I'm fucking dead, act independently, and send my mother flowers."

410

A mad grin split his face and he tossed the smoke grenade over the top and into the trench some thirty yards up.

Giving time for the smoke to obscure the view, he scuttled on his belly, hugging the ground as the Soviet defenders fired speculatively through the spreading cloud, adding random grenades for good measure.

His reflected view had been correct, in as much as there was a depression in the trench floor, framed by the bodies of Soviet guardsmen killed previously.

Sliding into the depression, he organised the dead body to give him both protection and a place to steady his weapon.

The smoke cleared slowly.

Höffman could clearly see two riflemen in cut-outs down the trench sides, but it was another minute before he made out the barrel of a DP light machine-gun some metres beyond.

He made a professional judgement, and settled himself for the shots.

The ST44 was a modern weapon designed for the modern battlefield, range less than a rifle but greater than a sub-machine gun. The intent was to provide improved firepower to the infantry facing the Soviet juggernaut, giving the Wehrmacht superior firepower in the 'middle ground' of battles.

The magazine contained thirty short-case 7.92mm rounds, capable of being blazed off on full automatic or, as Höffman intended, in semi-automatic mode.

He could see the enemy peering down the trench and felt that the left side rifleman was becoming far too interested in his hiding place.

He pulled the trigger and sent a burst into the DP position.

The MG fired, its bullets zipping through the air above the Sergeant.

Höffman fired again, assisted by the muzzle flash, silencing the crew.

A bullet nicked his shoulder, the enemy rifleman having got his bearings quickly.

The ST44, momentarily out of control because of the impact, lined up with the guardsman and fired. A bloody body tumbled out of the niche and onto the trench floor.

411

The second rifleman picked up a grenade, armed it, and threw it high.

Höffman was horrified to see it land the other side of the dead Russian he was using as cover.

He pressed his face into the mud and felt the shock wave as the grenade exploded.

Unharmed but disoriented, he struggled to aim the ST44, not realising that the foresight had been neatly removed by shrapnel.

None the less, he pulled the trigger twice, sending bullets into the right-hand niche, smashing the knee and shoulder of the rifleman, taking him out of the fight.

The sergeant retained enough presence of mind to shout to the assault group.

"Schnell Menschen! Vorwärts!

Needing no second invitation, Von Arnesen's group crashed around the corner at high-speed, closing down the deadly machine-gun position before it could be brought back into action. The first man there used his MP40 to repulse an attempt to man the DP, leaving three Soviet dead in the trench beyond.

Propping the damaged ST44 against the trench, Höffman selected a discarded PPSh, and slid an extra round magazine under his belt.

The second Soviet rifleman was crying tears of pain, moaning softly as his shattered knee and shoulder brought him to the extremes of agony.

The ex-SS man drew level with the noise and examined the Russian with emotionless eyes. He moved his PPSh into the crook of his left arm, grimacing as the extra weight provoked his new shoulder wound.

Höffman took out his pistol once more.

"Bastard Russich."

Hate replaced pain in the guardsman's eyes.

"Germanski bastard."

The Colt spoke twice, the naked fury in the Russians eyes inspiring Höffman to make doubly sure, the second shot masking the sound of the arming lever on the US issue fragmentation grenade, now dropping from a lifeless hand.

It rolled against his foot.

412

Höffman's impaired reactions gave him no chance.

"Du verdammter bastard Russich!"

0940 hrs, Thursday 30th August 1945, Soviet Defensive Position designated 'Rostov-5', south of Dagersheim, Germany.

The first assault had failed, falling short of the enemy position on a small rise two hundred metres from the main road out of Böblingen.

5th RdM's 3rd Battalion were tasked with Rostov-5 through to Rostov-9, a frontage of just under a kilometre, and they had fallen at the first hurdle.

In fairness, it was not their inability or lack of courage, but the fact that Rostov-5 was bristling with everything in the Soviet infantry arsenal.

Lange, his teeth gritted against the pain as the soldier bound his ankle, swept the approaches with his binoculars, the bodies of 7th Kompagnie's commander and some of his men still burning bright enough to be remarkable on the extensive battlefield.

A few metres behind Lange and his command group was his headquarters vehicle, its engine wrecked by shells from a light anti-aircraft gun brought into play against the easier ground targets.

Salvaging a couple of radios, the group set up in a shell hole, moving earth to form a raised ridge on the rim, behind which they could more safely observe the battle.

Lange had dislocated his ankle in the mad dash to escape the anti-aircraft gun's cannon shells, and the swollen joint stuck fast in his combat boots.

Refusing to have them cut off, he allowed one of the signallers to bind it tight with a bandage as he tried to organise his forces.

"Gelbkopf to Gelbbruder-one-two over."

The second in command of 7th Kompagnie did not have a radio, so no reply was forthcoming.

"Gelbkopf to any unit Gelbbruder come in."

"Gelbbruder-two-one to Gelbkopf receiving."

413

The commander of the 8th Kompagnie was an old soldier, and Lange's enthusiasm got the better of him, formal radio procedure suspended.

"Status, over."

"Gelbbruder-two-one to Gelbkopf, one-one is dead, one-two is wounded. I have command. I need Adler on this location immediately, and be aware, light flak is in the target zone, over."

"Gelbkopf received. I will advise."

Lange waited whilst the other signaller went to switch his radio channel to contact Adler direct. He was curtailed by an authoratative voice on the main scheme radio.

"Anton to Gelbkopf, Gelbbruder-two-one. Adler will be inbound. Mark Rostov-5 with red smoke, repeat red smoke over."

8th Kompagnie's Captain acknowledged and Rostov-5 was bathed in an expanding ruby red cloud within seconds.

Knocke spoke to the air controller, who in turn directed his last support strike in on target.

The self-propelled guns of the anti-tank unit were warned, and readied themselves to move closer still.

Three glass-nosed A-26 Invaders of the 640th Bomb Squadron lined up and attacked.

Many eyes were on their approach. The legionnaires of 5th RdM waited, coiled like a spring, ready to charge into the devastated position.

Knocke and Lange observed from their command positions, ready to react as needed.

The Soviet machine-gunners and flak crew waited, fearful for their lives if they should not knock down the aircraft.

The Invaders carried delayed-action bombs, enabling them to come in low and strafe as they attacked, each aircraft producing a devastating fire from eight nose-mounted .50cal machine guns, a heavy firepower bolstered by a further eight .50cal's in four wing pods. The combined effect being to place over nine thousand rounds per minute on the target area from each aircraft.

It almost seemed to the observers that the smoke was beaten down by the passage of lead, angular lines appearing in the redness, and often, other redness appeared marking the fatal passage of heavy bullets.

414

Experienced observers noted that the central Invader had its bomb bay open, and it was this aircraft that released eight 500lbs bombs, the weight loss causing it to swiftly rise above its comrades, receiving a line of tracer through its open belly for its trouble.

The three bombers turned sharply to starboard, moving over friendly territory, angrily pursued by a hail of Soviet bullets.

The fuses ran their course and exploded.

Rostov-5 rose into the air, or that was how it seemed to Knocke through his binoculars, the force of the bombs raising up earth, stone, metal and flesh, before it all came crashing back down again.

8th Compagnie's commander gave the order and his second in command charged forward, leading 7th Compagnie onto their objective.

The French officer shouted for all he was worth and plunged into the cloud of dust, closely followed by the 7th's legionnaires, shouting and screaming in the charge.

A Soviet guardsman staggered out of the smoke and dust, his hands holding his ruined face, ears bleeding from the concussion of the explosions.

He was shot down, and the legionnaires ran on.

A dead Soviet officer, his legs neatly severed at the top of both thighs, stood erect in a shallow pathway, acting as a diminutive gatekeeper and attracting humorous shouts as the legionnaires swept on.

The Invaders lined themselves up.

7th Compagnie pushed on, dispatching a few shocked guardsmen as they progressed.

The Invaders approached.

"Anton to Adler. Call the eagles off. Friendlies on target. Repeat, call the eagles off!"

Those on the command net who heard Knocke's words realised that a disaster was in the making, their commander's voice carrying a fear and worry that none could miss.

8th Compagnie's leader could only watch in horror as the USAAF bombers approached again.

All three opened fire together and ceased fire just as quickly, flying straight over the wrecked position without dropping any ordnance.

"Adler to Anton. Attack aborted. Eagles are low on fuel and returning to base, over."

The radiomen in the Command Panther heard a defined sigh of relief from their leader, and they shared one together.

The Invaders had fired for a split second, enough time to get nearly two hundred rounds on target. Enough to kill three legionnaires and wound five others.

7th Compagnie pressed on finding no resistance, dispatching a wounded man here and there, until they reached the edge of the position and could overlook the road to the south-east.

7th Compagnie's Senior NCO beckoned the radioman forward and reported in, confirming that their mission was accomplished, and also that he was in charge, the Invaders having killed the 8th Kompagnie's French officer.

Behind schedule, 8th Compagnie assaulted Rostov-6, taking the position with ease.

0947 hrs, Thursday, 30th August 1945, Soviet Defensive Position designated 'Leningrad', north-west of Dagersheim, Germany.

Von Arnesen's group was now down to thirteen on their feet. Whilst none of the others were fatally wounded, they were out of the fight, and the Soviet resistance was not getting less; far from it.

Allowing his men a few moments to get their breath back, he risked a swift look over the edge and saw just enough to know that they were close to their target.

He also saw a movement in the trench to their front and realised it was helmeted heads moving swiftly.

"Achtung! Counter-attack!"

His warning made all the difference.

Two experienced legionnaires, one, a man who had learned his soldering with the Leibstandarte-SS, and his loader, similarly versed in the art of war by his service with the SS-

416

Wiking, had just finished preparing their weapon for the new assault. They quickly deployed, in text book fashion, the loader kneeling, the gunner placing the weapon on the offered shoulder.

The MG42 had a phenomenal rate of fire, so much so that it super-heated the barrel if fired without pause. The German Army issued instructions to reduce rates of fire, and to use the weapon in short bursts.

Experienced or not, the gunner decided to ignore that particular instruction, and proceeded to unload the entire two hundred and fifty round belt into the group of Guardsmen that charged round the corner, holding grenades that remained firmly within dead hands.

The bullets literally cut some of the men to pieces.

The belt gone, the two machine-gunners dived for cover as the armed grenades started to go off amongst the recently fallen, transforming that piece of trench into something completely unspeakable.

More Soviet soldiers yet to emerge from the angled trench fell to shrapnel, and those that remained had no stomach for a further attempt.

'No time like now then.'

Von Arnesen rose swiftly, the pain stabbing his thigh and causing him to wince.

"Forward Menschen! No stopping, press hard!"

The two gunners already had another belt fitted and dragged another from a Legion corpse nearby.

At the front ran an ex-Hitler Youth soldier, screaming at the top of his juvenile voice whilst firing short bursts from his MP40 into the backs of the broken Soviet infantry.

He tripped and fell but the attack didn't falter, a French Caporal-Chef took up the lead, his recently acquired PPSh pushing the enemy on quicker than before.

The trench took a few more turns until they could see the log bunker just ahead.

At the next turn, a Soviet officer had stopped some of his men and they rallied.

The caporal-chef flew back round the trench corner, the impact of the bullets knocking him off his feet.

417

Through bloody lips he screamed as the Russians used his legs as a target, exposed as they were.

Von Arnesen and the medic dragged the man by his straps, but were horrified to see both his feet detach, severed by the stream of bullets.

"Grenate!"

A stick grenade was thrust into his hands and the cord was pulled. It was airborne with seconds, landing on the top of the trench and doing no more than distracting the defenders.

He risked another look over the top.

"Menschen, stay ready to charge. I'm going over the top here, you," he pointed to the ex-Hitler Youth soldier, "Young Fischer, I want you over that side. Come down in the trench behind them, but let's not shoot each other. Klar?"

Aloisius Fischer grinned like the child he was.

"Alles Klar, Sturmbannfuhrer!"

"And you all stay ready and attack when they have us to worry about. In the meantime, keep them busy as soon as we move. Klar?"

It was clear, and no further explanation was needed.

Von Arnesen checked his MP40 and took up another grenade, a British Mills bomb.

Fischer put a new round magazine on his submachine gun.

Both men ensured that their pistols were ready and correct, as such a weapon would be a life-saver and a life-taker in the environment they were about to create.

"Ready?"

A nod was sufficient.

"Go!"

Von Arnesen leapt up and out of the trench, half expecting to be instantly cut down by machine-guns.

Nothing.

He could see Fischer moving like a Gazelle, nearly halfway already, and so he drove himself forward hard.

Fischer was close to the trench now, and had his grenade ready, waiting for his leader.

His thigh protesting loudly, Von Arnesen got to his chosen position and signalled the attack with a simple nod.

418

Both man and boy pulled the pins on the grenades and threw them into the enemy position.

Both bounced into the trench, just as the defending DP started firing again after a reload.

The two Soviet soldiers who had covered that reload darted back into the trench and found themselves staring at death on the floor.

One threw himself back around the corner, falling in front of his machine-gun team who were busy firing at nothing in particular, just denying the French the trench on front of them.

The man died messily, and also blocked the DP's fire.

Both grenades exploded, sufficiently apart to be individual, and to do their own specific killing.

The Soviet officer was first, thrown up out of the trench.

Three of his men were killed or wounded by the same grenade.

Von Arnesen's grenade killed the DP gunner and badly wounded the loader, and spread its shrapnel equally between the remaining guardsmen.

Both attackers jumped into the trench and went about their grisly work, pistols barking in unison.

None of the defenders were in much state to put up any resistance, and so the two worked swiftly.

The main group arrived, less the medic, who remained to tend to the French NCO.

Quickly reloading his pistol as he moved, Von Arnesen found himself looking at the wooden structure rising out of the groun. Inside, the sounds of a huge fire fight broke out.

He halted his men, in order to understand what was happening.

'Durand?'

Rushing into such a position, when there is an uncoordinated friendly attack going on was a stupidity, and so Von Arnesen's group took cover and waited whilst their leader made an assessment.

Where the trench butted up to the bunker, a camouflage net hung, obscuring a doorway.

The netting ripped apart as a squealing Soviet officer threw himself through it, pursued by a bloodied Legionnaire.

419

The Soviet officer's scream was cut short as a bayonet sliced into his throat and trashed the base of his skull.

The Irish Legionnaire, one of the old 13th DBLE men, recovered his rifle and made to defend himself against the new enemy, not realising they were friends.

Von Arnesen leapt up and shouted as loud as he could, as the blood-crazed man seemed intent on killing his whole party.

"A moi la Légion!"

Words that burned through the legionnaire's bloodlust and brought him back to reality, which was just as well as Fischer was about to drop him dead.

With a slap on the shoulder and a gesture, the calmed man turned back to the fight and Von Arnesen led his men into the bunker.

Durand was using a rifle to deadly effect, his own submachine gun discarded for the moment in favour of the new weapon's longer reach and accuracy.

Soviet soldiers were in view through the bunkers openings, retreating as fast as they could towards Grafenau, some dropping as Durand's force opened more fire upon them.

The hedgehog had been taken.

Von Arnesen looked at his watch as he beckoned the radioman forward.

'0958. Time flies.'

He watched as Durand dropped another running figure, silently impressed with the Frenchman's skill.

Taking up the handset, he broadcast his success to Knocke, happily noticing more of his men popping up in positions to his left.

Turning to his right, he spotted more and, continuing his report, looked further on and saw the tanks of 1st and 4th Company in their defensive positions.

Some of them fired, and he looked to see what they were firing at.

"Mein Gott! Julius-zero-one to Anton. Russische panzers, at least two regiment's worth, heavy and medium types, moving south from Magstadt towards Dagersheim, straight at our panzers over."

"Roger Julius, Anton to Berta receiving over."

<u>0949 hrs, Thursday 30th August 1945, French First Army Headquarters, Hotel Stephanie, Baden-Baden.</u>

Saluting an arriving USMC Lieutenant Colonel, Kowalski strolled casually out of the Hotel Stephanie and, as was his habit, turned to the right and walked up Schillerstraße.

That was precisely what had been expected, but that didn't mean that other eyes weren't ready to follow him, had he turned the other way.

No chances were being taken with 'Leopard'.

Crossing the road near the junction, Kowalski took a left into Bertholdstraße, appreciating the fine lines of a classic Rolls-Royce that swept past.

He stopped to light a cigarette, turning back to the bin to deposit the spent match.

Kowalski had a lighter of course, but the walk past the bin and back permitted him to reverse direction quickly, just in case he was being followed.

He wasn't.

Satisfied he was not under surveillance, he drew in the rich smoke and watched a convoy of Military Police drive slowly by.

But he was, and numerous eyes feigned disinterest in his presence, but were keenly aware of his every move.

He passed the newspaper seller and repeated his u-turn exercise, again seeing nothing untoward.

Paying for the newspaper, more of a local news pamphlet in reality, he folded it neatly and resumed his stroll.

An obvious suspect for 'Deux', investigations had discovered that the newspaper seller had some interesting sexual preferences, something that they would revisit in less fraught times. But other than that, he was clean.

He crossed the junction of Ludwig-Wilhelm-Straße, increasing his pace, before turning right into Maria-Viktoria-Straße. He entered a small bakery.

421

Uhlmann dispatched an IS-II that had slewed sideways,
a single shell smashing the huge tank's engine.

He keyed the mike as his gunner sought another victim.

"Berta engaging eighty plus tanks, IS-II and T34 type, to
front. Approaching due south from Magstadt, over."

The crack of 75mm and 88mm guns could be heard all
over the battlefield, rising in frequency and urgency, punctuated
by the replying 85mm and 122mm weapons of the fast
approaching enemy.

"Anton to Berta. You must hold, repeat, you must hold.
Help is on its way, over and out."

Uhlmann already knew he had nowhere to go, for to
withdraw would leave the hedgehog outflanked, and the rest of
'Camerone' exposed.

The first part of Knocke's assistance became apparent as
shells from the Brigade's artillery started to fall.

"Anton to Berta over."

The response was not immediate, Uhlmann having more
pressing concerns as two T34's drove hard straight at him.

'Scheisse, you brave bastards!'

The first one was stopped dead by a direct hit, smoke
swiftly building and pushing out of the sprung hatches before
being replaced by urgent orange flames.

The second tank died within seconds, one of 4th
Company's Hetzer's joining the action late.

Knocke understood his Tank Regiment commander was
under pressure and so waited patiently.

"Berta to Anton receiving over."

"Anton here. Passing Artillery to you. Further, over."

Uhlmann looked at the shells landing and determined to
alter the barrage a little, although Knocke had made a good
attempt from distance.

"Berta here, roger, go ahead with further, over."

"Anton here, deploying part of Emil to your right flank, securing against 'Minsk', remainder of Caesar to your position, further, over."

Uhlmann processed that information. The rest of his First Company was coming to his rescue, and part of Third Company would seal any gap between his positions and Dagersheim.

"Berta here, roger, go ahead with further, over."

"Anton to Berta, Julius will..."

The next part of the message was lost as a huge force struck the Panther tank, rocking it like it weighed no more than a kilo.

"Berta to Anton, message lost, say again, over."

"Anton to Berta, Julius will hold in position and cover. Friedrich will move up through Leningrad and engage flank, over."

Uhlmann acknowledged his leader's information, pausing only to draw the gunner's attention to a flank shot on an IS-II.

'Excellent, that should do it. Now, the artillery.'

"Berta to Nordpol, over."

The slight correction brought the artillery of 'Camerone' closer to his tank line, creating a beaten zone to prevent the enemy from closing further, as well as causing casualties amongst those foremost.

Braun was getting vexed.

"Die, you bastard, die!"

For the eighth time the gunner put a 75mm AP round on target, and yet again it failed to have any apparent effect.

The IS-II seemed to have a charmed life.

"Again!"

The shell sped on its way, and struck, sticking hard in the gap between the turret and mantlet and jamming the gun in a raised position.

Another shell hit the nearside track, which came apart slowly, bringing the huge tank to a halt.

423

Braun encouraged the hull gunner to help the abandoning crew on their way with a burst or two of machine-gun fire.

An exploding shell flipped a T34 onto its side, the crew popping the hatches and exiting slowly, injured and in shock. Braun's machine-gunner had an easier target, and only two men made it safely to cover.

Seeking out another target, Braun spotted what looked like an ISU and ordered the gun laid on it. It burst into flames before he could fire, victim of one of 1st Company's Panzer IV's in Dagersheim.

This flanking fire drew the attention of a number of Soviet tanks, and the Panzer IV decided to retreat back into the town and relative safety.

Numerous enemy tanks lay smoking on the field. The legion tankers had certainly slowed up the advance, but the Soviets did not lack courage and still pressed on.

Their commanders got a grip, and the IS-II's became a wedge, moving inexorably forward, shrugging off many hits.

The range was now down to four hundred and fifty metres and the situation was desperate, with legion casualties mounting.

The lead IS-II, driven forward hard by the commanding Major, seemed to stagger, speed falling away and slewing off the direct path. A second shower of sparks betrayed a further hit, a solid shot boring into its flank and bringing havoc to the men inside.

The next IS-II in line required only one shot, its wrecked engine stoking up into a roaring fire within seconds, the stunned crew baling out, only to fall victim to vengeful machine-gunners in the Legion tanks.

The damage was being done by two anti-tank guns positioned in the hedgehog.

Von Arnesen controlled the larger gun's fire, and directed the 100mm anti-tank gun to shoot into the flanks of the heavy tanks. The other weapon, an ex-German 75mm Pak40 under the command of Lieutenant Durand, reached out at the T34's with equal success.

Some Soviet tanks turned to meet this new threat, exposing their sides to the tank line and paying the price for their stupidity. Others halted, trying to angle themselves to best effect against the two threats. Some lumbered on and some retreated.

Suddenly, the organised Soviet attack became a mess, one crew even quitting their intact vehicle and running back towards their lines.

The Soviet attack had quickly transformed from a serious threat to a shooting party, although the 'game' in question still packed a serious punch.

Taking advantage of the confusion, the Legion tanks repositioned, just in case, although the normally excellent Soviet artillery was proving strangely ineffective.

Uhlmann popped his head out of the hatch and gulped in the fresh air. The Hetzer beside him burned brightly. He hadn't even noticed that it had died, so intense had been the fight.

His gunner made his seventh kill, putting a solid shot into a reversing T34.

4th Company's Sturmgeschutz vehicles moved up and over the hedgehog, finding a choice of suitable firing positions, and lashing out at the trapped Soviet armour.

Knocke's experienced eye understood the field, and the fact that the enemy was on the verge of sheer panic.

However, mercy was not on his agenda.

He called the various elements, pushing them hard to finish the job, solely choosing to give his artillery the cease-fire order, and that only because his ammunition supplies were strung out for some kilometres and could not be up to the field in good time.

By the time he had finished with the artillery, the battlefield looked completely different. Everywhere Soviet tanks lay smashed or abandoned, burning or just silent.

About twenty or so tanks had made it back into the relative safety of the built-up area, but still men died, as the Sturmgeschutz and Panzers sent their shells into tender rear and side armour.

Shortly afterwards, Knocke ordered his panzers forward, following in the wake of the retreating tank units.

Moving up with his reconnaissance force in the lead, and an infantry group from the RDM's 1st Battalion, plus the Brigade's Assault Engineer force, the Legion Brigade found that the enemy force had melted away. It had left behind some wrecked vehicles, a few wounded men, and a few hastily laid booby traps.

Uhlmann organised the refuelling and reammunitioning of his tank companies, sought out the living and the dead, and began the process of putting his wounded regiment back together.

Elsewhere, other commanders, or in too many cases their deputies, began similar processes.

Knocke, his command Panther parked under the only stand of trees left in the park adjacent to Allgäuer Straβe, consulted a map in harness with Von Arnesen, combining their talents to extricate the Stuttgart garrison.

Uhlmann was still busy with his unit, and Lange was on his way to the rear with a twisted ankle and a nasty head wound, earned when leading an assault on Rostov-8.

Knocke's mind posed a question.

'Maybe I was wrong to have doubts about him?'

A radio transmission broke through his thoughts, bringing him quickly back to the problem in hand, and how to pass the 3rd Algerians through his positions.

The senior radio operator turned to report, but Knocke stopped him with a soft gesture.

"Thank you Lutz, I heard. Acknowledge and inform Commandant Uhlmann to direct them across the tank battlefield to pass south of 'Leningrad', where they will be met by elements of Julius and Otto with further instructions.

"Zu befehl, Standartenfuhrer," and he returned to his radio before he caught his commander's admonishing look.

Moving to the other radio operator, Knocke dictated a simple report to be passed to an expectant Lavalle.

Stuttgart had been successfully relieved.

With that simple message, ground-attack aircraft that had been husbanded for the secondary purpose, swept out over the surroundings kilometres, seeking out the Soviet artillery,

426

which could yet inflict heavy casualties on the escaping Algerians.

Most Soviet artillery units deliberately misconstrued their orders and kept silent. Those that didn't experienced a long enforced silence, as fighter-bombers visited themselves upon the ground forces with great effect.

<u>1505 hrs, Thursday 30th August 1945, Rüssel Bäckerei, Maria-Viktoria-Straβe, Baden-Baden, Germany.</u>

Kowalski purchased his normal pastries and tendered up his cash.

The standard procedure was for him to say 'Keep the change', which indicated that the notes that seemed stuck together actually were sealed and had a message inserted between them.

If there was a message in return then the offer would be refused and smaller denomination notes would be returned, similarly sealed.

This was the emergency communications route, and a back-up if there was a failure elsewhere. Although rarely used, it was a routine he undertook every day he was present in Baden-Baden. Otherwise, the baker passed the messages to a certain hotel employee when he attended the bakery in the early mornings.

Today there was no message back, but his message regarding the deployment of 'Camerone' was there, circumventing the hotel orderly because of its importance.

"Keep the change, Mein Herr."

"Danke, Herr Maior, danke."

A number of sweet pastries changed hands and he left, holding the door open for an old woman, who had also completed her purchases.

"Gnadige Frau."

"Dankeschön, Herr Maior."

'You Russian asshole.'

427

Despite having only one arm, Rüssel was an accomplished cyclist, and he undertook a number of deliveries for his special customers, once he had shut up shop for the day.

His wife would take any leftover product and sell it in the street, whilst he peddled through Baden-Baden, delivering special orders to those with sufficient means to pay for it, and he didn't mean money in most cases.

He most often exchanged goods for his wares, jams and preserves, with which he created his special cakes.

All except one customer, that was, a journey Rüssel hated because it involved cycling up to the four hundred metre line, following the winding Alter Schloβweg, to the main door of Schloss Hohenbaden.

As far as the entire house staff was concerned, the Oberst, as he was known, liked to meet with the tradesmen, as he enjoyed the haggling process. In reality, the trading covered the exchanges between him and the baker and other agents, information from a number of contacts one way, or orders and enquiries from GRU control going the other.

Oberst Christian Adolf Löwe summoned his manservant to have the baker seen off the premises, and returned to his drawing room, which was truly a room with a view, enjoying the all the sights of Baden-Baden in the valley below.

The gardener and his new apprentice didn't even seem to notice the cyclist's departure, so engrossed were they in their topiary.

The Oberst settled back into his favourite chair, enjoying both the view from his window and the obvious charms of the new member of the house staff, her splendid bosom so proudly on display in the uniform he had personally chosen for her.

He smiled disarmingly at the maid as she poured his traditional five o'clock coffee, one of the first things she had been told about on her first day of service.

"Thank you very much, my dear," he shoehorned the maximum amount of charm into the six words.

428

'I shall have those fat teats, my beauty, and more besides.'

Finishing up, the maid placed the cup and saucer in the right position and returned the coffee pot to its stand, smiling back at her employer.

"Will that be all, Herr Oberst?"

'I'll shoot your balls off if you so much as twitch.'

"For now, Anna-Maria, for now."

De Valois left the room and headed for a quick exchange with the new gardener's apprentice, also a member of 'Deux'.

1700 hrs Monday 20th August 1945, Headquarters of SHAEF, Trianon Palace Hotel, Versailles, France.

Eisenhower had finished up a briefing on the debacle that had been Operation Casino.

It was now wholly obvious that it had been an elaborate trap, from Station X's monitoring of the increased Russian radio traffic in the area, through dummy vehicles to draw the attention of aerial reconnaissance, and culminating in the agents talking of big numbers of Soviet tanks and soldiers, probably under the influence of Soviet Intelligence.

Tedder had grudgingly admitted that the subterfuge had been excellently worked out and carried through, displaying a flair hitherto unsuspected.

Clearly, the enhanced radio traffic was a carefully worked web of deceit, using radios and little else.

Elements of eight Anti-Aircraft divisions had now been identified by spies on the ground, although recent events meant that intelligence officers would turn jaundiced eyes to such intel until it was proven by other means.

Once bitten, twice shy on that one.

RAF Bomber Command had taken an awful beating, and would be dysfunctional for some time to come. It was an organisation used to taking casualties on unprecedented levels, but, with Operation Casino, it had exceeded its capacity to absorb the deaths of friends and comrades. In order to preserve the

429

Bomber Force, Harris had withdrawn it from combat for at least seven days.

'Poor Limeys.'

Bedell-Smith approached with a dead-pan face, partly annoyed because he had got it wrong, partly exuberant because of the end result.

He placed the report in front of his boss.

"What do we have here then, Walter?"

"Report on Stuttgart, Sir."

Eisenhower swapped his cigarette for the paperwork and tossed the first page.

"Wow!"

Coffee and fresh pastries arrived to sustain the two Generals until dinner.

"And this is all confirmed?"

"From De Lattre himself, Sir. It seems those boys gave the commies a damn good horse-whipping, and then some."

"Uh-huh."

Eisenhower shifted his gaze to the third page.

"Yeah, but they paid for it."

"Yes Sir, they did, but…"

The statement stopped ahead of schedule, drawing Ike's attention as Bedell-Smith had intended.

"Go on, Walt, spit it out."

"Sir, you know I was less than comfortable with this 'Legion' thing."

Eisenhower almost giggled.

"I seem to remember you mentioning it."

Bedell-Smith shrugged in acceptance of the point.

"Sir, these Legion troops may well have paid a high price for their success, and bear in mind that figure is probably not yet complete."

Ike nodded but let his man continue.

"The thing is, how many troops would it have cost us? More than three hundred dead? Certainly more than the final figure for the Legion troopers, whatever it may be."

Making to consult the report, Eisenhower slid it across the table so his CoS could see the evidence too.

430

"At the moment, the French report the loss of nineteen tanks, plus ten other vehicles."

Checking his way down the list, he found what he sought.

"Two hundred and one dead, fifty severely wounded, with another two hundred and thirty casualties. Less than five hundred as we stand, General."

Bedell-Smith considered the next statement carefully.

"Their figures on Soviet casualties are a bit hazy. But they do state at least eighty Soviet armoured vehicles, seventeen anti-tank guns, plus they have captured a lot of materiel."

He joined Ike in a sip of the scalding coffee.

"A rough estimate of over fourteen hundred Soviet dead upon the field. Top line Soviet troops too, so it is believed."

Eisenhower had missed that bit.

"Plus, they pulled the mission off to the letter, within time, and relieved the forces in Stuttgart."

Eisenhower held out his hands in mock supplication.

"Ok, Walt, I surrender. You have a point to make."

"Sir, I was anti, sure as hell. So, to a point, were you."

He didn't pose it as a question. It was a statement, and one that got Eisenhower's hackles raised.

'Jeez, I wanted the Germans in on the deal. It was my idea! Wasn't it? Was it?'

"Go on, Walt."

"There will be teething problems for sure, but I think we need to put aside our prejudices."

'Prejudices? Am I? Did I?'

"Sir, we are either allies with the Germans, or we are not, and the way I see it, our actions thus far have not borne out our faith and trust."

'Our actions have not borne out our faith and trust?'

Eisenhower felt angry and prepared to remonstrate before deflating swiftly, suddenly understanding that he had avoided using the German forces for anything specific, the committal of one of their infantry divisions in Denmark being at the behest of McCreery, rather than himself; the use of the Legion was because the French had done it themselves, not because he had made the running.

431

Even agreeing to move them up into the Ruhr…

'Goddamnit!'

"So, what do you suggest, Walt?"

His lack of denial being all the confession Bedell-Smith needed.

"Sir, these 'Legion' troops have shown that the German is still up for a brawl, and more units of the new Republican Army are forming as we speak. Get Guderian involved, and find out his views. Use his skills, his experience, until we get a handle on the new enemy."

"I hear you, Walter. But we are nowhere near ready to go over to attacking, even in a limited sense. We tried it with the 12th Armored, the Polish and Patton's boys, and each time we had our backside handed to us. We cannot yet successfully hit back."

Bedell-Smith raised his eyebrows and, in any other man, Eisenhower might have detected a mocking tone as his CoS indicated the report lying between them.

"I thought we just did, Sir?"

2002 hrs, Thursday 30th August 1945, Temporary Command post of 1st Legion Brigade du Chars D'Assault, Dagersheim, Germany.

Two salutes, immaculately prescribed, commenced proceedings.

"Good to see you, Ernst, and very well done today."

The two shook hands and moved to the folding map table, its rickety structure sufficient to provide a platform for a review of the situation map.

A drink was pressed into Lavalle's hand and he appreciated its cut, the dust and grime of the drive lying heavy upon him.

Knocke finished his brief, leaving out nothing that his senior might need to know.

Lavalle took another deep draught of the coffee, enhanced with something that had been liberated from a local hostelry.

"That's damn good!"

432

Knocke smiled. Finishing his brew and waving off a refill, he spoke softly.

"The Algerians don't look beaten."

He waved the empty mug towards the main road, down which a steady stream of vehicles and men moved towards safety.

Lavalle automatically looked at the same sight, delaying his response with another visit to the coffee mix.

"On my way up here I saw some who seemed to have little fight but, on the whole, I think you're right."

Lavalle then drained his drink.

"I did say they were tough soldiers."

Both men surrendered to a second attempt to refill, the insistent legionnaire taking it personally that his special coffee and Ansbach Brandy brew had been rejected.

"So, on the assumption that you didn't know we had special coffee, what brings the Corps Commander to the front, I wonder?"

The two shared a smile, a genuine one between two men who had become firm friends.

"Firstly, I brought with me a replacement for Lange. Legion Officer, extremely experienced and well-thought of, according to the reports he got from the Colloque Biarritz."

Ignoring the good-humoured grin on his commander's face, Knocke's mind, as sharp as a razor, processed that the symposium had only had two legion officers, and one of them had not completed the week due to a recurring malaria problem.

"St Clair?"

"Ah yes, the very same, St.Clair. I won't embarrass you with reciting your course report. He's over getting acquainted with his unit as we speak, just in case things start up."

Lavalle stretched, easing his back after hours sat in the jeep.

"So. Will they start tonight, Ernst?"

"My guess is harassing artillery fire will start once the sun goes down and we lose air. I really don't see them pulling anything major, but most of the unit will be on alert all night, just in case."

433

Knocke didn't need to add any more, his brief having covered the fact that he had withdrawn some units to safer positions to get rest and to recuperate.

"I must get back tonight, so I won't stay. However, one last thing."

Knocke, having moved slightly forward to bid Lavalle goodbye, checked himself immediately.

Slipping something out of his breast pocket, Lavalle pressed a folded envelope into Knocke's hand.

"Have a look at this, Ernst. It's an outline of the new order of battle for the Corps. Both you and 'Tannenberg' to be increased to divisional strength."

Ernst sought silent permission to open the envelope now, immediately signalled by Lavalle.

The Frenchman continued talking as the German read.

"I have suggested that 5th RdM stays with you and is absorbed into 'Camerone'. I assume you are satisfied with that?"

Knocke nodded as he consumed the written word.

"There will be a formalising of the structure so that command groups will be permanent, not be temporary as we have now."

His tone almost apologetic, Lavalle continued.

"To be frank, this was on the table a few days ago, but there was a feeling that we were running before we could walk."

The letter was refolded, put back into the envelope, and offered back to Lavalle.

"Keep it please, and let me know what you think when you have time to digest it fully."

Knocke placed it on the table and weighted it down with his empty mug.

"Anyway, your fight today has shown them that the Legion Corps can do the job, and the Generals are keen to give us our head."

"Can we sustain ourselves, Sir? Men? Equipment?"

"Since we left Sassy, a further seven thousand men have arrived, and there are more to come."

Knocke pressed again.

"And equipment, Sir?"

434

"More serviceable equipment has been discovered, and I am led to believe that there are plans to recommence vehicle production in the Ruhr, and some other places."

Something about the reply intruiged Knocke, but now was not the time.

Lavalle checked his watch and extended his hand once more.

"I must go, Ernst. Let me know your thoughts tomorrow. I should be back up here in the evening. Until then."

The hands parted and transitioned into precise salutes, marking an end to proceedings.

The waiting soldier saw his opportunity.

"Another coffee, Standartenfuhrer?"

"If I have another one of those you will have to pour me into my tank, Hässelbach!"

The man turned, grinning madly.

"And Hässelbach, if I have to tell you again that it's Colonel, you will be greasing the wheels ten times a day!"

The coffee manufacturer laughed as he disappeared to sample the rest of his wares.

The wrath was play, and those in earshot understood that it was just a small exercise in the art of leadership from one capable of great displays.

2047 hrs, Thursday 30th August 1945, Deuxieme Bureau operations house, Holzhofstrasse, Baden-Baden, Germany.

The meal had been created by a master chef, once noted as a rising star in Paris, before the jackboot descended on his country and truned him into a soldier.

Now he served in French Military Intelligence but, with an eye to less violent times, he liked to keep his hand in.

This, De Walle knew only too well, and he had played on it to get the man to create a wonderful meal for him and his guests.

A simple salad of lettuce and tomato, topped with hollowed boiled egg, the egg yolk creamed and mixed with roasted garlic and black pepper, all garnished with bacon and cheese. That was followed by baked whole Rabbit with

435

medallions of fresh venison, served with a beetroot and onion compote, Dauphinoise potatoes, and creamed cabbage. To finish off, a dessert of Crème Brulee accompanied by raspberries soaked in Benedictine.

It had been a working dinner, although the serious business had often been interrupted with moans of pleasure and favourable comments.

The man had worked wonders with the venison and rabbit, the gravy being almost worthy of bottling in its own right.

Now, filled with the finest cuisine, the five finished their discussions with cigars and the very finest Napoleon.

De Walle, stuffed to the brim and feeling extremely amenable, relit his cigar, creating a light smoke screen between his guests.

The man in the uniform of the Dutch Brigade stretched contentedly, Michel Wijers preparing his body for the short walk to the hotel.

"So, gentlemen. We have the basis of a plan, lacking only the most important details. Where and when?"

That was about the gist of it.

"We all have assets who could turn up the first piece of information, allowing us to fix the date."

Lieutenant Colonel Rossiter USMC, the merest hint of a gravy mark declaring defeat in his stalwart effort to keep his jacket clean, grunted his agreement and added to the winding-up.

"Find us the location and I can run the operation, once I have the assets in place. And I will get them ready on the basis of your present information, General."

The Luftwaffe Oberst, commander of the 40th Transportstaffel, had already declared his needs. Parts for his aircraft and experienced technicians to service the specialised craft. Promises to seek out both vital cogs in the plan reassured him, as did the presence of the fifth person.

Rossiter looked at the man, once a sworn enemy and adversary in the dark world of military intelligence, inviting the German's own closing statement.

"We will find them, rest assured Kameraden."

The dinner at an end, the five stood as one, exchanged handshakes and left to go to their billets.

436

De Walle remained, watching from the first floor window.

Rossiter and Wijers walked together, openly and without concern, their presence in Baden-Baden plausible even if their true identities were known to an observer.

Trannel, Luftwaffe Oberst, his uniform back at his squadron base, walked in an affected and uneasy civilian gait, his feet only recently venturing in the murky world of espionage.

Last to leave, and so slick in his field craft that De Walle almost missed the man, was Reinhard Gehlen, ex-GeneralMaior and one-time head of intelligence gathering for the Nazi regime.

De Walle tested a second glass of the Napoleon as he thought through the day.

It had been Uhlmann's idea, prompted by his belief that the USMC Lieutenant-Colonel Rossiter was something more than he presented. That was confirmed by asking a direct question in Versailles, bringing the Marine head of OSS an invitation to dine in Baden-Baden, along with an opportunity to run an important operation in Soviet-held territory.

Draining the glass, Georges De Walle decided enough time had elapsed for him to leave the building.

Speaking to no-one in particular, he nimbly descended the stairs.

"Much rests on you, Herr Gehlen."

2105 hrs, Thursday 30th August 1945, Headquarters, Red Banner Forces of Europe, Kohnstein, Nordhausen, Germany.

On entering the spartan room, her Commander in Chief greeted her with a huge, unforced grin.

Having returned her impressive salute, Zhukov stepped around his desk to pour some tea from a small service on the tatty wooden bureau to one side.

"You are looking well, Polkovnik. The doctors kept me informed, of course."

"Thank you, Comrade Marshall, I am feeling much better."

"You haven't met my right-hand, have you?"

437

Zhukov knew she hadn't, so it was delivered as a statement.

He indicated his CoS with a hand still containing an empty tea cup.

"Comrade Polkovnik-General Mikhail Malinin," his introduction interrupted by another formal salute from the intelligence Colonel, "This is Polkovnik Tatiana Nazarbayeva of the GRU."

Malinin was not actually in the habit of shaking the hand of any common Colonel, but he had heard much about the present company and it seemed appropriate.

Zhukov gave each a cup of tea and returned to his chair.

"Please sit. So what wonderful news do you bring me tonight, Polkovnik?"

"First, if I may, Comrade Marshall. My husband Yuri and I both wish to thank you for your kindness in granting him leave."

Zhukov smiled mischievously.

Wiping his lips dry, the smile remained throughout his words.

"The least I could do for a valuable asset of the Motherland, Comrade Polkovnik," his mock formality easily seen through by those present.

"Besides, I understand that Starshina Nazarbayev had a choice of documents to rely on."

"Indeed, Comrade Marshall, that is true, and my husband felt weighed down by them, truly."

Both men laughed freely, imagining how the man must have felt with such authorisations in his possession.

"In truth, Comrades, he surrendered the document from Comrade Stalin into my possession, so it can be preserved for our family when the war is over. He retains your document, Comrade Marshall, otherwise he would not get back to his unit."

That prompted Zhukov to speak more sensitively.

"Comrade Polkovnik, your husband's unit will soon be committing to the front."

If anything, the Marshall's voice took on even more of a sympathetic edge.

438

"I am conscious that you have lost a son already in this war, and that you have three others still serving."

Nazarbayeva's face was set, listening, harbouring her own thoughts without external display.

"If you wish it, I can arrange for your husband to be transferred to a rear-line formation, away from the possibility of harm?"

The silence was brief.

"Comrade Marshall. For myself and my husband, I thank you, but that cannot be. Neither of us would accept such a favour when the Motherland needs all her sons," and she smiled broadly, overcoming her inner grief with humour, "Even the old one's with bad attitude."

Zhukov understood and, in truth, he had expected such a reply, but he made the offer none the less, a sign of the esteem he had for the officer in front of him.

"The offer will stand always, Comrade."

As if by common assent, each cup was drained and set aside.

"Now then, what does the GRU have for me this evening?"

"Comrades, the RAF Bomber attack that was repulsed the other night was apparently called Operation Casino. Your figures on their losses are inaccurate. Here are the actual numbers that we have confirmed so far."

Zhukov's figures were supplied under the new regime of factual reporting, the NKVD having spread throughout the Red Banner Army, encouraging commanders to report correctly, an issue highlighted in early air war reporting.

Instead of the two hundred and thirteen confirmed kills, two hundred and seventy-three as reported in the GRU file was significantly higher, and marked an even greater destruction of Bomber Commands capacity to attack.

Handing the file to Malinin, and waiting for his CoS's startled look, he asked the obvious question, for which Nazarbayeva was ready.

"That is confirmed, Comrade Marshall, straight from an agent placed to gather such information directly."

439

Already the Soviet command had anticipated easier night movement and less attacks on laagers, but these figures would mean that such advantages were more likely to be for a longer period.

"The agent should be able to provide us good intelligence, although there is a delay in reporting that will limit the full usefulness of what will come to us."

"None the less, excellent, Comrade Polkovnik. And, unless I am mistaken, the original intelligence and basic plan came from your office?"

"Yes, I interviewed the British Intelligence Officer Comrade Marshall. The operational concept came about from that and I played my full part, I hope."

'No false modesty. I like that.'

Setting the folder aside, he saw a name he recognised on the next.

"Next Comrades, as you are aware, Comrade General Secretary Stalin instructed the GRU and NKVD to combine their skills in a joint operation involving the extraction of intelligence from this German Officer."

Nazarbayeva passed over the file bearing Ernst-August Knocke's name.

"The reports show that a GRU officer made contact with Knocke and received information in return for promises regarding the continued well-being of his family."

Again the file made it over to Malinin.

"There is an issue of information transfer. The product of our arrangement is of a type that would need to be in your hands as quickly as possible. Our departments will work on that, and we have already activated some sleeping agents for an alternate route that is higher risk but should be quicker in servicing the information."

"And will this Knocke play your game, Comrade Polkovnik?"

Malinin posed the reasonable question, knowing that the world of intelligence offered no guarantees.

"He is playing by the rules at the moment, Comrade General. My agent is at large and unhindered, reporting no undue activity since he first made contact. The NKVD report due to arrive tomorrow mirrors that. Everything points to a smooth operation so far, and one which should reap significant benefits for the Red Army"

Neither senior officer asked, but both wondered, how Tatiana had come by her information on the NKVD report.

"We have had reports that the NKVD agent provocateur plan has borne some fruit, but is overall disappointing in its results, although I believe that the NKVD report may not say that in so many words."

Neither senior officer asked but both were now dying to know how Tatiana had come by her information on the NKVD report.

"All the German units identified as forming have now mobilised towards the Ruhr." This was not news to either man, and had been the subject of hours of extra problem solving for them over the last few days.

"Plus unconfirmed reports from agents in the French and English ports state more Germans arriving by sea every day."

Tatiana sensed the two's confusion.

"Apologies, Comrades. Released prisoners of war returning from incarceration in the United States and Canada."

The GRU officer delved into a separate file and retrieved a heavily sanitised document.

"Apologies again that I cannot show you the originals for operational security reasons. These are précis of the reports we have received. Please note that all but one speak of the apparent physically healthy appearance of these men."

Malinin leaned in towards his boss, so anxious was he to read the reports.

"I am unable to say for sure, but I believe that these ports may have seen the transit of a minimum of thirty thousand German prisoners in the last two weeks."

An NKVD report had already set out the reinforcements arriving in Europe from the USA and Canada, as well as the shorter cruise from England.

Zhukov sat back in his chair, honouring Nazabayeva by discussing higher military matters in her presence.

"It seems that every day brings them more manpower. The situation is still militarily in our favour, of course. We have

441

more men and equipment, but they seem to be almost manufacturing bodies to throw at us!"

Malinin, not for the first time, found an opportunity to put forward his pet suggestion.

"We have 1st Southern and the Alpine. Is now the time to bring them forward and to hell with the main plan?"

Zhukov pondered, and took advantage of Nazarbayeva's presence.

"Comrade Polkovnik, the latest on the Italian forces if you please."

Without the slightest indication of triumphalism, the GRU officer extracted a folder from her collection.

"Comrades, as GRU predicted, all Italian forces have withdrawn behind the military demarcation line. Unconfirmed reports indicate that they are waiting for further indications from us before declaring themselves neutral."

A second document was extracted from her folder.

"This is a copy of the report Comrade General Pekunin sent to the Foreign Ministry."

The answer to Zhukov's question was satisfactory, and he conceded Malinin's point.

"It may well be that we will look to alter the master plan Mikhail. But that is not for now. Proceed, Comrade Nazarbayeva."

She selected a thicker folder entitled 'Enemy Losses'.

A wad of paper fell before Zhukov's gaze, listing every major enemy formation known or suspected to have been destroyed or badly damaged since the opening of the war.

Contained within the healthy sized report were casualty figures for air and sea forces too.

In isolation, it made excellent reading for hungry eyes.

However, Tatiana held a thicker report containing the losses sustained by Soviet forces over the same period.

Zhukov's eyes flicked up from reading about the loss of US reinforcements at sea, catching the title in her hands.

"I am only too well aware of the contents of that report, Comrade Polkovnik."

She waited unto both men had consumed her information and sat back, satisfied that all was well.

442

"I am afraid that you may not be aware of the contents of this report, Comrades."

Zhukov's eyes narrowed, his senses pricked by the sudden smell of danger.

"I have seen your combat casualty report and it suggests figures that are less than those GRU have, by as much as 10% in some cases."

A hand appeared, itself sufficient to demand possession of the file.

Malinin rose and retrieved the official Red Army casualty report for comparison.

There were some discrepancies, which were only to be expected in some ways, but there were some glaring problems with the numbers.

"How do you explain this difference in tanks, Comrade Polkovnik?"

"My understanding is that your field reports include all tanks available on the day of the report, and that includes tanks recovered from the field for repair and return."

"Yes, that is the case, and it always has been, Comrade."

"It would appear that means that tanks that are recovered but that prove irreparable are lost to this casualty accounting process, meaning..."

Malinin spoke this time, interrupting her flow.

"Meaning that the figures we have for tank strengths are higher than actual strengths in the line."

"Your commanders make reports on losses, detailed ones that are accurate. When compared with these general reports submitted to higher formation enquiries, the reports on which you base your strengths, we find discrepancies, such as this in tank strength."

"Ten percent difference!"

The two senior officers exchanged looks, aghast that something so simple could have such an impact.

The higher formations had apparently simplified the process of reporting, merely wishing for numbers to pass on to their own higher controlling formations.

443

"If I may point out, Comrades, Marshall Bagramyan has continued with the old system and so his returns are within +/- 2%, according to GRU calculations."

That was of little comfort, as Bagramyan's 1st Baltic had suffered the most casualties of any front so far.

"Thank you for bringing this to our attention, Comrade Nazarbayeva. Mikhail, no time like the present."

Malinin understood his boss perfectly and excused himself from the room.

Whilst the CoS commenced a number of haranguing phone calls to Front and Army commanders across Europe, Zhukov decided on more tea.

"Stupid, stupid, stupid."

Nazarbayeva, in the habit of all messengers in such circumstances, stayed silent, just in case.

The silence went on, with Zhukov deep in thought.

The tea arrived and Zhukov dismissed the orderly, taking advantage of the act of pouring to bring himself back from his un-soviet thoughts.

Taking a sip of his drink, Zhukov adjusted his jacket and looked at Intelligence officer.

"Tell me you have some good news for me, Tatiana," the use of her name being more indicative of Zhukov's distraction and annoyance than anything else.

"Comrade Marshall, the NKVD report you will see tomorrow will not include all matters of relevance regarding production, supply and reinforcement."

"Go on."

Behind his eyes, Tatiana could see the smouldering embers come to life, a growing fire of anger she had not seen before, yet spoken of in hushed whispers by others less fortunate than she.

"Ukrainian separatists continue to cause problems with the rail network. This week alone they have derailed or destroyed eight trains carrying supplies and equipment to the front."

That the figure was in excess of his briefing was apparent in Zhukov's silence. The fire spread inside.

"German partisan attacks are on the increase as you are aware, but the increase in security combined with the

444

centralisation of supply seems to have reduced their effectiveness."

That was not news to the man.

"NKVD inspection teams descended upon Chelyabinsk and made examples amongst some of the senior staff. Production has fallen by nearly 20% in the last two weeks, mainly lost in IS-2 and 3 output, and the new IS-4 production line will not be completed for some time to come it seems."

"Go on."

"The production of bridging equipment has increased since you insisted on it, but quality control has declined. So much so that our NKVD comrades have put units in place to ensure maintenance of production and standards. Unfortunately, they have shot a number of senior factory employees responsible for standards and, as of last Wednesday, the main factory has ceased production following a fire that is suspected to be arson."

The conflagration in Zhukov's head was now raging out of control.

"Tell me that is it, please Comrade. There is no more of this."

Tatiana took the plunge.

"Your request to employ Soviet prisoners of war who are engineering skilled is to be refused. Both the NKVD and GKO see such an acceptance of surrendered personnel as undermining the fighting spirit of the Red Army."

Total meltdown.

"Are they fucking mad? Do they not have fucking eyes and ears? I, we...", he brought his breathing under control, "The Motherland needs those men, and their skills, and we need them now."

Holding her ground, Nazarbayeva spoke firmly.

"I state the position of the GKO and NKVD on the matter, Comrade Marshall."

The door opened and in came Malinin, attracted by the sudden raised voices. He nodded to his commander, indicating that the wheels had been set in motion

The momentary lapse now history, Zhukov spoke softly.

"My apologies, Comrade Polkovnik."

445

She said nothing, only surprised that he had bothered to apologise at all.

"Listen to this, Mikhail," and he beckoned Tatiana into a repeat.

Malinin was as appalled as his boss, but didn't have the luxury of venting himself as Zhukov had done.

Professionalism rallied and extinguished the flames in an instant.

"Right, enough. I will tackle this and the other issues tomorrow in Moscow. Which of these reports can I officially have, Comrade Nazarbayeva."

"I will be in Moscow tomorrow presenting all of these reports myself, Comrade Marshall."

"All?"

"Of course. How can Comrade Stalin and the GKO make proper decisions if their information is flawed?"

"Such an attitude is excellent, but you do understand that Comrade Beria already seems to hate you, and pulling his NKVD report apart will be tantamount to a declaration of war?"

Both Zhukov and Malinin noticed the firmer set in her features and the resolution in her voice.

"We are at war with the capitalists and we must win, so I will take the risk of Comrade Beria's wrath to ensure that the Motherland is best served, Comrade Marshall."

'Balls of steel!'

"You will accompany me tomorrow then, Comrade Polkovnik. I am leaving at 0630 hrs."

"I am on the same flight, Comrade Marshall."

"Is there anything else, Comrade?"

Tatiana considered saying nothing, but she felt her relationship with the great man was such that she could share something less tangible with him.

"Yes Sir. I have a feeling that something is not as it seems with Spain. I have little to go on but a gut feeling and some low-level reports, but my instincts are telling me there is trouble ahead."

Zhukov, understanding that the woman had offered up a feeling based on intuition, recognised it as the privilege it was, and acted appropriately.

"What sort of trouble are you thinking of, Comrade?"

"At the moment, we have neutralised Spain. The NKVD are bragging about an operation they ran that brought Franco into a neutral position, removing the Spanish Army from the equation."

"Yes, so I heard. What operation?"

"As yet I do not know, Comrade Marshall, which in itself is unusual. Combine that with the fact my prime informants have dropped out of sight and there are some unusual circumstances in Spain."

"So, what makes your intuition tell you there is a problem?"

"Little things, like the possibility that some Allied merchant vessels still dock in Spanish ports, possibly with cargoes unloaded clandestinely. The absence of any information from GRU and NKVD agents in north-west Spain, and I mean absolutely nothing at all, Comrades."

"And?"

Zhukov pushed, knowing there was more.

"And a report from a low-level agent who describes an officer staying incognito in a modest villa on the outskirts of Saint Germain-de-la-Grange, which is near Versailles."

'Not bad from memory, Tatiana.'

"She is a cleaner and received an unfamiliar uniform to prepare, and her report seems to describe perfectly the uniform of a Spanish Army General."

Zhukov exchanged looks with Malinin, but neither ventured a comment.

"If I get further information, I will report it immediately, Comrade Marshall."

Standing to mark the end of proceedings, Zhukov ran his fingers across his pate.

"Thank you, Comrade Polkovnik. An excellent, if not unwelcome report."

Malinin moved to the door and opened it for the GRU officer, again, not something he ever did for run of the mill Colonels.

Nazarbayeva took her leave and the Chief of Staff closed the door behind her.

447

Turning back into the room, he found Zhukov sat at the desk once more, grinning widely, despite the bad news he had recently received.

"Well, Mikhail?"

He pursed his lips in thought, although none was necessary, his mind had already made up its mind.

"You were absolutely right, Comrade. That is one hell of a formidable woman."

"Balls of steel."

Zhukov laughed at his description.

"Balls of steel indeed, Comrade Marshall."

"There is no worthy man who has not once dreamt of himself in the jaws of danger, in order to triumph in the face of insurmountable odds. We, each of us, envy the brave the opportunity fate casts before them to prove their worth; those so exposed envy us the safety of our dreams."

Chris Coling.

Chapter 74 - THE APPROACH

0320 hrs, Saturday, 1st September 1945, aboard the 'Swedish' merchant vessel 'Golden Quest', 300 yards from shore, Glenlara, Eire.

"Your men are working well, Comrade Reynolds."

Judas Patrick Reynolds, commander of the IRA's Mayo Battalion, accepted the compliment, along with the glass of vodka, the second one the ship's captain had plied him with since he came onboard to supervise his men.

"That they are, Captain Lipranski, that they are, to be sure."

Perhaps it was the nature of the cargo that had inspired his men, or even the briefing he had given them, prior to the arrival of the darkened ship.

Whatever it was, the weapons and ammunition would soon be all landed, along with the additional Soviet personnel the 'Swedish' ship had brought.

Sinking the vodka in one, Reynolds moved to the other wing of the bridge, where he could look down on the starboard side. Efficient sailors were manhandling torpedoes from a cunningly concealed side hatch into the waiting shape of a partially surfaced submarine.

On shore, his second in command, Seamus Brown, was overseeing the concealment of the ammunition and weapons haul, or at least the part destined for use by the IRA units throughout the six counties, and beyond.

449

The munitions set aside for the Soviet Marines were organised and distributed by Senior Lieutenant Masharin, shortly to be replaced as the senior Soviet officer by a new arrival.

An experienced Starshina approached Masharin with a formal report, leading a party of forty businesslike soldiers, moving in an experienced silence born out of the experience of battle.

"Comrade Starshy Leytenant. My commander has been delayed on board. He asks that the men be directed to their quarters immediately, and then given opportunity to become aware of the position we defend."

"Comrade Starshina, the matter is in hand."

Masharin beckoned his own senior NCO forward, already briefed to lead the newcomers to their barracks.

The marines filed past, following the leader.

By 0512 hrs the supply ship had started to pull away, the second submarine having had its fill of the torpedo reloads.

The 'Swedish' vessel had refilled the ingenious fuel cell system, a set of large collapsible rubber bladders that were anchored to the seabed, their feeder hoses snaking up to the shoreline and concealed with prepared mock rough stone blocks.

Those submarines, there were now four of them, operating out of the Glenlara base, were well-provisioned for more strikes against the Allied supply routes.

<u>1615 hrs, Saturday, 1st September 1945, Headquarters, Red Banner Forces of Europe, Kohnstein, Nordhausen, Germany.</u>

Malinin and Zhukov were animated, the recent news from the front drawing them to the main operations room to consult maps.

As they took in the scenario, a further report from the Commander of 8th Guards Army arrived, confirming that a counter-attack had driven in the front of the 29th Guards Rifle Corps. The German forces had pushed them back nearly ten kilometres before the situation was retrieved, the employment of the nearby 12th Guards Tank Corps, and the profligate use of

450

ammunition by supporting artillery, eventually halting the enemy counter-attack.

Malinin cherry-picked items from Boldin's report, forwarded in its complete form from the 1st Red Banner Front Headquarters.

"Colonel General Boldin's report... he believes that Major General Shemenkov... 29th Guards Rifle... can hold... despite heavy casualties... he needs more time to organise... reinforcements... before he can start to push the enemy back."

"Hmm."

Zhukov's mind was working the problem.

There had been a few local counter-attacks over the weeks since the start of the offensive, and most withered with little or no gain. But this one was different, as the reports indicated that the enemy were pure German formations, part of the new Republican Army.

Combined with the appearance of German tanks and vehicles that had inflicted the Dagersheim debacle, for which the commanders of the tank units involved had paid the ultimate price, there seemed to be numerous Germans in the field.

GRU had sent over a special report that indicated the formation at Dagersheim was the French SS unit, and their performance unfortunately vindicated Zhukov's assertion to Beria that they would fight with their old élan.

For the moment, that unit had gone quiet, so the two senior officers concentrated on the setback on the road to Amsberg.

Some waving of fingers and palm movements conveyed Zhukov's orders, and his CoS noted them scrupulously, offering one small observation as an improvement, before moving off to get the plan in place, sending the commander of 1st Red Banner Central European Front specific instructions, as well as releasing some more assets to his control.

The Marshall took a seat at a modest desk and selected a biscuit from a plate set for his needs, a soft shortbread, sticky with raisins and honey.

A similar type had been laid out the previous day in Moscow, the only sweet taste in a sour encounter with the entire GKO.

451

The meeting had been planned as a full and comprehensive brief on the progress of Stage 2, and that section had gone as expected.

It was in the disputes with the dangerous Beria that the drama had developed, and the whole exchange reeked of threat and intrigue.

By the end of the meeting, Beria had created a climate of fear and distrust that obscured the initial purpose, and undermined the needs of the Motherland.

Zhukov's presentation on the need for utilising the engineers amongst the ex-prisoners had fallen on ears already burnt by the fire of the arguments between the Army and GRU on one hand, and the NKVD security apparatus on the other.

The ears were not receptive, and he failed to get what he needed.

'What the Rodina needed!'

He looked at the plate, making a selection.

'Why didn't they understand?'

Another biscuit sprang off the plate and into his mouth, the act of chewing bringing a moment of pleasure and relief.

Again he thought back to the tense meeting, and a moment when he had taken a back seat.

Fortunately, Colonel General Pekunin had taken onboard his late-night phone call, replacing Nazarbayeva, and presenting the GRU report, including the condemnation of the NKVD actions that Tatiana had listed the day before.

He had watched Beria carefully whilst Pekunin pursued the 'Spanish' matter, and he would tell the GRU Colonel that her intuition was correct, for the face of the NKVD chief had betrayed that all was not how it was painted.

Malinin returned and was directed to a seat by the pondering Zhukov.

"Shall I send for reinforcements, Comrade?"

Zhukov, broken from his thought process, responded brusquely.

"I think I have done all that is needed to ensure that the situation is rectified, General Malinin."

He caught the amused look on his comrade's face.

"Oh, the biscuits!"

452

Zhukov grinned in acceptance of his 'gluttony'.

"Why not?"

The intended replenishment process was suspended when a Staff Major ushered Nazarbayeva into their presence, a few beads of sweat present on her forehead, indicative of her haste to get to the Army Commander.

None the less, still buoyed by Malinin's comment, he decided to extend the good-humour.

"Ah, Comrade Polkovnik. Thank you for your report on the French SS, even if it arrived too late to be of use."

His light toying with Nazarbayeva did not survive her first words.

"Comrade Marshall, I need to speak to you on a matter of extreme urgency and interest to the Rodina."

Zhukov stood and moved off at speed.

"Follow me, you too Mikhail."

The three were quickly in his private office where Tatiana took the lead.

"Comrade Marshall, I came here as quick as I could. I thought it was vital that you should have this information."

Zhukov and Malinin could not help but exchange looks, their appetites whetted in expectation of something to balance the bad news of the day.

Nazarbayeva continued.

"This is from a GRU agent in Stockholm."

Both men inwardly deflated as their imaginations immediately reduced the significance of what was to come.

The agent's report was passed to the senior man, Malinin reading it over Zhukov's shoulder.

Both read it and saw nothing of substance; certainly nothing to agitate the GRU officer.

A second report was passed.

"This report is a brief note from Foreign Minister Comrade Molotov to Comrade Marshall Beria, apparently as part payment of a promise."

The two avidly consumed the second submission, spurred on by the identity of the writer and the recipient.

"I won't ask how you came by this, Comrade Nazarbayeva."

453

It was common knowledge that the GRU and NKVD spied on each other with as much enthusiasm as they did the enemy.

"Sweden again?"

Both remained puzzled but could see the correlation.

"What am I missing, Comrade Polkovnik?"

"Comrades, you have a report from an agent indicating that Sir Richard Carruthers is presently making a weekend business trip tο Stockholm on matters of modest importance. Also, that he has requested a private meeting with Östen Undén, the Swedish Minister for Foreign Affairs."

'Yes, I can read that Tatiana!'

"On receipt of that request, Undén cleared his schedule, confirmed his availability, and immediately took himself away to his holiday home on the Isle of Muskö."

Zhukov and Malinin looked on without understanding.

"Comrade Molotov states that his ambassador in Sweden has been summoned to an urgent Sunday meeting by the Utrikesdepartementet."

The two looked vacantly at her.

"Apologies Comrades, the Swedish Ministry for Foreign Affairs."

Zhukov's eyes narrowed, things clicking slowly into place.

"The venue for the meeting is the Isle of Muskö."

The link was nearly made, but they lacked a vital piece of information, one that Zhukov sought immediately.

"Who is this Carruthers?"

Nazarbayeva pulled out a dossier with a picture of the chisel-faced English politician clipped to the cover, with two more taken during a visit to Moscow before the Patriotic War.

"He is a member of their parliament, Comrades. But, more importantly, he is the personal private secretary of their Prime Minister Attlee."

Zhukov and Malinin physically relaxed as some of the confusion was cleared away. Two minds worked hard to assimilate the intelligence, unnecessarily, as Nazarbayeva had not finished.

454

"Comrades, Carruthers brings with him a proposal from the British, a proposal of a negotiated ceasefire."

"Govno!"

The two voices merged as the senior men reacted.

"Are we that close to victory? Is the whole capitalist apparatus so ready to fall Comrade?"

"No, Comrade Marshall, it is not. As I said, the proposal comes only from the British. The other Allies do not know of it."

As bombshells went, bombshells didn't get any bigger than the statement Tatiana laid before them.

Nazarbayeva left ten minutes later, leaving Zhukov and his staff hard at work, revising the military plan to heavily test the resolve of the forces of the British Empire.

1847 hrs, Saturday, 1st September 1945, Ottingen, Germany.

In the official orders, the 2nd Guards Tank Corps had been withdrawn to rest and refit, prior to the upcoming assaults in Northern Germany and Holland.

In reality, the survivors of the elite unit gathered themselves up and found time to lick their wounds in the area to the south-east of Visselhövede.

Yarishlov's Brigade was in the best shape of the Corps' major formations. Not because it had avoided the heavier combat, far from it.

They had just been lucky, far luckier than the 26th Tanks and the infantry of the 4th Motorised Brigade.

Those two veteran units, supported by a number of Army units, had been savaged in front of Zeven, enemy tanks and anti-tank guns being the least of their worries, as ground attack aircraft crucified the assault force.

The survivors of 26th Tanks would be merged into Yarsihlov's own brigade, just as soon as they reached his position.

Kriks, his normal noisy nature curtailed by the loss of many a comrade from the old days, occupied himself with the business of finding anything and everything of worth to sell and barter at a later date, whilst his commander, tired and dusty from days of sustained combat, sought to put his unit back together.

455

Kriks had selected one of the few undamaged buildings on the outskirts of the village of Ottingen, a large detached house, once the impressive home of a lady of obvious means. Yarishlov had welcomed the gesture from his staff, who set aside the master suite as his own, the huge and inviting four poster bed dominating what was an extremely large room.

Yarishlov sat up to an ornate dressing table, presently serving as his personal desk, sorting his paperwork, and concentrating hard on his brigade's needs. His aches and pains all but subdued by his overwhelming desire to sleep.

'I am so tired it hurts.'

Kriks arrived noisily some time later, his good-humour partially restored by the liberation of an extremely large smoked salami and six bottles of Beck's Bier.

Yarishlov woke with a start.

"Blyad!"

Kriks feigned horror, following it with the severe look that had made many a young soldier quake in his boots.

"Were you sleeping, Comrade Polkovnik? Sleeping on duty, Comrade Polkovnik? Wait until the Comrade Polkovnik hears about this. He will have your balls in a bag. A proper terror is our Polkovnik."

Yarishlov, his mouth like the inside of a Cossack's boot, looked mournfully at his senior NCO, resigned to the banter for the foreseeable future.

Kriks took pity on his commander, and made up for his comments with a Beck's, tapping the top off and passing it over.

It was the best drink Yarishlov had tasted in living memory, cutting the dryness of his throat and washing away the dust, the last dregs removed by worming his tongue in the neck.

He ran the cool bottle over his forehead, enjoying the sensation as a headache started to make itself known.

In response to the question he was about to ask, Kriks anticipated and spoke first.

"Sat them in the stream for an hour. Had to hide them well or those bastards from the sappers would have sniffed them out in a moment."

He offered another to Yarishlov, who accepted eagerly, consuming it at a slower pace to savour the full flavour.

456

"I thought I would wake the Comrade Polkovnik because our replacement tanks are about to arrive, hot from the train station."

In confirmation of that, the sound of growling diesel engines accompanied by the distinctive rattle of a T34's track pins grew until it became all-pervading.

"26th?"

"No, Comrade Polkovnik, they are still some hours away. These are replacement vehicles, so the Supply Officer wishes to inform you."

Walking to the window, Yarishlov looked down upon an approaching line of T34/85 tanks, replacements for those lost.

His professional eye approved of the tight formation.

But only for a moment.

"Job Tvoyu Mat! Kriks, are my eyes playing me up?"

Still feeling playful, the NCO feigned indignation.

"Such language from an officer. I am truly shocked."

The lack of response from Yarishlov was noted, and Kriks fell silent.

The recently promoted Praporshchik, the Red Army's highest Warrant Officer rank, careful to keep his bottle away from prying eyes, moved forward and sought to identify the problem.

That was easily done.

"Blyad! Your eyes are just fine, Comrade Polkovnik."

The tanks were clearly combat veterans, not new ones from the production line.

They also carried the very visible insignia of the Polish Tank Corps.

Both men retreated into the room, silently drinking and gathering their thoughts.

Kriks got there first.

"So, Comrade Polkovnik, now we recycle armour taken from our viperous Polish allies. I wonder why that is?"

Yarishlov, suddenly very awake, drained his bottle and grabbed his cap, ready to go out and get involved in the physical work.

Slapping it hard to remove as much dust as possible, he placed it on his head.

457

As his Colonel gathered up his written orders, Kriks opened the door and stood back respectfully, their private friendship once more on hold in the public gaze.

"Let us hope it does not mean what we think, Comrade Praporshchik!"

1920 hrs, Saturday, 1st September 1945, near Route 304, west of Wangmucum, China.

He was 21 years old and one of the final products of the officer production line that had tried to keep up with extreme losses during the closing year of World War Two.

His life had been spent studying the Samurai Arts and preparing for the day that he would bring his warlike skills to the field, for the benefit of the Emperor.

2nd Lieutenant Mori Sazuki imagined himself at the head of an army, driving all enemies before him, the men behind him in awe of his valour, his Emperor's eyes upon him as he swept the field.

His capabilities did not live up to his expectations, being only five foot four in his best boots, and wearing the trademark round glasses so beloved of his hero and mentor, General Tojo.

He was puny, even by Japanese standards, the rationing resulting from the American blockade imposing restrictions on his growing body that did not permit the proper development of muscle and fat.

None the less, he had made his way through the training process and now found himself entrusted with the responsibility of command, pushing his tank forward to support infantry units being penned back on Route 304, as Chinese Divisions rallied and fought back.

The advance divisions of His Imperial Majesty's Armies had invested Guiping, only to be pushed out; the first reverses anywhere in China since the new conflict erupted.

It had been decided to push Rainbow into a defensive line, using their talisman status with the troops, as well as their firepower, to halt the counter-attack.

458

Sazuki's Panther was an older model A, a tank that had seen active service in three armies to date, and taken lives with each.

The previous commander had fallen to enemy machine-guns, slain as he rose from the turret to get a better view. Traces of his blood could still be seen on close examination, or as Sazuki found out to his disgust, picked up by contact with various surfaces in the commander's position.

His sponsorship by General Tojo ensured he was placed in one of the German tanks, his survivability increased by its thick armour, although other officers disputed the inexperienced soldier's ability to handle and fight the prime vehicle.

Complimented by its own grape of infantry, riding high on the hull, the Panther named as 'Zuikaku' ploughed forward to its allotted position on the fringe of Highway 304.

It shared its name with an Imperial Japanese Navy Aircraft Carrier, the seaborne 'Fortunate Crane' proving less than fortunate, having been sunk during the Battle of Cape Engaño on 25th October 1944.

The dead officer's brother had served aboard the carrier, surviving the sinking, but not the injuries he sustained.

Sudden firing ahead focussed the minds of the tankers and rider infantry, Sazuki directing his driver to slow down in order to orient himself with the situation.

He felt the elation of his first battle wash over him, and he automatically checked that his Senninbari was in place around his waist, picturing the proud Tiger stitched into the cloth of his 'belt of a thousand stitches', the traditional Shinto good luck symbol.

Familiar uniforms suddenly emerged from the surroundings, a party evacuating wounded, and a senior officer bearing down on 'Zuikaku' with undoubted purpose.

Sazuki dismounted and took his orders, the Major's simple instructions being to move up to the road junction and hold it.

The senior man disappeared back into cover, quickly returning to where he was needed.

459

Climbing back aboard 'Zuikaku', Sazuki ordered the infantry group to dismount and deploy close behind, and pushed his tank forward again.

He ducked as one, and then two more bullets pinged off the armour in quick succession, strays not intended for him, but close enough for the first doubts to undermine his childish enthusiasm for the combat to come.

The tank emerged from the trees and bushes, sliding between two infantry positions with inches to spare.

At the road junction, there was a triangle where the three roads met, and the fallen trees upon it offered a reasonable firing position and lured Sazuki forward, ordering his driver to position behind the obstruction.

More bullets splattered on the armour, this time meant for 'Zuikaku', and a cry of pain indicated at least one of the infantry group behind had been struck.

The turret rotated and the gunner lashed out with his co-axial, putting down a group of Chinese soldiers huddled behind a bush.

Mori Sazuki was confused beyond words, his officer's brain registering the fact that the crew were fighting without orders, the child's brain wishing he were anywhere but where he was.

Raising his head above the hatch, he watched as more Chinese were chopped to pieces, a combination of the hull weapon and an infantry machine-gun ripping the bodies to pieces in front of his eyes.

'Uncle Tojo lied. It's horrible!'

To his front, a patch of the bushes grew darker and then disappeared as an enemy armoured vehicle worked its way forward into a firing position.

"Tank!"

His training forgotten, all he did was shout and point, attracting a swarm of bullets from vengeful enemy infantry.

The gunner, an experienced Corporal, caught the rough direction of his commander's arm, rotated the turret and picked up the shape of the tank-destroyer.

He fired and missed, concentrating more as a squealing Sazuki dropped inside the turret clutching his ruined right hand,

460

bullets having neatly separated the second and fourth fingers, as well as removing half the palm.

Despite the screaming in his ear, the corporal placed the next shot on target, knocking out the enemy Hellcat.

The fire fight around the junction was growing in intensity, and the tank crew knew they were in for the fight of their lives

All except Sazuki, who, having stopped screaming, seemed more interested in how he would now hold his sword than giving orders to his men.

As the loader laboured to serve the main gun, he stole swift glances at his officer trying to fit his wounded hand around the hilt of his sword, the face betraying the young man's shock.

The infantry grape had been decimated as the Chinese stepped up their attack, not put off by the presence of the powerful tank.

The infantry company had suffered badly too, and the Major chose to withdraw further, sending a runner to the tank with the order.

The runner took a rifle bullet in the thigh before he relayed the instructions, bleeding out from his destroyed artery before he could take his own life with a grenade.

It was the driver who first spotted the danger.

"Enemy infantry in close! Left side!"

The gunner screamed at his officer.

"Keep them off the tank!"

Sazuki, strangely comprehending the man's words, extended his head out of the turret, noting men in close.

The turret crew heard him shout at the figures scaling the side, ordering them off his tank like they were soldiers caught on a prank.

His brain seemed to comprehend what was happening, and the loader saw the ruined hand trying to free his Nambu pistol.

A dull thud overcame the other sounds of battle, and the young officer dropped back into the tank, his nose and jaw broken, front teeth removed by the powerful swipe of a rifle butt.

The loader had his own pistol out, shooting the first Chinese face that peered down the hatch.

461

"Move the tank!" He shouted, wondering why it hadn't already reversed away.

The driver was already dead, shot in the face at point blank range.

In an attempt to swat the unwanted passengers off, the gunner traversed the main gun.

A disembodied Thompson sub-machine gun hovered over the hatch, discharging two bursts of bullets.

The turret stopped turning, the hull machine-gun stopped firing.

Only Sazuki remained alive, unharmed by the bullets that claimed the other three crew members.

An accented voice spoke in Japanese.

"Come out now or you die. Speak."

Mori pulled himself upright as best he could but, his face swollen from the blow, was unable to speak.

His silence condemned him.

Rain descended through the hatch, falling on top of him and the dead loader.

He raised his face, appreciating its freshness, before realising that it was not rain and that death was about to visit him.

"Mother!"

A burning rag was dropped through the hatch and the inside of 'Zuikaku' became an instant and deadly inferno.

462

The betrayal of trust carries a heavy taboo.

Aldrich Ames.

Chapter 75 – THE TRAITOR?

1157 hrs, Sunday, 2nd September 1945, Legion Corps Headquarters, Hotel Stephanie, Baden-Baden, Germany.

The efforts outside Stuttgart had salvaged the Algerian Division, but only that, Soviet forces continuing their advances elsewhere and forcing back most of the French First Army.

De Lattre was already well into the process of moving headquarters, quitting the quaint town of Baden-Baden for the baronial surroundings of the Château de Craon, often referred to as the Palais d'Haroué. The relocation back to the Nancy area was considered appropriate by some, excessive by others.

However, for the Headquarters of the Legion Corps, it meant that buildings fit for purpose were becoming available and legionnaires now started to occupy rooms as the First Army personnel departed Baden-Baden.

'Camerone' had been pulled back, now floating around behind the front line ready to act as a fire brigade, should there be an issue. Its commander, Ernst-August Knocke, was also using the time to integrate the new units allocated to him according to the new order of battle, the former Alma unit. The 5th RdM was now permanently a part of 'Camerone', bringing it up to divisional strength.

'Alma' and 'Amilakvari were in the front line, but remained untested as yet. 'Tannenberg', the motorised-infantry brigade, had given up some of its armour and equipment to reconstitute Knocke's unit, so remained in the Rastatt area, its own headquarters now inhabiting those buildings in Waldprechtsweier previously used by 'Camerone'.

A further Legion brigade and division were in the making at Sassy, although heavy equipment was becoming scarcer to find. Ex-Wehrmacht engineers and civilian personnel were presently inspecting factories in the Ruhr area in order to

463

see what production could be accomplished, and some vehicles had been constructed by Allied military engineers already, although they were swallowed up by Guderian's larger force already in the Ruhr.

Rumours of Speer's efforts abounded, but Knocke preferred to see hard evidence.

In the main operations room, Lavalle and Bittrich discussed the military situation over coffee.

Knocke arrived at the front entrance and was immediately taken aside by Colonel Paul Desmarais, commander of 'Tannenberg', desperate to retain as much of his own resources as possible.

Knocke, sympathetic to the man's woes, listened with good grace, although his own unit had needs and was prioritised over 'Tannenberg'.

Two vehicles drew up together at the front of Hotel Stephanie, attracting the attention of the two Legion officers.

One was a military beast, muddy and bent, a kubelwagen that had seen better days. In the front seat was Lange, the newly appointed commander of 'Alma'. On seeing Knocke, he smiled widely, but the smile was heavily laced with the pain of his ankle injury. He gingerly slid out of the passenger seat of the battered staff car before attempting the two steps to the main entrance.

Both Knocke and Desmarais offered their hands by way of assistance, and Lange accepted thankfully.

The kerfuffle behind drew all three's attention.

The other vehicle was the first of six, all relatively pristine, as were the officers who dismounted from them. Some tugged tunics in place, others rushed to open doors, so that more important personages could dismount.

Knocke and Desmarais shook hands with Lange, none of the three taking their eyes off the growing sea of gold braid.

Eventually, the leader stepped forward, followed in order of seniority by the entourage.

The three Legion officers saluted as the unknown three-star General swept past; or rather tried to.

The two legionnaires on duty at the entrance challenged him immediately, barring the way, requesting his identification.

464

"Idiots! Step aside and let me pass. I am ..."

Both legionnaires were from 'Tannenberg', and both were old desert hands.

Neither intended to budge an inch.

The senior, a Caporal, took the lead and interrupted the bluster.

"Sir, my standing orders do not permit me to allow you entry without identification. Now, your papers please, sir."

"I will not give you my papers but you will give me your name, rank and number," the furious General eyed the obviously younger man, "And you too!"

The Caporal stood his ground.

"Sir, first I must request of you that you permit me to inspect your papers. Please, sir."

The crowd of French officers behind the General smiled openly, having witnessed their man destroy lesser beasts at will over the last few years.

The General's moustache trembled, either in his anger or in delicious anticipation of what was to come.

"Stand aside now, or I will have you both court-martialled and shot for interfering with my duties!"

Another man stepped forward and both sentries snapped to attention in deference, but remained placed so as to obstruct the General's progress.

"Sir, Colonel Knocke, Camerone Brigade."

The salute was magnificent, as was the figure that now made the human barricade into a strength of three.

The General touched his cane to his cap, angry and curious in equal measure, the more so as the figure in front of him sported more medals than an army, and medals of the enemy to boot.

"Order these men to remove themselves 'Colonel', or I shall be forced to act."

The emphasis on Knocke's rank was not wasted on anyone present.

"Sir, I regret, but I cannot."

The General grew red-faced immediately and went to speak.

Knocke cut him off in an instant.

465

"In the event that they permitted you to enter, in contravention of Corps standing orders, I would have no choice but to shoot them myself for dereliction of duty."

The General's eyes widened, and he wondered if the SS bastard would do it. Knocke could not see the two sentries behind him wondering the exact same thing.

An oppressive silence followed, during which the General stared into the eyes of the man in front of him, seeing there the character and resolve others had seen so often before.

Both Lange and Demarais spoke of it in hushed tones later, describing as best they could the silent battle of personalities, and trying hard to properly relate the discernable moment when the Frenchman knew he had been found wanting.

Knocke also relaxed, and gave the General a reasonable option.

"If I might offer an alternative, Sir? You were not to know of this standing order within the Corps. Perhaps Colonel Desmarais could examine your papers on their behalf, and then honour of both sides will be satisfied when they pass scrutiny?"

Colonel Paul Desmarais did not welcome being pulled into the confrontation but, in the spirit of the Legion, rallied to his comrade's side.

The General, to everyone's surprise, even his own, extracted his papers and passed them to Desmarais without a word, focussing his attention on Knocke.

"And what do these men know of honour, Colonel?"

The words could not have held more contempt.

Theatrically, Knocke turned abruptly to the sentries, who involuntarily stiffened, still expecting some sort of rebuke.

After spending a few moments examining each man in turn, exaggerating his close inspection of them from head to toe, he turned back and answered very deliberately.

"Sir, these men are legionnaires, and therefore they know more of honour than any fighting man in service today."

The whole situation was surreal to the General, defied by private soldiers, aided and abetted by a senior officer, a German, and ex-SS as well.

'I will shake these pigs up and make them into soldiers or my name isn't Molyneux!'

466

His thoughts would have moved to revenge but for the interruption from Desmarais, returning his papers with due formality.

"All in order, Mon Général."

The sentries snapped aside like hinged doors, presenting arms in the time honoured manner.

"You have not heard the last of this, Colonel Knocke, oh no."

The General swept forward, acknowledging the presented arms with another wave of his cane, penetrating deep into the Hotel Stephanie in search of Lavalle.

Lange and Desmarais looked at Knocke as a butcher looks at the likely turkey on Christmas Eve.

"You know how to make friends don't you!"

Desmarais' face didn't wholly convey the humour he intended, for Generals made terrible enemies.

The two sentries had recovered their stance and were motionless statues, mentally replaying the events that had tested them.

Knocke stood in thought before turning to his fellow officers.

"I think we are about to see a change around here, and not one for the better."

Neither man could disagree as they entered the headquarters, ushered in by Knocke who remained at the back.

The Caporal clicked into the general salute position, closely followed by the younger legionnaire, the two paying a soldier's homage to the man who had intervened on their behalf.

Demarais and Lange heard the movement and turned, witnessing an honour not normally afforded Colonels, but now being freely given by soldiers to one they held in high esteem.

Knocke was actually taken aback and stopped dead, examining each man in turn before his face split with a genuine smile.

He nodded, savouring the moment and made to enter, but again stopped.

His mind practised the words before he spoke them.

467

"Legio Patria Nostra, Kameraden," the Legion motto slipping uneasily off his tongue, the German sentiment at the end forgivable in his concentration.

The younger man could not bring himself to say anything; not so the Corporal.

"Honneur et Fidélité, mon Colonel," and in a lower, conspiratorial voice added, "Et merci. Merci bien."

Knocke nodded and headed off in hot pursuit of the new arrival, leaving behind him two men who would tell their comrades of what had come to pass, and thus increase the legend.

Soon to be Général de Corps D'Armée Albert Roland Molyneux was visiting himself upon the unfortunate Lavalle and Bittrich, haranguing them for anything from the colour of the wallpaper to the paperclip found on the carpet.

Eventually, Molyneux moved to the recent matter, ordering that Lavalle place the sentries on a charge for their impertinence.

Knocke and his comrades arrived at that moment, and discovered that Lavalle too could hold his ground.

"I regret you have been inconvenienced, mon Général, but the men were acting under my express instructions, so I am unable to do as you request."

"Then I will find someone who will! What sort of unit are you running, Lavalle?"

"The sort that obeys the orders of its commander, mon Général, and so I submit that I must also be arrested if my men are detained, as it was I that issued their orders."

The frontline officers in the room had all met the man's type before, and all dreaded being under the control of one so obviously useless and dangerously incompetent.

"Well. This time I will let it go. But, understand this!"

Molyneux turned around, scoping every man in turn.

"I will now be giving the orders around here."

Stout hearts sank all around the room, as the possibility became the reality.

"I, Acting Général de Corps D'Armée Albert Roland Molyneux, am here to take command of the Legion Corps with

468

immediate effect. I require a briefing from you and your unit commanders, with full details on all strengths and logistical stocks."

Calling on all the arrogance of a member of France's ruling class, bred into him within his mother's womb, through to the tolerance of his bullying all the way from Aspirant to the rank of Général, he added, "I will take coffee in my suite now and return here in thirty minutes precisely. Be ready or I will replace you with more capable officers."

Molyneux turned and strode out, satisfied that he had curbed the Legion officers for the moment, and determined to show them exactly who was boss, starting in thirty minutes.

Another officer arrived in the silence that held sway in the main staff room, the remaining presence of some of Molyneux's officers preventing the outburst that most needed to clear their minds.

Unpeturbed, the American General strode up to Lavalle and saluted.

"General Lavalle?"

"Yes, I am Lavalle, Général. How may I help?"

"John L. Pierce, 16th Armored Group, Sir."

The smartly turned out officer produced a sealed letter and passed it over with little ceremony.

"Coffee, Général Pierce?"

"That would be most welcome, Sir."

A cup appeared in front of Pierce, smaller in size than his normal brew. His disappointment lasted until he realised that the hot liquid was of the finest quality.

The staff had started to pull together all information needed for the briefing.

Lavalle handed the envelope and contents to Bittrich.

"Well, Général Pierce, it seems you have arrived at an opportune moment. The Corps has just received a new General and I am no longer in command."

Pierce had known about the change, part of which was brought on by his presence within the unit, and the need for a more senior rank.

He also knew a little of the new man, and did not like what he knew.

469

Molyneux had pestered De Gaulle constantly, his previous commands having been of lowly nature and experiencing little combat. De Gaulle saw the opportunity to rid himself of the annoyance and sent the man to De Lattre, with orders that the Commander of First Army could not ignore.

Pierce was a fair man, so decided to stay nothing of his inside knowledge, in order to give Molyneux every chance.

"As you will see, that may be our fault, General Lavalle."

"Never mind, it is of no import Général. Now, where is your command?"

Moving to a map already surrounded by Lavalle's staff, Pierce traced a route before stopping the other side of the Rhine.

"My lead elements were at Soufflenheim forty minutes ago. The rest of my unit is either debussing at Hagenau or en route to Hagenau from Landau, where we reconstituted."

"Reconstituted?"

"We were hit very hard in the opening days, General. My unit was still quite green, and we lost more than our innocence when the Russians attacked."

"And now, General Pierce?"

"Now?"

A look swept quickly across Pierce's face, carrying pain, hurt and anger in equal measure. It was quickly replaced with resolve.

"Now, we're light on everything, but my boys are itching for a scrap, General Lavalle. It's payback time for us, and from what I hear, this is just the right unit to go in harm's way with."

Lavalle accepted the compliment on behalf of his legionnaires.

"Apologies, I am at error. Let us meet those who do the soldiering in this Corps."

Introductions were made between the Legion unit commanders and the Americans, Pierce himself beckoning forward his previously hesitant seniors.

As the handshakes fell away, Bittrich informed Lavalle that the briefing was ready.

470

To a man, the ensemble checked either the wall clock or their watches, the fact that fourteen minutes had passed indicative of the way that the Legion Corps did its business.

"Excellent work, Willi! That leaves time for soldiers talk and more coffee."

Which talk and coffee occupied the intervening period before Général Molyneux descended the stairs and all was formality once more.

Bittrich's briefing, he insisted on doing it himself, was masterly, leaving no loophole for criticism, even from a man trying desperately hard to find one.

None the less, Molyneux managed to trash a lot of the staff work by producing the new order of battle, one of his aides taping it to the wall of the operations room.

Of course, at the head of the Corps and in bold letters was Molyneux's name and rank.

Beneath that there were now three commands, A and B discarded, now named formally as 'Normandie', 'Lorraine', and 'Aquitaine'.

Each senior officer was naturally drawn to his own particular section.

Knocke noted that 'Camerone' was now partnered by 'Alma' and the newly-arrived 16th Armored. And that Lavalle and Bittrich were at the head of Command Group 'Normandie.'

Demarais' command group, 'Lorraine', was headed up by a General Leroy-Bessette, the name a faint memory for no known reason of he could recall. 'Amilakvari' had been renamed as 'Sevastopol', but was still his running mate.

'Aquitaine' was presently unformed, awaiting the new units from Sassy before taking the field proper.

Some in the room started to notice a difference in atmosphere and became aware of another powerful presence.

Général d'Armée de Lattre de Tassigny stood silently, reading the body language in the room like a book and immediately understanding that Molyneux's arrival had not gone well.

"Attention!"

471

Salutes were thrown everywhere as total silence descended.

"Gentlemen, good afternoon."

De Lattre strode forward and offered his hand to the senior man, checking his surprised reaction when it seemed that instead of a hand in return, someone had slapped a wet fish into his palm.

"Général Molyneux."

"Général De Lattre."

Ever the politician, he prevented himself from recoiling, although he did clandestinely wipe it as he turned to Lavalle, catching sight of Pierce, and observed protocol for fear of upsetting the American.

"General Pierce, good to see you again."

"And you too, Sir."

Salute and handshake followed, both respectful, and the Frenchman noted the difference as his hand was held firmly.

De Lattre smiled and moved on.

"Général Lavalle."

His hand was again rewarded with a firm grip, the wet fish now a fading memory.

"Congratulations on 'Camerone's' recent achievement."

"Thank you Sir. May..."

The senior man interrupted before Lavalle could continue.

"Your sentries are formidable, Lavalle."

More than one man in the room cringed in anticipation. Only one man looked on in triumph at what he expected was to come.

"They wouldn't let me in without seeing my papers! Excellent fellows, stood their ground. Promote them both immediately."

More than one in the room shared the same thought.

'Does he know?'

Ever the politician, De Lattre's face continued to hide his prior knowledge.

The triumphant look departed Molyneux's face as quickly as it had appeared.

472

"Now, my apologies for not properly informing you of the change of command. Apparently, one of my Major's made an error in signal routing and then lied to cover it up. He is on his way here for you to use as you see fit, should you have room for another 2nd Lieutenant around here?"

It was posed as a question but De Lattre was sending the demoted man to serve in the unit he had wronged, and that was that.

"Before I am introduced to your officers, I notice that the order of battle is incorrect."

He strode to the wall and took a moment to take it in, absorbing the grandiose lettering of Molyneux's name, reading much into it that was wholly accurate.

'I must watch this man closely.'

Holding out his hand in expectation, one of his Captaine's pushed a grease pencil into it.

De Lattre went to work, turning to look at Lavalle and then crossing out the rank of 'Normandie's' commander.

"We can do better than that. Général de Division Lavalle it is."

Bittrich was next.

"For you, you are confirmed as the Corps' senior Général de Brigade. Your contribution has been invaluable. Thank you, General."

De Lattre then found the last man he sought, nodding at him in recognition.

'How long ago did we meet Colonel?'

"And finally we have Général de Brigade Knocke."

He completed his alterations and proffered the pencil to the Capitaine, who magically reappeared in place.

"Général Guillaume has done nothing but sing your praises ever since you got his Algerians out of Stuttgart."

Knocke, ever modest, shrugged slightly.

"My men did all the work, and my report on the conduct of certain individuals has been sent forward. Many men did their duty and more that day, Sir."

"I understand."

Nodding at the German Colonel, *'Général now of course'*, he stopped himself from engaging Knocke in

473

conversation and, once again businesslike, De Lattre turned to Molyneux and called him to attention.

"General, you are now confirmed as Général de Corps D'Armée, and commander of the Legion Corps D'Assault."

The Army Commander waited whilst one of his staff appeared on cue, removing Molyneux's three-star epaulettes, before stepping forward and placing the new four-star versions in place.

De Lattre formally announced, all the time remembering how De Gaulle had forced the issue.

"You have been entrusted with a splendid fighting machine. Use it wisely General."

He stepped forward, grasping the officer to him for a touch of each cheek, by way of congratulation.

No-one heard the whispered comment.

"Break it and I will break you, Molyneux."

De Lattre stepped back and exchanged formal salutes, all the time his eyes boring into Molyneux's, wanting to see some recognition of his concerns, as well as seeking some answers to his questions, but finding nothing of note within.

His mind was suddenly made up and he initiated his plan.

"I am leaving a number of my officers to assist you. Colonel Benoit Plummer will be your Chief of Staff."

From the back of the crowd stepped a bemedalled officer wearing the insignia of the Regiment de Marche du Tchad, a regiment now lying dead across southern Bavaria, once part of the destroyed 2nd French Armoured Division.

The man bore the pain of his loss stoically, and welcomed the chance to serve with such a fine formation as the Legion Corps.

He also had a number of other assets that would serve the Legion well in the months to come.

He was extremely competent, highly experienced, and, probably more importantly, had the ear of De Lattre. They had been friends since birth, having both enjoyed their childhoods in the sleepy French commune of Mouilleron-en-Pareds.

Finally, his credentials were impeccable, his full name being Benoit Hugues Kelly Clemenceau-Plummer, the grandson

474

of Georges Clemenceau, ex-Prime Minister of France and Conqueror of Germany in the 14-18 War.

De Lattre was introduced to all the officers present and engaged in small talk, enjoying a sample of the Legion's coffee. His own staff mixed in with those of the Legion Corps, officers from the First Army keen to hear about the recent victory.

When he took his leave, he was confident that the Legion Corps had the very best of leadership, with the exception of the man foisted on him from above. He also knew that Molyneux would be under close scrutiny every waking minute, and that the man watching him had a very special power that would be used wisely, if it proved necessary.

As the entourage left in De Lattre's wake, Kowalski caught the eye of his prize spy.

Nothing was said, but much passed between them in that millisecond, Kowalski breaking the contact and moving swiftly to ensure his place in the cavalcade. Lavalle caught a glimpse of the man as he left, seeking out Knocke, and finding that the German had seen him too.

A 'Deux' minder, immaculately turned out in the uniform of an officer of the Algerian Spahis, casually followed Kowalski outside, where another agent gunned the motor of the military Citroen, ready to take the 'Polish' Major back to Army Headquarters.

Knocke and Lavalle stood together in the window of the operations room, studying the agent's departure, unable to recognise who was watching him, but knowing that the watcher was there none the less.

Their train of thought was interrupted by a polite cough, the noise emanating from the throat of the door guard Corporal intent on attracting Knocke's attention.

"Sir, an officer gave me this to give to you, he forgot to do so when in here."

The man offered up an envelope marked for his consumption, and decorated with 'eyes only' markings, some of whose 'O's' were solid rather than hollow, an indicator of the sender and the nature of its content.

"Thank you. Your name and that of your fellow please, Caporal?"

475

"Caporal Jacquet, Sir, and he is Private Humbert. 3rd Compagnie, 7th Regiment du Marche, Tannenberg, Sir."

Knocke silently sought Lavalle's permission to continue, and it was given with a satisfied smile.

"I shall make sure your commander gets my full report, together with that of General Lavalle's here, endorsing your promotion to Sergent and that of Humbert's to Caporal, effective immediately, courtesy of General De Lattre. Congratulations, Sergent Jacquet. Dismissed."

Slightly confused at the heavyweight names that had just taken an interest in his well-being, Jacquet threw up a swift salute before retreating speedily, conscious that an officer's goodwill could evaporate as quickly as it distilled.

The smiles disappeared from both officers' faces, the envelope suddenly weighing heavy in Knocke's hand.

"My office?"

The question remained unanswered, both men moving quickly to the privacy of Lavalle's first floor suite.

Opening the door, they found Molyneux ensconced, already relieved of his tunic, enjoying a glass of claret with a splendid lunch, laid out on the exquisite marble-topped table.

Lavalle noticed two junior officers placing familiar items in a trunk.

"I expect you to give me the courtesy of knocking before you enter my room, Lavalle."

"Apologies, My General. I had not realised that I was no longer the resident. I shall remove my items immediately."

"Excellent. Now, please leave me in peace."

The two juniors threw a last handful of items on top of the pile, and the two senior men stooped to pick up the trunk.

A small sound from Molyneux indicated his obvious disgust that they should perform such manual labours themselves, the disdain clear on his face as they took their leave.

RSM Vernais strode around the corner and stopped in his tracks, both amused and perturbed by the surreal vision of two of his leaders dragging a large trunk with various possessions poking out from under the half-closed lid.

Keeping his thoughts to himself, he beckoned his men forward and, in his eyes, the officers were replaced by more suitable porters.

"Where to, Sirs?"

"I think it will have to be your private den, Major Vernais."

For a moment Vernais considered a bluster, but he already knew that, in Lavalle, he had an officer who knew more than he had a right to. Apparently including the fact that he and his cronies had set aside a bedroom for their own use as a private drinking parlour, amongst other things.

"As you wish, Sir."

"Room one-one-four please, Legionnaires," the simple words meaning so much to Lavalle as he saw the reaction on his senior Warrant Officer's face.

Smiling, he confided in Vernais.

"Just until I can get permanently settled somewhere else, Vernais. Then you can have your den back."

Turning to follow the trunk, Lavalle had second thoughts.

"Major Vernais, will you please locate Commandant de Montgomerie, and ask him to join us in one-one-four immediately please."

Acknowledging, Vernais went in hunt of the intelligence officer, all the time part of his brain working out where he could find an alternative venue with similar comforts to the recently requisitioned room.

Knocke waited until De Montgomerie arrived before opening the envelope.

Apart from the methodology of exchange with and contact details of a baker in Baden-Baden, there were also straight-forward requests for military information.

And a grainy picture of two girls called Greta and Magda, stood in front of an unknown Major in NKVD uniform.

What Knocke said was as much of a surprise as the way he said it, his voice taking on a sinister edge, not heard before by brother officers.

"I know where that is."

"Are they your daughters, Ernst?"

Lavalle enquired carefully, disturbed by the sea change in his friend.

Nodding sharply, Knocke looked up triumphantly.

"I know this place."

He brought the image closer, drinking in the peripherals more than the daughters he so missed, and the hated uniform in the background.

And then the penny dropped.

"Yes Christophe, they are my daughters." He held up the photograph for both men to see, "And they are stood in front of the old Gasthaus in Fischausen."

Fischausen, soon to be renamed Primorsk, had been virtually destroyed in the April fighting, the few surviving inhabitants moved on elsewhere.

The location provided the NKVD with the perfect hiding place, away from day to day public scrutiny.

The old guest house, away from the main area of fighting, had escaped damage, and was used to house the three 'prisoners', as well as the personal security detail.

The large building nearby provided warm and dry quarters for the thirty man NKVD guard force, charged with keeping the nosey at distance and 'disappearing' those who got too close.

Across the road from the Gasthaus, the relatively undamaged doctor's residence and surgery proved suitable accommodation for the two NKVD officers.

Other more distant eyes soon turned towards Fischausen, appreciating that its strength was also a weakness.

2037 hrs, Sunday, 2nd September 1945, Leconfield House, Curzon Street, London.

The thick curtains were drawn, and only a single table lamp salvaged the Victorian room from darkness.

478

The single occupant, relaxing with a modest single malt, had long ago switched off the radio, tiring of the new BBC Light programme, returning to the desk to finish the last of his work before heading to his London home.

At least that was the plan, which did not survive the urgent telephone call he received.

Placing his pen carefully in the holder, he lifted the receiver.

"Petrie."

Had another person been in the room they would have witnessed a metamorphosis, Petrie's gaze becoming hardened, his free hand stroking his moustache into place.

"Bring it up immediately, Jones."

He gently replaced the receiver and waited, estimating the time it would take the duty officer to make it from the decoding room to his office.

It was a game he played, interpreting the speed of arrival as a marker of their import.

The knock on the door came an unprecedented fifteen seconds in advance of schedule.

The duty officer entered and stood breathlessly before the desk of MI5's Director-General.

"Sir, this message was logged in at 2031 hrs and marked 'eyes only DG'."

That in itself was not unusual.

"It is also in Omega Code, Sir."

That was extremely unusual and the reason that Jones had taken the steps two at a time from basement to fourth floor.

Omega messages started in the code of the day and the message had been worked on by one of the duty communications team. However, the decoder soon found the 'Ω9Ω' mark that betrayed its extreme importance and specific recipient.

"Thank you, Jones. You may go."

Standing smartly, Petrie strode to his wall safe and extracted the necessary tools to unlock 'Omega', understanding that 'Ω9Ω' indicated Fenton, HM's agent in the sleepy hollow that was the Court of Bernadotte, in the presence of Gustaf V, King of Sweden.

Once the 'Omega' was decoded, the process of a full hour, Petrie realised that the message had transformed from the indecipherable to solid dynamite with the capacity to destroy much of what had been saved in the war years.

The receiver virtually leapt from its cradle.

The voice at the other end seemed half-asleep, it being a Sunday evening and nothing of note happening.

"Comms room, Charlton."

"Petrie here. Access to duty officer's cabinet. Authorisation code Picton. Acknowledge."

Charlton was suddenly very much awake, although not a little annoyed that a drill should be run at this time on a Sunday.

"Acknowledge receipt of authorisation code Picton. State your requirements, sir."

Jones looked up from his novel, the words attracting his attention.

"Access secure storage. My code 1830. Acknowledge."

Next to Charlton's position was a heavy metal cabinet, its eight-digit numeric combination lock built into the side. His free hand moved the dials, inputting first his, then the DG's numbers.

"1830, acknowledge."

The heavy lock clicked open and he tested the sliding door.

"I have access, Sir. File access name please."

'Still going, are we? Stupid time for a drill, old chap.'

"File access 'Hastings'. Contact both named members immediately. Message is 'Effingham'. They are to be in my office yesterday. Acknowledge."

Charlton was totally focussed in a micro-second, as 'Hastings' was just a rumour, spoken of in hushed whispers over drinks in the nearby pub.

"Access 'Hastings', both members to be contacted and given the message 'Effingham'. To attend your office immediately. Yes, Sir."

His 'Yes Sir' was spoken to a dead connection, Petrie having cut the line before dialling an outside number.

The phone rang unanswered.

'Damn, of course. Should have realised.'

He dialled another number, the one he should have dialled first, given the time of day.

This time it was answered immediately.

"The Guards Club, Good evening. How may I be of assistance?"

"Ah Squires, just the fellow."

"Sir David, how may I be of assistance?"

"Squires, is Sir Fabian there this evening?"

"He most definitely is, Sir. Presently engaging the younger members with his memories of Mons."

"This is most urgent, Squires. Please bring him to the phone."

"Sir."

The phone was placed carefully down, and Petrie could almost hear the man limp away as fast as his shortened left peg could carry him.

A disturbance in his ear quickly told him that his man had arrived.

"Callard-Smith."

"Jack, it's David. No time to explain right now. Just need to know you will be in town all week."

"Ah David! My dear fellow. I'm here until Thursday, and then I'm off to Roger's estate for some weekend shooting."

"Good. I may have need of you, so please don't disappear, Jack."

"I do hate mysteries, old chap. What's it about?"

"Cannot say right now, but I think it is as big as it comes, and I will need you."

"Righty ho David, mum's the word then. Got to go now, it's Percy's round."

Two men replaced their phones.

One, Sir David Petrie, started to work on a plan to sort out the abominable mess that had just landed in his lap.

The other, Colonel Sir Fabian John Callard-Smith MP VC, wondered what had got his dear friend in such an agitated state, and what part he was to play in the grand design.

Stirred by the faint cries of derision as Percy Hollander chalked drinks to his personal account, he stepped away from his thoughts and moved quickly to add to Percy's tally.

Petrie finished his scotch, enjoying the silence his
radical suggestion had brought about.

The other two members of 'Hastings', having been
summoned according to set procedure, had dropped everything to
deal with what was obviously a matter of the utmost importance.

The report had not been copied; Omegas never were. It
would not survive the end of the meeting, the cold fireplace to be
lightly warmed as it was destroyed within the sight of all the
Hastings Group.

But for now, the other two reflected upon Petrie's
drastic suggestion.

The first reaction had been shock, followed quickly by
anger.

After proper consideration, doubts had arisen.

"If we act against this, are we committing treason?
Becoming traitors in our turn?"

Lord Southam posed the questions to the head of MI5,
the confusion evident in a man of sound thinking.

"No, I think not, Will. We are preserving His Majesty's
Government in a time of National crisis. To not act, that certainly
would be a betrayal of our nation, and don't forget, there is no
democratic mandate for this, just the knee-jerk reaction of a
frightened man."

That may have been a bit strong, but Petrie didn't care.

Major General Colin Gubbins was, for the most part,
silent. He was having the most difficulty reconciling himself with
the contents of the Swedish report.

"I can't believe he would do it without Cabinet
approval."

Southam examined the empty nature of his glass, finding
a dribble to test his tongue.

"Well Colin, I can assure you that not even the Minister
has an inkling of this."

Gubbins looked mortified. None the less, having offered
little to the discussion but a word here and there, the Head of
SOE was not one to shirk responsibility.

He made his statement with a black humour.

"If this is how it is painted then your suggestion is acceptable. I will be hanged if I will see this happen."

Petrie nodded at Gubbins, having expected no less, his choice of words bringing a smile.

"If, and I stress if, I were to go along with this, will Callard-Smith do the job?"

Southam was a life-long civil servant, and he had learnt the political dance at an early age.

"Absolutely," stated Petrie with utter confidence.

Southam spent a few moments in quiet reflection before extending his glass.

The head of MI5 chuckled, refilling all three in a flash.

The three stood on cue, and it was Gubbins that offered the toast.

"God save the King, and to hell with Attlee."

The scotch seared their throats as they committed to Petrie's plan.

The Swedish report had detailed the intended secret meeting between British and Soviet envoys and the circumstances of it, complete with a Soviet intelligence report detailing their knowledge.

The reasons were unknown but could be guessed at, especially if reading intelligence reports on some of Attlee's private conversations in Number Ten.

His despair at the climbing casualty rates on land, his horror at the losses of capital ships at sea, and, possibly the last straw, his shock at the immolation of RAF Bomber Command in Northern Germany.

Whatever his reasons, it was patently clear what his solution was.

Clement Attlee, Prime Minister, had taken it upon himself to discuss the possibility of a separate armistice with the Soviet Union, taking his country out of the war.

And 'Hastings' was resolved to stop it at all costs.

483

Valour is superior to numbers

Flavius Vegetius Renatus

Chapter 76 - THE SURVIVOR

The 'Leopard' sat in his chair, looking like the cat that got the cream.

His surprise visit to Knocke's headquarters seemed to have caught the SS bastard on the hop and, for once, he felt in a dominant position.

'Always the superior air, you SS bastard. Not today though, caught you today, you bastard.'

Strangely, Knocke was of little use at the moment, as the ego of a certain newly promoted French General needed only the slightest of massages before indiscretions tumbled from the man's mouth.

As a professional, Kapitan Sergei Kovelskin of the GRU, or as he was normally known, Major Stanislas Kowalski of the 1st Polish Armoured Division, used General Molyneux as the excellent source he was. Privately, and in some ways, also as a professional, he had nothing but contempt for the fool, something he had in common with the man sat opposite.

With ill-concealed triumph, Kowalski revealed the depth of his knowledge.

"I already know that you have pre-movement orders for a relocation to Mühlacker, so I don't need that information."

Knocke's uncomfortable look gave him away immediately, something Kowalski noticed, whilst another part of his brain informed him that, in his arrogance, he had just made a mistake.

He quickly rectified it.

"What can I say, Knocke? The French are fools and I see a lot of paperwork, which is why I also don't need the revision of your Corps Order of Battle."

484

"Rear-line soldiers."

Knocke's simple statement was sufficient to portray his disgust, and also hide the smallest of lights in his eyes, put there by a possible error on the Russian's part.

'The German bastard is getting the idea.'

Kowalski relished the superiority of his position.

Knocke lit a cigarette to help gather his thoughts. By his right hand was a prepared and slightly sanitised version that he had set ready, once he had been informed that the Russian was on his way.

"So, you have no more use for me then, Kowalski?"

The laugh that greeted that statement bore no humour in it.

"Oh but we still have great use for you, Knocke. My next order to you is quite simple. Do not take your unit north of the River Enz."

"That will be impossible. I will have orders..."

"Fuck your orders Knocke. You will ensure that your men do not step over the water. I'm sure I don't need to remind you of the consequences."

Knocke conceded the point, his dangerous game best played with fewest words.

"If you relocate, I will come and find you, but use the relay here until then," and anticipating Knocke's protestation he held up a hand, "And don't tell me you can't because we know you can, even if it is just to get your favourite pastries."

Knocke methodically stubbed out his cigarette, using the dead end to bring together a coned-shaped pile of ash.

He dropped the butt, almost seeming to notice the agent for the first time.

"Was there anything else, Maior?"

"Just to say that if I don't report in regularly, the man in the photo will carry out some unpleasant orders. Don't forget that, Knocke."

485

The French pilot's sense of betrayal made them dangerous enemies and, combined with their knowledge of Soviet aircraft capabilities, they would soon establish a reputation second to none in air-to-air combat.

Having written briefing documents that were now circulating from frontline squadrons all the way to training units in Canada, the group of skilled aviators were determined to seek combat against their betrayers.

Finally, they were given some Mustangs, fresh from British service, the RAF pilots of necessity reverting to another type of which they had previous experience, brought out from mothballs because of the chronic shortage of aircraft and spare parts.

After some conversion, the 'Rapier's' were let loose on the battlefront, finally achieving their first air victories of the new war on 4th September.

The Il-4's were ripped apart, the fighters immediately going for the soft underbellies where they could attack with relative safety.

Four Ilyushin's were knocked down in the first pass, the commander screaming into his radio, partially to get help, and partially to vent his fear.

He ordered his Regiment to go lower, trying to remove the present attack option, and was immediately rewarded with the repulse of a hasty attack, the Mustang driven off smoking.

It was the sole victory he saw, his urgent radio transmissions stopped in mid-sentence as .50cal bullets smashed through his cockpit and exited the glass nose beyond.

Dazed and coughing blood, the Major could find no strength to move as his aircraft lazily rolled onto its back. He watched in petrified fascination as the ground came increasingly closer.

The surviving five bombers hugged the landscape and paid for it, the junior pilot clipping a church tower and fireballing into a row of houses.

486

Four now, as low as they dared, trading speed for height, or lack of it, safety the golden target.

Back over Soviet lines there was no chance of flak, so each pilot concentrated on the ground and the enemy who still pursued.

And then they were gone, the sky suddenly empty of the death bringers.

The surviving pilots flew on, leaving seven of their aircraft and twenty-nine of their comrades behind.

Each aircraft had a four man crew, the extra loss being a reporter from the 'Pravda' newspaper, who fell for the 'easy mission' briefing of the Divisional Commander, and who died cursing the man's name.

1153 hrs, Tuesday 4th September 1945, With 21st Guards Bomber Air Regiment, airborne over South-Western Germany.

The Lightning P38-J was an upgraded version of the famous twin-tail fighter, and much improved compared to the aircraft that had tested the Luftwaffe in the early days of the American commitment.

The general type was unknown to the crews of the 21st, not having been supplied within the lend-lease programme, although a few ex-USAAF models had been found damaged and made airworthy in the later years of the Patriotic War.

In the last years, the USAAF in Europe had mainly used the Lightning for reconnaissance, but now the ground attack and interceptor roles were more required, with other aircraft set aside to do the photo-recon work.

This particular unit was formed from training unit personnel and given a brand-new designation, that of the 601st Fighter Squadron.

Their first mission, a ground attack strike in support of a defensive battle north-east of Bretten, had been carried out with all the hallmarks of men either unused to combat, or rusty from an absence of it. Twelve had flown out and ten had come back, two aircraft lost due to mechanical failure, safely landing in friendly territory.

487

The 601st contained both sorts of pilots, new and veteran, and it took time to gel properly.

Their second mission had been an escort assignment, remarkable solely for a total no-show by Soviet fighters. Again, the entire squadron of fourteen aircraft returned.

This was their third, and they had thirteen birds in the sky.

'Tanya' was performing well, her twin engines sounding perfect as the squadron settled into line for the 'Carousel' attack.

Senior Lieutenant Istomin was checking the ground, observing numerous palls of smoke from the target area, markers of his comrade's success.

Like the veteran he was, Istomin calmly searched for something of note, his mind registering the tracers rising from the German town, suggesting the presence of military, and therefore justifying it as a target.

Istomin heard the call through a positive deluge of messages, the common radio channel sharing the destruction of the 9th Bombers, as well as adding a realistic commentary to the deadly fighter battle going on above them.

His head swivelled and his eyes tried hard to adjust to the approaching shapes, not knowing what exactly they were, but knowing exactly what they were about to do.

The bomber leader gave instructions for the 'Carousel' to commence and screamed into his radio for fighter assistance, receiving some hazy reassurance of 'help on its way'.

No help would come.

The Soviet fighter flight leader who acknowledged was already spiralling down in a fireball, dead before the bombers commenced their attack.

Istomin could see a disaster in the making, the regiment lined up preparing to follow the lead aircraft into a bombing attack, the enemy aircraft closing at high-speed.

"Zirafa-two-three to one-one, enemy fighters attacking head on, type unknown, over"

He made the call, even though the commander had to have seen them.

488

The man was a fanatic, and determined to discharge his duty, so he gave no countermanding order as he dived on his target.

'God fucking help us.'

Possibly God did help the 21st at that moment, although if he did it was by guiding the AA fire of the 'Camerone' flak unit into the regimental commander's diving aircraft, the 37mm shell striking the port engine on the propeller boss, its explosive power spent in wrecking the engine and sending fragments of itself and the propeller in all directions.

The Tupolev was a tough airframe, and the commander's aircraft almost seemed to shrug off the strike, continuing on its attack dive.

The regimental commander, the pain excruciating, his intestines already spilling out over the flight controls and pedals, issued one last order.

"Zirafa-one-one to all, continue the attack for the Rodina. Good luck comrades."

The 20mm quad flak guns now started to chew pieces off his aircraft, ending his suffering, and that of the three other crew, all victims of the shrapnel from the engine strike.

As the stricken Tu-2 buried itself in the ground, the second and third aircraft virtually came apart in the air as the enemy fighters struck.

Istomin acted.

"Zirafa-two-three to all, jettison bombs, break away, left, left, ground level, over.

Wide-eyed soviet bomber crews watched as the beautiful twin-hulled aircraft swept past them, more bullets striking home from quadruple .50cals mounted in each US aircraft's nose cone.

The tail end Tupolev received special attention from one of the three Lightnings that also had their 20mm Hispano cannon in place, the explosive shells biting deep into the wing spar and destroying the starboard wing's fuel tank.

For anyone on the Soviet radio scheme, the next few seconds were too horrible for words, and more than one pilot switched channels, be they in a bomber with Lightnings closing, or in a Lavochkin fighting for its life in the sky above.

489

Those who could observe, married the sight of the burning Tupolev losing height gradually with the animal screams of those being incinerated inside the metal tube.

Even those USAAF and Normandie pilots who caught sight of the aircraft immediately understood the suffering of those within, but none sympathised any more.

'*C'est la Guerre.*'

Four of the Tupolev's were either down, or going down, and the 21st Regiment had not even started to get itself down and heading back home.

The Normandie pilots concentrated on their own prey, pursuing the Il-4's away from the target area.

The 601st swept round and bore down again.

"Zirafa-two-three to all. Get down fast and turn left, course 100. Come on, comrades!"

Another Tupolev went, more spectacularly than the rest, cannon shells coming into contact with something that didn't respond well to the marriage, the sturdy aircraft disintegrating in the resultant explosion.

"Two-three, break left, now, now, now."

The column shifted instantly, the Tupolev no longer occupying the air now being thrashed by .50cal bullets.

A shape swept past Istomin and he instinctively flicked the aircraft to follow, pressing the firing button for his forward firing ShVAK cannon.

Whilst not as spectacular as his comrade's death, the shells did deadly work on the tail plane of the Lightning. Large pieces of the control surfaces fell behind in its wake, and the pilot quickly jumped out of his aircraft, taking to the air in silk.

Istomin jumped instinctively, the metallic rattle of bullets striking home on 'Tanya' preceding the anguished cries of one of his crew as the hot metal hit home.

Jinking the Tupolev left, he noticed no change in its performance following the enemy attack.

Sparing a look at his gauges, he saw no issues of note, the rise in engine temperatures because of his altitude and additional applied power.

490

Tracers formed a web ahead of him, more enemy Flak units taking the opportunity to contribute to proceedings as the P38's drew off to reform for a third pass.

Heavier clunks gave testimony to the accuracy of the allied ground gunners, and holes appeared in his starboard wing before the final strikes completely took off the wing tip.

Senior Lieutenant Istomin immediately felt the difference, the starboard engine gently dropping power, combined with a flutter on the starboard wing that was negligible, but none the less present.

His navigator had died behind him, despite the best efforts of one of the gunners.

The other gunner had already died quietly, hence the absence of any warning about the return of the Lightnings.

Bullets ate into the fuselage and right wing, adding to the damage and creating new, as the transit of US metal shredded part of the ailerons.

The sustained burst from the quadruple .50cal also left Istomin alone in the aircraft.

Now down low, he noticed that the other Tupolevs hugging the ground were pulling steadily away.

'I'm losing speed!'

Sparing extra time to study his gauges, he saw more problems.

'Engine is fucking hot! Losing revs?'

His eyes swept around further.

'Govno! Where's my fuel?'

The first strike had severed one of the fuel supply pipes to the right engine, wrecking the chokes designed to cut off any oversupply.

This was a problem that needed addressing immediately. He stopped the engine and isolated the fuel supply, conserving what was left and removing a source of ignition for the fuel that was sloshing around inside the wing spaces, just waiting for something to bring it into spectacular life.

'Govno! Work damn you!'

The blade would not feather, and now the Tupolev took on a partial sideways aspect as the idling propeller created tremendous drag.

491

Another metallic rattle as bullets struck home again, this time kissing the left wing. 'Tanya's' lack of speed was her saviour, as most of the .50cal, and all of the 20mm cannon shells, were spent in fresh air, the USAAF pilot getting his attack all wrong.

"Mudaks!"

Timed to the instant that the invective left his mouth, the propeller feathered, and Istomin could not help the thought that he should shout at 'Tanya' more often.

The Tupolev became more responsive again, shrugging off the lack of an engine and the damage to her control surfaces.

Istomin drove his aircraft lower still, too low, swiping some treetops and scaring himself, before rising a few metres for safety.

He shouted to his crew but there was no reply. He understood why but could not find a moment to mourn his comrades.

Ahead, an aircraft attracted the attention of three of the twin tailed aircraft.

Elation took hold as the Soviet gunner made a kill, the graceful US fighter turning over and plunging into the ground with its pilot.

Elation was replaced by horror as the Tu-2 was literally hacked to pieces, one of the cannon-firing Lightnings making it come apart in front of Istomin's eyes.

Horror was replaced by fear as more bullets beat their lethal rhythm on 'Tanya', the sudden inrush of cold air telling him that the glasshouse nose had been badly damaged.

Again, a change in performance, and more speed bled off as the drag increased.

Tracers swept past his right side, so close he could almost sense the heat from their passing.

The Lightning had bled off much of its speed, the new pilot anxious to show his comrades how well he had learned his craft.

Adding something extra, he had dropped his undercarriage, reducing his speed even more.

However, his attack had been badly lined up, and he still missed the struggling Tupolev.

His inexperience condemned his name to the wall of 'missing, believed killed', an aggressive quarter-turn from Istomin bringing the slow moving Lightning in front of his ShVAK cannon.

The low speed, the undercarriage drag, and the 20mm cannon shells combined to send the P38 into the small lake below.

However, the aviation spirit within the Tupolev's starboard wing finally found its ignition source with the firing of the cannon. A fire started; not an explosive ignition or the wing would have come apart, but enough to leave a growing trail of flame behind, a flame that started to melt everything of value that it touched.

Another two of Istomin's comrades were smoking, a single Lightning hitting both in one pass.

Following an aborte attack, one Lightning had hauled off, it's pilot working out how to fly with only one good arm, his left severed at the elbow.

Tracers again leapt skywards, ground positions seeking out kills amongst the hated enemy.

They struck home immediately, a P38 coming apart as something heavy exploded under the pilot's pod.

The USAAF fighters screamed away in a rising starboard turn.

Istomin understood immediately.

"Zirafa-two-three to all. We are over our lines, repeat, over our lines.

In front of Istomin's eyes were four Tupolev's, one apparently undamaged, the other three ranging from smoking to burning.

"Zirafa-two-three to all. Have no navigator. Communicate course to nearest airfield, over."

"Zirafa -three-three to all. Airfield immediately ahead, four thousand metres. We are perfect for land..."

The radio gave up working with a noticeable sizzle, leaving Istomin alone in every sense of the word.

He could see the undamaged lead aircraft make an adjustment and lose height, the other aircraft moving away to make their own approaches in their turn.

493

As protocol required, Istomin in 'Tanya' would land last so as not to obstruct the runway if he failed to make it.

He circled gently, alert for any return of the enemy aircraft, sparing a glance as his comrades touched down one by one.

'Two down, Come on, come on!'

The third aircraft, the flames almost extinguished, touched down and sheered right immediately, its damaged undercarriage giving way.

The fuselage ploughed up some grass before coming to a halt.

Spreading his attention equally between the air and the ground, Istomin saw only two running figures before the Tupolev was totally ablaze.

'Tanya' was starting to act up, the damaged right ailerons unresponsive, the right wing losing its integrity as the fire continued to wreak havoc.

Gently, he eased his aircraft into a left turn, losing an extra few metres of height, and lining up for a textbook landing.

Readying himself for any change in the flying characteristics, he lowered the undercarriage.

Or rather, he tried.

The starboard wheel was partially destroyed and refused to move, its operating system already consumed by the fire.

He tried to recover the port wheel.

'Govno!'

He tried again, remembering how to do it properly.

"Govno!"

The Tupolev did not respond.

The vibrations on the right wing were becoming worse, but Istomin had no choice except to go around again, his battle with the undercarriage bringing him to the overshoot point on his approach.

Turning to port, he found himself sweating and realised that the fire in the right wing was much larger than before.

The attempt to drop the undercarriage had merely opened the small doors, permitting additional oxygen to enter and feed the flames.

'Tanya' was dying around him, her systems failing as the damage increased by the minute, but she was still flying.

Istomin lined up again, his speed up, the single wheel down, the fire blazing.

As the aircraft dropped slowly, he found himself almost squealing, not a recognisable human sound, just the unmistakeable sounds of someone in the extremes of terror.

The pitch of his voice increased as his fear grew, the ground rising to meet him almost hand in hand with the increase in volume.

Teeth clenched in a brave attempt to silence his external display, Istomin went for the touchdown.

The survivors of the 21st Guards Bomber Regiment watched as the ravaged aircraft almost seemed to kiss the runway, no noticeable change from being airborne to being on the ground.

Still it was moving too fast but the engine sounds were dropping off as the pilot did what he could.

In silence, they and the soviet ground crews watched as the pilot skilfully cajoled his aircraft into losing speed, keeping the starboard wing above the ground until the last moment.

Spectacularly, fate took a hand, bringing the 'last moment' forward as cannon shells, cooked by the heat, exploded sequentially, opening up the ravaged wing and dropping the Tupolev to the runway instantly.

Dragging to the right, 'Tanya' ploughed the grass with a shorn-off starboard wing, the fire all but gone as the wing separated, courtesy of the cannon shells.

All across the airfield, men were running to his aid, mostly carrying nothing but their hopes.

The port wheel strut surrendered to the increased strain, bringing the fuselage down level and increasing the drag.

The Tupolev came to a sudden halt, settling into a dignified repose, surrounded by a cloud of smoke and grass.

The second fire truck had left the previous crash site, the fire crew determined to do what they could for the brave air crew of the latest arrival.

495

Overtaking running men, the elderly vehicle closed quickly on the smoking ruin and crashed to a halt, the crew quickly running out hoses to quell the flames, and arming themselves with tools to pry and cut open whatever needed to be pried and cut open in order to get the crew out.

The fire fighters swarmed over the fuselage and inside, bringing out the gunners and navigator, laying them down gently and covering them with their jackets.

More personnel now arrived and set to with helping. Others, members of the 21st, lifted a jacket here and there, confirming the identity of a dead comrade.

A wave of laughter grew throughout the responders, causing anguish with the bomber crews, who sought out those responsible for the disrespect.

Intending to right the wrong, the survivors of the 21st could only add to the growing sounds of laughter as, one by one, they became aware of Istomin.

Carrying signs of his close encounter, the blackened Senior Lieutenant was sat on the steps of a nearby equipment hut, sharing a bottle of vodka with the two air force personnel who usually inhabited it.

All three men sat there quietly praising fate for her benevolence, two for having survived the death they anticipated as the aircraft bore inexorably down upon them, one for being inside the blazing coffin all the way to the end.

The pilot had no boots, his bare feet a contradictory pink set against the more common black and brown of his ensemble.

The trio bore more than a passing resemblance to the 'three monkeys' of old, especially as Istomin massaged his head in an effort to relieve the headache brought on by the tension of his experience.

The doctor who checked him shortly afterwards also humorously observed that the heavy machorka tobacco he had obtained from the ground crew, combined with the vodka they liberally imbibed, probably also contributed.

However, in seriousness, he plainly put the headache down to the five inch gash in the back of Istomin's head, courtesy of the final lurch, the white of the skull plain for all to see before twenty-nine stitches pulled the flaps back together again.

The commander of the Donauworth airfield, a Colonel old enough to be his grandfather, wrote a report that would accompany him back to his base, once the transport arrived.

Two of the Tupolev's had already flown on, the crashed aircraft cannibalised to get the other damaged aircraft back to their base.

Whilst Istomin waited for transport, he was accommodated in every way, the whole base treated him like a celebrity for his skill in landing the ravaged aircraft.

A liberated US army jeep was placed at his disposal and his first journey took him back to the equipment shed, where he found his new 'friends' and shared the same pleasures as before, but under more relaxed conditions.

Together, the three strolled towards the silent and cold ravaged metal that had once been the sleek Tupolev.

Curiosity took over, and they questioned the evidence of their eyes.

So, the counting started.

Istomin pulled rank, insisting that his total of three hundred and seven would be the official total of holes in his aircraft and his report, the two deferring to him with exaggerated gravity, but continuing to speak of two hundred and ninety-one as the definitive figure.

"Either way Comrades, the lady brought me home safely against the odds."

A bottle did the rounds, each man toasting the fine aircraft in cherry brandy, although the two Air Force men confessed later that they celebrated her stopping powers in the slide more than her aerodynamic prowess.

"Perhaps, Comrade Starshy Leytenant, perhaps you should write and tell them, eh?"

Momentarily confused, Istomin screwed his face up.

The Serzhant passed over the bottle to the other man and moved to the silent airframe, tapping on each word as he spoke.

"For the Soviet liberation of Oryol from the Fascist hordes, as named by the People of Oryol."

497

Istomin hadn't flown out with the rest of his men because of his head injury, and the problems it had brought with it.

Those problems manifested themselves now as his brain could not comprehend what the Serzhant meant.

"Sir, the good people of Oryol bought and paid for that fine aircraft, and entrusted it to you."

The fog in Istomin's mind started to clear.

"Comrade Starshy Leytenant, their efforts gave you a good aircraft, one that brought you home when others wouldn't have."

"I understand, Comrade Voronov. You are right."

The three wise monkeys shared another drink together, pausing only to pour a small amount over the aircraft's unofficial name.

"To Tanya!"

And with the sound of the tribute ringing in their ears, the three said their goodbyes.

1221 hrs, Tuesday, 4th September 1945, Birkenfeld, Germany.

Casualties among the medical personnel and their wounded charges had been extreme, the targeted attack on the Castle wiping out the sick and the fit in equal measure.

'Camerone' suffered few serious casualties in the bombing attack, but five legionnaires were killed by a delayed explosion as they dug deep in the rubble to rescue trapped medical personnel.

The air-raid cut short the exchange between Knocke and Kowalski, the former moving off to attend to his units and organise the rescue efforts with no thought for the GRU officer.

Kowalski, satisfied he had got his message across, departed the area to report to his superiors.

It was sometime before Knocke had an opportunity to discuss the day's events with De Montgomerie, and specifically report that the GRU probably had another source within the Legion Corps.

498

The location had proven to be perfect, the sole occupant of the island being a lighthouse keeper for the Canadian government, whose understood that his continued existence was all about his usefulness at keeping the constant white light alive in order to not attract undue attention.

The few families that had once lived on what was actually two small islands joined by a small spit of land had long departed, leaving behind buildings whose apparent dereliction was only cosmetic, the secret Soviet base now flourishing behind peeling paintwork and advancing flora.

The submarines that were savaging the eastern seaboard replenished here, sinking to the bottom during the day, only rising to the surface when darkness hurled its protective cloak over them.

The woods provided more excellent cover, and the base easily accommodated the personnel from the other Soviet mainland base, threatened when a US Army unit moved in dangerously close. Their presence alone forced it to swiftly close, and, as yet, the US had no idea that they had even been there.

What could not be squeezed into the submarines was dragged into the water and sunk, leaving no trace that the base had even existed, save for the deeply buried body of the old man who had so surprised the landing party on the day they arrived.

The disadvantage was clearly the increased travel time to intercept southern state routes, but the undersea wolves found themselves close enough to Boston and New York to ensure that there were rich pickings for everyone.

All was activity once the sun set, the imminent arrival of a supply boat stirring the base into action.

The normal routine was for approaching submarines to surface and use the lighthouse for a bearing, ensuring precise navigation into the small south side harbour.

This evenings visitor was a unique craft, the only one of three sisters to taste the open seas.

Once U-1702, the type XX U-Boat had been a stop-start project for the Kriegsmarine, a project finally brought to

499

completion in a German shipyard under the watchful eyes of Soviet overseers.

She was a 'Milchcow', a supply boat, capable of carrying fuel, munitions, fresh foods and any number of the requirements of the clandestine base.

Schnorkel equipped, U-1702, or the Morž as she was now known, had nearly completed her maiden voyage from her Baltic home to the eastern seaboard of the Americas.

Deliberately riding low in the water, her tanks only partially blown, the Morž was being guided into the harbour by her nervous captain, the closeness of the enemy and the vulnerability of his vessel testing his firmness and resolve.

Around the conning tower, the watchers kept watch, eyes glued to binoculars, ears pricked for the sound of an approaching aircraft, all ready to drop into the dark hatch in a moment.

The lighthouse's constant light drew the Milchcow forward with its promise of safety, the projected Atlantic storm starting to make itself known with the increasing wind and milky grey hue to the moonlit sky.

The Starshina of the watch stiffened, his ears gently suggesting that they had heard something out of the ordinary, such as a buzz of a bee or the hum of an engine, but the suggestion withered as quickly as it arrived, the brain scolding the ears and pointing to the nothingness in the relative silence of the choppy sea.

2219 hrs, Tuesday 4th September 1945, three miles south of Cape Negro Island, Nova Scotia.

K-136 was in some difficulty, one of her engines doing nothing but adding dead weight, even though the mechanics were doing their best to get the dormant lump of metal back on line.

The hint of a storm added to the concerns as K-136 struggled to get back to base.

Naval Lieutenant Carlton E. Wetherbridge was nursing his fragile craft steadily northwards to try and make the emergency base at Barrington, accepting that, for tonight, Yarmouth was beyond him and his crippled charge.

That the approaching storm gave him some advantage and started to give him a push was immediately overridden by the failure of the second engine and the total silence which accompanied its loss.

Running on battery power one of the wireless operators continued his running commentary to the Yarmouth Operations room, the K-136 sinking lower and dropping below the cloud cover and into the surreal grey light of the impending storm.

<u>2223 hrs, Tuesday, 4th September 1945, two miles south of Cape Negro Island, Nova Scotia.</u>

"Errr Skipper, there's something ahead of us. I caught a look in the sweep of the lighthouse."

The voice belonged to Royston James, the crew's youngest officer and co-pilot of K-136.

"Come on Roy, you know better than that. Proper report, you know the drill."

Lieutenant [jg] Royston James kicked himself for not getting it right on his first combat mission as a second-pilot, and composed himself quickly, mentally rehearsing his sighting report.

Wetherbridge, irked by the delay, was about to press the young man's buttons when the silence was broken by a properly composed report.

"Yeah, sorry skipper. Possible submarine spotted at one o'clock. Range one thousand yards. Low in the water, moving at slow speed."

As the first words hit the intercom system, the crew started into instant action, the radar operator unable to find the tell-tale blip of the submarine, its partially blown tanks keeping its radar profile out of the detectable range.

Wetherbridge rapped out his commands, preparing the attack.

"C'mon boys, give me those engines, or even just one. I need some manoeuvring here!"

The mechanics understood that all rested on them, and worked quickly to get at least one of the Pratt & Whitney's turning in time.

501

"Skipper, Hernandez here. That looks like a U-Boat to me, boss."

"Roger. Chief, check the reports pronto."

Senior Chief Petty Officer Sveinsvold swiftly double-checked the movement reports and came up blank.

"Sir, nothing in movement, nothing on submarines, and, this is in a prohibited area, Sir."

Sveinsvold was unequivocal, and Wetherbridge concurred.

"Captain to crew, standby to attack. Radio Op, message, attacking submarine, confirmed U-Boat, give our position and timings, ok?"

As if to honour the decision, the port engine slowly growled into life, and Wetherbridge felt the response in his control's immediately.

2225 hrs, Tuesday, 4th September 1945, two miles south of Cape Negro Island, Nova Scotia.

The noise, sudden and terrifyingly near, was heard by ears other those of the Starshina of the watch, and a number of frightened eyes swivelled to scan for the source of what was clearly an engine coming up to full revs.

The rear observer punched out a report.

"Unknown object approaching at eight hundred metres, due south, height one thousand."

"Job tvoyu mat!"

The captain had joined the watchers and overheard the Starshina's expletive as his eyes sought to discover what was unknown about whatever it was that was approaching.

"No time to dive, Kapitan! He's on top of us already!"

His lens filled with something soft and circular, his memory banks stimulated by the sight of a USN Dirigible moving into the attack.

'Blyad! He's right! No time to dive!'

"Gun crews close up! General alarm!"

The klaxon sounded and the orders started to fly, men transformed by the imminence of danger.

"Fire!"

The Quad 20mm started to hammer out at the airship, a K-Class Blimp, the slowness of its approach confusing the gunners, whose first shots missed badly.

Machine-guns deployed to the bridge joined in, also without success.

The Blimp approached steadily and the flak gunners adjusted carefully, walking their fire into the attacking craft and being rewarded with obvious damage, closely followed by telltale smoke and flame in the pod slung underneath the gas envelope.

A machine-gun from the Blimp replied, making similar hits on the easier target below.

K-136 was dying, as was Wetherbridge, his stomach punctured by shrapnel from exploding cannon shells, and robbed of his sight by the impact of small pieces of Perspex and metal from his destroyed instrument panel.

James struggled across to help his commander, inhibited by pieces of his former comrades and the slippery nature of their present condition.

Hernandez was unrecognisable, save for the chest tattoo, declaring undying love for a girl called Iolanta, whom he had once courted in Florida long before he had met his present wife, the mother of his five sons.

Sveinsvold had taken a bullet in the thigh, but it didn't prevent him from pouring fire from his .50cal into the hapless sailors below.

The remaining living members of the crew were the mechanics, their work on the engine forgotten in favour of fire fighting within the pod.

Sveinsvold fired the last of his belt and then quit the post, moving painfully to help knock down the growing fire.

The 20mm crew had been flayed by the last burst, all five men falling around their weapon, some screaming, some forever silent.

503

The Starshina shouted for medical support and men rushed forward to recover the injured.

Two of the lookouts hung lifelessly in their straps but his attention was split between the descending airship and his dying captain, the noisy coughing accompanied by spouts of blood as his ruined chest let the essential fluid of life escape from his ravaged body.

"Get the Captain below, get the wounded below. Standby to dive!"

One man rushed to the two dead lookouts but was ordered away.

"No time! Get the living below now!"

Submariners live on their wits and their ability to move at high speed, and in seconds the Starshina was alone amongst the dead.

Sparing a last look at the airship, he screamed his command.

"Dive! Dive! Dive!"

Pulling the hatch shut behind him, he made fast the clips and dropped down further, leaving another to seal the lower hatch.

The captain had not survived the hasty evacuation.

The ship's first officer had taken command, ordering a turn to starboard.

It was of no import.

The fire was out, although it had cost the Norwegian his uniform, his shirt to beat out the flames, his trousers that had caught alight when some cleaning fluid spilled and flared. His white body, bereft of even a hint of a tan line, exposed now in a way that he studiously avoided whenever presented with choice.

A naked man wearing nothing but shoes and socks would have been comical in any other surroundings but the charnel house of the blimp's control pod.

James was crying, his captain and friends dead around him, the smells of tortured metal mingling with the metallic odour of blood, creating a special hell for the new officer.

504

Sveinsvold had pulled Wetherbridge's corpse from the chair and virtually thrown James into his place.

"Shit, they're diving."

Turning back to his surviving officer, the wiry Norwegian spoke firmly.

"Fly it Sir, get us over those bastards so we can have some payback."

Although new to combat, James was composed enough to assess his aircraft, and took her under control as best he could, the obvious rents in her envelope suggesting that a landfall may be beyond them.

He thought quickly.

"Chief, let's bomb these fuckers and lose some weight. Nearest land is to the east there. I'll try for that."

Sveinsvold spared the young man a momentary look, appraising him in the light of his sudden calmness.

"Aye Aye, Skipper."

The drop would be by eye, the release by emergency hand-pull, as the auto controls had long since ceased to exist.

James, his concentration blotting out everything else, watched and waited, the convenient new holes in the floor making his assessment all the easier.

"Ready, ready..."

Sveinsvold tensed.

"Now Chief!"

Pulling hard on the cables, Sveinsvold was immediately rewarded with all the signs of a successful release, confirmed as James whopped at the immediate gain in height.

"Now, let's get the lady down on that island, Chief."

The K-class blimp carried four Mark 47 depth-charges, each stuffed with 350lbs of high-explosive, One on the money would have been enough to sink the Morž, four proved excessive and the Milchcow succumbed, bent rapidly as explosions either side of her hull exerted irresistible forces, the fractures immediately becoming catastrophic and opening her watertight compartments to the sea.

There were no survivors.

The three men threw what they no longer had use for overboard, gaining precious inches in height. The airship brushed the water and slid slowly up the short beach, bouncing on into the edge of a wood and transfixing herself on branches.

"Well done, Skipper, really well done."

And Sveinsvold meant every word, for it had been a touch and go thing, James' hitherto unknown skill saving the day and keeping the four of them out of the water.

Detailing the two mechanics to salvage all they could from the pod, Sveinsvold took in the surroundings.

The Chief had already spotted an old building that seemed fit for purpose, and suitable to ride out the Atlantic storm that was coming ever closer.

The envelope was deflating rapidly, the penetration of the heavy branches proving the final straw.

Suggesting to the young officer that he might like to police up maps and weapons, Sveinsvold checked out the radios, quickly satisfying himself that neither were repairable.

The emergency rations pack had been one thing thrown out, its identity lost in the enthusiastic work to gain height.

Sveinsvold jumped down and screwed up his eyes, seeking out the small wooden box whose contents could make their life bearable if found.

Some items were floating close inshore, and he decided to take advantage of his naked state and go swimming in an attempt to recover the hastily jettisoned foodstuffs.

The cold water closed over him, and he immediately found the leg wound restricted his ability to swim against the incoming tide.

James laid out the flare pistol and spare flares, ready in case they were needed to attract attention.

The mechanics had shifted everything into the nearest building, and were pleasantly surprised to find clean beds and tinned foodstuffs available.

James stood the two men down whilst he waited for the Chief to return.

The growing wind had a soporific effect on the three survivors and the two mechanics, cosily laid out on the beds, were soon asleep and snoring.

James awoke from his lighter slumber as the door opened, and he adjusted his eyes to take in the figure stood there.

The uniform was unknown to him, but the sub-machine gun told him all he needed to know.

He slowly raised his hands.

Sveinsvold was tiring now, even with the assistance of the incoming tide and the buoyancy offered by the recovered wooden box.

His legs felt numb, all except the wounded thigh, which screamed with every little movement.

He traded time for the absence of pain, permitting the tide to slowly bring him closer to safety.

On the beach he saw two men patiently watching him, two men who bore no resemblance whatsoever to any of his crew.

Both men looked nonchalantly back as the unmistakable sound of firing rose above the howl of the wind.

'What the fuck?'

His mind was suddenly in overdrive.

As he drifted closer in, the two men moved to the water's edge.

A third man arrived and received a report from the senior of the two watchers.

The words carried on the breeze, a language Sveinsvold knew well from his time fishing on Lake Michigan with the crews of the various émigré groups, in friendly competition for everything from fish to women.

'Russian?'

507

The Russian Marines, for that was what they were, seemed relaxed, and in a moment of clarity Sveinsvold understood.

'They think I'm from the sub.'

In a moment, he took hold of his dog tags and jerked hard, releasing them to float to the bottom unseen.

The recently arrived Russian chivvied the others into the water, and soon strong hands were grabbing at the exhausted Norwegian, pulling him from the water and up to the beach.

Bjarte had decided to play the wounded man role to the full, in order to buy himself time.

His coarse mumblings in Russian slipped easily from his tongue, learned when the latest Michigan fisherman's fad had been the ability to insult all others in their own language. They served to reassure the Russians that they had indeed been correct, and that this man was the sole survivor from their supply vessel.

On his arm he bore a tattoo, his wife's name, and this served to further confirm his 'friendly' nature to the Russian marines, for they did not know that Riga was his wife, a pleasant Norwegian-American mother of four, as well as the capital of Latvia.

A blanket appeared and was wrapped round the ivory white body, and he was gently carried up to the road where two bicycles were lashed together to provide a base for a pair of floorboards, which were similarly tied in place, ready for him to lie on.

Sveinsvold suppressed his horror as two corpses were dragged in front of him, the two mechanics shot down by sub-machine guns as they rose from their beds.

The Russians spoke sympathetically to him, kicking one of the dead men to express their sympathy for the loss these Americans had caused.

A group of a dozen Soviet naval marines were now gathered around the centre piece of the bike litter, waiting for the command to set off.

Two more Russians emerged from the tatty building, bringing with them a bloodied James.

508

Last out was the unit's commanding officer and owner of the submachine gun that had taken the lives of Sveinsvold's crew mates.

An NCO reported to the Captain with a salute, indicating the bike litter, which received a nod of approval from the officer.

James, spotting the chief but not understanding the predicament, became agitated, growling sounds coming from his ruined mouth.

"Ah Comrade Submariner, I am sorry for the loss of your comrades."

Surprisingly, his Russian was more than up to the job of understanding and he decided to risk conversation.

"Thank you, Comrade Kapitan," grateful to the NCO for speaking the man's rank earlier, "The Amerikanski fought well and had the luck this time."

Expecting a torrent of abuse to be aimed at the surviving American, the Captain was confused.

"But they killed all your comrades, and this one's life is forfeit."

Sveinsvold made his play.

"It is war, Comrade Kapitan. This time they won, and I will mourn the loss of my comrades while this one," he pointed an exaggeratedly accusing finger at the now quiet Lieutenant, "Spends the rest of his war as a prisoner."

The Captain frowned.

"I think not, Comrade Submariner. We have no need for prisoners here. Anyway, we must get back now. Prepare to march."

Hands took hold of the Chief and gently eased him onto the bike litter, occasionally obstructing his view of James, as the young officer was pushed to his knees between the two dead mechanics.

No sound escaped either man's lips. Not James', as the cold muzzle touched his hairline, nor Sveinsvolds', as part of his Lieutenant's face detached with the passing of the heavy Tokarev bullet.

509

As the party swiftly closed down upon the main base, the Soviets pushing the litter assumed that Sveinsvold's tears were those of pain.

The Captain, actually the second in command of the base security force, sent more men out into the night, tasked with sanitising the scene, and removing any trace of the blimp or its crew before the sun spread its wings once more.

They did an excellent job, with one small exception.

Great men are not always wise.

Job 32:9

Chapter 77 - THE HOUSE.

<u>1055 hrs, Wednesday, 5th September 1945, Hotel de Limbourg, Sittard, Holland.</u>

Crisp dropped heavily into the worn but comfortable armchair and surveyed the town square, acknowledging the arrival of a freshly brewed coffee with the politest of grunts.

Before his eyes was a hive of activity, vehicles and men coming and going, supplies and reinforcements arriving for distribution and allocation, all part of the process of getting the 'Screaming Eagles' back on their feet.

The 101st had been withdrawn from the fighting in Southern Bavaria, and had been moved back into the Netherlands, although Sittard was an unfamiliar billet for them.

One in five of the Eagles were still in Germany in one way or another. The casualties amongst the parachute and glider infantrymen had been higher than the other service arms, as they had borne the brunt of the Soviet attacks.

The newly displaced 4th Indian Division slipped into line in their stead, fresh from a forced march from Northern Italy. The 101st gathered themselves up and made the journey back into the reserve, where they could reconstitute and prepare themselves for whatever they were next told to do.

With a professional but exhausted eye, Crisp noted the men jumping down from the back of two 6x6's, each and every man sporting the patch of the 82nd US Airborne on his arm, their faces wearing the looks of men who had been exposed to hell.

It was these men that Crisp had come to find, as they were to be assimilated into his battalion, trained men to keep his jump qualifications up, but he worried if they were too much like damaged goods inside.

With a burst of energy that he somehow found within the empty recesses of his body, he sprang out of the chair, driving

511

himself out of the bar, down the steps into the square and across to the slowly assembling replacements.

Baldwin and Hawkes noticed the Acting Lieutenant Colonel on his way, and harangued the new arrivals into some semblance of order.

<u>1159 hrs, Wednesday, 5th September 1945, House of Commons Chamber, Palace of Westminster, England.</u>

The members of 'Hastings' were present in the spectator area, although neither seated together nor acknowledging each other.

Lord Southam's presence had been noted by more than one of those representatives on the floor below, his unexpected and unusual appearance being put down to the important statement the Prime Minister was just finishing.

The Speaker indicated that the leader of the Opposition could rise, and Churchill did so, to sounds of encouragement from both sides of the house.

Normally, Winston would provide the highlight of the day's business, and most in the gallery and, indeed, on the floor of the house, listened appreciatively to his summation of Attlee's delivery, and his dissection of its contents.

Only six people there understood that something momentous was about to happen, and the Speaker only knew part of it to ensure he did what he had to do.

The Member of Parliament for Woodford took his seat again, permitting Attlee to either address or rebuff the concerns raised.

The Prime Minister countered Churchill's points and reseated himself, prepared to be attacked a second time.

Churchill, being one of the six, decided not to rise again.

Murmurs of discontent grew on the opposition side of the House, the former prime minister clearly, and most unusually, passing off an opportunity to roast the present encumbent

Attlee made an error in interpreting Churchill's silence, believing that he had won the exchange. Despite the

512

confusion, his confidence received a boost, misplaced as it was, and perhaps contributing to what was to come.

The Speaker gave the floor to Clement Davies, the new incumbent Liberal Party leader, elected in after their recent drubbing at the polls.

He was similarly scathing about the Government's position on the war.

Those third, fourth and fifth in the know felt their anticipation building, as Davies took his seat to permit Attlee another opportunity for rebuttal.

The Prime Minister concluded his follow-up, still off-balance from Churchill's response, or lack of it.

The floor was open and, as had been requested, the Speaker called others to speak, before discharging the simple request the head of MI5 had put to him.

"The Honourable member for Wroughton."

The sixth man stood, receiving the usual recognition and adulation due a man who wore his country's highest bravery award.

Colonel Sir Fabian John Callard-Smith MP VC coughed gently and composed himself.

"Mr Speaker, I can only agree with my Right Honourable friend, the member for Woodford, and find myself asking the Prime Minister to reassure this house that the spirit necessary for a successful prosecution of this new war still exists in both himself and his cabinet colleagues."

The Labour benches howled in defence of their man, and Callard-Smith gave way to the rising Attlee.

"Mr Speaker, I can assure the Honourable Member for Wroughton that the Government is fully resolved to ensure the preservation of our Country and the Kingdom of our Sovereign, and that we will not shy away from any measure in order to secure the same. I just gave the same reply to the leader of his party, which reply obviously was acceptable, given the lack of further exchanges."

Four men smiled ever so gently, one wondered what he had just set in motion. The sixth pursued the plan.

The uniformed MP shot to his feet, and Attlee gave way instantly.

513

"Mr Speaker, can the Prime Minister clarify that, for the sake of an ill-educated old soldier," the laughs from both sides creating a more relaxed atmosphere instantly, just as he had intended, "What measures are presently being considered to secure the future of our country?"

Attlee smiled disarmingly.

"Mr Speaker, the House will, of course, understand that I am unable to be open in this setting, but that such matters are diligently discussed during the meetings of the Committee for Imperial Defence. But I can assure the House, and especially the Honourable member for Wroughton, that no stone is left unturned in the preservation of our nation state."

Callard-Smith pushed again.

"Mr Speaker, I thank the Prime Minister for his assurances thus far, but find myself in need of further clarification."

Those MP's with limited attention spans started to mentally drift away, mainly to thoughts of the lunch to come.

Callard-Smith continued.

"Can the Prime Minister confirm that there has been no discussion between the Allied powers regarding any negotiated settlement with the Soviet Union?"

As was the habit of cabinet members giving a swift answer, Attlee slid upright to the stand, gave his reply, and slid back in place on the front bench, all in one movement.

"I can confirm that is the case, Mr Speaker."

The retired Army officer coughed gently and composed himself.

"Mr Speaker, I would like to thank the Prime Minister for his responses. Might I ask one more question, and seek his report on the progress of the Honourable member for Mortimer's mission to the Court of Bernadotte?"

Some of those dreaming of lunch did a double-take, processing the question, and coming up none the wiser.

Others who were more attentive saw the Prime Minister pale.

The few that were astute understood that they were in the presence of history in the making.

Four others waited in delicious anticipation.

514

Attlee's delay in rising, spoke volumes.

"Mr Speaker, the Honourable member for Mortimer is presently returning from a trade mission to Sweden, and he will be making his own report in due course."

All in the house now realised that what was about to come to pass would be something special.

The stunned Attlee resumed his seat, his mind in turmoil.

The chamber was as silent as a morgue, no one's mind on anything but what was going on in front of their eyes. Indeed, people started to arrive as if by magic, the electricity in the air drawing them forward from the outer chambers like fish into a net.

Everyone's attention was on the Member of Parliament for Wroughton, as they waited for him to rise.

Callard-Smith stood and looked at the waiting Attlee. Very slowly, and with practised theatre, he tugged his jacket into place and slowly examined his VC. The Colonel then seemed to suddenly realise where he was and stiffened, addressing the Speaker, the central figure of authority, but fixing his gaze most firmly on the man across the floor.

"Mr Speaker, can the Prime Minister confirm that the report of the Honourable member for Mortimer will also include the results of his discussions with Soviet Foreign Ministry officials, and that a full transcript of the meeting, recording our tentative offer of a separate armistice, will be made available to this House?"

Every eye, every fibre, every sense, was directed at the Prime Minister, who almost seemed to shrink under the intense scrutiny.

He rose like a fox who knew that the pack had him cornered.

"Mr Speaker, I can confirm to the House that the Honourable member for Mortimer was secretly tasked with exploring certain possibilities, should the war situation become untenable, and that he will be reporting back to me personally on his return. I will then present the results to the Committee for Imperial Defence and, in due course, the King."

515

Attlee felt he should admit the fact and try to control it as best he could, not thinking straight, as he had just admitted openly misleading the House on the matter.

The attention again switched to Callard-Smith, by common assent, now appointed as the judge, jury and executioner in the matter.

"Mr Speaker, can the Prime Minister confirm that he acted with the compliance and agreement of the War Cabinet, and that the matter has been," he searched his memory for the quote and found it instantly, "As he so eloquently stated a few minutes ago, 'Diligently discussed by the Committee for Imperial Defence?' "

Attlee continued to sit, his mind seeking a solution, and Callard-Smith took the opportunity with both hands.

"No, Mr Speaker, the Prime Minister cannot confirm that. He cannot confirm that because his personal private secretary, the member for Mortimer, was sent to Sweden to negotiate terms for an armistice involving solely this country and our dominions. Without discussion with his Cabinet. Without the knowledge of the Committee for Imperial Defence."

His third thrust was delivered with open contempt, the sort that only a man of uniform, who has given his all for King and Country, can have for someone he sees as a traitor.

"Without regard to our fighting allies or the indomitable spirit of this island nation!"

The house remained silent, the tension, disgust and anger tangible in the very air they breathed.

With a sense of the dramatic, Callard-Smith picked up the tempo, and the volume.

"Look at his cabinet colleagues. See how appalled they are, the looks on their faces betray the facts of the matter here!"

He pointed at the opposition front benches, filled with horrified-looking men, either heads bowed in anguish or raised and focussed in anger upon the balding leader of the government.

"Without discussion, the Prime Minister has set our country on a path of betrayal from which we will not recover, unless it is stopped right now!"

The House members howled, venting their own pent-up passion at last, concentrating their anger on the same diminutive figure.

The Prime Minister rallied and took to his feet, using the dispatch box as a support, enduring the cries of derision until they faded away and he could be heard.

"Mr Speaker, I asked the Honourable member for Mortimer to meet with a delegation from the Soviet Foreign Ministry, in order explore the possibilities of a separate negotiated peace for the island."

Again he had to wait for the anger to subside.

"Mr Speaker, I did so in order to gauge the Soviet Union's stance and reaction, as well to ensure that all options were properly explored."

This time he did not just stop, but raised his voice over the throng.

"There has been no commitment at all, and there is no harm done."

The hounds bayed louder, drowning out his defence, and much was lost although, in truth, no-one cared.

"Mr Speaker, I considered it prudent to embark on this undertaking, in order to explore all options for the preservation of freedom in our lands, and in the wider world. I repeat, there has been no commitment to any course of action, neither would there be without full and frank consultations with all our allies, and within this house."

Attlee rallied, his argument convincing him of the astuteness of the move, although the continued jeers indicated that the opposite was true of his political colleagues from both sides of the house.

"Mr Speaker, by exploring all possibilities I have acted properly and within the remit of my office. No harm has been caused by this course of action and none will result, regardless of what approach His Majesty's Government now chooses to take."

The noise dropped away as Callard-Smith rose to his feet, holding a piece of paper given to him by someone who had supplied the hangman's noose for just this very moment.

"Mr Speaker, the Prime Minister informs the House that there is no harm done, but I fear that I must contest that."

517

Someone coughed gently and everyone heard it and suddenly realised that the spectator chamber was full, and yet in total silence.

"Mr Speaker, I hold here a draft copy of an urgent military report from the European Front, due to be placed before the Prime Minister this afternoon."

No-one bothered to ask where he had acquired it from.

"Mr Speaker, before I pass on the contents of this document, I am aware that the first of three meetings between the Honourable member for Mortimer and representatives of the Soviet Foreign Ministry and NKVD took place last Sunday at the private residence of Östen Undén, the Swedish Minister for Foreign Affairs. Subsequent meetings took place on Monday lunchtime and Tuesday morning."

Callard-Smith paused to permit the assembly to digest that information. More than one mind digested the introduction of the NKVD into the equation.

As the house descended into expectant silence, he played his part to the full.

The Colonel brandished the sheet of paper, high enough for all to see writing upon it, and for Attlee to imagine it as a headsman's axe destined for use on him.

"Mr Speaker, this military report indicates that since Sunday evening, a disproportionate number of air raids and ground attacks have been made against our forces, causing heavy casualties amongst our Army and Air Force units."

Pausing to theatrically consult one important section, Callard-Smith quoted to the assembly.

"If I may Mr Speaker, and I quote, *'Soviet ground forces have commenced uncoordinated and hasty attacks on a wide front, adopting an offensive system and style not previously seen, and not conforming to any pattern previously identified during the Second War."*

He risked a look at the crestfallen Attlee and continued.

"Prisoners have been taken and talk only of urgent orders from command authorities to maintain attacks on British units, regardless of position or cost, just to maintain pressure at all times."

518

A growing noise within the chamber gave him a moment's pause, and he held his hand up to appeal for silence.

"Activities in American and other Allied sectors conform to previous expectations and doctrine, so this report concludes that British and Dominion forces are being deliberately targeted."

He turned the report outwards, presenting the written word in Attlee's direction, his spare hand addressing the paper, highlighting the phrase he loudly and precisely repeated.

"This report concludes that British and Dominion forces are being deliberately targeted."

The noise returned, louder and more earnest in nature. Callard-brown concluded that the job was nearly done.

"Mr Speaker, the Prime Minister has acted alone and without the consent or agreement of the official organs of state, and in so doing has placed the lives of our fighting troops in extreme jeopardy!"

The headsman's axe fell, swift and deadly.

"Mr Speaker, as a direct result of the Prime Minister's ill-advised and unsanctioned mission to Sweden, the British and Dominion Army and Air Forces have suffered heinous losses in men and equipment. Far from, as he states, '*No harm being done*', this country and her dominions have experienced losses that are directly associated with the Soviet perception of our weakness created by," and Callard-Smith deliberately sought eye contact with the broken man opposite, "This lunacy!"

The hounds bayed, louder than before.

The beaten Attlee remained seated, suddenly a solitary figure, his Cabinet colleagues having moved away until he alone occupied the wooden front bench.

"Mr Speaker, this House must act now to ensure this betrayal is stopped and that our Allies are comforted and reassured as to our commitment to the shared cause of Freedom."

He pressed on, talking over the shouts of agreement.

"This House must take the appropriate steps to ensure that such betrayal of our national cause never happens again."

The shouting grew, almost screaming for what they all knew he was about to propose.

"Mr Speaker, we must also expunge ourselves of the cause of this problem and so, to that end, I propose an immediate vote of 'no confidence' in the Prime Minister and earnestly implore him to resign so that our Country may hold its head high again."

The shouts of 'Aye' dominated the next few minutes, each individual word driving home into Attlee as his political career collapsed around him.

Even hard-line supporters of the Labour leader chanted 'Out, Out, Out,' and pointed at him with open malice, condemning him for their perception of his treachery.

The members of 'Hastings' remained seated, awaiting the final section of their orchestration, the finale which would set Great Britain back on course, and start the process of healing the wounds that Attlee had opened wide.

In the chamber, the voices bounced back and forth, words lost as echoes clashed head-on with echoes, producing an unintelligible cacophony.

Through the wall of sound, a single word emerged, lightly at first, beaten aside in precedence by the noisier neighbours of '*out*' and '*shame*', but gradually gaining ground, until it burst forth into everyone's consciousness and the whole chamber, including those watching from the balcony, were joined together as one.

"Winston, Winston, Winston..."

British politics is not renowned for its swiftness but on this day it was hit by an inexorable whirlwind of targeted activity, commencing with Attlee's abject resignation, and completed by the forming of a 'war-duration' coalition government.

Winston Spencer-Churchill would not install himself in Downing Street until the following day, when the disgraced former incumbent left by the back door and the new Prime Minister could move in and start bringing his special energies to the battles ahead.

520

His first task was to address the peoples of Free Europe and Britain's allies, and explain honestly what had happened, and what now lay ahead for all.

<u>This is not the beginning of the end...</u>

List of figures

Appendix-1 German Republican Army - Units becoming available for Deployment from 13th August 1945 onwards.

German Republican Army units in Germany and the Low Countries.

71 Armee [assigned to US 12 Army Group.]

101 Korps
102 Korps.

116 Panzer Division. [101 Korps].
Panzer-Grenadiere Division 'Germany'. [101 Korps].
3 Fallschirmjager Division. [101 Korps].

319 Infanterie Division. [102 korps].
346 Infanterie Division. [102 korps].
159 Infanterie Division. [102 korps].
509 Panzer Abteilung. [102 korps].

German Republican Army Troops in Germany and the Low Countries [Unattached]

Panzer Brigaden 'Europa'
501 Schwere Panzer Abteilung
519 PanzerJager Abteilung
101 Nebelwerfer Abteilung
14 Nebelwerfer Regiment [Reduced]
551 Pioniere Regiment
Grenadiere Brigaden 'Berlin'
1st Gebirgsjager Brigaden

German Republican Air Force in Europe.

1 Jagdstaffel – FW-190 HE 162 [9]
2 Jagdstaffel – FW190 [15]
3 Jagdstaffel – Me 262 [11]
4 Kampfstaffel – HE 111 [9], AR 234c [6]
5 Kampfstaffel – JU 88 [13]
6 Nachjagdstaffel – JU 88 [7], FW ta 154 [5],
7 Jagdstaffel - FW190 [11], FW ta 152[3], DO 335 [6]
8 Nachtjagdstaffel – HE 219 [12]
9 Aufklarerstaffel –ME410 [5]
10 Kampfstaffel – HE177 [18]
11 ZBV Staffel – HS 129 [12]
12 Nachtjagdstaffel – JU88 [5], Ju388[4]
13 Storkampfstaffel – JU87 [7]
14 Transportstaffel – JU52 [14]
15 Transportstaffel – JU52 [13]
16 Jagdstaffel – FW190 [8]
17 Jagdstaffel – ME262 [7]
18 Kampfstaffel – HE111 [7]

[Figures in square brackets represent number of aircraft of type deemed fit for flight duties on date of report.]

German Republican Army Forces in Denmark.

1 Korps

160 Reserve Division. [1 Korps].
264 Infanterie Division [1 Korps].
Special Division Staff 614 [1 Korps].
233 Reserve Panzer Division. [1 Korps].
169 Infanterie Division [Attached to British 2nd Army.]

German Republican Army Forces in Norway.

HeeresGruppe 'Norwegen'

ArmeeAbteilung 'Narvik'
20 GebirgsArmee.

169 Infanterie Division. [HG Norwegen.]
196 Infanterie Division. [HG Norwegen.]
199 Infanterie Division. [HG Norwegen.]
7 Gebirgsjager Division. [HG Norwegen.]
296 Infanterie Division. [HG Norwegen.]
Special Division Staff 613. [HG Norwegen.]

Army Abteilung 'Narvik'

19 GebirgsKorps
71 Korps.

6 Gebirgsjager Division. [19 Gebirgskorps]
270 Coastal Defence Division. [19 Gebirgskorps]
193 Grenadiere Brigaden. [19 Gebirgskorps]
388 Grenadiere Brigaden. [19 Gebirgskorps]
210 Coastal Defence Division. [71 Korps]
230 Coastal Defence Division. [71 Korps]
140 ZBV Division. [71 Korps]

20 GebirgsArmee

33 Korps
36 Korps
70 Korps

274 Infanterie Division. [70 Korps]
280 Coastal Defence Division. [70 Korps]
613 ZBV Division. [70 Korps]
295 Infanterie Division. [33 Korps]
702 Infanterie Division. [33 Korps]
14 Air Force Field Division. [33 Korps]

Panzer Division 'Norwegen'. [36 Korps]
Maschinengewehr Ski Brigaden 'Finland'. [36 Korps]

German Republican Army troops in Norway [unattached].

203 Schwere Werfer Batterie
224 Schwere Werfer Batterie
Gebirgsjager Werfer Abteilung 10
162 Flak Brigaden
92 Flak Brigaden
152 Flak Brigaden
83 Flak Brigaden

German Republican Army Forces in Italy.

91 Armee

201 Korps
202 Korps

1 Fallschirmjager Division. [201 Kps]
5 Gebirgsjager Division. [201 Kps]
1 [Austrian] Bundes Division [201 Kps]

90 Grenadiere Division [202 Kps]
162 Infanterie Division [202 Kps]
334 Infanterie Division [202 Kps]

German Republican Army troops in Italy [unattached.]

504 Panzer Abtleilung.
129 Panzer Abtleilung.
15 [Motorised] Infanterie Regiment
67 Panzer-Grenadiere Regiment.
289 Grenadiere Regiment.
17 Nebelwerfer Regiment.
56 Nebelwerfer Regiment.
Artillerie Gruppe Italia.
Bundes [Austrian] Alpenjager Brigaden

Bibliography

Rosignoli, Guido
The Allied Forces in Italy 1943-45
ISBN 0-7153-92123

Kleinfeld & Tambs, Gerald R & Lewis A
Hitler's Spanish Legion - The Blue Division in Russia
ISBN 0-9767380-8-2

Delaforce, Patrick
The Black Bull - From Normandy to the Baltic with the 11th Armoured Division
ISBN 0-75370-350-5

Taprell-Dorling, H
Ribbons and Medals
SBN 0-540-07120-X

Pettibone, Charles D
The Organisation and Order of Battle of Militaries in World War II
Volume V - Book B, Union of Soviet Socialist Republics
ISBN 978-1-4269-0281-9

Pettibone, Charles D
The Organisation and Order of Battle of Militaries in World War II
Volume V - Book A, Union of Soviet Socialist Republics
ISBN 978-1-4269-2551-0

Pettibone, Charles D
The Organisation and Order of Battle of Militaries in World War II
Volume VI - Italy and France, Including the Neutral Conutries of San Marino,
Vatican City [Holy See], Andorra and Monaco
ISBN 978-1-4269-4633-2

Pettibone, Charles D
The Organisation and Order of Battle of Militaries in World War II
Volume II - The British Commonwealth
ISBN 978-1-4120-8567-5

Chamberlain & Doyle, Peter & Hilary L
Encyclopedia of German Tanks in World War Two
ISBN 0-85368-202-X

Chamberlain & Ellis, Peter & Chris
British and American Tanks of World War Two
ISBN 0-85368-033-7

Dollinger, Hans
The Decline and fall of Nazi Germany and Imperial Japan
ISBN 0-517-013134

Zaloga & Grandsen, Steven J & James
Soviet Tanks and Combat Vehicles of World War Two
ISBN 0-85368-606-8

Hogg, Ian V
The Encyclopedia of Infantry Weapons of World War II
ISBN 0-85368-281-X

Hogg, Ian V
British & American Artillery of World War 2
ISBN 0-85368-242-9

Hogg, Ian V
German Artillery of World War Two
ISBN 0-88254-311-3

Glossary.

.30cal machine-gun	Standard US medium machine-gun.
.45 M1911 automatic	US automatic handgun
.50 cal	Standard US heavy machine-gun.
105mm Flak Gun	Next model up from the dreaded 88mm, these were sometimes pressed into a ground role in the final days.
105mm LeFH	German light howitzer, highly efficient design that was exported all over Europe.
128mm Pak 44	German late war heavy anti-tank gun, also mounted on the JagdTiger and Maus. Long-range performance would have made this a superb tank killer but it only appeared in limited numbers.
2" Mortar	British light mortar.
39th Kingdom	See Kingdom39
50mm Pak 38	German 50mm anti-tank gun introduced in 1941. Rapidly outclassed, it remained in service until the end of the war, life extended by upgrades in ammunition.
6-pounder AT gun	British 57mm anti-tank gun, outclassed at the end of WW2, except when issued with HV ammunition.
6x6 truck	Three axle, 6 wheel truck.
Achilles	British version of the M-10 that carried the high velocity 17-pdr gun.

Addendum F	Transfer of German captured equipment to Japanese to increase their firepower and reduce logistical strain on Soviets
Alkonost	Creature from Russian folklore with the body of a bird and the head of a beautiful woman.
Anschluss	The 1938 occupation and Annexation of Austria by Germany.
Anthrax Bombs	Factual Japanese weapons, believed used against the Chinese by Unit 731. Both the US and Britain carried their own tests on the same weapon.
Aquitania, RMS	Cunard liner that saw service in both WW1 and WW2. She was scrapped in 1950.
BA64	Soviet 4x4 light armoured car with two crew and a machine-gun.
BAR	US automatic rifle that fired a .30cal round. It was an effective weapon, but was hampered by a 20 round magazine. Saw service in both World Wars, and many wars since.
Battle of the Bulge	Germany's Ardennes offensive of winter 1944
Bazooka	Generic name applied to a number of different anti-tank rocket launchers introduced into the US Army from 1942 onwards.

Beaufighter, Bristol	British twin-engined long-range heavy fighter, saw extensive service in roles from ground attack, night fighter, to anti-shipping strikes. Also served in the USAAF in its night fighter role.
BergePanther	German Panther tank converted or produced as a engineering recovery vehicle to service Panther Battalions in combat.
Bletchley Park	Location of the centre for Allied code breaking during World War two. Sometimes known as Station X.
Blighty	British slang term for Britain.
Boyes	.55-inch anti-tank rifle employed by the British Army but phased out in favour of the PIAT.
Brandenburghers	Rough German equivalent of commando, who were trained more in the arts of stealth and silent killing.
Bren Gun	British standard issue light machine-gun.
Browning Hi-Power	9mm handgun with a 13 round magazine, used by armies on both sides during WW2.
Buffalo	British term for the LVT or Amtrak, the amphibious tracked vehicle which became a mainstay of the Pacific War, and featured in all major Allied amphibious operations from Guadalcanal onwards.

Bund Deutsche Madel	The League of German Girls, young females' organisation of the Nazi Party.
C47	US development of the DC3, known in British operations as the Dakota. Twin-engined transport aircraft.
Camel	US cigarette brand
Caudillo	Political-military leader, in this case, referring to Franco.
Cavalry	The German army had cavalry until the end, all be it in small numbers. The SS had two such divisions, the 8th and 22nd.
Chekist	Soviet term used to describe a member of the State Security apparatus, often not intended to be complimentary.
Chesterfield	American cigarette brand.
Chickamauga	A battle in the American Civil War, fought on 19th to 20th September, 1863. It was a Union defeat of some note, and second only to Gettysburg in combined casualties.
Colibri	High-class men's accessories producer, initially specialising in cigarette lighters.
Colloque Biarritz	The fourth symposium based at the Château du Haut-Kœnigsbourg.
Combat Command [CC]	Formation similar to an RCT, which was formed from all-arms elements within a US Armored Division, the normal dispositions being CC'A', CC'B' and CC'R', the 'R' standing for reserve.

Corvette	Small patrol and escort vessel used by Allied navies throughout WW2.
Court of Bernadotte	The Court of the Swedish Royal Family.
Deuxieme Bureau	France's External Military Intelligence Agency that underwent a number of changes post 1940 but still retained its 'Deux' label for many professionals.
Douglas DC-3	Twin-engine US transport aircraft, also labelled C-47. [Built by the Russians under licence as the Li-2]
DP-28	Standard Soviet Degtyaryov light machine-gun with large top mounted disc magazine containing 47 rounds.
Duke of York	British battleship of the King George V class. Survived WW2 and was scrapped in 1957.
Edelzwicker	Alsatian wine that is a blend of noble and standard grapes, and as a result is sometimes hit and miss, sometimes superb.
Elektroboote	A Type XXI U-Boat
Fallschirmjager	German Paratroops. They were the elite of the Luftwaffe, but few Paratroopers at the end of the war had ever seen a parachute. None the less, the ground divisions fought with a great deal of elan and gained an excellent combat reputation.
Fat Man	Implosion-type Plutonium Bomb similar in operation to 'The Gadget'.

FBI	Federal Bureau of Intelligence, which was also responsible for external security prior to the formation of the CIA.
FFI	Forces Francaises de L'Interieur, or the French Forces of the Interior was the name applied to resistance fighters during the latter stages of WW2. Once France had been liberated, the pragmatic De Gaulle tapped this pool of manpower and created 'organised' divisions from these, often at best, para-military groups. Few proved to be of any quality and they tended to be used in low-risk areas.
FG42	Fallschirmgewehr 42, a hybrid 7.62mm weapon which was intended to be both assault rifle and LMG.
Firefly, Fairey	British single-engined carrier aircraft, used as both fighter and anti-submarine roles.
Firefly, Sherman V	British variant of the American M4 armed with a 17-pdr main gun, which offered the Sherman excellent prospects for a kill of any Panzer on the battlefield.
Fizzle	Failure of a nuclear device to properly explode, but which can result in radioactive product being distributed over a sizeable local area.
Flak	Flieger Abwehr Kanone, anti-aircraft guns.

Fuhrer-Begleit-Brigaden	German army armoured formation, formed from the Wehrmacht's Fuhrer Escort. Considered an elite formation, it was part of the Grossdeutschland detachments.
Gamayun	Creature from Russian folklore with the body of a large bird and the head of a beautiful woman.
GAVCA	Grupo de Aviação de Caça [Portuguese] Translated literally means 'fighter group', the 1st GAVCA serving within the Brazilian Expediationary Force.
GAZ	Gorkovsky Avtomobilny Zavod, Soviet producers of vehicles from light car through to heavy trucks.
Gebirgsjager	German & Austrian Mountain troops.
Gestapo	GeheimeStaatsPolizei, the Secret Police of Nazi Germany.
Gitanes Mais	French cigarette brand
GKO	Gosudarstvennyj Komitet Oborony or State Security Committee, the group that held complete power of all matters within the Soviet Union.
Grease gun	US issue submachine-gun, designated the M3. Cheaper and more accurate than the Thompson.
Green Devils	Nickname for the German Airborne troops, the Fallschirmjager.

Großdeutschland	Literally, 'Greater Germany', the elite Grossdeutschland Division was not an SS formation although it wore a cuff title on its right arm.
GRU	Glavnoye Razvedyvatel'noye Upravleniye of Soviet Military Intelligence, fiercely independent of the other Soviet Intelligence agencies such as the NKVD.
Halifax, Handley Page	British four-engined heavy bomber
Hapsburg	European monarchy that ruled Austro-Hungary amongst other European states.
Harai Ritual	Harai or Harae are rituals for purifying and removing factors such as sin, uncleanliness and bad luck from objects, places, and people.
Hauptmann	Equivalent of captain in the German army.
Hellcat Tank-Destroyer, M18.	US tank destroyer armed with a 76mm gun. Capable of high speed.
Hero of the Soviet Union award	The Gold Star award was highly thought of and awarded to Soviet soldiers for bravery, although the medal was often devalued by being given for political or nepotistic reasons.
Hitler Youth [Hitler Jugend]	Young males' organisation of the Nazi Party.
Hohenzollern	Noble house of Germany, Prussia, and Romania.

Horsch 108	German transport that served throughout WW2 in a variety of roles from officer's car to ambulance.
IL-4, Ilyushin.	Soviet twin-engined medium bomber.
Infected Fleas	Factual Japanese weapon. A load of infected fleas were dropped on Quzhou in 1940, resulting n the deaths of over 2000 people.
IR	Infra-red, a technology that the Germans pursued late in the war.
IS-II	Soviet heavy tank with a 122mm gun and 1-3 mg's
IS-III	Iosef Stalin III heavy tank, which arrived just before the German capitulation and was a hugely innovative design. 122mm gun and 1-2 mg
IS-III	Iosef Stalin tank, armed with the fearsome 122mm gun.
Jeep	½ Ton 4x4 all terrain vehicle, supplied in large numbers to the Western Allies and the Soviet Union.
Job tvoyu mat	With apologies, this is translated in a number of ways, and can mean anything of the same ilk from 'Gosh' through to 'Fuck your mother."
Kalibr	Codename of David Greengrass, US Army Sergeant who was a Soviet Spy.
Kangaroo	Allied infantry carrier, either converted from a tank, mainly M4 Shermans and M7 Priest SP's, or purpose built from the Canadian RAM tank.

Kar98K	German standard issue bolt action rifle.
Katana	The main sword of a samurai or Japanese officer.
Katorga	Soviet penal system, also accepted as a noun for a place of hard servitude.
Katyn	1940 Massacre of roughly 22,000 Polish Army officers, Police officers and intelligentsia perpetrated by the NKVD, Site was discovered by the German Army and much propaganda value was made, although in reality there was no sanction against the USSR for this coldblooded murder.
Katyusha	Soviet rocket artillery weapon capable of bringing down area fire with either 16, 32 or 64 rockets of different types.
Kavellerie	German translation of Cavalry.
K-Class Blimp	US Airship [dirigible] used in reconnaissance and anti-submarine roles
Kerch	Soviet peninsular that juts out into the Black Sea, known in English as the Crimea.
Ki-84	Japanese single-engined fighter aircraft, considered to be the finest fighter in the Japanese inventory.
King Tiger tank	German heavy tank carrying a high-velocity 88m gun and 2-3 machine guns.

Kingdom 39	The Fairytale Kingdom in Russian Folklore.
Kradschutzen	Motorcycle infantry, term also applied to reconnaissance troops.
Kreigie	US slang for a German prisoner of war.
Kriegsmarine	German Navy
Kriegsspiels	Wargames
LA-7	Single-engine Lavochkin fighter aircraft, highly thought of despite poor maintenance history.
Lavochkin-5	Soviet single-engined fighter aircraft.
Leutnant	German Army rank equivalent to 2nd Lieutenant.
Liebfraumilch [Liebfrauenmilch]	German semi-sweet white wine.
Lightning, Lockheed, P38	US twin-engined fighter, most successfully used in the Pacific Theatre.
Lisunov Li-2	Soviet licenced copy of the DC-3 twin-engine transport aircraft,
Little Boy	Uranium based fission bomb.
Luftwaffe	German Air Force
Lysander, Westland.	British single engine monoplane designed for Liaison activities, but best known for its use in ferrying agents into Occupied Europe.
M-10	Known as the Wolverine, this US tank destroyer carried a 3" gun with modest performance. It was subsequently upgunned in British service, and the more potent 17-pdr equipped vehicles became known as Achilles.

M13/40	Italian light tank with a 47mm gun and 3-4 machine-guns.
M-16 half-track	US half-track mounting 4 x .50cal machine-guns in a Maxon mount. For defence against aircraft at low level it was particularly effective against infantry.
M1Carbine	Semi-automatic carbine that fired a .30 cal round, notorious as being underpowered.
M20	US 6x6 Armoured utility car, which was basically an M8 without the turret.
M21	M3 halftrack with an 81mm mortar mount, providing mobile fire support.
M24 Chafee	US light tank fitted with a 75mm gun and 2-3 machine-guns.
M26 Pershing	US Heavy tank with a 90mm gun and 2-3 machine-guns. Underpowered initially, it had little chance to prove itself against the German arsenal.
M3 Halftrack	US standard half-track normally armed with 1 x .50cal machine-gun and capable of carrying up to 13 troops
M3A1 sub-machine gun	Often known as the Grease Gun, issued in .45 or the rarer 9mm calibres with a 30 round magazine.
M4A4	US medium tank, last of a number of developments, Armament ranged from 75mm through 76mm to 105mm Howitzer.

M5 HST	US fully-tracked high-speed artillery prime mover.
M5 Stuart	US light tank equipped with a 37mm gun, and capable of high speed.
M8 Greyhound	6x6 Armoured car with 37mm main gun and 1-2 machine-guns.
Maior	German Army rank equivalent to Major.
Manhattan Project	Research and development project aimed at producing the first atomic bomb.
Market-Garden	Montgomery's failed plan to drop paratroopers and secure river crossings into Northern Germany, thus ending the war by Christmas.
Maskirova	Soviets have a fondness for deception and misdirection and Maskirova is an essential of any undertaking.
Matrose	German naval term for a common sailor.
Mauthausen	More properly known as Mauthausen-Gusen Concentration Camp, the camp grew to oversee a complex of Labour camps throughout the area. The high estimate of persons dying within the Mauthausen camp system is 320,000.
Maxon mount	A single machine gun mounting which could be installed on a half-track of a trailer, by which means 4 x .50cal were aimed and fired by one man.

Merville Battery	German gun battery assaulted by the British 9th Para Battalion on D-Day.
Meteor F3, Gloster	British twin-engined jet fighter, which first flew in 1943.
Metgethen	Scene of a successful German counter-attack in 1945, where evidence of Soviet atrocities against the civilian population was uncovered.
MG.08	German WW1 machine gun. Many survivors were employed during WW2.
MG34	German standard MG often referred to as a Spandau.
MG42	Superb German machine gun, capable of 1200rpm, designed to defeat the Soviet human wave attacks. Still in use to this day.
Mills Bomb	British fragmentation hand grenade.
Minox	Gained notoriety as the first 'miniature' spy camera.
Mitsubishi Ki-46	Japanese twin-engined reconnaissance aircraft.
Mlad	Codename of Theodore Hall, Nuclear Physicist, and Soviet Agent.
Molotov Cocktail	Simple anti-tank/vehicle weapon, consisting of a bottle, a filling of petrol, and a flaming rag. Thrown at its target the bottle shattered on impact and the rag did the rest.
Moscow Crystal Vodka	Highest quality triple distilled vodka.
Moselle	Mainly white wine originating from areas around the River of the same name.

Mosin-Nagant	Russian bolt-action infantry rifle.
Mosquito	DH98 De Havilland Mosquito was a multi-purpose wooden aircraft, much envied by the Luftwaffe.
Mosquito Mk NF30, De Havilland	British twin-engined night fighter.
Mosquito Mk VI	British twin-engined fighter-bomber.
Mosquito Mk XXV, De Havilland	British twin-engined light bomber.
MP-40	German standard issue submachine-gun.
Mustang, North American	P51 Mustang, US single seat long-range fighter armed with 6 x .50cal machine-guns.
Nagant pistol	Standard Soviet revolver, very rugged and powerful using long case 7.62mm ammunition.
Natzwiller-Struhof	Concentration camp in Alsace.
Nebelwerfer	German six-barrelled mortar weapon, literally translated as 'Smoke Thrower' and known to the Allies as the Moaning Minnie, ranging up to 32cms in diameter.
NKGB	Narodny Komissariat Gosudarstvennoi Bezopasnosti, the Soviet Secret Police, separated from the NKVD in 1942 and absorbed once more in 1946.
NKVD	Narodny Komissariat Vnutrennikh Del, the People's Commissariat for Internal Affairs.

Normandie Squadron [Normandie-Niemen Regiment]	French Air force group that grew to three squadrons and served on the Russian Front throughout WW2.
OFLAG XVIIa	Offizierslager or OfLag No 17A, prisoner of war camp run by the Germans for officer detainees.
Operation Anvil	August 1944 landing in Southern France.
Operation Apple Pie	US project to capture German officers with specific knowledge about the Soviet Union's industry and economy.
Operation Kurgan	Soviet joint-operation to employ paratroopers, Naval Marines, NKVD agents and collaborators to attack and neutralise airfields, radar, communications and logistic bases throughout Europe. Subsequently enlarged to include assassinations of Allied senior officers.
Operation Paperclip	OSS project to recruit German Scientist to the Allied cause post May 1945.
Operation Sumerechny	Soviet plan to remove German leadership elements from their prisoners. All officer ranks from captain upwards were to be executed.
Operation Unthinkable	Study ordered by Churchill to examine the feasibility of an Allied assault on Soviet held Northern Germany.

Operation Varsity	The largest single airborne operation of WW2, undertaken in in March 1945, Varsity involved dropping over 16,000 paratroopers to the east of the Rhine.
OSS	US Intelligence agency formed during 2, The Office of Strategic Services was the predecessor of the CIA, and was set up to coordinate espionage activities in occupied areas.
OT/34	T34 variant with a medium flamethrower in the hull.
P.O.L.	Petrol, oil and lubricants.
Panther	German medium tank, considered by many to be the finest tank design of WW2. Armed with a high-velocity 75mm, it could stand its ground against anything in the Allied arsenal.
Panther Tank	German heavy-medium tank carrying a high-powered 75mm gun and 2-3 machine-guns, considered by many to be the finest all-round tank of World War 2.
Panzer IV	German tank, which served throughout the war in many guises, mainly with a 75mm gun.
Panzer V	See Panther Tank
Panzer VI	See Tiger Tank
Panzerfaust	German single use anti-tank weapon. Highly effective but short ranged.
Panzerjager	Antitank troop[s] [German]
Panzertruppen	The German tank crews.

PanzerVIb	See King Tiger Tank
PE-2	The Soviet Petlyakov PE-2 was a twin-engine multi-purpose aircraft considered by the Luftwaffe to be a fine opponent.
PEM scope	Soviet sniper scope for Mosin and SVT rifles.
PIAT	Acronym for Projector, Infantry, Anti-tank, the PIAT used a large spring to hurl its hollow charge shell at an enemy.
Plan Chelyabinsk	Soviet assault plan utilising lend-lease equipment in Western Allies markings.
Plan Diaspora	Soviet overall plan for assaulting in the East and for supporting the new Japanese Allies.
Plan Kurgan	Soviet joint-operation to employ paratroopers, Naval Marines, NKVD agents and collaborators to attack and neutralise airfields, radar, communications and logistic bases throughout Europe. Subsequently enlarged to include assassinations of Allied senior officers.
Plan Zilant	The Soviet paratrooper operations against the four symposiums, detailed as Zilant-1 through Zilant-4.
PLUTO	Acronym for 'Pipeline-under-the-ocean', which was a fuel supply pipe that ran from Britain to France, laid for D-Day operations and still in use at the end of the war.

Pointe-du-Hoc	Cliff face and bunker position near Omaha beach, Normandy, assaulted by US 2nd Ranger Battalion on D-Day.
PPD	Soviet submachine gun capable of phenomenal rate of fire. Mostly equipped with a 72 round drum magazine but 65 rounds were normally fitted to avoid jamming. It was too complicated and was replaced by the PPSH.
PPS	Simple Soviet submachine gun with a 35 round magazine.
PPSH	Soviet submachine gun capable of phenomenal rate of fire. Mostly equipped with a 72 round drum magazine but 65 rounds were normally fitted to avoid jamming.
Pravda	Leading newspaper of the Soviet Union, Pravda is translated as 'Truth'.
PS84	Passenger Aircraft built at factory 84, the initial designation of the Li-2 transport aircraft.
PTAB	Each Shturmovik could carry four pods containing 48 bomblets, or up to 280 internally. Each bomblet could penetrate up to 70mm of armour, enough for the main battle tanks at the time.
PU scope	Soviet sniper scope for Mosin and SVT rifles.
Puma	German eight-wheel armoured car with a 50mm and enclosed turret.

Ranger, USS	US Aircraft carrier [CV-4], Survived WW2 and was scrapped in 1947.
RCT	Regimental Combat Team. US formation which normally consisted of elements drawn from all combatant units within the parent division, making it a smaller but reasonably self-sufficient unit. RCT's tended to be numbered according the Infantry regiment that supplied its fighting core.[See CC for US Armored force equivalent.]
Red Devils	Nickname for the British Airborne troops, the Red berets.
Red Star	Standard issue Soviet military cigarettes.
Rodina	The Soviet Motherland.
Schmuck	A Jewish insult meaning a fool of one who is stupid. It also can literally mean the foreskin that is removed during circumcision.
Schwere Panzer Abteilung	Heavy tank battalion [German]
SDKFZ 234	German eight-wheel armoured car equipped with a range of weapons, the most powerful of which was a 75mm HV weapon. Of the four variants, the Puma with its 50mm and enclosed turret is probably the most well known.
Senninbari	Japanese good luck charm given to soldiers, rooted within the Shinto religion. Each one carried 1000 stitches, each from a different woman. Typically, they were waist belts but could also be headbands, vests and flags.

Sherman [M4 Sherman]	American tank turned out in huge numbers with many variants, also supplied under lend-lease to Russia.
Shinhoto Chi-Ha	Upgraded Japanese battle tank, based on the Chi-Ha. The Shinhoto had a 47mm gun superior to the 57mm in its forebear.
Shinto	Japanese religion [Shintoism].
Shturmovik	The Ilyushin-2 Shturmovik, Soviet mass-produced ground attack aircraft that was highly successful.
ShVAK	Soviet 20mm auto cannon that equipped aircraft, armoured cars, and light tanks.
Skat	German card game using 32 cards.
SMLE	Often referred to s the 'Smelly', this was the proper name of the Short, Magazine, Lee-Enfield rifle.
SOE	British organisation, Special Operations Executive, which conducted espionage and sabotage missions throughout Europe.
Spitfire, Supermarine.	British single-engined fighter aircraft.
SS-Hauptsturmfuhrer	SS equivalent of captain.
St Florian	Patron saint of Upper Austria, Linz, chimney sweeps, and firefighters.
ST44 [MP43/44]	German assault rifle with a 30 round magazine, first of its generation and forerunner to the AK47.

Standard HDM .22 calibre pistol	Originally used by OSS, this effective .22 with a ten round magazine is still in use by Special Forces throughout the world.
Starshina	Soviet rank roughly equivalent to Warrant Officer first Class.
Station 'X'	See Bletchley Park entry.
STAVKA	At this time this represents the 'Stavka of the Supreme Main Command', comprising high-ranked military and civilian members. Subordinate to the GKO, it was responsible for military oversight, and as such, held its own military reserves which it released in support of operations.
Sten	Basic British sub-machine gun with a 32 round magazine. Produced in huge numbers throughout the 40's.
Stroh rum	Austrian spiced rum.
Studebaker	US heavy lorry supplied to the Soviets under lend-lease.
Studebaker	2.5 ton truck built in USA and USSR [under licence] and often used as platforms for the Katyusha.
Stuka [Junkers 87]	Famous dive-bomber employed by the Luftwaffe.
SU-76	76mm self-propelled gun used as artillery and for close support.
Sunderland	British four-engined flying boat, used mainly in maritime reconnaissance and anti-submarine roles.

SVT40	Soviet automatic rifle with a 10 round magazine.
Symposium Biarritz	Utilisation of German expertise to prepare wargame exercises for allied unit commanders to demonstrate Soviet tactics and methods to defeat them.
T.O.E.	Table of Organisation and Equipment, which represents what a unit should consist of.
T/34	Soviet medium tank armed with a 76.2mm gun and 2 mg's.
T/34-85 [T34m44]	Soviet medium tank armed with an 85mm gun and 2 mg's.
T-44 [100]	Soviet medium tank, produced at the end of WW2, which went on to become the basis for the famous T54/55. Armed mainly with the same 85mm as in the T3485, a few were fitted with the devastating 100mm D-10 gun.
T-70	Soviet light tank with two crew and a 45mm gun.
Tallboy	British designed earthquake bomb, containing 12,000lbs of high explosive. It weighed five tone and proved effective against the most hardened of targets.
Thompson	.45 calibre US submachine-gun, normally issued with a 20 or 30 round magazine [although a drum was available.]
Tiger I	German heavy battle tank armed with the first 88mm gun, capable of ruling any battlefield when it was introduced in 1942.

Tokarev	Soviet 7.62mm automatic handgun [also known as TT30] with an 8 round magazine.
Trimbach	Quality Alsatian wine.
TU-2, Tupolev	Soviet twin-engined medium bomber. Extrememly successful design that peformed well in a variety of roles, the TU-2 is considered one of the best combat aircraft of WW2.
Type 97 Chi-Ha	Japanese main battle tank, armed with a 57mm gun.
Type XXI submarine	The most technologically advanced submarine of the era, produced in small numbers by the Germans and unable to affect the outcome of the war.
Typhoon, Hawker.	RAF's most successful single seater ground attack aircraft of World War Two, which could carry anything from bombs through to rockets.
U-Boat Type XX	30 such U-Boats were planned, but none produced during WW2. They were intended as pure supply boats, shorter than the Type XB but with a wider beam.
U-Boat Type XXI	Advanced U-Boat design capable of extended underwater cruising at high speed.
UHU	German 251 halftrack mounting an infra-red searchlight, designed for close use with infra-red equipped Panther units.
Unicorn, HMS	British light aircraft carrier and aircraft repair ship, seeing service throughout WW2. Scrapped in 1959.

USAAF	United States Army Air Force.
Ushanka	Fur hat with adjustable sides.
Vampir	German term for the ST44 equipped with an infra-red sight, also used to refer to the operators of such weapons.
Venona Project	Joint US-UK operation to analyse Soviet message traffic
Vichy	Name of the collaborationist government of defeated France.
Vickers Machine-Gun	British designed machine-gun of WW1 vintage. Extremely reliable .303 calibre weapon, standard issue as a heavy machine-gun.
Vitruvian man	Da Vinci's sketch of a man with legs and arms splayed.
Wacht am Rhein	Literally, 'Watch on the Rhine', a codename used to mask the real purpose of the German build-up that became the Ardennes Offensive in December 1944.
Waffen-SS	There will always be much debate over these troops. Ideologically driven, politically inspired, pathological killers with an unshakable faith in the superiority of the Aryan race or highly motivated troops with an incredible 'esprit de corps'? Whatever your point of view, the military achievements of the SS Soldiers were without parallel in WW2. That others wore the same uniform as they tended the camps and satisfied the despicable agendas of the Nazi party has, in many ways, tarnished the Waffen-SS. None the less, they

	have their own crimes to pay for, as do all who wore a uniform in WW2, for no side came away with clean hands.
Walther P38	German 9mm semi-automatic pistol with an eight round magazine.
Wanderer W23 Cabriolet	German vehicle designed for civilian use, sometimes pressed into military service, particularly as a staff car.
Wehrmacht	The German Army
Yakolev-9	Soviet single-seater fighter aircraft that was highly respected by the Luftwaffe.
Yakolev-9U	Soviet single-engined fighter aircraft, probably the best Soviet high-altitude fighter.
Zilant	Legendary creature in Russian folklore somewhat like a dragon
ZIS3	76.2mm anti-tank gun in Soviet use.
ZSU-37	Soviet light self-propelled anti-aircraft vehicle, mounting a 37mm gun.
Zuikaku	Japanese fleet aircraft carrier of the Shokaku class. Present at Pearl Harbor, she succumbed to air attack during the Battle of Leyte Gulf, sinking on 25th October 1944.

About the Author.

Colin Gee was born on 18th May 1957 in Haslar Naval Hospital, Gosport, UK, spending the first two years of his life at the naval base in Malta.

His parents divorced when he was approaching three years of age, and he went to live with his grandparents in Berkshire, who brought him up.

On 9th June 1975 he joined the Fire Service and, after a colourful career, retired on 19th May 2007, having achieved the rank of Sub-Officer, Watch Commander, or to be politically correct for the ego-tripping harridans in HR, Watch Manager 'A'.

After thirty-two years in the Fire Service, reality suddenly hit, and Colin found himself in need of a proper job!

As of today, Colin is permanently employed doing night shifts for NHS Out of Hours service.

At this moment in time Colin has a wife, two daughters, one step-daughter, two step-sons and two grandsons, called Lucas and Mason, who are avid Manchester United fans, although neither know it yet.

Four cats complete the home ensemble.

He has been a wargamer for most of his life, hence the future plans for a Red Gambit wargaming series.

In 1992 Colin joined the magistracy, having wandered in from the street to ask how someone becomes a beak. He served until 2005. The experience taught him the true difference between justice and the law, the former being what he would have preferred to administer.

Red Gambit was first researched over ten years ago, but work and life changes prevented it from blossoming.

Now it has become six books, instead of one, as more research is done and more lines of writing open themselves up.

Though the books are fiction, fact is a constant companion, particularly within the biographies, where real-life events are often built into the lives of fictitious characters.

Colin writes for the pleasure it brings him and, hopefully, the reader. The books are not intended to be modern day 'Wuthering Heights' or 'War and Peace'. They contain a story that Colin thinks is worth the telling, and to which task he set his inexperienced hand. The biographies are part of the whole experience that he hopes to bring the reader.

Enjoy them all, and thank you for reading.

Extras available on the website www.redgambitseries.com and also on www.facebook.com - group name 'Red Gambit'. https://www.facebook.com/#!/groups/167182160020751/

Please register and join the group or the forums. If on the website, remember only to visit the areas relevant to your book or you may pick up spoilers.

'Stalemate' - the story continues.
Read the first chapter of 'Stalemate' now.

For all those that take up the sword shall perish by the sword.

Matthew 26:52

Chapter 78 - THE TERROR

1017hrs, Friday 7th September 1945, Headquarters, Red Banner Forces of Europe, Kohnstein, Nordhausen, Germany.

Colonel-General Malinin consumed the GRU report dealing with the dishonoured British peace negotiations.

"Your thoughts, Comrade?"

Zhukov sat peeling an apple, having already read the document.

"I see no reason to doubt her report, Comrade Marshall. Even though it is hard to imagine such an act without a mandate, our Nazarbayeva sets out the reasons quite clearly, and the reinstatement of Churchill seems to bear out all she states."

"So, we lost many men for no good reason, Malinin. Bagramyan is hopping mad and threatens our lives, so I'm told."

Whilst Zhukov delivered that with humour, both men understood that the old Armenian Marshall was extremely upset at having lost so many good men for something that, in the end, produced no tangible advantage.

In actual fact, it had produced some advantages, in that the Britsh and Dominion formations had been given a very hard time and, by all accounts, were exhausted beyond measure.

That at least three times as many casualties had been suffered by the attacking forces was of no comfort to the British, but they had not folded under the pressure and now, with the return of Churchill, they seemed almost inspired to higher things.

"We must send the Armenian Fox some more troops. Draw up a list of units we can release for his use."

Malinin raised an eyebrow at his superior, knowing he was husbanding his reserve forces for the right moment.

By way of reply, Zhukov adopted a conspiratorial tone to lighten the moment, but he didn't carry it off.

"Just enough to shut him up, Comrade. Just enough to shut him up, and not a soldier more."

Malinin looked at his commander, realising for the first time that the strain of command was laying heavier than normal on his shoulders.

1957hrs, Friday 7th September 1945, Junction of Routes 317 & 323, East of Unterankenreute, Germany.

The 4th Indian Division had given up Bergatreute and Wolfegg under pressure, dropping back into the woods to the west, protecting the major highways that led to the remaining parts of South-Western Germany still under Allied control.

They had yet to take serious casualties, their retreat caused by logistical problems that saw some frontline units without more than a few minutes worth of ammunition.

Food was also just beginning to become an issue, the restrictions of their faiths meant that it was less easy to scavenge or accept gifts from the friendly population.

A serious enemy thrust on Vogt had been bloodied and repulsed, the combination of British tanks, Indian artillery, and USAAF ground attack proving too much for a large mechanized force that withdrew in disarray.

Those units melting into the cool shadows of the trees found ample munitions and hard supplies waiting, product of a magnificent effort by the Division's logistical chain, meaning that this was a line that they could hold.

Bullets and explosive had taken priority over bread and meat, so only modest amounts of food reached some units, whilst others waited in vain. Many men went hungry that evening, partially because there was nothing to eat, and partially because of the presence of the enemy.

They were known as the 'Red Eagles', a homage to their divisional badge.

Their service during the Second World War was exemplary, from the 1940 campaigns in the Western Desert, through East Africa and the rout of the larger Italian Forces, Syria and finally Italy, where the division earned undying glory in and around the bloodbath that was Monte Cassino.

The 4th was considered an elite formation, but it had taken heavy casualties in the process of acquiring its illustrious reputation.

Returned from a stint of armed policing in Greece, the 4th Indian Division had slotted back into the Allied order of battle alongside sister units with whom they had shared the excesses of combat, only to be swiftly transferred north and into the cauldron of the new German war.

It performed well against the new enemy, and swiftly relieved the exhausted 101st Airborne.

The new positions assigned to the 7th Indian infantry Brigade covered the routes out of Wolfegg, and the approaches to Vogt.

The 4th/16th Punjab Regiment, ably supported by two platoons of the 6th Rajputana MG Battalion, had stood firm in and around Vogt, British tanks from the 26th Armoured Brigade causing heavy casualties amongst the attacking T34's.

As the Soviet probes continued, the 2nd/11th Sikhs were pushed hard along their defensive line, set in parallel with Route 324 to the north of Vogt.

On Route 314 to the north, British soldiers of the 1st Royal Sussex Regiment folded back, but did not give, forcing the attacking Soviet infantry and cavalry to retreat, leaving scores of dead on the field.

An unusual error in Soviet attack scheduling had delayed the central assault, enabling the defending artillery to concentrate on assisting the Sussex Regiment before switching to the aid of the forces defending Routes 317 and 323.

2007hrs, Friday 7th September 1945, astride Altdorfer Strasse [Route 323], 2 kilometres south-west of Wolfegg, Germany.

Company Havildar Major Dhankumar Gurung looked around him, able to make out the shape of one of his men here, a weapon ready and manned there.

8th Platoon was quiet, safely hidden behind their tree trunks, protected by the hastily scraped foxholes, or comfortable in the old German trench.

Not one man had suffered any injury as the Soviet artillery, weak by comparison to normal, had probed the defensive positions of the Sirmoor Rifles.

Part of their line was a trench dug months before their arrival, eight foot deep, wood reinforced and with firing steps along its length, a relic of the previous conflict.

Gurung's soldiers had extended the trench, and taken advantage of natural depressions in the ground, as well as fallen tree trunks, creating a strong position from which to resist.

Thus far, the battalion had not seen an enemy, apart from the occasional flash of an aircraft overhead.

According to the legends of the British Army, no enemy relished fighting these wiry hillmen from Nepal, and, to a man, they were keen to get to close quarters with the new foe to put their marshall skills to the test against a strong and cunning enemy.

The Sirmoor Rifles, also known as the 1st/2nd [King Edward VII's Own] Gurkha Rifles, waited in anticipation of the battle to come.

[Book Three of the Red Gambit series, 'Stalemate', should be available by January 2013 on Amazon Kindle as a download, and createspace.com as a book.]

Fig #50 – Rear cover graphic

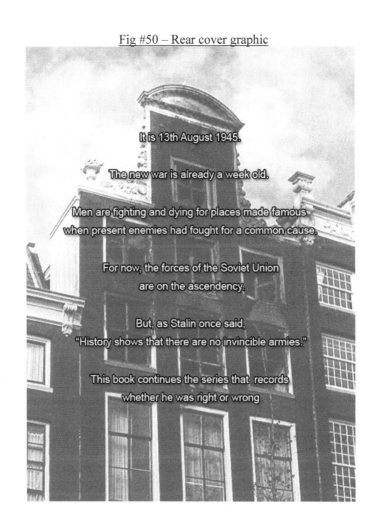

It is 13th August 1945.

The new war is already a week old.

Men are fighting and dying for places made famous
when present enemies had fought for a common cause.

For now, the forces of the Soviet Union
are on the ascendency.

But, as Stalin once said,
"History shows that there are no invincible armies."

This book continues the series that records
whether he was right or wrong

15147723R00316

Made in the USA
Middletown, DE
25 October 2014